THE
CHANGE

AN UNBOUNDED NOVEL

BOOKS BY TEYLA BRANTON

Unbounded Series
The Change
The Cure
The Escape
The Reckoning
The Takeover

Unbounded Novellas
Ava's Revenge
Mortal Brother
Lethal Engagement

UNDER THE NAME RACHEL BRANTON

Lily's House
House Without Lies
Tell Me No Lies
Your Eyes Don't Lie
Zoey's Place (Novella)
Bianca's Hope (Novella)

Noble Hearts (Royals of Monterra)
Royal Quest (Novella)
Royal Dance (Novella)

THE CHANGE

AN UNBOUNDED NOVEL

TEYLA BRANTON

WHITE
STAR
PRESS

This is a work of fiction, and the views expressed herein are the sole responsibility of the author. Likewise, certain characters, places, and incidents are the product of the author's imagination, and any resemblance to actual persons, living or dead, or actual events or locales, is entirely coincidental.

The Change (Unbounded Series #1)

Published by White Star Press
P.O. Box 353
American Fork, Utah 84003

Printed in the United States of America
ISBN: 978-1-939203-28-1
Year of first printing: 2013

To my baby daughter Lisbon, who has been my constant little shadow while preparing this book for publication. I probably would have finished a lot faster without your "help," but all the distractions remind me

of

what

is

really

important.

I LOVE YOU!

CHAPTER 1

ON THE DAY I SET FOOT ON THE PATH TO IMMORTALITY, I WAS WITH Justine in her car driving down 95th on our way to pick out her new sofa. Ordinary. That's what the day was. The plain kind of ordinary that obscures the secrets lurking in the shadows—or behind the faces of those you love.

Justine was the sister I'd never had, and our relationship was close to official since her brother had asked me twice to marry him. Tom was sexy, persuasive, and best of all, dependable. The next time he asked, I was considering saying yes.

A van came from nowhere, slamming into Justine's side of the car.

Just like that. No warning.

Justine jerked toward me but was ultimately held in her seat by the safety belt. My head bounced hard off the right side window. A low screeching grated in my ears, followed by several long seconds of utter silence.

An explosion shattered the world.

When the smoke began to clear, I saw Justine's head swing in my direction, though not of her own volition. Her blue eyes were open but vacant, her face still. Fire licked up the front of her shirt. Her blond hair melted and her skin blackened.

"No!" The word ripped from my throat.

I tried to reach out to Justine, but my arms wouldn't move. Heat. All around me. Terror.

Pain. The stench of burning flesh.

Fire and smoke obscured my vision, but not before I saw something drip from the mess that had been Justine's face. We were dying. This was it. The point of no return. I thought of my parents, my grandmother, my brothers, and how they would mourn me. I couldn't even think about Tom.

A premonition of things to come?

I lost consciousness, and when I came to I was lying flat on my back. A sheet covered my face. I was suffocating.

"Witnesses say . . . in flames almost on impact," a man's voice was saying. "A fluke . . . not for the fire . . . might have survived."

I turned my face, struggling to move my mouth from the sheet. Searching for air. Agony rippled up my neck and all over my head and down my body, the pain so decimating that it sapped all strength from me. I couldn't move again, but that little bit had been enough.

"What the freak!" the voice said. I could barely hear the words, but they gave me something to focus on through the pain. I clung to them. "Gunnar . . . the oxygen . . . thought you said she was dead."

The sheet lifted and air rushed into my tortured lungs. I could sense people all around me, though I couldn't see anything except a hazy light. My throat was tight and burning, reminding me of the time I'd had both strep throat and tonsillitis as a child. Only far worse. Blinding pain so intense that I couldn't even moan.

More snatches of conversation filtered to my brain. "Black as a crisp . . . try an IV . . . have to be amputated . . . University of Kansas . . . Burn Center."

Motion. The blare of a siren. Then blessed nothing.

When I awoke the next time, my throat still hurt, and so did every single inch of my body, though not with the all-consuming pain that made me wish I were dead. Probably they'd given me drugs. Or maybe too many nerves were damaged. I could feel an oxygen tube in my nose and cold seeping into a vein in my right shoulder. How could that be? I'd had IVs before and I'd never felt the liquid. It was so good, so necessary, that for a moment I concentrated all my attention on that small, steady flow. Life seeping into my body. But far too slowly. I wanted more.

Abruptly the sensation was gone. The pain cranked up a notch.

I tried to open my eyes, but only the right one was uncovered. From what I could tell, I seemed to be completely swathed in bandages and unable to move. My single eye rested on Tom, who was standing near the window, staring out with the unfocused expression of a man who saw nothing.

Tom shifted his weight, his muscles flexing under his T-shirt and jeans. In the past months I'd learned his body almost as well as my own, and even now I felt a sense of wonder at the miracle of our relationship. He didn't push me for commitment, didn't question why I was so hesitant to take the next step, and I loved him for that perhaps more than anything. It was also why I didn't know if things would work out between us.

A tiny rush of air escaped the hole they'd left in the bandages near my mouth. He turned toward me, his face stricken, looking older than his thirty-five years. "Erin? Are you awake?"

I tried to nod, but found I couldn't. I lay mute and helpless. Finally, I thought to close and open my single eye.

He was at my side instantly. "Oh, honey. Thank God! I thought I'd lost—" He broke off, struggling for control. "Erin, can you understand me?"

I blinked again.

"Okay, good. That's really good. Do you remember what happened?" He took a shaky breath and hesitated before adding, "Blink once for yes, twice for no."

I remembered the accident. I remembered the fire and how

Justine had burned, but I wanted the rest explained. I wanted to hear if Justine was in a bed like I was. I wanted to hear if we'd be okay.

I blinked twice.

He leaned closer, not touching me, his eyes rimmed in red. His eyes had a tendency to change color with what he wore, and today they were the inviting shade of a lake on a hot summer day. My favorite color.

"This morning you and Justine were in a car accident. There was a fire. You were burned."

Over seventy percent of my body. The thought came from nowhere, and I wondered if I'd unconsciously heard someone talking about my condition. If that was true, my chances weren't good. I'd heard of a formula at the insurance company where I worked: take your age, add the percentage of your body burned, and the sum was your chance of fatality. I'd be over a hundred percent.

I'm still alive. I'm the exception.

"Your parents just stepped out for a while. Your grandmother was here, too, almost all day, but they finally convinced her to go home. Chris is on his way."

Had that much time passed? My older brother, Chris, had left that morning to pilot a charter flight from Kansas City to Tulsa. I'd been planning to go over tonight when he returned so I could spend time with him and Lorrie and their kids.

"They called Jace. He'll be here soon."

Jace was on his way from Texas? My younger brother had barely arrived at his new unit, and the army would never allow him to come home.

I knew then what Tom wasn't saying: I was dying. Was that why there wasn't as much pain? Or had my limbs been amputated? I tried to move my legs, but they felt heavy, and I wondered if that was the sensation the nerves sent to the brain after amputation. I concentrated on moving my arms, and though they were sheathed in bandages, I managed to move my right one slightly.

Tom's eyes followed the movement, swallowing so hard I could see the lump in his throat go up and down. He wet his lips, started to speak, stopped, and then tried again. "It's going to be okay, Erin. You'll see."

The lie was so bad I felt sorry for him. I knew it was killing him not to do something useful for me, to somehow alleviate my suffering, but there was nothing he could do now, nothing either of us could do. This was one of those moments you endured and survived. Or you didn't.

A nurse entered, and Tom eased away from the bed. "She's awake," he said. A pleading kind of hope had come into his face, and it was painful to see. More painful than the lie. "She understands what I'm saying."

The nurse leaned in front of my good eye, doubt etched on her round face. Two bright spots of red stood out on her plump cheeks like awkwardly applied blush. "Well, that's a good sign," she said, but hesitantly, as though I was somehow breaking the rules by regaining consciousness.

Her eyes lifted toward something behind me. "What happened to the IV? It shouldn't need changing already. That's the third time we've run out in the last hour." She shook her head. "Must be something wrong with the valve. I'll check it and get another bag."

After she left, Tom said more encouraging words, which only made me feel worse because I'd seen the truth in the nurse's face. *Talk about something real,* I wanted to scream. *Talk about the things we didn't do. Talk about Justine. Tell me she's okay.*

He didn't, and I guessed what that meant. A tear slipped from my eye into the bandage. She was gone. Justine was gone.

Meeting the siblings at the Red Night Club six months earlier had been a changing point in my life. Tom hadn't been able to tear his eyes away from me that night, or since, and over the past months Justine had loved and bullied me into thinking seriously about my future, something I'd lacked the confidence to do since leaving law school in disgrace. So what if I was thirty-one and living in the basement apartment at my parents' house in Kansas City? Or that I worked a boring job as an insurance claims clerk when I'd always longed to do something more adventurous? I could change all that. I bought new clothes, took up biking, and began looking for a new apartment.

Tom couldn't see my tear, but it really didn't matter. I was dying. I'd lost my best friend, my almost sister. I'd lost any future I might have had with Tom. I couldn't wrap my understanding around either loss.

The nurse returned, and shortly I felt cool liquid seeping into my veins again. Purely imaginary but sweet all the same. I closed my right eye and concentrated on that lifeline, as though I could suck it into me and repair the damage to my body from the inside out.

"Don't worry." Tom's voice came from far away. "I'm here for you. We're going to make you well again. No matter how long it takes." I couldn't hear the lie in his voice anymore. Maybe it made him feel better to believe.

I wished I could.

The next time I woke, it was dark except for a dim light over the sink that stood against the wall. I sensed someone in the room but couldn't move my head to see who it was. Tom? My brother Chris? More likely my mother or father.

The door opened and light sliced into the room. In walked a short, broad man with longish dark brown hair, intense brown eyes, and a trim mustache. Not good-looking, exactly, but so sure of himself that he exuded an animal attractiveness. A stethoscope hung from his neck and down his white lab coat. If anyone could accomplish a miracle, this man could; his presence was almost palpable.

Behind him came a similarly dressed blonde, and my single eye riveted on her in surprise. She carried her head and lean body with the same regal confidence of the man, but her face was familiar, though I had no idea where I might have seen her before. The fierce, possessive way her eyes fixed on my unmoving body gave me the unnerving feeling that she'd been looking for something for a long time.

And had found it.

The woman turned on the overhead light, and I shut my eye momentarily at the brightness. "We need to take her for a few tests," she said to the person at my bedside.

"More tests?" The voice was my mother's, exhausted but not quite devoid of hope. I opened my eye, straining to see her, but she was out of my line of sight. "She woke up earlier. Isn't that a good sign? Could the doctors be wrong?"

The woman shook her head. "I don't believe so, but I promise we'll do everything we can for your daughter." Her smooth, clear skin was wrinkle-free, and I pinpointed her age near mine, or perhaps a few years older. Could she be a doctor? A specialist maybe? Her attitude suggested absolute authority. Even if I could have moved my head, I doubted I'd be able to look away from her for long.

"Thank you." My mother sounded unhappy. Things weren't perfect between us, but I would give anything to be able to console her, anything not to be trapped in this ruined shell of a body.

"Dimitri," the woman said. "The IV."

The man nodded and moved around the bed, but not before I caught a glimpse of another IV bag in his hands, though it seemed different. Larger, maybe.

"The bags keep running out before they should," my mother said. "I'm worried it's not helping her condition. Where's all the liquid going?"

Was that a flash of excitement in the woman's eyes? It was hard to tell with my monovision. "We're monitoring it carefully," she assured my mother.

Within seconds I could feel the drip of the liquid again—different this time. Sweeter, thicker, and coming faster. I closed my eye and drew the liquid into my body, though I knew the effect had to be entirely in my mind.

"Don't I know you?" my mother asked the woman. "You seem familiar."

"I must have one of those faces."

"No, I've seen you before. I know I have. Aren't you my mother's neighbor? The one who teaches karate?"

"I have a sister who teaches taekwondo. People often confuse us."

A lie. I couldn't hear it in her voice, but I felt it all the same. An unease, a hint of uncertainty that marred her perfect confidence. What was she trying to hide? Or maybe my imagination was kicking in again.

"That must be it," my mother said.

"Probably. If you'll excuse us? We should be back within the hour."

"I'll be here." My mother's hand briefly touched my shoulder as I was rolled from the room. I wished I could see her face.

The hallway was quiet, nearly deserted, though the lights overhead blazed brightly. We passed several tired-looking nurses and an orderly mopping a section of floor.

"Ava," the man said from the head of my bed. "The bag's half gone."

"Then we were right." The woman walking beside me fell silent a moment before adding, "It's about time."

"Too bad it had to happen like this. She's suffered a lot."

"At least we're sure. And there won't be anything to explain to her family. They're already prepared for the worst."

"She might not cooperate. It wouldn't be the first time."

"She *must* cooperate. There's too much at stake."

I didn't like her clipped tone, or any of their words. They were talking about me, but I couldn't understand the context. None of it made sense. Maybe the drugs had scrambled my brain.

When they began discussing transfer papers with another man, icy suspicion crawled through my mind. Where were they taking me? Maybe they weren't with the hospital at all. As they loaded me into an ambulance, panic ramped up my breathing, but no one noticed my distress. My mouth refused to utter a sound.

The woman sat near my head out of sight while the man stayed at my side. I didn't see who was driving. "This bag's gone," the man said. "I'll get a new one. I'll start another IV, too. The idiots already amputated half her left arm. She'll need the extra."

My left arm was gone? Bile threatened to choke me. *No!* This was too much. I couldn't survive another minute.

Yet when the man put the second IV in my upper chest, I felt another rush of cool liquid, and my body gulped it down as though it were life itself. My fear numbed at this relief, and I dozed as the ambulance cruised through the streets, rousing a little each time we stopped at the traffic lights. I heard honking, a snatch of music, the throb of the engine, and my own breathing, which seemed loud and fast in the small confines of the ambulance.

Something was very wrong. They'd told my mother I'd be back within an hour, but we'd been driving too long for that now. Not to mention that removing me from the burn center would lower what minimal chance I had of survival. Yet whoever these people were, they didn't seem to want me dead—for now.

I tried to move, but the only limb I could get to obey me was my right arm. I lifted it halfway in the air before the man grabbed it.

"It's okay, Erin. I really am a doctor. Best one in the world, I daresay. I'm Dimitri, and my friend is Ava. We're here to help you." To the woman, he added, "She's a fighter."

"So it seems." Satisfaction laced Ava's voice, and I felt a sudden and distinct hatred for her. What did she want from me? Was she an organ harvester? It was the only rational explanation—though utterly terrifying.

Dimitri laid something on my chest. Another IV bag. "Hold onto this." He placed my right hand over the bag. Immediately, a delicious coolness entered my fingertips even through the plastic bag and the bandages. I blessed him silently and gave myself up to this drug-induced hallucination.

The next thing I knew, I was being rolled into a cavernous room. I had the impression of large crates and of a woman sitting in front of several computers which she seemed to be using all at once. One of the computers was connected by a thin black cord to a woven metal headpiece the woman wore on her head like a crown. Her chair turned toward us, one hand twisting up a circular section of the headpiece that obscured one eye. "Good, you're back." A smile spread over her face.

I stared. I'd been wrong thinking Ava and Dimitri were the most assured, compelling people I'd ever seen. This new woman had the same confident bearing as the other two, but it was coupled with straight dark hair, a heart-shaped face, slanted Asian eyes, and flawless golden skin. Her revealing green tank showed an ample bosom and a torso that fell to an impossibly thin waist, flaring again for perfect hips. Her delicacy and utter perfection was the kind that inspired poets and started wars between nations—and made me feel completely inadequate.

I knew that feeling well. I felt it often in the presence of my mother.

"Cort's got the room ready," the woman said. She was younger than the others, perhaps in her late twenties, though her dark eyes were far too knowing for true innocence. A chill shuddered in my chest.

"Thanks, Stella."

I knew Stella meant star in some other language, and the name fit her perfectly.

We were moving away, and Stella vanished from my line of sight. My thoughts of her cut off abruptly as I was wheeled into a smaller room, bare except for what looked like a coffin on a long table.

A coffin!

My heart slammed into my chest, its beating furious and erratic.

Ava withdrew scissors from the pocket of her lab coat and started cutting the bandages from my feet and legs. Dimitri began at my head. I caught a glimpse of blackened tissue, the bloody stub of my left arm. Tears leaked from my right eye, but I couldn't see anything through my left and I doubted I still had tear ducts there. Now I knew why Tom had felt the need to lie. No one could be this badly burned and survive.

If by some cruel twist of fate I did live, I would be a monster.

I tried to struggle against them, but any tiny movement sent shards of pain in every direction until it seemed pain was all I had ever known. Neither would my mouth open to scream, though hoarse sounds of distress issued from my throat, sounding grotesque and panicked. My chest convulsed wildly with the effort. Before too long, my throat became too raw for sound, and even that haunting noise ceased.

"It's okay," Dimitri said, his voice gentle. "It'll be over soon." Somehow I didn't feel comforted.

When I was nothing more than a mass of burned and bleeding raw flesh, Ava and Dimitri lifted me into the coffin. Exquisite torture. My vision blurred and darkened. Nausea gouged at my insides.

A gelatinous substance oozed around me and the pain slightly eased. Dimitri pushed it up against my chin and smoothed a layer over my entire face. *They're drowning me in Jell-O,* I thought, but Dimitri made sure I had ample space beneath my nose to breathe. The syrupy sweetness I'd felt with the IV bags was increased a hundredfold, as though each of my damaged nerve cells had become a conduit for an IV.

Dimitri's face leaned close to mine. "I've added something to one of these IV bags to put you out. It'd be impossible for you to sleep in this stuff otherwise. But you'll heal better if you aren't awake." Already I struggled to keep my good eye open.

Ava stood by the coffin looking in. "Don't fight it, Erin. You'll have your answers soon. Sleep, Granddaughter. Sleep."

Granddaughter? I must not have heard her correctly.

Well, I suppose there could be worse ways to die than cradled in a coffin full of sweet gelatin. I gave up fighting and let my right eye close.

CHAPTER 2

MY HEAD POUNDED. NO, IT WAS MY HEART. BEAT, BEAT BEAT. I was alive.

I must have been drinking. I always had such vivid dreams after I drank. At least three other times in my life, I'd made a vow to give up alcohol. This time I meant it.

My eyes blinked open. The first thing I saw was the white ceiling above me, but the slick sides of the coffin came a close second.

I hadn't been dreaming.

I looked down, surprised that my neck obeyed the command. Sure enough, I was lying in a coffin full of greenish gelatin, except instead of burned limbs and torso, my naked skin was pale pink and smooth like that of a young child.

My arm.

I lifted my left arm and sighed with relief. It was whole and normal. In fact, on closer examination it was better than normal. The thin, half-inch scar that had been on my thumb since I'd tried to open a tuna can with a knife when I was eleven was missing.

What was going on?

Easing myself to a seated position, I felt disoriented but no pain. Nothing except the pull of the IV tubes going into my chest beneath each clavicle, though their liquid seemed less important now. I began working at the tape that secured them to me. The sooner I got these out, the sooner I could leave this place. The gelatin was cool and slimy and sticky against my flesh, making me feel dirty and uncomfortable.

"Ah, you're awake. Good afternoon, Erin."

My hands froze as the woman who'd taken me from the hospital glided into the small room, followed by her partner Dimitri. The beautiful Stella and a pale blond man I hadn't seen before came in behind them. Each of them was smiling at me as though it was the most normal thing in the world to be burned beyond recognition, put into a coffin of gelatin, and wake up healed.

Not to mention naked.

To a roomful of strangers.

I crossed my arms over my chest. "Do you mind?" I willed my voice to be demanding instead of fearful.

Ava and the others stopped walking, confusion and then amusement running over their faces. "I'll take it from here," Ava said, flicking her gaze toward the door.

The blond man cleared his throat. "We have to remember how it was for us in the beginning. How interesting to see it first-hand." His piercing blue eyes lingered on my body before locking onto my face. He was of average height for a man, slightly taller than Dimitri, but nowhere near as muscular or eye-catching. His face was too ordinary. If not for the eyes and the confidence I'd come to expect from this impressive crew, he would have been relegated in my mind to the nerdy realm. Minus the glasses, of course.

"You can talk to her about it later, Cort." Ava continued toward me alone, apparently expecting full obedience. I wasn't surprised when the others turned and left without another word.

Ava was as striking up close as from a distance. I'd give a lot to look like that and have her confidence. She wore a black karate uniform of some kind, though without a belt, which meant she'd lied about not being my grandmother's next-door neighbor.

"Sorry about the coffin," she said. "It was all we could find at such short notice."

I did rather feel as if I'd walked into one of the popular vampire novels my fellow claims clerks at the insurance agency so eagerly devoured on their breaks. Maybe I'd been bitten and that's why I wasn't dead. Good thing I didn't believe in any of that nonsense.

I lifted a handful of gelatin and watched it ooze slimily between my fingers. More yellow than green once it was away from the blue lining of the coffin. "And this?"

She grinned. "Cort's invention."

"Jell-O?"

"Not quite, but not far off, either. We call it curequick. Besides a heavy amount of sugar, it also contains proteins reduced to their most usable form. This mixture and the IVs are the best thing for a wounded Unbounded."

"Unbounded?"

Impatience swept over her face, but I sensed it wasn't directed at me. "Look, why don't I take these IVs out, and you can shower and get dressed before we talk. You'll probably feel more . . . comfortable that way."

"Okay." I *would* feel better, even if I wasn't really safe. I got the idea that simply walking away wasn't an option.

"When you're finished, I'll tell you a story. My story. This whole thing might make more sense that way." Ava eased off the IV tape so smoothly I didn't feel discomfort, pressing a cotton square over the needle site for several seconds before proceeding to the next. "There, you won't need bandages. The bathroom's through there. I'll put some clothes for you by the door."

I was glad she'd pointed to a different door than the one everyone else had exited. She scooted a chair next to the coffin so I could climb out, and I wondered if I'd been wrong to mistrust her.

In the small bathroom, I headed straight for the surprisingly spacious shower. I'd prefer a hot bath, but there wasn't one here—which was probably why they'd needed the coffin. The warm water hit my body, whirling the yellow gelatin over the white tile and down the drain.

Examining myself carefully, I seemed to be the same. Same toes, thighs, stomach, and breasts, though these were a bit sore and tender, and, if I didn't know any better, I'd say firmer, too. Definitely not burned, though there were a few pinker patches on my calves and thighs, which ached now that I thought about it. Nothing, however, compared to the pain I'd experienced when I'd awakened near the crash, or when they'd lowered my blackened body into the gelatin.

I shuddered. Was any of this real?

Using a towel from a stack sitting on the built-in shelves near the door, I patted my skin dry. Afterward, I ran the towel over the steam-covered mirror to study my reflection. My face was also the same, except the eyebrow over my left eye was short and sparse, and my lashes there had only begun to regrow. The right eye was fine. Normal. I peered closer, trying to spot any other difference, but there was nothing to see. Then it occurred to me that the chickenpox scar under my right eyebrow was missing. Yet that eye hadn't been burned—at least I didn't think so. My hair was ultra short, and some of it felt prickly, as if the hair had only recently begun to grow again, but other parts, especially in the back, were slightly longer. My skull was nicely shaped, and despite its unevenness, the hair didn't look half bad. I should have taken Justine's advice and cut my long hair months ago.

Justine.

My face crumpled, becoming almost unrecognizable in the mirror. Closing my eyes, I fought to contain the huge sense of loss. Or at least to keep breathing. Justine would want that.

Turning purposefully, I strode to the bathroom door to retrieve the clothing Ava had set on a chair outside the door. I noticed a camera on the far wall, angled toward the coffin and the bathroom door. No wonder they'd known so quickly that I was awake. I swept up the clothes and shut the bathroom door again.

The black cotton pants and short-sleeved blue blouse were a little large, and there was a snug black tank instead of a bra, so apparently they expected my new skin to be tender.

New skin?

I didn't believe any of this. Or want to believe. Yet the pounding of my heart seemed real enough. Not a dream.

I fought the urge to collapse to the bathroom floor and weep with fear and uncertainty. There was no one here to help me—not Tom, not Justine, not my brothers, or even my mother who could always pick up the pieces when things went wrong, even if she didn't always get them back in the right places.

There was just me. I exhaled slowly and opened the door.

This time Ava was waiting outside the bathroom, her gray eyes as cold and somber as gravestones. Eyes like my grandmother. Like me. "Come on," she said. "Let's go somewhere more comfortable."

I followed her into the cavernous room. It wasn't as large as I remembered, but still warehouse-like, with cement floors and exposed iron support bars on the walls, reaching far above our heads where florescent lighting hung on long chains. Wooden crates stacked high against two of the walls, including the one with two huge automatic doors, leaving only enough space for the doors. Tables loaded with smaller crates and bundles of folded boxes took up another wall.

Close to the fourth wall was a carpeted area, lined with couches, several large metal lockers, and an oversized television screen. Near the couches, Ava's friends grouped around the computers I'd seen earlier. The conversation died as we passed, and I could feel their eyes on me. No one spoke, but the nerdy one who'd checked me out earlier smiled.

I inclined my head without returning the smile, saving my judgment until I knew why they'd brought me here. They might have saved my life—or they might be perpetrating a giant hoax.

"Stella, if you could cue the video for the office?" Ava said.

Stella was wearing the woven crown I'd seen before, with the single, semi-transparent eyepiece in place, and lines of code were appearing on the computer in front of her. I had the sense she was controlling the machine, though I knew that couldn't be right. "Already done."

"Thank you."

I tore my gaze from the computers and continued after Ava. Walking took effort, as though I had new muscles that needed training.

Ridiculous.

I studied Ava as she led the way. She was taller than me by a few inches, and her golden blond hair was short and stylish. She carried herself with unmistakable grace, while, by contrast, I tripped on a cord taped to the cement floor. Ava's glance flickered toward me, her eyes taking on a bit of warmth. "Sorry about that."

We arrived at a door, which led to a narrow, antiseptically clean office with all the amenities: carved oak desk, client chairs, a comfortable couch near several metal filing cabinets, pictures of exotic places on the wall. Unexpectedly nice, except the only window looked into the warehouse instead of outside the building. She closed the door behind me and went, not to the desk, but to the couch. "Have a seat."

I did as she requested, keeping an arm's length between us. "That stuff, the gelatin. Does it heal burns? And scars?"

"Not exactly."

"If the gelatin didn't do it, how—" I stopped and looked down at my clothed body. "I *was* burned, wasn't I? My arm was . . . gone. Or did I imagine it?"

"No, but whether or not you were put into the gelatin you would have healed, though it would have taken a lot longer than three and a half days. Weeks at least. The curequick gives our bodies enough nutrition to speed up our already accelerated recovery by as much as five times."

I blinked, digesting that fact. The prickly hair on my head told me I hadn't been here long, but healing from such massive burns, even sped up five times, would have taken months at the very least.

"That's impossible. What really happened to me? Who are you people?" Every muscle in my body tensed for the answer.

She held up a hand to still my panic. "The story, for me at least, begins a long time ago, when I was your age."

Frustration momentarily overcame my fear. "What do you mean? You're my age now."

"Things aren't always what they seem, Erin. Now do you want to hear this or not?" She spoke as though to a child, and I nodded, feeling oddly abashed at the disapproval in her voice.

"When I was thirty, I had a near-death experience, and like you, I survived. It was then I met a couple who claimed to be related to me—my eighth great-grandparents. They said that because I recovered, it meant I was Unbounded."

"Unbounded. You used that term before." I ignored for the moment the claim about her long-lived relatives.

"A derivative of the early Greek word boundary. Our temporal boundaries are not like those of regular mortals; thus, we are unboundaried. The word has been changed and shortened over the centuries."

"Temporal boundaries. What does that even mean?"

Her chin lifted with an elegance I could never hope to emulate. "It means I'm your fourth great-grandmother, I'm three hundred years old, and I have every intention of living until I'm two thousand."

What kind of an idiot did she think I was?

I jumped to my feet. "Look, I don't know who you are or what you're trying to do, but I don't want any part of it. If you don't mind, I'd like to leave now."

Ava arose and went around the desk, sitting in the chair and tapping on the computer keyboard. "Come here. You need to see this." Her calm tone hadn't altered in the slightest at my outburst.

Reluctantly, I obeyed. My eyes skimmed past a mug full of pens, a stack of papers, a black cell phone and came to rest on the computer monitor. A video was playing of Ava and Dimitri bringing in a bandage-wrapped form on a hospital bed. I watched as they cut off the bandages and slipped the grotesque figure into the slimy curequick. Ava touched something on the keyboard, and the image zoomed in on the mass of burned flesh. Me. I remembered the torture, and if nothing else, one side of my face was clearly recognizable. I was surprised anyone could be that destroyed and still live.

Another key speeded up the film. Before my eyes, the body shed the black shell and new pale skin gleamed underneath. As the curequick disappeared, more buckets of the gelatin were dumped into the coffin over the unmoving body. The amputated arm regrew, pushing and stretching out grotesquely in the sped-up video.

I swallowed hard. On some level I knew all this; I'd lived it. Yet seeing it on the screen made it all too real. Either they'd gone to great lengths to create a realistic hoax, or they were telling the truth.

"I should have died."

Ava shook her head. "There are only a few ways Unbounded can die, and fire isn't one of them. I'm sorry we didn't discover your nature before the accident. I know it was painful."

"Are you saying I was, uh—"

"Unbounded," she supplied.

"So I was already Unbounded before the accident?"

"Obviously, or you wouldn't have survived." She stopped the video at the point where she was helping my naked self out of the coffin, and another picture popped into view. "This is you on your thirtieth birthday." My face filled the screen, a close up, including the chickenpox scar in my right eyebrow. "We took pictures every few months. Unfortunately, it seems we missed the fading of your scar. We spotted it only after we brought you here." She ran through several more photographs. "There, that was you four months ago. Barely noticeable."

"Could have been the light."

"It wasn't. We call it the Change, and it usually takes place between the thirty-first and thirty-third birthdays, though sometimes it happens as early as twenty-eight and as late as thirty-four. I personally know of two cases when it happened even a few years later, but that's rare. When the Change occurs, scars disappear, wrinkles fade, your muscles become tighter. Surely you've noticed a difference these past few months."

I had noticed, but I thought it was because of the biking and boating with Tom and Justine. Dancing into the early morning after a long day at work. A good diet.

"We keep an eye on all potential Unbounded in our blood lines," Ava continued in her sedate voice. "Generally, that means those closely enough related. But unlike some who regrow lost fingers or suddenly stop limping, there was nothing to make your Change noticeable. The accident was unfortunate, but at least it revealed that you have the active gene. If we'd realized before, we would have contacted you and maybe the accident never would have happened."

"Why is it so important that you find Unbounded? What do you get out of it?" There had to be a motive I wasn't seeing, something she wanted from me. I was certain she hadn't been blowing off steam at the hospital when she'd told Dimitri that I must cooperate.

Her eyes widened, whether in surprise or offense, I couldn't tell. "We have a need for every Unbounded, but our primary goal is to teach them what they are. They have a right to the protection we can offer. The right not to be studied in a lab because of their abilities." She leaned back in the chair behind the desk, now completely relaxed, not seeming to mind that on my feet I towered over her. "Can you imagine what happens when a new Unbounded suddenly regrows a missing hand? When they come back to life from an accident like yours? Or begin to be noticeably younger than their aging spouse? We want to make transition as easy as possible. Usually we must fake their deaths and obtain new identities."

"What about their families?"

Her expression softened as though she knew I was thinking of my parents and my brothers. My grandmother. "We have a different view of family than mortals. We value them every bit as much, but we recognize that sometimes the best thing we can do for them is to let go."

I could not imagine a world where I would ever walk away from my family, despite some of the problems we'd had. "I can't do that. I won't." My eyes felt drawn to the cell phone on the desk, but I didn't give in to the urge to look at it. A plan formed in my mind.

She sighed. "You are much like me in that. Unfortunately, even if you could convince everyone that you hadn't been burned so badly and your arm hadn't been amputated, the Jane Doe we put in your place at the hospital took a turn for the worse yesterday and died. I'm sorry, but there's no going back as yourself."

The fact left me numb. "Jane Doe?"

"An unidentified victim of a forest fire. Believe me, we had to scramble to find someone who was a close enough match."

"My family thinks I'm dead?" The words hurt.

She nodded.

It was all wrong—both that a stranger would be buried as me and that moving her might have hastened her death. "What about her family?"

"The clinic we supposedly transferred you to will officially record that she died there and will file her records in case her family is ever found. Don't feel bad, Erin. There was no way she'd survive in any case. For the two days she was you, she had the absolute best care. After your funeral, we'll make sure her body is returned to its proper place."

I clenched and unclenched my fists at my sides. "And Tom? I suppose he thinks I'm dead, too? I have to see him."

"I'm sorry, but the one thing you can't do is contact Tom or your family right now."

"Why?" I demanded. "Because it would cause problems for you? That's the real issue here, isn't it? All that forging of documents and transfers."

She stood abruptly, finally meeting my anger with her own. "You aren't getting the whole picture. You have a destiny, Erin. Inside you is a power far greater than you can even begin to comprehend. It's a priceless gift, or a great curse—make of it what you will."

Before either of us could speak again, there was a rap on the door and a brief pause before it flung open to reveal Dimitri. For a moment, I felt a silly rush of gratitude toward the broad man who'd given me the IV bags and comforted me in the ambulance.

I fought the feeling. I wasn't grateful. He was a part of why I was here. If Ava was telling the truth, they hadn't saved my life at all, but were the reason my family was mourning my death.

"Sorry to disturb you," he said to Ava. Though he didn't acknowledge me, his dark eyes rested briefly on my face, the act as solid as any greeting. "Stella has identified signs of Emporium presence at the burn unit."

Ava's face went rigid. "Does she suspect pursuit?"

"We're not sure. I've put security on alert, but we need to do an on-site check."

Ava opened the desk and withdrew a handgun. My stomach twisted when I saw how casually she checked the chamber before shoving in a magazine. Whoever these folks were, they meant business.

She walked past me, as graceful as ever. "Come. You'll wait with the others."

"Who's the Emporium?" I reached out to the desk, presumably to steady myself, but I made sure it was near the black cell phone. My heart pounded, but I didn't allow my mind to dwell on even the shape of the phone touching my fingers. I was too afraid my intentions would show in my expression.

"The Emporium is who you really need to be afraid of, Erin." Ava's gravestone eyes locked onto mine with an intensity I couldn't escape. "If they've been to the burn unit, make no mistake—they are looking for you. If they find you, you'll wish you really had died in that accident."

It was no answer, but all I was going to get from her. I followed her to the door, the tiny cell phone a slight bulge in the narrow pocket of my black pants.

CHAPTER 3

"UNBOUNDED AGE AT THE AVERAGE RATE OF TWO BIOLOGICAL YEARS for every hundred years," Stella explained.

I sat on a chair near her in front of the computer screens. Dimitri and Ava had disappeared a half hour ago, but they'd left Cort and Stella with orders to answer my questions. More likely, they were supposed to keep an eye on me. I had no idea how long I'd be kept in the warehouse, but I was definitely a prisoner. For now, I would play along because I wanted to discover everything I could about what had happened to me.

Or what I'd supposedly become.

"Two years for every hundred?" I repeated. "Impossible."

On the chair next to me, Cort cleared his throat as he always seemed to do before speaking. "Nevertheless, it's true. In about two thousand years, you'll die from old age."

"Yippee for me. What's the drawback?"

"You'll watch everyone you ever loved die." This from Stella, uttered with a gravity too real to be faked.

My levity vanished, leaving me feeling like an idiot. "I see."

Without my family, the appeal of near immortality lessened

considerably. Sure, I'd disappointed my father by dropping out of law school to work a dead-end job, and my mother with my obsession for old jeans and for failing to provide her with grandchildren, but in the end none of that was important. They still loved me. Yes, my much older brother, Chris, was busy with his family, and my younger brother, Jace, was off on his own now, and neither of them needed me on a daily basis. But they were still my brothers, a permanent part of me. I needed them.

And Tom. What would it be like to live without him? Of course there was always the chance he wouldn't want me when he discovered what I was. I couldn't believe that, though. Tom was solid, and he was mine. It was always me who wasn't quite sure.

I rubbed my finger over the place on my thumb where I'd once had the scar from opening the tuna can. It felt absurd to be upset that it was gone, but it had been with me for so long, a part of who I was. Who I'd been.

Cort cleared his throat and scooted closer to me. His leg touched mine in a way that seemed accidental but I knew wasn't. This was the first human contact I'd had in days, and the sensation startled me. It also comforted me, and I let several long seconds pass before I moved away.

"One of the first things you might have noticed," he said, "is that you don't feel hunger anymore. Your body will absorb sustenance from the world around you. Like you did with my curequick in the coffin."

So much for thinking my lack of appetite these past months was because I was too busy with Tom and Justine to care about food. "Obnoxious name," I said. "Curequick."

He laughed. "You name it then."

"Maybe I will. So are you saying we don't eat?"

"Oh, we eat." Cort looked amused. "When we do, our bodies absorb less around us. But we don't *need* to eat. Of course, that doesn't stop some of us from overeating anyway."

"He's talking about Laurence," Stella said, glancing at me before typing something on her keyboard. Her woven metal crown lay discarded on the desk, and I could see tiny metal probes jutting wickedly from nearly the entire inner circumference. Definitely not a sound device. Maybe it recorded brain waves.

I glanced at what she'd written but it was in some kind of computer code and didn't mean anything to me. "Who's Laurence?"

"Laurence is one of us—the newest besides you." She looked around the warehouse. "These crates are part of his paper business."

"He hates that being Unbounded messes up his eating urges," Cort added. "So he pretends it doesn't. On the bright side, he's an excellent cook."

"Ah, an overweight stepbrother," I said. "But still family."

Cort nodded. "Something like that."

"Maybe he's happy the way he is." I'd always been a sucker for the underdog. Maybe I felt an affinity with them because I was there so often myself.

Stella smiled and the effect was powerful. Even with minimal makeup, every feature was perfect, from her wide brown eyes and high cheek bones to her sculptured eyebrows and smooth golden skin. She had good genes, or maybe an excellent plastic surgeon. "Laurence is happy. Besides, it's not as if the weight is physically unhealthy for him, though the extra pounds would make him vulnerable in an attack."

"Attack?"

"From the Emporium."

"Ava was talking about them earlier. Sounds like some kind of retail conglomerate."

She shook her head. "They own a slew of retail businesses, to be sure, but they're a group of Unbounded like us, except they have a completely different agenda."

"They're bad guys." Cort leaned forward, resting his elbows on the armrests of his chair and rubbing his hands together as if anticipating his tale. "Basically there are two types of Unbounded—our people and the Emporium. We allow regular humans—mortals—to live their lives as they choose, interfering only to make their lives better. Almost every medical and technological advance since the Renaissance can be traced to our Unbounded. On the other hand, the Emporium doesn't share what it learns. Their people use medicine and technology to gain money and power. They meddle constantly in politics and aren't above making certain people disappear—permanently. Their stated goal is to create a utopia for all humans, mortal and Unbounded."

"Utopia doesn't sound bad," I ventured.

Stella snorted and even that was attractive in her. "They can succeed only by severely limiting freedom, and that is never justifiable."

"Yet Emporium Unbounded would say they protect more people than we do." Cort pierced me with his blue eyes, as if challenging me to make a judgment call.

"They want to set themselves up as gods," Stella retorted.

Cort shrugged. "You have to admit that living so long does make us seem almost like deity. People have worshipped far worse."

"The Emporium will do anything to control the world," Stella said, ignoring Cort's last comment, "and they almost succeeded with the Greeks and Romans. Basically our job is to block their politics where we can and give the world technology and advances so they can better protect themselves."

I took my time to digest this information. The idea of two secret groups battling under the uncomprehending noses of ordinary mortals seemed a bit farfetched—unless I considered it in the light of my miraculous recovery. "What's your group called?"

"Renegades," Cort said. "A name the Emporium gave us. Meant to be derogatory, of course, but it sort of stuck. We like it."

"I see." For me, the title Renegades said a great deal about their ideology. I'd never been considered a renegade until I was forced to quit law school, and even that had been only a matter of self-preservation. Regrouping. Escaping the stares and embarrassment.

For a while no one spoke. Stella stared at her computer where the figure of a gymnast now flipped gracefully from side to side. Cort studied me instead of Stella, which I found unnerving. He was probably immune to her beauty by long association.

"Stella, how old are you?" I asked, more to distract Cort than from curiosity.

Her eyes left the computer and found mine, a tiny smile on her lips. "I discovered I was Unbounded earlier than most. I was twenty-eight. That was about two hundred years ago."

I gaped but felt none of the indignation I'd experienced when Ava shared her story. Perhaps because I'd actually begun accepting this whole idea of immortality. In my mind, Stella looked barely twenty-eight, though at the two for one hundred rate, her body would now be approaching thirty-two.

My gaze shifted to Cort, who cleared his throat and said, "I'm almost five hundred, but who's counting? Time isn't something that binds us." He rubbed his hands together again. "Though, you know, the term Unbounded didn't come from the word bound or bind. It came from—"

"Unboundaried," I interrupted. "I know. So you're older than Ava." I couldn't think of her as my fourth great-grandmother yet. Maybe I never would. "But she seems to be in charge."

He cleared his throat. "After the first hundred years, seniority hardly matters. But yes, she's the mother of our little family, as you might call it."

"And Dimitri's the father?"

Stella laughed. "That's as good a description as any. Dimitri and Ava coordinate our efforts here. And before you ask, Dimitri's over a thousand years old. As the saying goes, he's forgotten more than most of us have ever learned." She glanced at Cort and grinned. "If Ava and Dimitri are the mom and dad, and Laurence the ugly stepbrother, who's Ritter?"

Ritter? There was another one?

Cort took up the game. "Ritter's the prodigal son who returns after extended absences only for the pure joy of beating the hell out of the Emporium."

Stella laughed again, but I didn't get the joke. "We're fortunate Ritter's on our side. You shouldn't tease him so much, Cort. One of these days, he'll squash you like a fly."

"I'd just get up again."

"Ava, Dimitri, Laurence, Ritter, and you two," I said, "How many more are there?"

"There's you," Stella said.

"Besides me."

Her face lost all amusement. "Here in Kansas City, that's all, though we do employ some non-Unbounded security personnel—most of whom formerly worked for our government in secret operations. Not stuff you'd ever hear about. There's a larger group of Renegade Unbounded based in New York and several other groups spread throughout the world. Less than a hundred total now, with fewer and fewer being born every century. We don't practice inbreeding like the Emporium."

"Maybe you should."

Cort cleared his throat. "I've told everyone I'm perfectly willing." Stella shot him a disgusted stare, but he only shrugged and continued speaking. "Anyway, our low Unbounded birth rate is why you're so important, Erin. You're the first Unbounded to Change in America since Kennedy in 1999."

"President Kennedy?" My jaw was hanging, but I didn't care.

"No. His son, but yeah, the father was Unbounded, too. Back in sixty-three, we had to get President Kennedy out of the public eye before it was too obvious. Makeup just wasn't working to age him anymore, and a few aides became suspicious."

"You faked his death?"

"Technically he did meet the mortal criteria of being dead long enough to fool the doctors, but yes, that was our doing. However, the son's plane accident was real enough, a little gift from some enemies. Fortunately, we were able to get to him in time. But besides the Kennedys there were only three other American Unbounded born to our side in the past century. During those same hundred years, we lost more than a dozen to the fight against the Emporium—including the older Kennedy. We need you."

"Need me for what?" The survival and re-death of an American icon was more than I could assimilate at the moment, much less the idea that I could actually be of value to these assured people. "For my genes?"

"Well, that too, I suppose." Cort's eyes focused briefly on my lips, and I found myself wondering how many women he'd kissed during his half millennium of life. Talk about practice. "But it's more of what you can become after we train you. Your potential."

Ava had hinted at something similar, but I had trouble believing either of them. I didn't have too much confidence in my potential—law school was only one example of my failures.

"Saturday morning we're flying to New York to deliver software to a company in exchange for something they've developed," Stella said. "You'll be coming with us. We need an Unbounded they don't recognize."

"But I don't know anything about it."

"By Saturday you'll know enough."

"Why don't you just e-mail or Fed-Ex the program to them?"

They shared an amused glance that irritated me. "Too risky," Stella said. "We must be sure they fulfill their part of the bargain. I can't give you details now, but suffice to say, it's to our good fortune that you've joined us at this time."

I hadn't actually "joined" anything. Not of my own will. But already I could tell that these people excelled at using whatever— or whoever—was at their disposal.

Standing, I paced a few steps under the pretense of stretching. They didn't move to stop me, and my gaze shifted to the automatic doors. If I made it outside before they stopped me, I could get away and call my family. I could be safe in Tom's arms, this nightmare behind me.

Yet what if everything they'd told me was real? What if I was different? Special. Not the ordinary middle child in a family of overachievers. I'd seen the video. I'd watched my burned body heal, felt my body absorbing that sticky gelatin and the clear substance in the IV bags. My two most notable scars—on my thumb and my eyebrow—were gone, and more miraculous, my arm regrown.

I ran a hand over the stubble on my head, abruptly feeling

naked and exposed. Vulnerable. I didn't know how much more strangeness I could take without losing it.

Stella made a sympathetic noise in her throat. "Your hair should grow back pretty fast now. All the curequick will affect that, too."

"Only as a side effect of your entire body speeding up to make repairs," Cort clarified. "Give it another few days, and it'll look like any short haircut."

"Meantime, I have something you could wear." Rising to her feet, Stella motioned me to one of the large metal lockers against the wall. Numerous pieces of clothing hung inside, some obviously period pieces. She laughed when she saw my wonder. "I'm a bit of a packrat. I keep them here so my husband doesn't—" She broke off, the smile vanishing, and I knew I'd learned something about her. Stella was married, and not to an Unbounded. Did he know her true nature?

That made me wonder how it would be telling Tom. I wondered if he'd believe or if I'd have to cut myself or something to prove it. Yet wasn't the accident proof enough?

Stella took out a red-and-black checkered hat, a thing I'd never be caught dead in before, but I let her put it on, and when she angled the mirror on the door to the locker so I could see myself, I decided it looked good. But the short hair reminded me of the accident, the terror I'd experienced, and what I'd lost. Who I'd lost.

The now-familiar pain exploded in my chest, and for a moment I was stunned at its magnitude. My heart, apparently, was one thing they couldn't fix with any amount of protein concentrate. I struggled for breath, struggled not to collapse to the floor and curl into a fetal position. "I have to see Tom," I said, forcing the words between clenched teeth. "His sister, she was in the car. She's dead. He grew up in foster homes until she found him. He doesn't have anyone else but me."

Because I'd been trying not to repeat mistakes that had caused me so much embarrassment and pain in the past, he'd barely met my family. They had no idea how I felt about him—which I guess put them about even with me since I didn't know how I felt either.

"I know. He's holding her funeral tomorrow." Stella's eyes showed pity. "Yours is tomorrow, too."

I whirled then and started for one of the huge automatic doors. I was leaving, going back to Tom and my family. That was more important than any secret software or Unbounded struggle for control. Afterward, I would return to learn more—on my own terms, and not as their prisoner. Because a part of me desperately wanted what they were saying to be true. I wanted to *be* someone. To make a difference as I hadn't attempted doing since leaving college.

Stella didn't move to stop me, and Cort only kicked his feet up on one of the computer desks and leaned back, his hands folded over his stomach. I received a brief impression of somber amusement and hoped that didn't mean all the exits were locked.

Next to the huge outer doors, I spied a smaller one with a regular knob. I angled toward this, praying it would open. It did. In a second I was through and hurrying over a cement loading dock that connected to the parking area by means of a concrete ramp.

It was early evening, as far as I could tell, and the day had been a hot one even for early September. Heat radiated off the parking lot, the hot air rising in visible distorted waves. In every direction I saw buildings and cement, and only one road leading away. Though no people were in sight, the honk of a horn and the racing of distant engines were welcome sounds after the isolation of the warehouse. I might have to walk some distance before I knew where I was, but with the stolen cell phone, it would be only minutes before Tom was on his way to me. I quickened my pace.

A rush of air blew against me, and a man stood in my way. He was tall and tanned and muscular, and his black hair was longer than I generally liked on a man, yet it fit him perfectly. Power poured off him like the heat from the tarmac. By the hard lines of his square jaw and his determined stance, I knew he wasn't there to wish me well in my bid for freedom.

CHAPTER 4

I TRIED TO MOVE AROUND HIM, BUT HE STEPPED IN FRONT OF ME AGAIN. He was closer now, his wide shoulders level with my eyes, his muscles tight under the navy T-shirt. I let my eyes trail downward, taking in hiking boots and faded jeans that he filled out to good advantage before moving back to his tanned face. Despite my irritation, I couldn't help but stare. If Stella could possibly have a male opposite, this man would be a good candidate for the job. His face wasn't as perfect as hers but it was attractive in a rugged, compelling way, the bronze skin marred only by beard stubble.

"You're Ritter, I take it." I didn't hide the bitterness in my voice. He certainly wasn't the overweight Laurence, whom I'd presumably have the chance of outrunning.

His face twitched in what might have been a poor attempt at a smile. "Ava wants you to stay here."

"Ava doesn't own me."

Irritation echoed in eyes so dark I had to call them black. "Sometimes people have to be protected from themselves. So they won't do something stupid."

I searched for something to say, and Cort's comments about

Ritter's hatred for the Emporium came to mind. "Oh, but wouldn't that be Emporium rhetoric?" I said it mockingly because I had no idea really who the Emporium was, except what the others had told me, and for all I knew they were making everything up. I was pleased to see Ritter flinch.

"Stay put before you get us all killed." The confident way he spoke told me he wasn't accustomed to being disobeyed.

I turned and went the other way, sprinting now. But somehow he was there before me, blocking my path. I ran into him before I could halt my momentum. Strong hands grabbed my arms. I beat at his chest. "Let me go!"

His hands tightened on my arms, his fingers biting painfully into my skin and bringing my struggle to a quick end. "You'll have enough time to act like a mindless idiot later," he gritted. "You aren't starting tonight."

"What kind of monsters are you? My family thinks I'm dead! Do you know the pain they're going through?"

His face was expressionless. "Right now the only thing I care about is that you're wasting my time."

"What do you care about your precious time? You're Unbounded, remember?"

"Am I?" He lifted one dark brow.

More mind games. I yanked myself from his grasp and lurched into a run. I hadn't gone five steps before he blocked my path again, one strong hand gripping my arm, his mouth twisted in a grim smile. It was no use. He was too fast. I'd never seen anyone move the way he did. "How?" I asked.

"Years of practice."

"See? Unbounded."

He shrugged. "You'd better go inside."

"Or you'll *make* me?" I didn't know what had overcome me. Usually, I wasn't into confrontations—or hadn't been since law school. In my family, I was the peacemaker, the one to smooth everything over. The one who felt guilty when she didn't deliver what her parents expected. What was happening to me?

I didn't want to change. I wanted to remain who I'd always been. I wanted my life back.

My turmoil must have shown in my face because Ritter's grip loosened slightly on my arm and something akin to pity chased across his face. "It'll be okay."

"It's not okay!" I went up on my toes to shout as close as I could to his face. With luck someone in the neighboring buildings would hear and come to investigate. "I want my family. I want Tom. I want out of here!" Tears came then, the flood I'd been holding back. I felt the fabric of my heart rip, a small hole becoming as large as the missing pieces of my life. What if they meant to keep me from my family forever? I started to slump to the ground, my hands coming to my face to block out this whole terrible nightmare.

As if I weighed no more than a bag of salt, Ritter picked me up, slung me over his shoulder, and stomped back to the warehouse, barely halting to fling open the door. I struggled half-heartedly, but it did me no good. Every part of him was solid as if he'd been working out for years.

Probably centuries.

I hated him. I hated all of them.

I closed my eyes, forcing away the tears, already angry at myself for giving into despair. No. I would not give up. I'd find a way around whatever Ava chose to put in front of me, especially this block of human stone.

"Sheeze, Ritter." Stella looked up from her computer screen, once again wearing her headset. "I hate to remind you, but that sort of behavior went out of style centuries ago."

He set me down, his eyes running over my body. "If you ask me, there's something to be said for throwing them over your shoulder and doing with them what you will."

Stella snorted. "Barbarian!"

Ritter bent and scooped up the hat that had fallen from my head when he let me go, and I caught a gleam of a gold chain previously hidden under his shirt. There was a fluid magnetism in his movement and for a moment all thoughts of escape deserted me. Our eyes met, my furious gray ones to his cold obsidian. We were standing close—too close. At that moment I became aware of him, not as an obstacle, but as a man. A living, breathing man with more confidence and sexuality than I'd ever encountered in anyone before. The power I'd felt from him outside drew me in, beckoned me to touch. I couldn't breathe.

A flare of something in Ritter's eyes. What? I couldn't say. It didn't matter. I despised him and everything he represented. I needed all my energy to get back to Tom and my family.

"This isn't over," I muttered. Even so, it was all I could do to step away.

He gave me a mocking smile. "I'm sure it isn't."

Cort, his feet still ensconced on the desk next to one of the computers, cleared his throat before adding his two cents, "I think you've met your match, Ritter."

"Shut up," Ritter growled.

Cort laughed. "You're just mad 'cause she's not batting her eyes at you like every other female you meet."

"Shut up both of you." Stella was staring at an e-mail. "Listen. This morning in New York there was another attempt on John Halden's life."

Ritter swiftly made his way to her computer, bending over with his hands on the wide desk, his face moving only slightly as he read the words. I couldn't help but notice what a striking couple Stella and Ritter made, both so attractive and completely sure of themselves. There was an easy familiarity in their manner toward each other, and I wondered if they'd ever been romantically involved.

I didn't know why I cared.

"I should have been there." Ritter threw me a look of disgust.

"You were needed here," Stella said.

I debated whether or not to make a dash for the door, but given his uncanny speed, I doubted I'd succeed. Besides, curiosity burned inside me. I went to stand between Stella and Cort. "Who's John Halden?"

"The world's richest man," Cort answered. "Though you'd never be able to track all his companies to him. We keep tabs on him through several of his employees. Pass him technology when we need to. He has a huge network."

I was beginning to understand. "You use him to develop Unbounded inventions."

"He's currently our main contact." Stella sent a quick reply to the e-mail as she spoke, though her hands weren't touching the computer. Her uncovered eye was slightly out of focus, and I could see movement through the lens of her eyepiece. "From time to time, Halden comes up with technology on his own as well. He's the man we're going to see in New York."

Ritter glanced at Stella. "What have you told her?"

She calmly removed her headset. "Only that we need her to go with us, and that Halden has come up with a program we must have." She looked away from Ritter to meet my gaze, rolling her eyes where he couldn't see. "Anyway, in exchange for Halden's software, we're giving him a virtual reality program I've designed with some help from my counterparts in New York, London, and Italy. It's going to make Halden's company a fortune in video games alone."

I felt a distinct disappointment. "More video games. Isn't that the last thing people need?"

Stella smiled. "Oh, but the program has far greater potential than just for gaming. Especially in medical and science applications. Imagine students being right there when a doctor performs an actual surgery, or as scientists conduct a dangerous physics experiment. You'll be able to experience dozens of scenarios, and that means better training and more lives saved. There are limitless possibilities in all areas of education."

My disgust became embarrassment at my ignorance. I needed to remember to keep my mouth shut around these people.

"Unfortunately, Halden is all too mortal." Cort gave me a wistful smile. He'd taken his feet from the desk and scooted his chair closer to Stella's monitor. "Like Archimedes, Gutenberg,

Franklin, Jenner, Tesla, Edison, and all the rest we've worked with over the years. That means we have to protect him from the Emporium."

They'd worked with Thomas Edison? If that was true, it would certainly explain why he'd taken out so many patents. "Why don't you start a company of your own?"

Ritter's eyes narrowed. "Too many want us dead. We have other enemies besides the Emporium."

"Ritter's right," Stella said. "We'd be too exposed. It'd take all our resources and personnel. This works for now."

"Until Halden's dead." Ritter's voice held no emotion, but I received an impression of inner fury that frightened me with its bleakness.

"Then go save him, by all means." I waved my arm at the door. "Don't let me keep you."

"Halden will be all right," Stella said. "Our people were there in time and he'll be extra careful now for the next little while. He has bodyguards."

Ritter snorted. "No match for Emporium Unbounded."

"I don't know," Stella said lightly. "He's got access to really good body armor. New design. And our guys are in the wings. Besides, you know as well as I do that we're grooming someone to run his company when he does die."

"If the replacement can be trusted, you mean." Ritter's tone implied that such a thing was doubtful.

Stella folded her arms. "I think he can be."

"Regardless, he's not ready to run the company yet." Ritter backed away from the computer, his eyes falling on me. "I'll be outside in case you decide to run away again."

"Wait a minute," I said.

He lifted one brow, impatience in the taut lines of his impressive body.

"How old are you?"

"Does it matter?"

Why did the man have to be so difficult? "Humor me."

"Two hundred and seventy-three."

So, several decades younger than Ava, but older than Stella by nearly fifty years. When I didn't say anything further, he turned and stalked away.

"What's his problem?" I asked the others.

Cort laughed. "The better question is what isn't Ritter's problem?"

Stella wasn't amused. "He has a past. Many Unbounded do."

"What happened to him?" I was more interested than I wanted to be.

"It's his story to share," Stella said. "Or not."

Cort cleared his throat. "Maybe it's better if she knows the risks."

"It's his story," Stella repeated.

"Just tell me already." I didn't bother to hide my annoyance at this exchange. How could I learn about the Unbounded if they didn't give me enough background?

"Ritter was a kind of policeman, I guess you'd call it." Cort didn't look at Stella as he spoke, but I knew he couldn't miss the way she sat up stiffly in her chair. "One day when he was working, he was stabbed numerous times, which killed him, or so they thought. When his family started laying him out at their home before the burial, his mother discovered he wasn't really dead but only badly injured and healing quickly." He glanced at Stella, who relaxed, and I knew there was more, a lot more, but they weren't going to tell it to me. Even so the story made my irritation at the man subside a notch. Almost dying like that had to affect a person. I knew.

"Do all Unbounded have such a horrible beginning?" Ava had said something to the contrary, but so far I wasn't encouraged.

Stella shook her head. "I was born here in America, the descendant of an Italian Unbounded grandfather and Japanese mortal. As a child, I lost movement in my arm falling from a horse, and when I was suddenly healed as an adult, I thanked God for the miracle. Ava approached me the next day and explained that I was

Unbounded and had undergone the Change. My father didn't have the active gene and was never let in on the secret, so my grandfather and uncles in Italy had asked her to watch over me when I neared the age of Change. I was excited to learn the truth. My parents never knew, though I confided in my younger sister."

"You didn't go to Italy to be with your Unbounded relatives?" I asked.

"I've spent some years there off and on, but this is my family now. Besides, I have my sister's posterity to look after. Two in Oregon are nearing the age of Change. Now that you're safely with us, we'll be moving there to keep an eye on them."

I looked at Cort, but he shook his head. "No trauma here, either, except that I had no one to explain what was happening to me. My Unbounded ancestors either weren't aware of me, or they were killed long before I came along. I was born in Germany and lived a normal life—until I stayed young while everyone around me aged. Fortunately, my talent is in the sciences, so I made accurate conclusions rather quickly. I moved to America during the revolution, but it wasn't until about thirty-five years ago that I heard a story of two high school buddies meeting after fifty odd years and one swearing the other hadn't aged. That led me to Laurence and eventually to the group."

"He was lucky he found us and not the Emporium," Stella said. "Or that they didn't notice him first."

The scariest thing was that I utterly believed them.

Not that believing them would stop me from being with my family or Tom. Leaving them behind wasn't an option, and neither was waiting until we returned from whatever Ava wanted me to do in New York. Tomorrow my mother and father would bury what they thought was me, and I couldn't let them endure that horror for a second longer than I had to. As for Tom, the idea of him mourning both Justine and me by himself gnawed at me constantly.

"Erin, are you okay?" Cort took my elbow and led me to the couch, sitting so close to me our thighs nearly touched. "I thought you were going to faint there for a moment. Stella, can you bring her a drink?"

"Thank you." I touched his hand in gratitude before easing away from him. Tension winged between us, like a current of electricity I couldn't see.

"It'll take a while to get your normal strength back. Even though you may look and feel well, you're not a hundred percent. You'll recover soon."

I had the odd sense that he was hiding something, but as I studied him, his face showed only sincerity, his eyes an eagerness to please. Maybe it was his physical closeness that made me uncomfortable, and the odd heat that reminded me of soft sheets and blanketing darkness.

Or maybe I'd landed on the wrong side of the Unbounded issue. It was possible that the Emporium were the good guys, and I was being set up by the Renegades to do something in New York that I'd regret forever. Something that would hurt not only my family but all humanity.

Because in all the talk about John Halden and the software, I realized that everyone had carefully avoided mentioning what program we would receive from him in return.

CHAPTER 5

STELLA RETURNED WITH A CLEAR LIQUID IN A TALL CRYSTAL GLASS. "It's curequick, but this tastes better than the gelatin version."

The other had tasted good enough, so I eagerly drank down the liquid, feeling energy seep through my body. "You really invented this?" I asked Cort.

He shrugged modestly. "I had a little extra time on my hands."

My unexpected laugh was cut short when Ava entered the warehouse and strode toward us, unzipping a white lab coat.

"Well?" Cort asked.

"Definite tampering with files," Ava replied. "However, no one at the burn center is aware of anything amiss, and we can't find a link to Erin."

"There has to be a link." Stella crossed to the desk and clapped on her headset, not appearing to mind the probes that must dig into her scalp. As she sat in front of one computer, the computer linked to the headset also came to life and began running code. "No way it's coincidence."

"Agreed. But I was unable to extract any valuable information from the employees. Dimitri stayed behind to do a little more investigating since he's the one with the medical license." Ava's gaze focused on me. "Feeling better?"

"I'll feel fine when you let me go." I tried to keep my face expressionless like Ritter, but I failed miserably. Ava's complete self-assurance provoked too much resistance in me.

She sighed. "How about I take you someplace else? Now that you don't need around-the-clock supervision, you'll be more comfortable staying with me until we leave for New York."

"What if I don't want to go to New York?"

Ava frowned before crossing over to the desk area to stand behind Stella. "For the moment, you have no choice, but I'm confident you'll make the right decision. Sooner or later you're going to need us." Her exasperation was clear, and that slip of control made me feel victorious.

Stella rose from the computer, setting down her headset. "I've given the computer a few search parameters to look for indications of what might have happened at the burn center, but I have to leave in a minute. Bronson made dinner." Her voice became painfully bright at the mention of her husband. I didn't understand why, but I liked her enough that I was curious to know the reason.

"Be extra careful on your way home," Ava advised her.

"I always am."

Ava set a comforting hand on Stella's arm, and though the contact lasted only fleetingly, I knew it was genuine. Turning, she said to me, "Let's go."

With a farewell nod at Stella and Cort, I followed Ava out the small door and down the concrete ramp to a white sedan. I'd barely opened the passenger side door when Ritter appeared and threw a black duffel into the backseat. It clinked heavily as it landed.

Great. Just great, I thought as he ducked into the car. His presence would make any escape attempt that much more difficult, but at least I still had the phone in my pocket, and I would use it the moment I had the opportunity.

As she started the car, Ava said, "I have a late class tonight, so Ritter's going to stay with you."

"I don't need a babysitter."

"But you do need to begin training. Tonight will be your first lesson."

"What kind of training?" I tried to keep the resentment from my voice, but I didn't think I was fooling Ava—or Ritter who hadn't yet spoken a word from the backseat.

Ava kept her eyes on the road, shifting down as we approached a red light. "Every Unbounded is genetically predisposed with an ability. Some are good at science or medicine. Some have a way with computers and technology. Languages, combat, patterns, numbers—you get the picture."

I rolled my eyes. "People aren't genetically predisposed for careers."

"Oh, but they are. Even among mortals many sons and grand-sons follow in their parents' footsteps."

Since I'd wanted to follow my father into law, maybe she had a point.

"Unbounded really don't have a choice." Ava glanced at me and then back at the road. "We often think we'll go into something different—we may spend years fighting it—but we always end up in the same or similar profession as one of our Unbounded ancestors. It's tied up with the gene. Most of us develop many different skills over our long life spans, but we are truly talented at whatever drives us, so we focus on our dominant trait. Playing to our strengths makes sense."

"Let me guess. Stella's has something to do with computers."

"She's what we call a technopath—an ability that wasn't even understood until the past fifty years or so. Not only does she under-stand anything to do with computers, she can connect directly to them with a neural receiver and, through electrical impulses and eye movements, increase the rate of processing, program-ming, searching, or whatever by dozens of times. The rest of us see gobbledygook if we try to use a neural receiver, but her brain manages to make sense of the information."

That explained the metal probes and the eyepiece. "So what's our family trait?" With my luck, my ancestors were all chefs. I hated cooking.

"You will be learning combat."

I choked back a derisive laugh. I'd tried a self-defense class once and quit after ten lessons. The relief in the teacher's expression hadn't been in my imagination.

"I hope you will apply yourself tonight." Ava's voice contained ice. "You'll be surprised how much Ritter will teach you in a few hours. He's an exceptionally gifted fighter."

From the corner of my eye, I caught a glimpse of Ritter. His face was expressionless, but I knew instinctively that he found this whole situation amusing. I doubt he'd think it funny when I finally managed to escape.

"I guess that explains your interest in karate," I said to Ava, as she turned the car into an area where the houses all had to be worth several million dollars. I would have gaped if my whole world had not already been turned upside down. "But I don't understand why you waste time teaching. If you're basically at war with this so-called Emporium, why bother with anything else? A karate class can't change the world."

"It's actually taekwondo."

"It's still a waste of time." I had the sense that I'd irritated her, though I could see no sign of it on her face. "Tell me, what's the point of teaching self-defense classes when on other days you're out saving the world—a world that doesn't even know it's being saved?"

That it seemed anticlimactic was only part of the issue. As an almost immortal, a demigod, shouldn't there be something more in her life? At the very least I'd expect prominent positions on important boards or think tanks. Or even a life of utter luxury and indolence.

When Ava didn't immediately respond, I glanced at Ritter, who met my gaze without blinking. A shiver of awareness tingled down my spine, but I didn't know if it was because I knew he was ready for me to make a move, or because he was so frighteningly attractive. I wasn't imagining his hands running over my body. I wasn't. There was Tom to think about.

I gave him my best cold stare and turned back to the front.

Ava pulled up to a gated drive, rolling down the window and punching a code into a little silver box. The black wrought iron gate swung inward, but Ava didn't move the car forward. "You really want to know why I teach, Erin? Because there comes a time when the newness wears off, and you will have to decide what to do with the rest of your very long life. Fighting the Emporium is my main purpose and always will be, but there are many days when we simply watch and wait. Stella and a few others like her do most of that, informing us when we need to act. I could concentrate on amassing wealth like Laurence, and I did that at one time—we all did—but each of us comes to a point where we have to find our life's ambition. To use what we know. To make our lives meaningful." Her gray eyes had become black shadows in the dimming light. "I like teaching women to defend themselves. Especially against the men in their lives, the men they should be able to trust. If I have the chance to save even one woman's life in my spare time, I'm willing to make the effort." Without another word, she edged the car down the long, tree-lined drive.

Against my will, I felt the tiniest bit of admiration for this woman who claimed to be my relative.

We rounded a bend and the house came into view. All other thoughts vanished from my mind. To say the building was huge would be an understatement. Nothing short of a mansion, it was many times grander than all the other houses we'd passed. I had the impression of endless manicured lawns, towering trees, elaborate flowerbeds, ornate pillars, and many windows before I was whisked inside.

"We'll meet you in the gym," Ava told Ritter. "I'll show Erin to the main floor guest room. Will you be staying tonight?"

"Yes, but don't bother to make up a room. I probably won't use it." Another glance at me had my face flaming. Was his comment related to me and my strange attraction to him?

"Unbounded can't read minds or anything, can they?" I asked as Ava led me down the hall.

Her step hesitated ever so slightly. "A few Unbounded have the ability of being sensitive to others' feelings, depending on the situation and how well they know the person. Extreme emotion or stress can accentuate or hinder the ability. It's unreliable even in the best of times, but still helpful, even vital, for many operations. It's a talent the Emporium most desires, though fortunately their inbreeding hasn't been successful at giving them enough of what they want." Two seconds of silence, and then she added, "Why do you ask?"

"Ritter makes me uncomfortable."

She laughed. "He makes everyone uncomfortable. But don't worry—his ability is combat, not mind reading. Besides, anyone can learn to block a casual reading, and there are other methods we use when going up against the Emporium to protect ourselves."

"And I guess they use those same methods against you."

"Of course."

Some part of me noticed the details of the carved wood panels that bordered the hallway, the elaborate crown molding, the many light fixtures, and the elegant furniture, the exquisite paintings that were probably originals, but for the most part I felt numb to the sensory information. What was opulence when compared to near immortality?

"Ah, here we are." She pushed open a door to the guest room, or guest suite, rather, since we entered a spacious sitting room that connected to a bedroom. The walls were papered in here, but they had the same crown molding and elegant furnishings in shades of calming blue. "Dimitri bought you clothes today, and I had the housekeeper put them in the closet. You won't be disappointed. Dimitri has a good eye."

"He's had enough years to learn, I guess." I kept my words light, but I was touched that he'd taken the time.

"Hurry and change into something appropriate, so I can show you to the gym before I leave." She didn't trust me. I could tell from the deliberate casualness of her comment, the alert way her body moved.

"When can I see my family?"

She sighed. "Be patient. You have a lot of time."

"They don't."

She gave me a wistful smile. "No. They don't. Look, go along with this meeting in New York on Saturday, and then we'll set something up with your family."

"I have no skills. I can't help you."

At that she smiled. "I believe you have the potential to become one of the most valuable Renegades alive today. Your talent just needs to be awakened."

I snorted. "Even if fighting is my talent, I'd hardly have the corner on the market. You and Ritter are far more skilled." Something didn't add up here. There was more I didn't understand, more she wasn't willing to tell me.

"Don't worry about your skills, or lack of them. Ritter will prepare you well enough physically. I'll brief you more thoroughly on the plane to New York, but for now, only a few of us know all the details. It's safer that way."

Safer? Or an excuse to lead me on?

Keeping my doubts to myself, I took a few steps toward the bedroom door. "Whose house is this? Dimitri's?"

"It belongs to a friend of ours."

"Unbounded?"

"Of course. He lent it to us when we came to Kansas."

"Yet you also have that house next to my grandmother's."

"You visited her often. It was a good way to see you."

Keep tabs on me, she meant. My grandmother probably confided a great deal about my personal life to Ava, as she had to the other neighbors who all knew me by sight. I wondered if Ava had learned why I'd left law school.

My emotions seesawed again, and I glared coldly at her. "I will never forgive you for making my family suffer any more than they already have."

The compassion in her face didn't ease my anger. "That is your choice. Regardless, *you* are my primary concern right now, especially after the anomalies in the burn center records. We closely guard our genealogy, and we don't think they can connect you to us, but for the time being, it's vital that your parents go through with the funeral."

Vital for the Unbounded, she meant.

"I could at least call them," I said.

"No, because you couldn't explain. Even on secure lines we use code. The Emporium has enough technology to make countries like America and Japan look backward in comparison. Please just wait until after New York. This operation is extremely important."

"Why?"

"I can't tell you that. Not yet."

"Because you don't trust me."

She sighed. "Because you haven't decided yet what side you're on."

Having no answer, I turned and went farther into the suite. The centerpiece in the spacious bedroom was a huge bed with a wrought iron headboard, the mattress so thick I'd need a step stool to climb under the golden quilt. A door on the far side opened onto an oversized bathroom and a closet bigger than the bedroom in my basement apartment. Clothes filled a two-foot portion of one rack, and several drawers held underclothes and socks. Apparently, Dimitri felt our relationship would be long term.

Removing the cell phone from my pocket, I hid it under the socks. Better to keep it here as it was unlikely I'd have a chance to be alone during the training session. Besides, I hadn't exactly decided who I'd call and what I'd say. It wasn't every day I had to inform people I wasn't actually dead.

Minutes later, dressed in loose gray sweat bottoms and a red sports bra, I reentered the sitting room where Ava waited. In silence, we went through the house again, going down a wide staircase that opened into a family room. Beyond that was the gym, its floor lined with mats and exercise equipment running the length of the walls. Ritter had changed into sweat bottoms as I had and was on his back lifting weights, his blue T-shirt darkened with sweat, his triceps gleaming with the effort. He was beautiful to watch.

"Ritter, not too hard yet," Ava warned.

He cast me a mocking glance. "I'll go easy on her."

I only hoped I had the opportunity to "accidentally" hurt him. Really hurt him.

Ava was smiling as she left, as though she suspected my determination, which irritated me even more. "So what does a combat ability mean exactly?" I asked when she was gone.

Ritter put aside his weights and came toward me. "It means having fast reflexes and good coordination, anticipating your opponent's moves, and knowing the best way to kill."

If that was true, my chances for escape should be increasing by the minute. "Okay, let's do this."

Ritter took two long shiny sticks from a rack on the wall, tossing one to me. His was black, mine a deep blue with white marbling. I ran my hands along the smooth surface that tapered to a blunt point on each end. "This is a bo staff," Ritter said. "We'll begin with this since your skin is still healing. Hold it like this. No. Look at my hands. About this far apart. Spread out your feet. If they're together, you'll be knocked off balance too easily."

I readjusted my hold and my stance. I felt good. Steady. Maybe I could do this.

"Come at me. I'll show you how to block."

I hit his stick with a satisfying thump.

"Not like that! Hit me like you mean it. You can't hurt me."

I attacked, slamming the stick into him, aiming for his inflated head. He blocked me easily.

"Harder!"

I swung at his stomach, his chest, his feet. His groin. Anywhere I could think of, but each time my staff rebounded off his, the shock reverberating throughout my body until I wondered if my teeth would fall out.

"Now you try to block me."

I could tell he wasn't trying hard, because several times he had a clear shot and didn't take it. "Faster," he urged. "No, bring your staff up like this."

Sweat slicked all my exposed skin as I tried to comply with his demands. I understood the basic moves easily enough, but I didn't have the muscles or the speed to even begin competing with him. At one point when I blocked, I tripped over my own feet, slamming backwards onto the mat, my lungs screaming as my body struggled for breath.

Ritter stood over me. "You okay?"

"As soon as . . . I figure . . . out where . . . they put all the air," I gasped. "Are you sure I have a talent for this? Because it really doesn't feel like it." Nothing was clicking. I received no inner warning as to where he might strike, felt no intuitiveness about where to place my staff. Next to Ritter, I was slow and clumsy.

"Better not depend on anything they say about genetics. All Unbounded must learn to defend themselves. It will come easier in a few weeks." He offered his hand. "Let's take a rest. Get a drink."

I let him help me up, still wheezing. Regardless of what he said, my talent had better kick in soon, or I might not live much longer.

Except maybe I couldn't die from something as mundane as exhaustion or lack of air. Or maybe suffocation was one of the ways the Unbounded could be killed. As soon as I could breathe properly again, I'd ask. I'd run out on Stella and Cort before we'd covered that vital tidbit.

I followed Ritter to a large alcove in the gym that housed a kitchenette. Peeling off his shirt, he took a can from the mini fridge and sat at the table, stretching out his legs. Now I could see the gold chain I'd only glimpsed before; on this hung two small gold bands and an even smaller ring that might have fit a child. I wondered who the rings had belonged to.

"Curequick?" I asked. He looked even better without a shirt, and I knew Tom would hate that I noticed. He'd become a bit possessive of late.

"Beer."

I frowned in disappointment. I really wanted the kick Cort's mixture gave me. Instead, I drank water, though it had the strange taste of rose petals and beer anyway. I knew I was absorbing some of Ritter's drink, but I didn't know where the roses came from. Probably outside. Strange that I didn't feel the least bit hungry, though I hadn't eaten anything solid in days. Not that I wouldn't mind a big steak about now. There was comfort in the familiar.

"So," I said, leaning back against the counter, "how exactly is it that Unbounded can die?"

His dark eyes studied me for a few seconds before replying. "By completely severing all three focus points."

"Focus points?"

"Yes, focus points store everything we are—our thoughts, feeling, memories, intelligence. We have a triple system backup in case we're wounded. These are located in the heart, the brain, and the reproductive organs. Even if you sever one of these completely from the others, the body will heal and become exactly as it was before. But separating all three from each other is fatal."

I stared at him. "You're saying if I cut off your head, it'd grow back exactly like it is now?"

"Or if you drown me, cut me in half, or stick a stake in my heart. As long as any two focus points are connected, an Unbounded will survive."

"You expect me to believe that?"

He shrugged. "It doesn't matter what you believe. It's true." There was bleakness in the words, and I wondered exactly how damaged he'd been when he'd been taken home for dead all those years ago. Or what had happened to him in the centuries since.

"That would mean if you lost your kidney or your heart, your gallbladder—"

"They'd grow back."

I wanted to tell him he was nuts. They were all nuts. Yet I'd seen my arm, and unless they had a way of manipulating memories, I was living proof of these claims.

"What if I'd burned so much that the tissue between my focus points burned away?"

Ritter shook his head. "Unlikely. Dimitri could explain it better since he's a physician, but in a trauma situation, the Unbounded body protects that link. The only way, really, is to sever it."

With something really sharp, I was betting.

"What's the second way?" I hoped it didn't get any worse.

"Starvation."

"But we're absorbing from the air constantly, aren't we?"

"Hard to do if you're in a sealed metal room or a cement room over two feet thick. Food molecules can't get through."

"How long would it take to starve?"

He thought for a moment. "Double or triple what it takes a normal human body to rot to pieces. Depending on the temperature, it could take years."

I shivered. What a horrible way to die.

Worse than being hacked to pieces? The world of an Unbounded was much darker than I'd suspected. No wonder Ava was so cautious.

Ritter downed the rest of his beer and tossed it into the garbage. I set my glass in the sink. "Let's work on a few kicks and hand-holds," he said. "Ways to get away if someone grabs you."

I was glad to leave the staff behind. Muscles I didn't know I had ached, and my lungs still felt tight.

He was waiting for me on the mat, and I walked toward him with trepidation. I wasn't sure I wanted to work so closely with him, especially when he wasn't wearing a shirt. The staff at least allowed me to keep some distance.

"Grab me," he said, holding out his hands.

He had good hands, with long, well-shaped fingers, and strong wrists that curved gracefully into muscled arms. Not bulky enough to be ungainly or grotesque, but powerful and all man. Not a scar on him, of course—at least not on the outside. He was whole and untouched, not a man who had apparently been stabbed and left for dead.

"Go ahead. Give it all you got," he urged.

I hesitated.

"Grab my wrists!"

I did as he asked, and at once my hold was thrown violently off, my arms protesting at the abuse.

"Now you try."

I did without much success. We repeated the movements several times until he was satisfied. Then he grabbed me from behind and told me to break free. I could feel the warmth of him, the moistness of his skin, his heart beating against my back, his arms heavy and strong around me. My heart thundered—and not just because of the workout. I didn't know him well enough to be comfortable with this kind of intimacy, but at the same time I craved it. Craved him.

We went over every single hold I could imagine and then some. Next, we worked on kicks and punches. Rivulets of sweat ran down my neck and between my breasts. Before long I was too exhausted to notice when his body touched mine. Besides, his manner had no room for me as a person, as a woman, and I wondered if his life's experiences had created a monster, a killing machine that survived only to train more killers. More than anything I wanted to quit, but something about his cold determination forced me to continue.

At last he nodded and said we were finished. I gently ran my hands over my arms and they came away smeared with traces of blood. My skin felt raw everywhere, but especially my arms.

He saw the blood and the hardness left his face. "You should have told me you were hurting."

"It wasn't important."

We were standing close. I could smell his sweat, feel my own dampening my entire body, mixing with the blood on my arms. Neither of us moved away. Tension sprang between us like something with a life of its own.

Against my will, I thought of him touching me, of gliding my own hands over his sweaty chest. I ran my tongue along my parched bottom lip, and his eyes followed the movement. Pressure built until it screamed in my head.

I clamped down on my emotions. He was physically appealing—I wasn't fooling myself on that score—but this blatant desire coming out of nowhere wasn't me. I preferred to actually know a man before starting something more. Another lesson learned during my bitter stint in law school. Another reason I hadn't said yes to Tom.

Yet I wasn't ready to back down, either. To move away would be another kind of defeat. A show of fear. I met his gaze head on, my eyes narrowed, my lips pressed together.

In the end, it was Ritter who stepped away, his black eyes dark and unreadable. The moment he did, all the emotions fell away, as though they hadn't been mine to keep. Blood still rushed through my veins and my breath came shallowly, but I could think clearly again.

I knew only one thing—I had to get out of this insane place and back where I belonged. I didn't like what I was becoming.

CHAPTER 6

AVA MET US AT THE TOP OF THE STAIRS. HER EYES LOOKED ME OVER, faltering on the red rashes and streaks on my arms. "I thought you said you'd go easy on her," she said to Ritter.

"I did."

She gave him a half smile. "You joining us for dinner?"

Now that she mentioned food, I could smell something delicious in the air. My stomach didn't growl in anticipation, but my mouth watered. I wondered if the others still had that ability—to have their mouths water at the thought of food. Certainly some of their bodily functions were still very much in place, if my attraction to Ritter was any indication. I didn't dare look at him as he spoke.

"I'm going to do rounds," he said.

"George and Charles are doing them here. And Marco and Gaven are still outside the warehouse. They all know what we're up against."

"Never hurts to double up. I'll also check in with Dimitri. Be back in an hour. Two, tops."

Ava nodded. No false hostessing here. No reason to make a plea that he needed to sustain himself when he could get anything he needed from the air around him.

His leaving meant that Ava was the only obstacle to my sneaking away, but I couldn't leave until she retired and that meant there was time for dinner.

"I'm hungry," I said. "I mean, I could eat." Because I wasn't really hungry.

Ava smiled. "Why don't we both shower and meet in the dining room? I'll show you where it is on the way to your room."

She wasn't going to watch me? Then I remembered the men she'd talked about. No doubt they were monitoring inside as well as outside the house. That might complicate my plan.

I looked for cameras on the way back, noticing several. Not favorable to an escape, but in the dark, wearing black, I shouldn't be too noticeable if I kept to the shadows along the walls.

I hoped.

I dressed in dark jeans and a thin, zippered jacket to hide the bright white of my skin. The jeans were stiff and new and a little loose, but the stretchy material of the black jacket fit my body like a glove. Dimitri had bought hats, too, and still very much aware of my ultra short hair, I pulled on a black French beret, feeling gratitude toward the man. He'd been so kind to me in each of our few encounters, and his detailed purchases for me, from shoes and hair elastics to face cream and sanitary supplies, were uncanny.

I entered the dining room five minutes before Ava arrived. It seemed rather ostentatious to use the enormous room for two, but neither Ava nor the cook, a kindly rounded woman with graying hair and sagging cheeks, seemed to think it strange. The cook, whose name turned out to be Janice, was practically invisible as she served the steak and potatoes, gliding along and anticipating our every need. I wondered if she knew what Ava really was.

What I really was.

I soon forgot her as I dug into my second steak, so tender it almost melted in my mouth. One could grow used to this.

By the time I'd finished the meal, I peeked under my sleeves and saw that the rashes on my arms had faded, the tiny smears of dried blood flaking off the skin. I felt a lot better.

I yawned. "I think I'll turn in."

Ava's eyes settled on me. "You don't want to talk?"

"I'd rather sleep." Escape.

She walked me back to my room. "Don't take offense. I just want to make sure you get there okay. Please stay in your room until I come for you in the morning. I promise to make things right. Trust me."

Fat chance of that.

"Sleep well, Erin."

When she was gone, I went to the closet to retrieve the cell phone I'd stolen. My father would be the best to call, but he'd be the most suspicious and probably contact the police. Chris would be angry and think it was a prank. My mother—well, she probably wasn't answering the phone.

Tom, I decided. *I'll call Tom.* While he'd be spooked, he'd be willing to come and get me—provided I could make it out of the mansion and off the grounds. And provided we could figure out where I was. There had to be a house number down by the gate. Once I told him the story, we could go see my family. Besides, I wanted to see Tom. I needed his arms around me.

The cell phone wasn't in the sock drawer. I searched all the other drawers just in case, but I had a sinking feeling I hadn't fooled anyone. How had they known about it? Anger and fear twined together, paralyzing me for an instant until I managed to push the emotions to the back of my mind. I had to be calm. I had to think.

Okay, I'd walk to Tom's. Or hitchhike, if I needed to. I'd wait until later, though. The sun was setting, but there was still too much light coming through the windows to be sneaking around with any stealth. I climbed up on the bed and lay down fully dressed, planning to rest only a few minutes.

Sleep claimed me immediately. I dreamed I was in the car with Justine's head lolling toward me. Fire sprang from our clothes.

"Help me, Erin," she pleaded. "Please help me." I reached toward her, but my arm blackened and crumbled before I could free her from the safety belt.

I awoke with a start, and I could see by the lack of light in my room that it was much later than when I'd hefted myself onto the bed. The clock on the nightstand told me it was ten-thirty.

Time to go. I hoped Ritter wasn't back yet, or I might have blown my chance. Pulling on a pair of black running shoes, I slipped out the door, pressing my body against the wall. I hurried past the first camera. Then the second. Were there more I hadn't seen? At last I reached the front door and opened it. The moment of truth.

No alarm sounded. It could send a silent signal, though, and I worried about that as I ran across the yard, keeping to the shadow of the trees. When I arrived at the gate, I saw immediately that the stone fence was high and didn't offer any footholds and the trees weren't close enough to use. There was no way out but to climb the metal gate itself. I swallowed hard, hoping I could make it over before whoever monitored the cameras noticed me.

Using the hinges where the gate attached to the stone fence, I began climbing. It wasn't as hard as I thought; my reformed muscles were strong and able. Then I reached the top—and almost threw up. Apparently, becoming Unbounded hadn't removed my deathly fear of heights. I teetered there for dizzying seconds, my heart racing, before my sweaty hands lost their grip and I made it down the other side the hard way.

Cursing under my breath, I picked myself up from the ground. Nothing seemed broken. Another Unbounded miracle. Behind me at the hidden house, an alarm sounded.

I started running.

Now what? I had no money and no cell phone. *Think!* I told myself.

Two blocks over, where the houses had shrunk to more normal sizes, I slowed and began to walk. I wasn't tired but a lot less likely to draw attention that way. Besides, there was a long stretch of bushes here, and if I saw a car, I could jump inside to hide. Good thing I wore long sleeves, though they were damp from the effort of my run.

The residential neighborhood seemed to go on forever, and so far I was alone in the streets. My mind raced over the possibilities, but short of going up to a house and asking to use their phone, I didn't see what I was going to do. I didn't recognize this part of town, and I might have to walk for hours before I even knew where I was.

When the bushes ended, I saw two teenagers on a sloped front lawn, a boy and a girl, their dark heads close together, cell phones gleaming in the darkness. Maybe one of them would let me use a phone, though I'd begun to have second thoughts about calling. What if Tom thought it was a prank? What if the Emporium really was listening and was able to pinpoint my location? I still didn't know who I could trust. I needed another plan.

The teenagers were staring at me now, though I didn't look threatening. Even in my dark clothing, I was just a woman of average build with an odd French beret on her head.

"Excuse me," I said. "My car broke down back there, and I don't have a cell phone. Could I use yours?"

"Sure." The boy pressed a few more buttons on his phone and handed it to me.

I punched in a number and held the phone to my ear without pressing send. After a while, I shut the phone and handed it back. "No answer. I guess I'll have to wait. I'm too tired to walk all the way there. Truthfully, I'm a little lost. I've been distracted since my cancer treatments." I pulled off the beret so they could see my short, uneven hair, and then put it on again quickly, as though embarrassed. All an act, except the tears of frustration stinging my eyes.

"Man, sorry about that," said the boy.

The girl next to him nodded. "You going to be okay?"

"Well, if you can call living with my parents okay." And the fact that I was now Unbounded and presumably had other Unbounded hunting me who wanted to either use me or cut me into three precise pieces.

The boy laughed. "I hear you on that. I'm leaving for college at the end of the month, and it'll be a relief to finally be on my own. Hey, why don't I give you a ride? You can come back and get your car later."

"Would you? That would really help." My gratitude was real.

"Sure. We got nothing to do anyway. Just got back from a movie, and she's got an eleven-thirty curfew. Talk about strict parents."

"You live close?" The girl asked, obviously concerned now that her curfew had been brought up.

I had no idea. "I think so." I gave them Tom's address, and to my relief the boy nodded. "I know where that is. About ten or fifteen minutes from here. No problem."

Minutes later, I was standing in front of the white clapboard house Tom had shared with Justine. It was as large as my parents' home, but nicer inside since Justine had remodeled it with dark wood flooring, plush carpet, and granite countertops. I hoped Tom would be home alone, yet I also hoped he wouldn't be. Maybe a friend at the firm where he worked as a stockbroker had thought to spend time with him so he wouldn't have to mourn alone.

I went up the walk and rang the bell. No answer. I couldn't tell if he was home because the garage was shut, but I tried the door anyway. The knob turned under my hand. "Tom?" I called as I stepped inside. "Tom, are you here?" The house was dark, and no alarm sounded, so I turned on the cast iron lamp by the brown leather couch. "Tom? It's me, Erin. Don't be frightened. I'm okay. There was a mix-up at the hospital. Tom?"

He came from the master bedroom down the hall, his brown hair askew, his blue eyes bloodshot. Something felt different about him, but after what he'd been through, that didn't surprise me in the least.

"Erin? Oh, Erin!" He pulled me into his arms and we were touching, kissing. The familiarity of him soothed the terror of the past days. "I've missed you so much," I whispered against his lips, pressing myself against him. His hands kneaded my back.

This is exactly what I needed.

We fell to the soft carpet, kissing in earnest. "I don't want to ever wake up," he murmured, rolling on top of me.

He thought I was a dream?

I pushed him away. "You're not dreaming, Tom. It really is me. Look."

"I don't need to look." He started kissing me again.

I evaded his grasp and turned on the brighter overhead light. "I'm alive." I pinched him hard. "See?"

His ragged face paled. "You were burned." His eyes went to my left arm. "They cut off your arm. Said it couldn't be saved."

Did I tell him it was a mix-up or give him the truth? I had no time to consider the options, but I didn't like deceiving the man I was considering marrying. "I have a certain gene in my body. It healed me."

"Your funeral is tomorrow. After Justine's." He could barely get out the words.

I lifted my hands to either side of his face. "I know it doesn't make sense, Tom, but I'm alive. I woke up today, and I've been trying to get back to you ever since." I pulled off the beret to show him my head. "See? We've been given a second chance."

"This is a nightmare, isn't it?" Tom looked at me with a mixture of both longing and sadness. He slumped to the couch, his face in his hands. When he spoke, his voice was a hoarse whisper. "I can't take this. What if I keep losing you every time I dream?"

I sat and put my arms around him. "This isn't a dream. I promise you—it's going to be okay. I know you're doubting your sanity right now. I've been doing the same thing all day. But it really is me. Look, feel." I took his hand, running it up my arm, over my shoulder, across the top of my neck to the other shoulder. He began touching me of his own accord, his hands going to my face and my head, feeling the stubble there.

"I can't believe it," he said. "Yet here you are." He didn't make any move to kiss me again, and I tried not to feel offended. It was a lot to take in.

"Look, drive me home. I can't let my family go to that funeral tomorrow thinking I'm dead."

"Justine?" His face was suddenly hopeful.

I shook my head. "This gene isn't something you can be injected with. You have to be born with it. She wasn't."

An odd aloofness settled between us as he drove to my parents' house. After his reaction, I felt nervous about how my family would deal with my return from the grave. I was also tiring, so perhaps my nutrients were running low. I closed my eyes and concentrated, pulling in from the air around me. The sensation was vague, probably because there was no obvious food source nearby, but after a while I did feel stronger. I hoped I wasn't stealing body mass from Tom. Yuck.

We pulled up in front of the house. Everything appeared the same, from the roses lining the walkway, to the weeping willow in the middle of the front lawn. It was an older, red brick house, well-tended and loved, and had been a part of my life for as long as I could remember.

"Are we going to ring the bell?" Tom asked.

The night was warm and beautiful, the overhead stars shining with a promise that I didn't feel at the moment. In fact, I was beginning to dread the coming scene. "Let's go through my apartment." I scanned the streets, feeling nervous. I didn't think I'd led anyone here, but Ava was bound to guess where I was the minute she discovered I was missing.

We went around to the back of the house. Our dog, Max, began barking as we went through the wood gate, but he stopped when he saw it was me. He bounded up, tail wagging, trying to lick my cheek, but I averted my face and gave him a good scratching instead. The Collie-Chow mix had long golden hair and a beautiful face with none of the pointy sharpness of a full-bred Collie. My younger brother had found Max sick and abandoned on the side of the road a few years earlier and now we were stuck with him.

He wasn't much of a guard dog, and he couldn't even fetch, but he loved us all with single-minded devotion.

I snagged my spare key from under the decorative frog in the flowerbed, jogged down the stairs, and opened the door. "Stay outside," I told Max.

"Is the alarm on?" Tom asked.

"Probably. But I know the code." I punched in the numbers and a tin voice said, "Disarmed. Ready to arm." Without stopping to see if Tom followed, I headed for the stairs that connected my apartment with the main house. I reached the upstairs kitchen only seconds before my mother came into the room, turning on one of the overhead lights.

"Who's here?" she called. "Jace, have you been out? Was it you who disarmed the alarm? It woke me up."

I could see her now, her hand clutching the top of her white robe. Her face looked worn, her blond hair carelessly swept up with a comb instead of her usual careful styling.

"Mom," I said quietly.

Her head turned and her mouth fell open, one hand going up as though to stifle a scream. Then she did scream. "Erin!" She launched herself at me crying and squeezing me all over. "Is it really you?" Her hands continued to wander over me.

"It's me."

Her hands held my face still so she could look into my eyes. "My baby," she whispered. Tears rolled unchecked down her face. She took off my beret and ran her hands over my head, then pulled me close again and sobbed.

"Annie," my father called from the hallway. "I'm coming! What's wr—" His words cut off as he saw me.

I broke partly away from my mother and held out an arm. "It's me, Dad."

"But the hospital."

"They made a mistake."

He grabbed me and my mother, holding us tightly. All of us were crying.

My mother looked up at Tom, who was staring at us. "Thank you," she whispered.

His head swung back and forth. "I didn't—she came to me."

"I can explain everything," I said, "but we need Chris and Jace here. I don't want to tell it twice. I don't know how long I have."

"What do you mean?" My mother blinked frantically.

"Just that I'm tired, and there are some people who've been . . . uh, helping me. They don't know I left, and they might come looking for me. You'll understand when I explain." Ava and her friends had gone through a great deal of trouble to get to me in the first place and wouldn't give up easily. Whether that made me feel hunted or special was still up for debate.

My father disconnected himself from us. "I'll call Chris. Annie, go wake up your mother and Jace."

"Grandma's here?" I wiped the tears from my face.

"At a time like this, where else would she be?"

He had a point.

My mother hugged me again tightly before she left the kitchen, as if worried I might disappear. That she didn't say anything about my cat burglar appearance said a lot about her state of mind.

"Don't mention my name," I said as my father dialed Chris's number. "It's not safe."

"Not safe?"

"I'll explain when he gets here. Tell him to bring Lorrie, if he can, but not the kids." I would make sure I saw the children at some point, though, because I loved them and I wasn't willing to give up my role as their favorite aunt. Okay, their only aunt. But still.

"Lorrie," my father said, "it's Grant. Can I speak to Chris? Thanks." As he talked to my brother, his eyes never left me. Neither did Tom's. I put my beret back on to hide my shorn head, but I still felt uncomfortable. As though a neon sign above my head screamed abnormality.

"See you in a few minutes," my father said. "Drive carefully." His voice cracked on the words, and my stomach twisted.

He hadn't lost me, but if I hadn't been Unbounded, I would be as permanently dead as Justine.

My mother appeared in the doorway, a sleepy Jace behind her. I hadn't seen my little brother since Mother's Day when he'd made a surprise visit, but we e-mailed almost every day. We were born only three years apart, both the result of fertility treatments, and we'd always been close. The past four months had made a big difference in my brother. His white-blond hair was shorter and he'd gained ten very needed pounds—probably all muscle. He was scrubbing a hand over his head and yawning when he caught sight of me.

His blue eyes popped open and he choked on his yawn. "Erin? But you're—"

"It's me."

He whooped and crossed the kitchen in four steps, swooping me up into his arms and twirling me around and around. He really had gained muscle if he could do that. "I can't believe it. You're alive! I thought I'd lost you!" He crushed me to him, tears coming fast.

It was the reaction I'd expected—craved—from Tom.

My mother was crying again, prying me from Jace's grasp. She kept touching me all over, patting my arms and shoulders. Then I was in my father's arms again, and back to Jace. It felt so good. For the moment, the disappointments I'd caused in the past didn't matter. I'd done this thing right at least. I'd survived.

My grandmother entered the kitchen, still buttoning the top of her old-fashioned robe. Her gray eyes widened and she immediately began to sob. Then we were off again, hugging and crying.

My mother ran a finger across my left eyebrow. "Your eye. They said you'd lost all use of it. How could they be so wrong?"

That started another round of questions, but I refused to answer. "Wait for Chris."

My mother squeezed my shoulder. "Let's have something to drink. What would you like?"

I couldn't very well tell her I'd like some curequick, though I was craving Cort's mixture.

"Have a seat," my grandmother said to Tom. "There's a chair next to Erin." She began making coffee, and as I breathed in, I felt the coffee, not only as a smell, but seeping into my body, and a bit of my tiredness vanished.

Tom sat by me, still wearing the stunned expression he'd had since I turned on the light at his house. His hand lay on the table, and I put mine over it. He didn't respond. After a moment I took my hand away.

By the time Chris and Lorrie arrived, Grandma had made coffee for us, tea for herself, and had also filled the table with food that no one but Jace seemed to want. My father stood behind my chair, and my mother sat next to me. She said she'd thought I'd lost weight. After days of mostly only absorbing nutrients through my skin, she was probably right, but I told her it was because the new jeans were loose.

When Chris entered the kitchen, I noticed his blond hair was longer and darker than I remembered. How long had it been since I'd really seen him? His face was worried and lined and he looked every one of his thirty-eight years. When he saw me, his eyes, gray like mine, widened and his jaw went slack. Behind him, Lorrie, my blond-haired sister-in-law gasped. "Erin!" They hugged me, the questions flying around my head until I felt dizzy.

"Let's all sit down," I said. "I'll explain everything."

More chairs were brought in and somehow Tom and I were separated. It was just as well. His silence made me nervous.

"I need a knife," I said.

Jace handed me a butter knife, but I took the cheese knife from the cutting board instead. I turned my palm upward and, my lip between my teeth, pressed the knife into the fat at the base of my hand.

"Erin!" my mother said sharply. My grandmother gasped, and everyone else stared at me as if I had gone crazy.

The knife wasn't making very much headway on my skin, so I dragged it across, wincing as it finally brought blood, slicing deeper than I'd intended. Pain registered, making me suck in my breath. Boy, I was bad at this. I grabbed a bundle of napkins and pressed it against the wound.

My father grabbed the knife from the table where I'd dropped it, placing it beyond my reach. "Are you crazy?"

"It's okay, Dad."

"That's going to need stitches." My grandmother took off the napkins to examine the wound.

"It's fine." Already I could feel the flow of blood slowing. "Don't worry. It's part of the story." I replaced the napkins and turned my hand palm down on the table.

A movement came from the basement stairway. I was the only one who saw it because everyone else was focused on me. I knew who it was—or at least I hoped I did. I jumped up from the table. "Come out," I ordered.

Just in case, I reached for the cheese knife again.

CHAPTER 7

MY FATHER HELD THE KNIFE OUT OF MY REACH, SO I HAD NO choice but to face the intruder unarmed. Murmurs swept through my family as Ava stepped into view, dressed similarly to me. She gave me a wry smile. "Hello, Erin."

My grandmother stared at her. "What are *you* doing here?"

"You're the woman from the hospital!" My mother arose and stood slightly in front of me, as though preparing to come to my defense.

"No, she's my next-door neighbor," my grandmother insisted. "She teaches martial arts. I took a class from her once. Why are you here, Ava?"

"Erin was about to explain," Ava said calmly. "But it's too dangerous for her to be out on her own, and by coming here, she has, unfortunately, put all of you in danger."

"Are you threatening us?" My father took a step closer. "Maybe I should call the police."

"You have that choice, but I hope you won't. If you do, everyone here will probably die." Ava looked at Lorrie. "Your children, too."

Jace and Chris came to their feet, and I knew things were about to get ugly. After sparring with Ritter and seeing how they trained, I doubted all of us together had a chance against Ava.

"Wait," I said, holding out my hands in a pleading gesture. "Please. Everyone, be calm and sit down. Ava isn't going to hurt anyone." I hoped that was true. She didn't look angry, but she had followed me, after all. What would she be willing to do to keep me under her control?

"I hoped you'd trust me more, Erin," she said, as if no one else were in the room.

"I couldn't let them go on not knowing."

She sighed. "You may come to wish you had."

"Will one of you please tell me what is going on?" My father's eyes were narrowed and his hand gripped the portable phone. "Or should I call the police now?"

I swallowed hard. "It's okay, Dad. Please put down the phone. Everyone, I'd like you to meet Ava."

"Ava O'Hare," Ava added. "I'm Erin's fourth great-grandmother—Chris and Jace's, too—and I'm three hundred years old, give or take a few."

More confusion erupted. My family was anything but quiet and docile. I could usually disappear in all their conversation. Or hide, rather.

"Stop!" I banged my hand on the table.

Everyone stared at me as though I'd grown two heads.

"Your hand," my grandmother said. "Be careful of it."

"I don't have to." I turned my hand over, holding it out for them to see. The bleeding had stopped and the edges of the cut had begun knitting together. Already the gash was noticeably smaller.

Complete silence fell—until my father said, "I think now's a good time to tell us everything."

I did, with Ava filling in the details, and by the time I finished, they were stunned and speechless, all but Jace, who thought it was the most wonderful thing he'd ever heard. "What about me?" he said, eyes bright with eagerness. "I'm only twenty-eight. Could I be Unbounded?"

Not knowing anything about the statistics of the Unbounded gene pool, I looked at Ava helplessly. "Even if both parents are Unbounded," she said, "the offspring Unbounded rate is only thirty percent without genetic manipulation. With so many generations removed, the chance is much slimmer."

"But it still happened." Jace's voice was full of wonder and hope.

"We'll watch you for the Change, just as we did Chris and Erin."

Chris and I both gave a start at the mention of his name, though I should have realized he'd been included in their observations.

My mother suddenly snapped her fingers. "I know where I've seen you before."

"I told you—Ava's my neighbor," Grandma said.

"That's not it. I remember seeing her when I was a child riding my bike." Mother looked intently at Ava. "I didn't see the car, but you did. You pushed me out of the way. The car hit you instead. At first we thought you were dead."

"I remember that." Grandmother stared in amazement at Ava. "I called the hospital later, and they said you'd been released. I was very relieved."

Ava smiled at her. "I was in town because you were thirty. When you were little, you looked a lot like my first daughter. I probably visited Kansas more because of that."

"So you're saying," Tom said, looking at me and not Ava, "that this woman doesn't age—that you will never age, or not so we'll notice. Does it mean you become stronger, too? Physically?" His mouth had a pinched whiteness about the edges and his voice was tight and hard. I'd never heard him sound so ill or controlled.

I didn't know the answer, but Ava did. "Unbounded are generally stronger and have more endurance than they did before the Change because their cells are continuously regenerating."

"Even if they don't eat?"

"Unbounded are always absorbing. Food consumption is immaterial."

Tom didn't like that answer, but when I tried to catch his attention he didn't seem to notice. He stared past me at something only he could see. Was he thinking about Justine? Or did he now regard me as some kind of a freak?

Silence again, and then my mother spoke, tears in her voice. "Why didn't you tell us about Erin? It's been so hard these past days."

Ava sighed. "Because it's not safe yet. Our enemies would be thrilled to get their hands on her—or any of you. But also because of the funeral. Do you know how difficult it's going to be pretending to mourn, unable to tell anyone that Erin is very much alive?"

My father's lip curled. "We'll manage. But you need to understand right now that we refuse to be cut out of our daughter's life."

"That's between you and Erin. She'll be able to keep in contact by phone for now—as long as you don't mention her name or anything related to the Unbounded." Ava's gaze met mine. "I'm sorry, Erin, but we need to leave. It's vital that no one sees us here."

Everyone stared at me, my mother looking ready to cry, and I knew the time had come to make a choice. I wanted more than anything to go downstairs to my familiar bed and curl up, forgetting any of this had happened. Or go somewhere with Tom and work things out. But I couldn't. I'd fulfilled my goal of telling my parents and Tom that I was alive. They were okay, and now I had to discover where the rest of my life would take me. Even if it was away from them for a time.

I gazed at the healing cut on my hand. "Don't worry. I'll call you soon." I expected an argument, especially from my father, or a guilt trip from my mother, but they were apparently too shocked for either. Everyone began hugging me goodbye.

Only Tom stayed apart, his lips clenched tightly shut, his face stony. When he walked out to the hallway, I followed. "I wish I could be at Justine's funeral for you," I said.

"It doesn't matter."

"Of course it matters."

He grabbed my hand, turning my palm upward to expose the nearly healed cut. "The Erin I know would never do something like this. I don't even know who you are anymore." There was a trace of horror in his expression.

"I'm the same person. I still feel the same about you."

"What, so you'll be out fighting mysterious bad guys, repeatedly getting cut up or shot, disappearing for days on end—and all the while I'll be at work selling stocks? Growing older every year? I'd be nothing more than useless baggage to you." Something new in his demeanor now, something greedy, almost envious. Hateful. I was stunned with its intensity. In the months we'd been together, I'd never seen this side of him.

"So you were willing to stay by my side for months of recovery and operations, but all bets are off now that I'll live longer than you will?"

"Look, I wish you well in your new eternal life, but let's not pretend I can be a part of it." He pushed past me roughly, heading toward the front door.

His rejection was like law school all over again. I'd given up then, unwilling to endure the disbelieving faces of my peers and the public disgrace inflicted upon me, but being Unbounded wasn't something I could run away from—even if I'd wanted to.

"What aren't you telling me?" I yelled after him. Because I felt there was more, though I couldn't explain why, except that his loathing hadn't seemed entirely directed toward me.

Jace appeared behind me, his arms sliding around my shaking body. "If he can't accept this, he's not worth it."

I leaned back into his arms. Trust Jace to say what I needed to hear. Justine would have said something similar. She would have embraced this opportunity, not broken under it. That's what I chose to do.

"This is your chance," Jace added in my ear. "Your chance to do something big. To shine. You've always had it in you. Stop worrying about past mistakes. Stop worrying about our parents' dreams for you. Do what *you* need to do. I'm so proud to be your brother. I wish I could go with you." I clung to him. I wished he could, too.

"And by the way," he added. "That thing with the knife. So cool."

"I know." I'd been showing off, and leave it to Jace to appreciate my effort.

"Erin." Ava was waiting.

We took the downstairs exit and found Cort, Dimitri, and Ritter waiting for us in the backyard. Cort looked amused, while Dimitri appeared exactly the same as always—I guess after a thousand years, you aren't easily ruffled. Ritter was squatted down in the grass, a machine gun slung across his chest, giving Max a good rub. Since Max normally barked like crazy at strangers and especially men with his bulk, this was amazing, but no more so than the relaxed expression on Ritter's chiseled face. I wouldn't have taken him for a dog person.

"How did it go?" Dimitri asked. I wanted to thank him for the clothing he'd bought, but now didn't seem the time.

"As well as can be expected." Ava glanced at me. "I'm worried about the boyfriend. If we hadn't already been keeping track of him, I'd think he has something to hide. There was so much going on, I couldn't get a good read on him."

Dimitri nodded. "I'm on it."

"What are you going to do?" I was mad and hurt at Tom's reaction, but that didn't mean I could let them hurt him.

"Just make sure he doesn't endanger you," Dimitri said.

Cort laughed. "Don't worry, Erin. We don't knock people off."

"No." Ritter came to his feet, his expression hardening. "Usually we leave that to the Emporium. Now can we get out of here?"

"Ritter's right," Ava said. "I haven't waited hundreds of years to see my last blood line eradicated."

I lifted my chin. "You keep talking as if the Emporium cares about my family. I thought it was us they wanted."

Ava's eyes glittered. "The Emporium would wipe out an entire family line if they so much as suspected it might carry the

Unbounded gene. That's why we're willing to leave our families completely, or to see them secretly until enough generations pass that we can bear the separation. By coming back to your family tonight without proper caution, you've put not only yourself but all of them in danger. If the Emporium learned anything about you at the burn center, your reappearance may give them all the verification they need."

I felt frozen, numb at the information. "What about the police? Won't they protect my family?"

"They can't." Ritter's voice was clipped and hate gleamed from his eyes. "No mortal police can prevent an Emporium massacre, if that's what they choose." He turned on his heel and started toward the back gate, the one I'd gone through to my best friend's backyard as a child. Max followed him, but the others hung back for a few moments, as though to give Ritter space.

"How do you know?" I called after Ritter's retreating back. He didn't look around, so I turned to the others. "Will someone please tell me what's going on? Why is he so angry?"

They exchanged looks and finally Ava nodded at Cort who began speaking. "After Ritter started to heal from the attack I told you about, word of his survival found its way to the Emporium. They went to his house and killed everyone, including the Unbounded ancestor who'd come to protect him."

"Not just killed," Ava added. "Slaughtered, in case there were any potential Unbounded among them, or anyone who might someday give birth to an Unbounded. The woman Ritter was supposed to have married was at his bedside when they burst in. Our people arrived barely in time to save Ritter."

Cort cleared his throat. "Ritter didn't even know what an Unbounded was or why he'd survived the attack in the first place, but he blames himself, of course."

We'd reached the gate where Ritter had disappeared. Max was sitting there, brown eyes mournfully awaiting his return. To my knowledge, the old gate hadn't been used in years, yet it opened as though it had been oiled recently and often. Ava reached down to pat Max's head, and he licked her hand in a farewell he reserved for friends.

"You should have told me before," I said. "I'd never have put my family at risk."

Ava shrugged. "I asked you to wait, to trust me. Even now you don't really believe. You still think the law would step in to save them."

She was right. It all sounded impossible.

Dimitri motioned me through the gate to my neighbor's dark yard. No lights gleamed in their windows. "There have been more recent occurrences similar to Ritter's experience. Those massacres are one more reason we fight the Emporium."

"We'll do our best to make sure your family remains safe," Ava added quietly.

I blinked. "You mean, as long as I go to New York."

"It's not a bribe, Erin. It's a promise."

I thought of how she'd saved my mother's life as a child and nodded. "Okay. I'm in." For now. Because no matter her promise, she couldn't speak for all the Renegades, and I was willing to do anything to protect my family from all the Unbounded in this crazy world I'd stumbled into.

We walked through our neighbor's yard to Ava's white sedan parked out on the street. Ava slid into the driver's seat and Dimitri sat next to her. I climbed in the back next to Ritter, who avoided my gaze.

"How did you find me anyway?" I asked Ava, as Cort wedged into the empty space next to me.

"Every entrance to the house is monitored. Someone followed you on foot until you met those kids and got a ride. We thought you'd come here first—a small miscalculation."

"So you *let* me leave."

She sighed. "I'd hoped you wouldn't make that choice. Living as long as I have, I sometimes forget how immediate things seem for mortals. Or those who were recently mortal."

It was surprisingly comfortable sitting between Ritter and Cort, but gradually my awareness of Ritter's presence became acute. Knowing his story and how much he must have suffered watching his family being slaughtered troubled me. Besides, I couldn't get the image of him petting Max out of my head, or how I'd felt standing close to him after our training session. The way I'd felt at that moment—well, I wasn't sure I'd ever experienced that kind of pull even with Tom.

Tom, who seemed to be hiding something. Or who simply didn't want anything to do with someone like me.

Exhaustion finally took over, and I was half asleep when we arrived at the gate to the mansion. Ava rolled down her window but before she could punch in the code, men dressed in camouflage rose up all around the car. They carried heavy rifles, which I knew couldn't kill us but could incapacitate us long enough to allow them the pleasure of cutting us apart at their leisure.

A clear image came to my mind of a beautiful young woman with long dark hair lying on a floor running with blood, her head separated from her body. Sightless eyes open, framed by dark lashes. The sword coming down again on her motionless torso.

Blinding rage fought with an urge to vomit.

I gasped and the scene vanished, leaving behind a dull ache in my head. Where did that come from? More Unbounded tricks?

"Get out of the car," a gravelly voice ordered. "And keep your hands where we can see them."

I heard a metallic click in the vicinity of Ritter's waist before he opened the door. Whoever these people were, he wasn't planning to go down without a fight.

CHAPTER 8

"**N**OT EMPORIUM," AVA WHISPERED AS SHE SLIPPED FROM THE CAR. I wondered how she could tell. There were more than a dozen men, and looking over them I saw most were in their mid-twenties. Only two appeared old enough to be Unbounded, but neither had the confident presence. In fact, one of these was pasty with fright.

"What's the meaning of this?" Ava demanded.

"Shut up." This from the older man who didn't seem afraid. He leveled his gun at Ava's chest. "Oh, I know this won't kill you, but it will be enough for now." To his men, he added, "Secure them."

One of the men reached for my hands, and I wondered if I should struggle. Ritter looked at Dimitri and Ava and Cort briefly in turn. His chin dropped infinitesimally. A sign.

The world exploded into motion.

Ritter slammed his fists into two men, dropping them before anyone had the chance to move. His knife whipped out as he threw another man into the path of bullets fired from the leader's silenced rifle. He was liquid in motion, a black blur that somehow avoided the soft pops of the rifle fire. A foot went up, then an arm, each connecting with their target. A deadly dance with men dropping all around him. If I weren't seeing it for myself, I'd never have believed anyone could move like that—or anticipate the attackers' movement so accurately. Five down already and a sixth falling, his neck twisted at an impossible angle.

Beyond him, Ava was also in motion, her foot flying backwards into a man's stomach. Two others lay unmoving at her feet. Dimitri had taken out two men as well but had collapsed, grabbing his stomach. Cort grappled with his third opponent over control of the man's weapon.

Only I seemed to be rooted to one spot. *Think,* I told myself. *Do something.*

The next minute, a man grabbed my hands and started dragging me toward a black car barely visible next to the shrubbery. The engine revved. I slammed on the man's foot and pain exploded there as my shoe connected with his boot. Was that a grunt of amusement from my captor? I made my knees go weak, my body heavy, a trick my nephew had pulled in his younger years when he didn't want to go somewhere.

The man swore and leaned to pick me up. I was in position, so I tried the elbow jab Ritter had taught me mere hours before. I didn't have much hope of it actually working, but I felt a momentary thrill of success when the man grunted in pain and jackknifed forward. Twisting from his weakened grasp, I swung my freed hands into his head. I felt them connect, but the blow didn't faze him.

With a growl, he launched himself at me, tumbling me backwards. I kept waiting for a miracle, for one of the others to save me, or for my so-called Unbounded talent to kick in and tell me what to do.

Nothing.

Sitting on my stomach, my assailant punched me hard in the face. Fury burst through my fear. I'd been burned practically to death, lost my best friend, held prisoner, separated from my family, trained till my arms bled, and finally rejected by a man who'd claimed to love me. I wasn't going to let myself be kidnapped by a twenty-something idiot I didn't even know.

I feigned semi-consciousness but was really absorbing nutrients from the grass I laid in, the trees looming above, the air I breathed. My assailant came to his feet, dragging me with him. In seconds, I'd be in that car, all hope of escape gone. There were no convenient rocks or heavy sticks nearby to use as a weapon. But there was the car.

Faking a stumble, I grabbed at him and used my body to ram him into the car. Then I grabbed his head and shoved it into the window with all my strength. After a sickening thump, he slid down into a heap.

I was free.

A man leapt from the other side of the car, a pistol in hand.

Crap, I thought.

He pulled the trigger, too soft a sound for the hot fire that sliced into my right shoulder. While I stood in shock, he rounded the vehicle.

The crack of an unsilenced gun split the false quiet of the night, and the man crumpled, a bloody hole blossoming on his chest. I glanced and saw Ritter turning back to his own opponent in time to smash a pistol into the man's face.

Everything was still. I counted eighteen men lying dead or unconscious.

Ava was seated by Dimitri. "You shouldn't have jumped in the way like that," she told him. "He might have missed me."

He gave her a pain-filled smile. "Ah, well, you know me."

"We've got to get this looked at."

"I'm fine. Or I will be."

Ava laid her hand on his cheek, and in that moment of unguarded tenderness, I saw what I hadn't seen before. I wondered if they knew it themselves.

Behind them Cort was on the phone, no doubt rounding up our security. He was also pulling out a dark green bag from the trunk of the car. He threw it to Ava, who removed a bottle of something and passed it to Dimitri. Then she brought out a familiar bag of liquid. When Dimitri had finished the drink, she pressed the bag over his wound.

I tried to take a step toward them, but my knees buckled under me, the fall sending what felt like shards of glass into my arm and chest. I touched my right shoulder and my hand came away slick with blood.

Ritter came toward me, knife in hand. He knelt down, cut off my sleeve, and tied it around my wound. "Ouch," I said.

He closed his knife and tucked it into a pocket of his black pants. "Next time act sooner. Before the guy gets out of the car."

Next time? Who was he kidding? "I'll remember that," I said, deciding not to thank him for saving me. "Who are they anyway?"

Ritter sighed heavily. "Hunters. An organization that kills Unbounded. See that insignia of a man with a rifle on their uniforms? It's a secret code to identify members."

"How'd they find out about the Unbounded?"

He gave a bitter laugh. "Years ago the Emporium's inbreeding program began to result in dozens of children who were kept locked away and then abandoned when they grew up and didn't Change. A few eventually discovered the secret of their birth and started hunting us, recruiting anyone they could get to believe them. For fifty years now their hatred for Unbounded has been like a religion. Emporium, Renegades—we're all the same to them. They're the ones who shot down Kennedy Jr.'s plane when they discovered the Unbounded link. Fortunately they're largely untrained, and they die easily. We wouldn't have survived tonight if they'd been Emporium."

"I see." The pain in my shoulder was intense, and the knife wound in my hand had torn open again during my struggle. I'd thought I'd never feel as much pain as I had while burning to death, but this came close. Funny how the mind bowed to immediacy. Patches of black floated before my eyes, and Ritter's voice came from far away. I forced myself to take a deep steadying breath and the black receded a bit.

Cort came toward us. "Stella's waiting for us at her house. She thinks if this place is compromised, the warehouse probably is, too. She's calling Laurence and our security guys to give 'em a heads up." He bent down to check the pulse of one of the downed men before continuing on.

Why would Stella's place be safe? But almost without trying, I understood. She was married to a mortal and would always take extra precautions. Unlike us, her husband didn't have infinite lives.

Dimitri was struggling to sit up despite his wound and already looked stronger. By contrast, I didn't think I could make it to the car on my own two feet.

"You don't have any more of that curequick, do you?" I asked Cort.

He grinned. "That bad?"

"I'm not accustomed to getting shot."

"The trick is not to get hit," Ritter said.

I glared at him.

"You have to be careful with this stuff." Cort handed me a bottle. "It's addictive. Even for Unbounded."

So now I was a druggie? That explained a lot. "How addictive?"

"Ten times stronger than caffeine. With repeated overuse, the effects can be devastating. I can't figure out exactly what causes it, so Dimitri's going to do some tests when he gets a chance. I may understand connections on an atomic level, but I'm still basically a scientist, not a medical doctor."

"Your talent is to see stuff at an atomic level?"

"Understanding the connections and interactions between atoms is the important thing, not just seeing them." He gave me a bland smile. "Anyway, with what you've been through, it's okay to depend on curequick a while longer. Just don't make it a habit."

"I won't." I chugged down the liquid, feeling strength seep into me, a tiny thing at first, followed by a flood. I might even be able to get to my feet in a moment.

Cort checked the man I'd shoved into the side of the car. "This one's alive. Should come to shortly."

Ritter jerked his chin at one of the others. "He's alive, too. Unfortunately. And probably most of the others."

"Held back, did ya?" I mocked.

Cort laughed. "Hey, that's my line."

Ignoring us, Ritter glanced at Ava. "Cort and I'll get Dimitri into the car. Keep an eye on these guys." She nodded and removed a gun from her waistband. Ritter took the rifle from the fallen man in front of us and handed it to me.

I was still shaking inside, wondering if I was going to be sick, but I took the gun. Jace had taught me how to shoot both a rifle and a handgun several summers ago, and we'd gone shooting every time he came home. I'd become a good shot—but shooting a living, breathing, moving man was far different from knocking cans off a log.

Ritter and Cort hefted a white-faced Dimitri into the front passenger side of the car. He didn't let out a sound, but I could see pain in the rigid lines of his body and in the way his arm curled around Ritter's neck. The guy next to me moaned, and I tore my gaze away from them to watch him more closely. "He's awake," I called, hoping they wouldn't tell me to shoot him.

In seconds Ritter was leaning over the man. "Wake up," he said, slapping his face.

The man's eyes opened and filled instantly with fear. "Please don't kill me. Please!"

Ritter's jaw worked as though expending great effort. "You jumped five people with eighteen armed soldiers, and you're asking us not to kill you? Isn't that exactly what you planned for us? A little appointment with an ax and a lot of blood?"

"Well, uh . . ."

"Can it. Look, I have a message for your people. Same as always. The Renegades are not Emporium. We do not harm people unless we're attacked. But we're getting sick and tired of your insistence."

"You're an abomination," the man choked out. "You can't be allowed to survive! All Unbounded must die."

"Okay, message delivered." With a casual blow, Ritter knocked him unconscious.

"We really should kill them," Cort said.

My breath caught in my throat. I believed in self-defense, but these men were helpless.

Ava shook her head. "We'd be no better than they are if we did. It's one of the things that separates us from the Emporium."

"I know, I know," Cort grumbled.

Ritter slapped him on the shoulder. "None of us will feel so charitable the next time we're dodging their bullets. And there *will* be a next time. Let's see that we're better prepared." I felt a little surprised that he didn't ignore Ava and slit their throats. Instead, he took the rifle from my hands and walked toward the car, gathering the Hunters' weapons as he went. Cort followed his example, piling firearms into the trunk. I stumbled to the car. Ava lingered next to the unconscious men, going from one to the other, placing a hand on each forehead and closing her eyes briefly. I was in too much pain to ask what she was doing, but the image stuck with me.

"We're just leaving them there?" I asked, once more in the backseat between Cort and Ritter. I was glad they weren't going to kill the men, but leaving them like that seemed rather unsafe—for the neighborhood, the mansion's servants, the world in general.

Ritter shrugged. "They'll call their people when they come to. They're of no interest to us. If we hadn't killed some of them, we'd call the police, but we don't want to get caught up in that now. Let the Hunters deal with their own dead."

"And the house? What happens to it?"

"Don't worry." Dimitri lay in the front seat that was reclined as far as it could go. "My friend will sell it to himself under another name, and when he comes to visit, he'll come armed. He'd do that anyway. He lives in England and goes years without coming to the States. Decades even. This mansion represents only an infinitesimal portion of his wealth. He will have many years yet to enjoy it."

I guess I had to start thinking in completely new terms. All the Hunters we'd fought today would shrivel and die before my body aged another year.

"How'd they find us?" Cort said.

Ritter shook his head. "I don't know. We'll get Stella on it. Probably they've got this house listed in their archives as belonging to Unbounded and check it periodically for occupancy. They could have been watching us for days."

"Stella and I searched before we came," Cort said. "There's never been any Hunter activity near that house."

"Maybe we need to dig deeper." There was no accusation in Ava's voice, only a grim determination.

"Would they really have killed us?" I had a hard time comprehending that so many people I didn't know wanted me dead.

"Yes," Ritter said shortly.

So we would have died. All of us, cut in three pieces, like Ritter's family. Could such evil exist in the world?

"What about the families of Unbounded? Do Hunters go after them?" I was unable to hide the tremor in my voice. As an army-trained officer, Jace would be able to fight, but the rest would be helpless.

"Depends on the leader," Cort answered. "They'll either kill anyone connected with the Unbounded, or they might test them first. You know, shoot them and see if they heal."

I shivered, wondering how close I'd come to exposing my family to these Hunters. What if they'd tracked us there?

Ritter's eyes gleamed in the light of the oncoming headlights, and when he spoke, his voice was unusually gentle. "Some are no better than the Emporium, but for the most part they are bound by human laws, and wiping out a whole family is too dangerous for them."

Unlike the Emporium, of course. What kind of mad world had I entered?

Yet already it was a part of me. I wanted to fight the Emporium and stop the Hunters from hurting us. Tom was right.

I wasn't myself. The Unbounded gene had penetrated all that I had been, moving things around, altering me, creating something quite different, perhaps similar to the way a child changes into an adult. Maybe it hadn't been Justine's influence that had begun to make me reach out, to search for more, to become less inhibited, more assertive. Maybe the real reason was written in my DNA. I had Changed. And despite all the horror and suffering and heartache, I knew deep down that I was glad. Glad to be different.

That scared me most of all.

Ava drove around a good while before she was satisfied that no one was following us. I couldn't help but let my head rest against Ritter's shoulder. It was at the right height and on my left side away from my wounded shoulder. Ritter didn't comment on it, and for that I was grateful.

Stella's house appeared normal on the outside, even rather small, though when she opened the double garage for us, the interior was quite deep, easily fitting our car behind two others already there.

Stella came into the garage, beautiful as ever, and I could tell by her lacy nightwear that she'd been in bed. "Laurence called from the warehouse. He and the security guys did have a run in with Hunters and were all pretty beat up but alive, thanks to your warning."

"Good," Ava said.

"On his way here, Laurence is taking the guys to the hospital for a few bandages since Dimitri's in no condition to patch them. They ended up reporting the ambush to the police, though, so Laurence will probably need a new ID—especially if they killed too many Hunters."

We were inside now, and I could see that like her garage, Stella's house wasn't ordinary on the inside either. No expense had been spared. Sweeping arches, crown molding, elaborate wallpaper, vaulted ceilings with ornate designs. Furniture that looked like it came from a house in a design magazine. I was too exhausted to take it all in. It was after two in the morning and would be light soon. I'd been out of that coffin little more than fourteen hours.

I stumbled and Stella steadied me. I clung to her gratefully.

"Need to see if the bullet is still in her shoulder." Behind me Ritter's voice showed the strain of Dimitri's weight.

"I can do that," Dimitri said.

"No, you can't." Ava locked the outside door behind us. "We know enough to take care of her. You, however, have a bullet in you for sure, and it has to come out if you want to heal fast."

"Bronson's prepping now," Stella said.

"Your husband's a doctor?" I asked.

"No, but he's got a steady hand from years of working with electronics, and he's good with blood." Stella glanced at Dimitri. "Though tonight he's a little nervous."

"He's taken out bullets before," Ritter said.

"Not from the stomach."

Dimitri gave her a pale smile. "I'll walk him through it. Shouldn't be bad if the bullet hasn't shattered. If it has, a piece or two left inside won't kill me. My body will eventually expel them."

Since I was battling to stay conscious with my smaller wound, I had a hard time picturing Dimitri awake during a stomach operation, much less directing the extraction.

"In here, Erin." Stella guided me into a room furnished with a twin bed with a white headboard and matching dresser. "Stay here. We'll be right back."

I heard the others move down the hall with Dimitri. Mentally apologizing to Stella, I drew up the blanket over my bloodied arm and let myself float into the warmth of the bed.

The next thing I knew Ritter and Stella were tugging at my shirt. When I groaned in protest, Ritter used his knife to cut the rest of it off. Dressed only in my bra and jeans, I shivered, and Stella drew the blanket over all of me but my shoulder.

Turning me onto my side, Ritter removed the sleeve he'd tied over the wound outside the mansion. Gently, he probed the area with his fingers, and agony reverberated throughout my entire body. "There's an exit wound. Bleeding's all but stopped. An injection of curequick and a few bandages should do the trick. I can take care of it if you want to get back to Dimitri."

"I'll do that. Bronson will feel better if I'm there." Stella smoothed my hair and was gone.

Ritter cleaned and bandaged me in silence as I floated on memories of the evening. His touch was so gentle that I hardly flinched when I felt the point of the needle. Inevitably, my thoughts came to dwell on Tom. I hadn't known that I'd said his name aloud until Ritter bent down and spoke in my face. "Forget him."

A tear slipped from my eye and rolled to the pillow under my head. I wanted him to leave so I could cry in peace. I didn't want anyone to see my longing, my deep hurt at Tom's rejection. At the same time I was terrified of being alone. I kept reliving images of what the Hunters had planned for me and the others. Severed into three pieces. Ugh.

Ritter edged onto the bed, sitting close to me. His hand rested on the blanket covering my body. After several long moments of silence, he said, "Believe me, leaving your family now is better. Watching those you love die is a worse hell than what you feel now. You'll see tomorrow with Stella and Bronson."

My eyes came open. He was looking at me, his black eyes somber. There was more to him than I'd understood at our previous meetings. For the first time, I could see him as a man who'd probably fought to rise from his sick bed in an effort to save the woman he loved. To save his entire family. I wondered whose rings he wore on the chain around his neck.

"I'm sorry about your family," I whispered.

His body stiffened, and his expression became impassive. "My family is not your concern."

"I'm still sorry. No one should have to—I wish . . ." I didn't know what I wished.

"Even if they'd lived, they would all be gone by now. Go to sleep. I'll make sure you're safe." His soft voice and the pressure of his hand did make me feel safe.

I shut my eyes and obeyed.

Sometime during the night, I awoke and became aware of Ritter lying beside me, the comforting sensation of his hand draped carelessly over my bare stomach, his sleeping breath in my ear. His smell was different from Tom's, and I fought tears as memories engulfed me. It had taken me months to trust Tom enough to get close to him. Even then I'd been wrong.

I rolled slightly so I could see Ritter, careful not to push my new wounds against his chest. He was more likeable asleep, devoid of his imperturbable day mask, his features relaxed and unstressed. Even in repose he was compelling, his features beckoning to be touched. I reached out, drew a finger down the stubble of his cheek, cupped his face with my hand. That's all I dared. I didn't want him to wake up and get the wrong idea.

Or maybe I did.

I turned away, but this time sleep was long in coming. When I shut my eyes I saw the dark-haired woman's sightless eyes, pleading. Her blood dripped like water. I wanted more than anything to help her.

But I didn't even know who she was.

CHAPTER 9

I EXPECTED ACHING MUSCLES WHEN I AWOKE, BOTH FROM TRAINING and my encounter with the Hunters, but only a mild soreness remained in my shoulder, marked by a fading bruise. There was no trace of the cut I'd made on my hand at my parents' house. I still wore my bra, but my jeans had been replaced by comfortable pajama bottoms. My bandages had vanished.

So had Ritter.

"Ah, you're awake." Ava was sitting on a chair beside my bed, dressed in her black martial arts uniform, which I'd learned during our dinner at the mansion was called a *dobak*.

I squinted at her in the bright light coming from the window. "Not going to my funeral, huh?"

"That was yesterday, and yes, I was there."

Now that she mentioned it, I did seem to vaguely recall getting up several times to use the bathroom. "Friday already?" I must have been really out of it. Tomorrow would make an entire week since the accident, but I only remembered Wednesday, the day I'd awakened.

"Dimitri made us give you a sedative. He was worried about you.

You were calling out about blood and death during some apparently nasty dreams. We couldn't wake you."

"Dimitri's the one who should be sleeping."

"He has been. He's almost well."

"So how was my funeral?"

"Sad. Thankfully." She grinned. "I talked to your grandmother for a minute."

"You didn't tell them I was hurt, did you?"

"Of course not."

"So everyone's okay?"

"Yes."

I breathed a sigh of relief and made myself sit up. Not even sitting up hurt. In fact, I felt wonderful.

Ava saw me studying the unbroken flesh on my shoulder. "No more curequick for you, especially drinking it."

"I know," I said regretfully. "So what's on the agenda today?"

"After Wednesday's attack and with all the record tampering at the burn center, we've decided to move the group to Oregon now instead of next week."

"What about New York?"

"Still on. Our appointment isn't until midnight tomorrow, so there's plenty of time to get our operation heading to Oregon before we leave on our plane tonight."

"Isn't midnight a little late for a business meeting, even for New York?"

Ava laughed. "John Halden's rather eccentric. I'm surprised you haven't read about him in the tabloids. Rumor has it he's a vampire. Completely unfounded, of course, since there are no such things as vampires, though Unbounded are the basis of that particular folklore. Anyway, tomorrow Stella, Ritter, and I will spend the day preparing for the meeting and introducing you to our counterparts in New York. Meanwhile, Dimitri and Laurence will head to Oregon to set up camp."

She gave a little sigh as she arose. "Well, I'll leave you to shower and dress. Dimitri's trying to get up, so I think I'll go use some muscle on him. I put a few of your outfits in the closet here. They'll have to do until we get to Oregon."

I was pulling on a T-shirt in preparation to find the bathroom when a knock came on the door. "Come in," I called.

Stella entered, carrying a tray. "Good to see you vertical. Ava told me you were up, so I brought you some breakfast. Hope you like bacon and eggs. And don't give me any mortal nonsense about calories. Your training will burn more than you could ever eat."

I groaned. "Do you train with Ritter, too?"

"We all do. It's not a matter of choice. It's survival." She set the tray on the bed.

"What's this?" Besides the promised bacon and eggs, the tray also held official-looking documents.

"Your new identity. An Oregon driver's license, California birth certificate, social security number, passport, concealed carry permits from several different states, debit card—everything you'll need. Oh, and under all that somewhere is your new cell phone."

"Debit card?" I wasn't even going to think about the concealed weapons permits.

She laughed. "We've had centuries to amass wealth. We have royalties on everything from books to patents, not to mention dividends on stocks. The card gives you access to a monthly allotment from a trust. Enough for anything you need as long as your requirements aren't too lavish. Anything beyond that is up to you. Or you could ask your grandmother for funds."

I knew she meant Ava, not the woman I'd called Grandmother all my life. I picked up the card. "What if I took it and left?"

"Do you feel ready to be on your own?"

Good point.

She shrugged. "The money is a gift from your Unbounded family, even if you decide to disappear. You may not feel the way we do, yet, but I hope you'll give us a chance."

I sat down on the bed. The aroma of the bacon swirled deliciously around me, though I didn't feel hungry despite not having physically eaten for more than a day. "She's so . . . businesslike," I said, for lack of a better word.

Stella pushed the tray toward the wall and sat beside me. "She's waited a long time for an Unbounded descendant. Many of us have."

"Maybe your sister's descendants in Oregon will Change."

"That's my greatest hope."

"There've been no Unbounded in her line yet?"

She nodded. "A few. But we lost them a long time ago."

"What about having your own children?" I realized as the words left my mouth that she might have already raised a dozen for all I knew.

"When I married Bronson, he had two grown children and a vasectomy." She looked at her fingers lying in her lap and then back at me again. "At the time I was glad. I watched my little sister grow old and die, and her children do the same. Putting off childbearing seemed to make sense. There was no rush."

"You wish you'd had Bronson's child, don't you?"

She gave a slight nod. "He's ill—dying."

"Cancer?"

"I wish." She saw my confusion and added. "We found a cure for most cancers years ago, but sick people make the medical community rich, so scientists are forced to sweep their research under the couch to save their grants. We'll get the cure out there eventually, but right now the people opposing us have more weight and money behind them."

I was stunned. My grandpa had died of cancer. "You mean the Emporium, don't you?"

"They're always involved wherever there's a huge amount of money at stake. Anyway, Bronson has a rare autoimmune disease that affects his heart and several other major organs. Medication isn't working well, so he's sick quite a bit of the time now, though this week's been pretty good." She was silent for a moment before adding, "If we'd had a child, I'd have something of his after he's gone."

Until the child grew old and died. The words hung between us, unspoken, but I heard them as clearly as if she said them aloud.

"Your child could be Unbounded."

"Twenty percent chance with an Unbounded and a mortal." She hesitated before continuing. "About children—there's something else you should know. Shortly after the Change, birth control methods no longer work for Unbounded."

I blinked at her. "What are you saying?"

"Barrier methods have a high failure rate. Implantation happens despite an IUD, often with frightening results. Keeping careful track of your cycle can help avoid pregnancy a percentage of the time, but the only sure method is sterilization—if your partner is mortal, that is, because an Unbounded's organs simply regenerate."

"Then why don't you all have more children?"

"Partly because it's hard watching those you love grow old and die—again and again. Also, we come from a different age, an age where family was all-important, where people married and stayed together. Most Renegades have watched the world change, families falling apart, and the resulting weakening of society. We reject that. To us duty to family is everything. We feel a deep responsibility to track our descendants for at least six generations, which is generally how long it takes before the gene is too diluted to create an Unbounded. We refuse to allow our Unbounded posterity to be killed or recruited by the Emporium. Or left alone to discover their nature."

"Like Cort."

"Exactly. So we're very careful. Laurence is already on his second marriage and has eight children that will probably result in more posterity than he'll ever be able to look after by himself. His current wife is only thirty and they have one child together. She had her uterus removed two years ago. The next time he marries, he'll look for someone who's finished bearing children."

The next time. How could she be so casual?

My thoughts must have shown in my face because she nodded.

"It's a paradox. We desperately want more Unbounded to stand with us against the Emporium so we keep marrying and trying, but many of our children aren't Unbounded and as the generations go on, there aren't enough of us to keep watch over our posterity." She patted my leg and stood. "Enough seriousness for now. You should eat. When you're finished getting ready, come meet my husband. He's quite pleased with himself for getting all the lead out of Dimitri. Ritter's in a mood, though. He's insisting everyone double up on defense training for the next few weeks—especially Dimitri."

"And me, I suppose." I was the weak link, no doubt about that. Perhaps the family talent had skipped me altogether.

Stella smiled. "Don't mind Ritter. He takes it personally when any of us get hurt." She grabbed my hand, squeezing it briefly. "I'm glad you're here, Erin. I've missed having a sister, and while I love Ava dearly, she can never be that for me."

I'd always wanted a sister. I'd almost had one in Justine.

After Stella left, I stared for a long minute at the phone she'd given me. It was thin and black and very much like the one I'd stolen from the office at the warehouse. At least I'd moved up in their estimation if they trusted me this much. Then again, after hearing about Ritter's family and getting up close and personal with the Hunters, I wouldn't likely be running to my family again anytime soon.

I dialed and waited until a familiar female voice spoke. "Sorry, no one's home right now. Leave a message and someone will call you back. Tom probably." A laugh that made me smile. Justine.

"Hi, Tom," I said when the beep signaled. "It's me. I wanted to see how it went yesterday. If you're okay. Call me later on this number if you want to talk."

I hung up feeling pretty pathetic. He'd made his point quite clear, and hoping that he'd been unbalanced because of Justine wasn't doing me any favors. Even if he begged on his knees, I didn't know that I'd ever be able to trust him again. Not really. I told myself the only reason I was calling was because of Justine. She'd want someone to check up on her little brother. But in the end, I failed her because I'd called the home phone Justine had insisted on, which Tom never picked up, instead of his cell. I wasn't sure I wanted to talk to him at all.

MY SHORT HAIR WAS STILL WET FROM MY SHOWER WHEN I EMERGED into the hallway and ran into an extremely large man with the thickest, brightest, most beautiful curly red hair I'd ever seen in a natural color. His red shirt contrasted unfavorably with his hair and his pale skin. I knew he must be Laurence, for he moved his impressive bulk with the same casual confidence as the others.

He held out his big hand, which completely enveloped my own. "You won't remember me, but I've seen you several times. I'm Laurence Green, and Dimitri's my fifth great-grandfather from his tenth wife's line. Our family tree is rather lengthy and wide. Takes a computer program to track everyone for even six generations these days."

"I can imagine, with him being so old."

Laurence had Dimitri's brown eyes, though not nearly as dark. He was also taller and a good deal rounder. "Old?" He laughed, leaning up against the wall, folding his arms over his ample stomach. "Dimitri hasn't even had his mid-life crisis yet."

"Are you a doctor like he is?"

"No way." He lifted a hand as though to wave away a pesky fly. "I'm not giving in to that for at least another century. I'm a hundred and ten already, you know. Right now I'm amassing a huge fortune so that when I do give in I can spend the rest of my life throwing unheard of amounts of money at my research." His voice lowered. "Although, I do own, in one form or another, every relevant medical text in the world. They're fascinating. Only don't tell anyone, okay? It's our little secret."

I liked him. I liked him a lot. There was no tension, no hidden agenda, no sexual desire emanating from him. He was a lot like my brothers, despite the fact that they looked nothing alike. My eyes felt suspiciously moist. "I'm pleased to meet you, Laurence. I really am."

He took my hand again and leaned forward, his face nearly touching mine. "I know. They're all a little too intense, but you and I will get along just fine. As soon as we're settled in Oregon, I'll set you up in business. There's nothing better than being in control of your own destiny, and as long as they hold the purse strings, you won't feel that way."

Impulsively, I hugged him. "Thank you."

He smiled and winked at me, the fat on his face jiggling slightly. "Enough of that. I'm a married man. You're going to love my wife, by the way. She's a sweetheart."

Something about the way he said it made an impression on me. "She doesn't know, does she?"

"I'll have to tell her soon." He smiled, but this time his expression was infinitely sad. "I'll introduce you as one of my many cousins. Won't be far from the truth, I'm sure." He patted my shoulder. "You're a lot more like your grandmother than I thought. But I like you anyway. Come on, let's go find the others. Take my advice, though, and don't back down. Fight for what you want. Even if it's not important."

He was a curious man. Affable and friendly one minute, sad and serious the next, and definitely not afraid to show his emotions. Maybe he was too young to have developed the habit of hiding them.

Too young. When did I start thinking of a hundred and ten as being young?

In a sitting room adjoining the kitchen, we found Ava and Dimitri together on a couch, Cort in an easy chair, and Ritter pacing along the shuttered window. Stella was on the loveseat next to an arresting white-haired man, who was older than I'd expected but much more handsome. In his younger years, he would have been a heartthrob; now he was the epitome of old-fashioned stateliness and grace. Stella snuggled in the crook of his arm, one of her smooth hands lying atop his wrinkled, age-spotted one in casual intimacy.

"Ah, this must be the famous Erin," Bronson said, coming to his feet and extending a hand.

"You mean infamous," I said with a smile.

He chuckled. "Or soon to be. Goes with the territory."

My stomach lurched as our hands made contact. On the outside he appeared at rest, but touching him showed me his pain, as though it were my own. I drew my hand away, trying not to yank it. My imagination must be working overtime.

"Well, I have to be off," Laurence said.

Ritter opened his mouth, but Laurence beat him to it. "Don't worry. I'm armed, and I'm taking two of the guys. They know the score." He leaned over and kissed me on the cheek. "Bye, dear cousin. We'll talk later."

I watched his bulk amble from the room, wishing I could go with him.

"When are we leaving?" I addressed no one in particular. Ava was talking to Dimitri, and Ritter gazed sullenly out the half-open blinds on the window, so my gaze settled on Cort who at least appeared happy to see me. "I want to call my family before we go. See how they're doing." What I really wanted to do was tell them about the Hunters and about Ritter's family so they would be more careful, but I couldn't say those things over the phone, and that meant some kind of a visit.

"We won't leave until late tonight," Cort said.

Ritter picked up his machine gun from the windowsill and turned in my direction. "Time for your lesson."

"Can't that wait until Oregon?" I asked.

"No."

I was going to argue the point, but Ava nodded. "I agree with Ritter. You never know when you'll need to protect yourself. Our encounter with the Hunters has proven that. We have things well enough in hand that we can spare Ritter for a while. You might even be able to arrange a quick visit with your family, if you must."

At first I was startled that she had guessed my true intentions, but then she'd spent a good deal of time studying me. "Okay. Let's train," I capitulated with bad grace. "I'll go change, but you have to remember I was shot a day and a half ago, and burned nearly to death before that. I'm not exactly feeling my best." This was a lie. I actually felt quite well.

Ava smirked at me. "Don't worry. Ritter will go easy on you."

I sighed. I'd seen what his "easy" entailed.

"You know," Stella mused aloud. "Eventually your family may want to consider moving. That way, you would be able to visit them more readily."

At once I felt lighter. It would take time, but maybe my life could be put back together.

Five minutes later, Ritter led me down to Stella's walkout basement. The whole floor was one open room, with a long line of windows and glass doors along the far wall. Another wall was lined with combat instruments, and still another sported a wooden mannequin with knife cuts marring both its body and the cork wall behind. There was a punching bag, a wrestling mat, and in the corner, looking very out of place, a pool table.

Ritter gave me a flat smile. "Everything but a shooting range. But you know how to shoot, don't you?"

"A little."

"More than a little." He strode to a black duffel near the rear wall by a drinking fountain, reaching inside to pull out a pistol. "This is yours. When we get to Oregon, I'll train you on the other guns as well, and show you how to take care of them, but this will do for now. It's a nine mil, but it's compact, so you can carry it at all times. Use your purse, a shoulder holster. Whatever. We have a bunch to choose from in that bin over there. Next time a Hunter attacks, you'll be ready."

I scowled. I didn't feel comfortable enough with a weapon to carry it around, but more importantly I didn't like him telling me what to do. "And if I don't want to?"

"Please, Erin."

I hadn't expected that. Though the expression on his face hadn't changed, there was a sudden shift in the way he held his body, and I knew the attack had shaken him. Not because there had been so many Hunters or the manner of the attack, but because he hadn't expected it. He hated surprises. I was beginning to suspect Ava had made me train today only to assuage his conscience, to give him something to focus on.

My anger died, and I decided not to remind him of how many gun owners had their own weapons turned on them. "About the other night, after the shooting," I said, checking the chamber of the gun to make sure it didn't have a bullet inside. Some people carried guns loaded, but I preferred to be two steps away from firing. That meant I'd have to rack before pulling the trigger. "Thanks for staying with me."

"It was my pleasure." He looked at me through half-lidded eyes that sent an involuntary heat surging through me as I remembered the heaviness and warmth of his hand on my bare stomach, the relaxation in his face. His smell.

Not good.

He turned from me and grabbed two bo staffs off the wall. "Set the gun over there. We won't need it today."

He stood in the middle of the room waiting for me but didn't seem to be in a hurry to begin. "About your family," he said. "Stella's suggestion to move them may sound simple now, but it's more complicated than you realize. Eventually, your parents will have to move again and again, so their new neighbors won't catch on to the fact that you never age. Every few years they'll have to become accustomed to calling you by yet another name, and when your face becomes known among the Emporium Unbounded and the Hunters, they'll have to worry about the lives of your siblings and their grandchildren. They may feel they have to choose."

I hadn't thought about Chris and Lorrie. Would they be willing to uproot their children? My parents wouldn't want to leave them. Was constantly moving fair to my family? I glared at Ritter, hating him for being my conscience, for making me see that my parents were better off where they were. Better off without me.

He tossed me a staff, and this time I went after him with force, not holding anything back. Why should I? It wasn't as if I'd really be able to hurt him. Yet. For now he was too fast and too good, but the day would come. Until then, he was skilled enough not to hurt me as I made my wild, uncontrolled attacks.

Or so I hoped. I was really tired of getting hurt.

After twenty minutes, he put away the bo staffs and tossed me a black stick about two feet long. "This is an escrima stick. We'll start with one, but eventually use two."

We went at it again. Overhead strikes, under strikes, use of the butt to hit your opponent in vital places. Sweat dripped from my body, but I was determined not to stop until he told me to. It was a matter of pride. Pride like the kind that had forced me to leave college. I longed for curequick, but knowing its addictive properties kept my craving manageable. I settled for sips of water from the drinking fountain, and absorbed whatever I could from the air. I was glad I'd had the bacon for breakfast.

After the sticks, we worked on hand-to-hand combat. My skin was tougher today, and though we worked strenuously, there were no beads of blood. He corrected my technique every few minutes, but he didn't seem to tire or become angry at my repeated mistakes. "Good," he said, as I blocked a blow that would have leveled me during our first session. Instead it only shoved me into the wall. "Of course, you'll need to twist out of there immediately after the block. You can't afford to be pinned against any solid surface."

For demonstration, he faked an uppercut to my abdomen that probably would have meant the end for me in a real fight. We stood inches away. I could taste the hint of mint in his hot breath, see the glistening of the skin of his neck, face and arms. Emotions waved over me. Possessiveness. Desire. I wanted to run my hands over the tautness of his chest. I wanted to taste his lips, his cheeks, the softer-looking skin in the hollow of his neck.

Where did that all come from?

I clamped down on the emotions. Had becoming Unbounded messed up all my hormone levels? Or was I simply attracted to Ritter in a way I never had been attracted to any man before?

Whatever it was, I didn't like it.

I steeled myself for what might come next. I didn't know how I'd react if he touched me. My skin was already on fire. I tried to think about Tom, but all that did was make me feel angry, betrayed. Tom may have taken himself out of the running, but that didn't mean I would fall into the arms of the nearest available killing machine, no matter how deathly sexy he might be. I didn't need Ritter or Tom. I would have dozens of lifetimes to find someone else. If I even wanted anyone else.

Ritter moved closer, his hands reached out. Instead of touching me, they went above my head, removing something from a shelf above my head. A leather holder containing two knives.

"These," he said, hoarsely, "are something else you shouldn't be without. Guns make a lot of noise, especially without a silencer, and they're harder to hide, but these you can strap around your thigh like this." He touched me then, settling the leather over my stretch pants. "Works especially well if you're wearing a skirt."

I wasn't sure if he was teasing or not. Frankly, I was glad for the layer of cloth between us, but only because I was afraid of how I would react to his fingers on my flesh. He didn't look at me as he fastened the buckles, and I knew he was avoiding my stare.

"Come over here," he said, backing toward the mannequin in front of the cork wall. "I'll teach you some basic moves. You'll be keeping these knives. I already talked to Stella about them."

So I learned the basics of knife-throwing. I was worse at this than at combat, and even Ritter's calm was beginning to show a few cracks as yet another knife bounced off the wooden dummy without penetrating. "You'll have to start working out your arms. You're simply too weak."

That jab hurt more than I wanted to admit. I glanced at the clock someone had so kindly hung on the wall. It was past one. "That's what I've been doing for the past four hours." I shoved a knife back into the leg sheath, nearly cutting through my pants in the process. "I'm finished here."

We glared at each other for several long seconds before he nodded. "I have things to do anyway before tonight. Go ahead and say goodbye to your family, if you must. But don't go to their house. Take Cort with you wherever you decide to meet. He'll make sure you're not followed."

"Fine. But I'm agreeing only because I *want* to take Cort, not because you're ordering me to." I knew he didn't exactly deserve my anger, but my hormones were raging, and I was sick of being taught to kill by a man who was half dead inside.

He sighed. "You are just like your grandmother."

"My *fourth great-grandmother*. And we are nothing alike."

I stomped up the stairs in a rather childish fashion, but I didn't care what Ritter thought. In the kitchen, I stumbled into Cort. "Finally," I said, "somebody sane. Take me away from here."

He smiled, his eyes roaming with interest over my sweaty body. "I don't know about sane, but I'm game. Everyone else is busy. No one has need of a scientist right now."

"I do. Besides, according to Ritter, you're my appointed baby-sitter if I want to see my family."

"Couldn't think of a better way to spend my afternoon than with you. How about lunch first?"

"Sounds great." Beautiful. Normal. "Give me ten minutes to shower."

"Tell you what, take twenty and dress up. I want to take you someplace nice. Besides, you'll need time to come up with a disguise in case we run into someone who might recognize you."

In my room I had a message on my cell. From Tom. I played it back, a knob of anxiety cranking inside me.

"Erin, I'm sorry I missed your call. I do need to talk to you. It's very important. Look, I've done some checking and no matter what you do, don't trust those people. They aren't who they say they are. Call me." A hesitation and then, "I'm sorry about what happened at your house. I can explain everything. I—I love you."

CHAPTER 10

CORT MIGHT BE A LITTLE NERDY, BUT HE CLEANED UP WELL. He wore a tan suit with a brown shirt that matched his hair and set off his blue eyes. I knew he wore a gun strapped to his calf because I'd briefly seen the bulk stretch against the cloth of his pants when he'd climbed into the green Lexus.

"Nice car," I said.

"Thanks." Cort glanced at me quickly and then back to the road. "You look really beautiful. I mean, you've always been attractive, but with this disguise, you look mysterious. Unrecognizable."

You'd think that at nearly five hundred years old, he'd be better at compliments. "You can blame Stella for that." She'd made up my face with far too much makeup, given me sunglasses, and tied a silky red scarf around my head to show off my new blond fuzz. Okay, curls. I barely recognized myself. I also had stylish red glasses with clear lenses to wear in the restaurant. "But I don't think I should have worn this red dress. I mean, it's good for these"—I pulled up my dress a few inches above my knee to show the leather knife sheath that I'd decided to wear at the last moment—"but it sort of makes me noticeable."

"That's the best way to hide. Out in the open. But you shouldn't do that."

"Do what?"

"Show me your leg. I may be old enough to be your tenth great-grandpa, but my hormones say I'm only forty."

I laughed, feeling flattered. "Like you haven't seen it before. Are you married? And how many children do you have anyway?"

"I had ten children, two Unbounded, one still alive and living in Europe, and a slew of great-grandchildren and other posterity. I've been married several times now, each time to mortals." He shrugged. "Not for a while though. It's tough in the end."

Always it came down to loss. I was beginning to understand what the Unbounded faced, and that there would eventually come a time when they would be afraid to take another risk. Too many hurts piled up. Too many losses. Yet being alone was a terrible way to live, even if it took a thousand years before you could resign yourself to saying goodbye without that bitter regret.

So how could regular humans, whose lives were comparably short, be satisfied with such a brief time with their loved ones? Merely a week ago, I'd been resigned to exactly that. Perhaps because I hadn't realized others had far more.

"Now I'm thinking of saving myself for just the right Unbounded," Cort said with a laugh that sounded only a little forced.

His stray glances had become a little pointed, and I wished he'd pay more attention to the road. I hadn't banked on being the hot new commodity on the Unbounded single scene. It was sort of like being sought after because I had money, only this time my wealth was measured in potential years of life.

I shook off these thoughts. Right now my body was sending me strong signals I couldn't ignore. Not hunger, but something else. "We have to stop by a grocery store. I need gum or mint, or something. Maybe chocolate."

"Protein. It's always that way after you've been hurt."

"I could just absorb it, couldn't I?"

He smiled. "I've forgotten how it felt in the beginning. It's as natural as breathing now. I never feel in need of anything."

"Well, I'm aware of absorbing every second, at least when I'm awake. It's like I'm reaching out to bring it inside me. Very physical. Calculated." I hesitated, debating on whether I should confess the rest of my thoughts. I decided to go ahead. "I've been wondering—do we take sustenance from other living beings? I mean, I know we absorb from the air and plants and everything, but I'd hate to think we were absorbing people, too."

His chuckle was deep and warm and inoffensive. "No wonder you're so aware of it, if that's what you've been thinking. Don't worry. Absorbing from another live human or an animal would be a last case scenario. There's too much else that's easily accessible to us in the air from decaying matter, even through glass or ordinary walls. Our systems go for easy first."

"What if we were in a sealed room with someone, and no other food source was available?"

"We do have some innate control over our absorption, so you would instinctively avoid absorbing from them unless you were unconscious."

"And then?"

"Then your body would do whatever it took to keep you alive. That's part of the Unbounded gene. But by the time you started absorbing the other person, they'd be dead from starvation or suffocation, and you'd be doing it unconsciously as their body decomposed and became part of the air." He made a face. "Hey, I thought this was supposed to be a nice outing, not a morbid one."

"Sorry. Are we almost there? I'm not hungry, exactly. I just want to eat."

"We're almost there."

He drove to Café des Amis, a French restaurant on the Missouri side of Kansas City that I'd never eaten at before, though I'd seen the outside, which sported wooden decks lined by trees where diners could supposedly experience the atmosphere of a real French restaurant. As Cort parked, I made a decision. "Maybe my family could meet us here—I mean, after our meal. Join us for a drink or dessert. It would probably be one of the last places anyone would look for us."

"The attack scared you, didn't it?" Cort's blue eyes were intent again, piercing as I remembered them from that first day.

I nodded slowly.

"Go ahead, call your family. I'm sure we haven't been followed."

I considered a moment before dialing Jace's number. I was closest to him, and I knew he wouldn't pester me with more than a few questions about my welfare.

"Hello?" he answered, a bit of impatience in his voice.

"It's me, Blondie." I used the nickname I'd had as a teenager. We'd both enjoyed the comic strip, and because I was blond, the name stuck, though we hadn't used it much since leaving high school. I hoped he'd remember.

"Blondie, hello. Been wondering when I'd hear from you. How is everything?"

"Good. Thanks. Look, I called because, well, what are you up to right now?"

"Packing. I'm heading back to Texas tomorrow. The army only let me have a week off for my, uh, sister's funeral."

"I was sorry to hear about her death." More sorry to have experienced it, but I couldn't very well say that with the Emporium possibly listening in. "Look, I'd really like to see you and your parents. I was hoping you could meet me. Right now, if you can."

"My parents are out. Some school play for my brother's kids. But I can come."

Maybe it was better this way, since neither of my parents would be happy I was leaving the state. "Okay, meet me at Café de Amis. Know where that is?"

"Do *you* know what that place costs? I'm on a serviceman's salary, you know." There was a note of teasing in his voice that calmed me.

"Cheapo. Never mind—it's on me. Besides, by the time you get here, we'll be finished eating. You can have dessert with us."

"Us?"

"A friend. Someone I want you to meet."

"Okay. I'll be there soon. Later, Blondie."

Cort arched a brow as I shut the phone. "Well?"

"Just my brother's coming. It'll be better this way. But I wish I didn't feel so unsettled."

"In what way?"

"I don't know. I feel strange, like I'm not myself. I'm sure it's all these changes." My quick healing proved I was Changed, but it was still hard to wrap my thoughts around living for two thousand years.

He reached out a hand and placed it on my leg. "Let me know if you think of anything I can do to help." His touch felt good, too good, and that confused me further.

"Thanks, Cort. I appreciate it."

He nodded and opened his door, moving swiftly around the Lexus to help me out of my seat.

"I have a château in the south of France," Cort said minutes later as a waiter led us outside onto one of the decks at the restaurant. "I lived there for more than eighty years, and I still go back as often as possible. Lovely place. When you go to France, you'll have to visit." I noticed he said "when" not "if," as though it went without saying that I'd eventually go there in my extended lifetime.

As Cort pushed in my chair, I lifted my gaze, scanning the people around us. The restaurant was comfortably full, but no one was paying us extra attention. I set my small red purse gently on my lap, all too aware of the gun inside. But instead of feeling nervous, I was surprised to find both the gun and the knives gave me a sense of power.

Totally not like the old me. If I'd had any doubt about having undergone a complete physical and emotional change, this proved it beyond doubt. But it was still all kinds of weird.

We began our meal with an assortment of French cheeses, fruit, and wine, to be followed by a salad and a dish of wild boar, which I'd always wanted to try. Cort watched me, a smile on his face. "I've been wanting to tell you that I'm sorry about your, uh, boyfriend."

I shrugged, unwilling to talk about Tom. On the phone, he'd hesitated before his declaration of love. I'd felt a lie in the words, as I had in the hospital when he'd assured me I would live. Whether because of the lie or his desertion, I hadn't called him back. It didn't make sense that he could have discovered anything about the Unbounded when for all our lives we'd never heard of their existence. Could there possibly be something about them on the Internet? Had he been contacted by Hunters? Whatever the case, I was finding it hard to trust him. That didn't mean I wasn't going to call. I would, but not yet. I had plenty of time before the exchange in New York.

"I'm more worried right now about surviving this week than I am about Tom." I nibbled a piece of cheese. "Ritter's determined to kill me with all this training. I don't seem to have any talent at it, though they say I should."

"Well, let me know if it kicks in." Cort set down his wine. "In fact, I'm interested in recording everything that happens to you— for science's sake, of course. If you notice anything happening, in your physical makeup, your abilities, your senses, please tell me. It could help new Unbounded adjust more easily in the future."

Except that I wasn't feeling comfortable enough to talk about my strange hormone shifts with anyone, much less with a man who'd as much as admitted he was attracted to me. "Someone should write an Unbounded manual, that's for sure." I'd finished most of the cheese and was looking around for something else to eat. Fortunately, the waiter was coming our way with our salads and steaming entrees.

I'd made good headway on my food by the time Jace arrived. My little brother greeted me with a hug and kiss on the cheek that he had to lean down to give me, even though I'd come to my feet. I grabbed his hand as we sat down, knowing we looked more like lovers than siblings, but I couldn't help myself. He was the only thing I had to cling to from my past life. My normal life.

"What's with the paint and the glasses?" he asked. "Almost didn't recognize you."

"That's the point." I introduced him to Cort, and he released my hands to shake Cort's, but already I was feeling steadier.

"So," Jace said. "What's happened?" My brother was nothing if not direct.

I glanced pointedly at Cort, but he shook his head. "Sorry, can't leave you two alone. Ava's orders."

"Because you don't trust me?"

"Do you trust us?"

I sighed and turned back to my brother. "I'm leaving town tonight for a little trip. I wanted to say goodbye and remind you to keep your eyes open."

The waiter chose that moment to ask Jace if he wanted anything. Jace ordered coffee and pastry puffs filled with vanilla ice cream and drizzled in chocolate sauce. "Make that two," I said.

Jace arched a brow. "Glad to see you're back to eating dessert. You're looking a little thin. What about that absorption thing?"

"Still getting the hang of it. Plus, I've been working out a bit." I gave a wry smile at the understatement. At least my Unbounded body had so far endured Ritter's training. "So about Mom and Dad . . ."

"I'll keep an eye on them, as much as I can from a distance. And Chris always looks in on them. We have to keep working, of course."

My old life may have completely stopped as though I'd really died, but not his or Chris's, or Lorrie's, or my parents' lives. Only I had changed. Or Changed.

I leaned toward him and whispered, "After we left the house the other night we were attacked. Eighteen men with guns. Jace, you have to understand—this is far more serious than I ever realized." I grabbed his hand under the table and placed it on the leather sheath around my leg.

He looked confused until he recognized the shape of the knives. He pulled back as if bitten. "What the—you're serious!"

"I was shot in the shoulder, but that was nothing compared to what they were going to do to us if we'd lost. Remember what Ava and I told you about the only ways to kill an Unbounded?"

"Got it." His face was ashen. A little louder he added, "I wish I could come with you. I don't like you being out there alone."

"She's not alone," Cort said. "I assure you of that. We're looking out for her."

Jace didn't seem comforted.

"They do hire security," I told him. "Maybe when you decide you've had enough of the army—"

"I've had enough of it now. I'm not sure how I can go back knowing what's really out there. You're different, Erin. I see that. And I'm not ashamed to tell you I'm jealous as hell. If I hadn't signed that contract with the army, I'd go with you right now."

I leaned close to him, put my cheek against his. "I'm sorry."

That's when I noticed the man. He was two tables over to my left, nowhere near us. He wasn't looking our way, and I couldn't see his face clearly because he was framed by the light coming through the trees behind him, but the confident way he held himself, the way his mouth moved when he spoke to his red-haired female companion, told me he was Unbounded. I fought a burst of panic. They weren't part of Ava's Renegades. Could they be from the Emporium?

"Cort!"

"Yes?" He looked at me sharply.

"I think we have a problem."

"What problem?" Jace hissed.

I glanced at him and then at Cort. "Don't look around or anything, but I think we're being watched. By an Unbounded. Someone I don't recognize."

Beside me Jace tensed, but I could detect no reaction from Cort. "Where?" Cort asked.

"To my left. Two tables back—by the trees. Gray suit, open collar, dark hair speckled gray."

Cort wasn't in a good position to see the man, but Jace was.

"I see him," Jace said. "No jewelry except a big ring. Can't see his face clearly, but I'd say from the way he carries himself he knows how to fight. Army trained, or something. Can't see anything of the woman he's with, except for all that hair. Is she Unbounded, too?"

I hadn't noticed her, and I didn't dare turn now, but as I recalled the glimpse I'd had of them, I was fairly certain she was. "I think so."

"How can you tell?" Jace asked.

"More of a feeling than anything else."

"If they're watching us," Cort said, "did they follow us here, or did they follow Jace to get to you?"

I shook my head. "I didn't see if they got here before or after us, and I can't tell by what's on their table. Coffee maybe? Could be waiting for food or already finished."

On the pretext of looking around for the waiter, Cort glanced their way. "I don't recognize them from our files on the Emporium. You might be mistaken."

"Maybe they're new," I said. "Like me."

Cort shook his head. "Guy's too old to be new."

There was silence at our table, and I felt doubt creeping in. If Cort didn't think they were Unbounded, who was I to insist? Still, I wanted to be sure. "I want a closer look. Where are the bathrooms?"

"You can't go alone," Jace said.

I opened my purse, tilting it so he could glimpse the gun there. "Don't worry little brother, I won't be gone long."

Jace stared at me in shock, and I knew that was not only because of the gun, but because of my confidence. I hadn't been sure of my actions for a very long time. Before either man could object, I arose and strode across the restaurant, clutching my bag like a life preserver. As I approached the gray-haired man, I could see absolutely nothing about him that would signal his true identity, but I was even more sure he was Unbounded. The woman's nature was more difficult to determine, as she was framed by a mass of dark auburn hair that covered her back and shoulders. As I passed, she leaned down for something in her purse so I was unable to see her face, but her movement exuded Unbounded confidence. Why couldn't Cort see that?

I almost expected the man's arm to whip out and grab me, but nothing happened. I went past them into the main restaurant, searching until I found the bathrooms. Once there, I blew out a shaky breath of relief and waited an appropriate period of time, one hand inside my purse, before starting to leave. As I moved toward the door, it opened.

"You should have seen him," a thin blonde was saying to her dark-haired friend. "It was the funniest thing ever." She froze when she saw me.

Oh, no, I thought, releasing the gun and snapping shut my purse.

I knew her. Her name was Judy—we'd worked at the insurance agency together in claims until last year when she slept with one of the bosses and was promoted to his personal secretary. Never mind that he was married and had two kids. Her sharp sarcasm, incessant prattling, and constant criticism of coworkers had just about alienated her from everyone who worked there. But she did have a fabulous figure and rumor said she knew how to use it.

She stopped talking and put a hand on her heart, her eyes growing wide. "Oh, you gave me a scare! I'm sorry, but for a moment you looked like a close friend of mine who just died. I attended her funeral yesterday."

Close friend? Right. "I'm sorry for your loss," I said coolly.

"Of course, I see now that you don't really look much like her. She was a sweet girl, but she didn't wear glasses or have fabulous clothes like that dress, and she certainly didn't have your style." Envy dripped from the words. "You're much thinner, too. And she had a skin problem."

I'd never had a skin problem, though my skin did look clearer now, unblemished, all the scars gone. Most women would never realize how those tiny, nearly imperceptible flaws added up over the years.

"A lot of people have look-alikes," said Judy's companion. "Everyone tells me I look like Julia Roberts."

I blinked. If she resembled Julia Roberts, I looked like, well, Stella.

Judy laughed. "You do, Lizzy. Really."

"Well, I hope everything works out for you," I said with a touch of ice. "Please excuse me."

They moved away from the door. "Great head scarf by the way," Judy called as I swept past them. I inclined my head in acknowledgment, but I didn't reply or slow my progress. I was grateful now that Stella had insisted on all the makeup and the glasses. The encounter had been too close for comfort, even though I barely knew Judy.

As I approached the strange Unbounded's table, the woman straightened from kissing the man's face, and I caught a glimpse of smooth white cheek before she turned and made her way from the restaurant. Definitely Unbounded. I wish I'd gotten a better look at her face, though. I had the nagging feeling I'd seen her somewhere before.

Jace frowned when I sat down. "What took you so long?"

"Saw someone I knew in the bathroom."

He gaped in alarm. "And?"

Cort didn't speak, but his body tensed and his eyes rapidly scanned the restaurant for danger. His hand went below the table where he would have better access to his weapon.

"It's okay," I told them. "Apparently, I'm too put together to be me. Besides, she attended my funeral. That's hard to ignore."

"We'd better leave," Cort said.

With a calm I didn't feel, I ate the last couple bites of my pastry. "We have to be sure no one follows us."

Cort met my eyes. "Not a problem." I knew this was an old game for him.

"I'll be fine," Jace said. "I know this town like the back of my hand, and I've learned a thing or two in the army."

His letters and e-mails home verified that. I remembered only too vividly how on his last tour of duty in Iraq, we'd prayed every night for his safe return. "You have a gun?" I asked.

"In my trunk."

"Put it up front with you."

"Okay." His expression was odd, and I understood that despite his excitement about the Unbounded and the support he'd offered, he was having trouble seeing me as I'd become: giver of orders, woman with a plan, confidence incarnate. I didn't blame him. I had difficulty accepting the changes in myself, which was why I was trying not to think about any of it too closely.

We left the restaurant together, making sure the suspicious man wasn't following. In the street there was no sign of the woman with the auburn hair.

I hugged Jace. "Please be careful."

We made him leave first to be sure no one followed him, but that didn't guarantee they weren't waiting for him down the road. Or what if they'd followed him here in the first place? I sighed. "I really hate this."

"It'll be over soon." Cort put an arm around me, and I leaned into him before remembering it might not be a good thing to let him get the wrong idea. I was enjoying his touch far too much for someone I didn't think I was attracted to.

I was seriously messed up.

Or maybe just missing Tom.

"Don't look now," Cort whispered, "But our friend is coming out of the restaurant. Time for a little creative driving."

CHAPTER 11

THE SHAKING DIDN'T START UNTIL WE WERE BACK AT STELLA'S, and even then it was only on the inside, so I tried to ignore it. I didn't know if I could ever grow accustomed to constant fear. Was this the usual life of an Unbounded?

Cort had been careful driving away from the restaurant, and I'd learned more than I cared to about doubling back on my route, but the truth of the matter was that the man hadn't tried to follow us. I called Jace, and though he didn't say so directly, he didn't believe he'd been followed either.

"I think we were mistaken," Cort said as he turned off the engine.

By "we" he meant me.

"Maybe." I suppose I could have been so tense that I'd imagined everything, but Cort's certainty bothered me somehow.

"Well, no one followed us or your brother, so even if they were Unbounded it makes no difference in our plans."

He came around the car to open my door, but I jumped out too quickly. I didn't want him to touch me as he had at the restaurant. I was too edgy, too nervous, and too aware of the hormones chugging through my body. I'd have to ask Stella about this. Maybe it was a normal adjustment all Unbounded had to make. A genetic urge to carry on the species.

Ava was waiting for us in the kitchen, standing before several small boxes on the counter. She'd changed from her *dobak*, so I knew she'd taken care of whatever classes she'd had to teach that day. "Good, you're back," she said. "Cort, Stella needs your help supervising the loading of the equipment down at the warehouse. They're in a hurry to finish."

Cort nodded, smiled at me, and disappeared. I noticed he didn't tell Ava my suspicions regarding the people at the restaurant. Maybe he didn't want to worry her for nothing.

I went to the counter where Ava had placed several stacks of documents. I could make out airline tickets, several dozen passports, birth certificates, and a two-inch stack of driver's licenses. As she organized the items, I noticed not only her picture but also the pictures of others from our group. Aliases.

"How's Dimitri?" I asked.

"He's fine. Or nearly. He insisted on checking security details at the private airport with Ritter. With the exception of the warehouse and these boxes here, we're all ready to go. A moving company can be trusted with the rest." She paused before adding. "Is everything okay?"

"I saw Jace." My doubts stopped me from telling Ava more about the restaurant. Surely Cort knew better than I did, and if I told her, she'd probably put me on a shorter leash than she had already.

"I trust that made you feel better. Well, I've gone through all this stuff. Why don't you help me load these boxes in the car? As soon as Ritter and Dimitri are back, I'll drop them at the warehouse before the truck leaves." She took a small pistol from one of the boxes, checked the magazine, and then tucked it into the pocket of her jeans. I felt ill at the sight, though I vividly remembered my own empowerment when I'd shown Jace my gun.

When we finished loading the car, Ava made some fresh

lemonade. "Reckon I'd best use up all those lemons," she drawled, sitting beside me at the small table and taking a long drink. She'd set her handgun down and it lay on the table between us, looking oddly out of place in Stella's immaculate kitchen. "Ah, this brings back memories. I always did cotton to fresh-squeezed lemonade."

"Is that a southern accent?" I asked with a wide smile. "It's as thick as Cort's curequick."

"I lived there for a time." She laughed, dropping the accent, her smile bright. "I've lived in a lot of places, but being a southern belle was fun. The beautiful dresses, the servants, lemonade on the lawn, the big plantations. No TV, or Internet, or telephone. Of course we always treated our workers well. It was a simpler time—at least until the war."

I rubbed my thumb over the condensation on the outside of my glass. "I wish I could have seen it."

"Oh, don't wish that. You'll see a lot more. The advances in the world in the past sixty years alone have been incredible, and we'll see far more progress. We may even leave this world eventually. Maybe find more of our kind out there."

That surprised me. "You think the Unbounded might not have come from earth?"

"Don't look so shocked. There are a dozen theories, and that's just one. None of our people have been able to trace the origin of the gene. Dimitri is sure it's a fluke of evolution. Some believe it came from a human-dragon union at the dawn of time." She rolled her eyes at this. "Still others believe our ancestors saw the finger of God. Maybe you'll live long enough to learn the truth."

"Maybe." I put my elbows on the table, which put me closer to her, though still at a comfortable distance. "So, Ava, do we have any other Unbounded relatives?"

Ava smiled and I knew the question pleased her. "We have two in England, a woman and her grandson, both in their seventh century. Locke and Kelsey Whittard. Locke would be your thirteenth great-grandmother. Her parents were the Unbounded who first contacted me. They're gone now. Lost in a battle with the

Emporium along with so many others. Our genealogy before them was never recorded."

"Do you know them well, Locke and Kelsey?" My tongue tripped over the unfamiliar names.

"Locke was once like a sister to me. I lived with her parents for over four decades."

"You mean after you nearly died." I leaned against the counter across from where she stood. "I'd like to know what happened, if you don't mind."

She hesitated, and I felt her reluctance.

"Was it fire?" I asked.

"No."

"Then what?"

She appeared to make a decision. Leaning on the counter herself, so our hands were inches apart, she began. "My parents married me off to a farmer. That was how it was done in those days. Women often didn't have a lot of say. You obeyed your parents, and that was that. To be honest, my parents thought he was a good catch. He had land, was older than I was, and prosperous. He'd been married before, but his wife didn't last long on the frontier."

"Frontier?"

She quelled me with a look. "Yes, the frontier. My family originally came from England, but some of them immigrated to America as early as the late sixteen hundreds. Anyway, I didn't want to marry the man. I was in love with another boy, but he was a year younger than I was and had no land or prospects. So at almost eighteen, I was married to the farmer. I was fortunate enough to wait that long. Many of my childhood friends married much younger."

She fingered her glass of lemonade, and I had the feeling she was gathering strength to go on. At last her eyes met mine. "He wasn't a good man. I spent the next twelve years being raped and abused. I rarely saw anyone. I worked all day in the fields or in the house. Several times I was pregnant, but he'd hit me and I'd always miscarry."

"Oh, Ava!" I struggled to take in this information. This confident, beautiful, forceful woman was the last person I would have seen as a victim, yet I knew by the solemn lines of her face and her grave tone that she was telling the truth.

"One day when I was thirty and thinking I would like to die, I found out I was pregnant again, and I began to hope."

Something in her expression told me that was a terrible thing.

"I was careful not to anger him. I talked a lot about the son he'd have to carry on his name. I finally had the child— a beautiful little girl. I never knew I could love anyone so much. I did everything I could to keep her safe. I'd hide her at night when he'd come home, so he wouldn't think about her. I'd make her stop crying before he could hear and become angry. But a man like that doesn't need much provocation. One night he became upset because his pot roast had grown cold while he'd discussed a cow with the neighbor, and he beat us. My baby was dead at his first blow. For me it took much longer. I'd thought I'd known pain before, but I was wrong.

"He left us both in the woods, but I wasn't really dead. I could sense the life around me—in the earth, the air, the trees. I absorbed it all, pulled it all in. When I finally came to consciousness weeks later, I found the rotting corpse of my child lying next to me, and I knew it was time to make sure he'd never hurt another person again."

She paused, and I waited, wondering what she had done. I knew it had to be something horrible. I wanted it to be. Our eyes met with total understanding.

"After I buried her, I staggered out of the woods and went to the house. Imagine his surprise when he saw me. I walked inside and started making a stew for dinner. I put herbs in it to make him sleep—probably enough to kill him—but to make sure, I burned down the house. It was while I watched it burn, that the man and woman came up to the house—Locke's parents. They spoke to me with proper English accents, asking if I needed help. I was crazy with grief for my baby and told them what I had done.

I hoped they would turn me in, and that I'd hang for my revenge. Stop the hurting.

"Instead, they told me I was special and took me home. I didn't believe them at first, but they were kind, and I needed to be cared for. I think I lost my mind for a time. Months. When the years went by and none of us aged, I finally understood what being Unbounded meant. That's when I became an active part of the Renegades."

"That's why you teach," I said, softly so as not to break the bond that had sprung between us. "To enable women to defend themselves."

Her mouth curved in the slightest of smiles. "You understand."

"I do now."

"After a hundred years I found a mortal I trusted enough to marry. We had a child, your third great-grandmother. She was Unbounded like me, and one of her children was, too, but both of them eventually died at the hands of the Emporium, leaving my mortal granddaughter to carry on the bloodline."

So much loss. No wonder she was fixated on me. "What will happen to your studio here?"

"I have an assistant who will continue on. Like in every other city we've been to."

"I'm glad." I grabbed her hand. "Thank you for telling me. I'm sorry I've been such a pain."

She laughed. "You wouldn't be my descendant if you weren't tough."

"I don't know about that. The last time I should have been tough, I ran away."

"You mean from law school, when that man you were dating refused to back up your claim that the professor had stolen your paper and published it under his own name."

I wasn't surprised that she knew. "He betrayed me for a good grade and a recommendation. I regret every day that I wasn't strong enough to fight back. That I let my hurt give me an excuse to quit."

"You learned an invaluable lesson, Erin. Some things you must fight for—even if you know there's no way to win. Otherwise all you have left is regret. It's a lesson you never have to learn again."

We'd nearly finished our lemonade when the garage door swung open. Ava reached for her gun, and I went for one of the knives still strapped to my leg. I wished I hadn't left my purse with my gun on the counter.

"Relax," Ritter said as he and Dimitri entered.

Ritter wore a gun in a holster under his arm and had the usual machine gun slung over his army green T-shirt. He looked big and dark and dangerous—except for the potted plant he carried in both hands. As his eyes followed my hand to where it disappeared under my red dress, a smirk filled his face, and I knew he was recalling our workout this morning and my failed attempts with the knives. I eased the knife back into the sheath and smoothed down my dress.

Ava stood to greet them. "I didn't hear the car."

Dimitri smiled. "Must be the good company."

Ritter removed his machine gun and lowered it to the table before sitting down to the glass of lemonade Ava poured for him. His eyes didn't leave me, and I could feel heat from him even across the table. Or was that coming from me?

"Dimitri," I said, coming to my feet. "How are you feeling?"

"Better. Much better. Almost normal. Great stuff, that curequick, though it makes me jumpy afterwards."

"Tell me about it." Maybe that's what was wrong with me, an overdose of curequick. "I've wanted to thank you for the clothes," I added, glancing down at the dress. "Everything fits well, and not a lot of men would think of accessories. The purses are very handy for my new gun."

He laughed. "You're welcome. I have a lot of daughters and granddaughters, and I know what they like. It's always a pleasure to dress a beautiful woman."

I smiled at the compliment, glad the feeling with the words didn't set off the hormonal alarms I'd experienced with Ritter and Cort. "Thank you."

"I would have thought you'd find more pleasure in *undressing* a beautiful woman," Ava said dryly. Her eyes flicked to mine as she added, "He is certainly an expert in the fairer sex."

"Except for one," Dimitri said.

Their gazes met and held for several long seconds before Ava stood and pocketed her gun. "I have to get to the warehouse."

"I'll go with you." Dimitri followed her to the door.

"Guess you're the babysitter now," I said to Ritter when they were gone.

"You don't look much like a baby." He leaned back in his chair and smiled up at me, which softened his expression. The light coming through the blinds lit his face well, and I noticed the slightest droop at the corner of his left eye. Not a wound that Unbounded genes would have fixed, but a feature programmed into his genetic makeup at birth. His black hair parted on the left side, the hair falling to the right, grazing a mole on his cheek, and already there was a shadow of growth on his face. "Red suits you," he added.

More heat, which this time might have reached my cheeks, but I kept my gaze steady as I poured myself more lemonade and sat across from him. "Thanks. That your plant?"

He shrugged. "I like watching things grow." He ran his finger slowly down the length of a leaf, still watching me. Almost, I felt the touch on my skin. "I wanted to tell you that you did well in training this morning."

"You're a good teacher. Patient."

"Patient?" He arched a brow. "You don't know me very well."

"Then you better get a new hobby. Plants take a long time to grow."

"Fortunately my main pastime doesn't require patience." No doubt he referred to killing Emporium Unbounded. His voice was harder now, but his eyes didn't tell me anything about his feelings, as many people's did. They were deep and dark and that was all. Yet that didn't stop the compelling urge to move closer, to touch him as I had when he'd slept.

"I thought I saw an Unbounded today," I said, searching to break the spell. "Two actually. A man and a woman."

"Where?"

"At a restaurant where Cort and I ate. My brother was there, too. They didn't seem to notice us."

"It can't be coincidence." At last his eyes held emotion, a burning hatred, and I regretted my words.

"That's what I thought, but I was probably mistaken. Cort didn't think they were Unbounded. He didn't recognize them." Pressure was growing in my right temple and I brought my hand up to massage it.

His head tilted to one side as he regarded me silently. "Was there anything specific about them that made you suspect they were Unbounded?"

"Nothing I can pinpoint."

"Not the way they looked? Acted?"

"The man was just sitting there, not even looking at us. She had her back to us, and I couldn't see her face because she had so much hair. Not even when I walked by their table."

"Cort let you do that?"

I narrowed my eyes. "He had no choice." Now the pressure had spread to my other temple.

"Okay, forget that. Why would you think they were Unbounded?"

"I don't know exactly. You and the others—you exude a kind of confidence. I can just tell you're different. I *felt* it."

He stood, sweeping up his machine gun, his face becoming rigid. "Excuse me. I need to check in with my men."

I leapt to my feet. "What is it? What did I say?" I reached out to touch his arm, to slow his flight to the door, but he stepped away as though my fingers burned. The pressure in my temples built. Pain sparked from the center of the pressure, spreading across my skull and down the back of my neck. Brightness, and then I saw another flash of the headless dark-haired girl. She'd been wearing a blue dress. I bit my lip to prevent myself from crying out.

More frightening thoughts whirled together in my mind, but only one rose to the surface: Ritter's men were watching my parents and my brother and he wanted to check in with them.

I stumbled after Ritter. "It's my family, isn't it? Do you think those Unbounded followed my brother to the restaurant and now that they've seen me my family is in danger?"

"I won't know anything until I check in with my men."

"Call them."

"I will. But I'm going over there, too, even if they answer. They might need backup."

Fear shuddered through me. "I'm going with you."

"No. You're staying here."

"Maybe I can help."

He turned and put his hands on my shoulders, staring into my face. "You won't be any help. Not yet. There's a reason you aren't any good at fighting, Erin. Believe me, we'd both know already if you had a talent for it."

"What does that mean?"

"I can't say anything more—Ava'll have my head—but regardless, I'm not risking your life. You aren't ready."

"It's *my* family!" I yelled in his face. We glared at each other for several long seconds. More calmly I added, "If you leave me here, I'll just follow you. Or go myself."

He was still for a moment, but any internal indecision was completely masked from me. I was going to have to practice that casual blankness for future use—if I lived through the night. At least the pressure in my head had vanished.

"Okay," he agreed finally. "But you do as I say. Obey every word."

"Sure," I lied, knowing that when the time came I'd have to trust my own instincts. No way would I live with more regrets.

"Bring your gun."

Inside the garage, he ushered me to a sturdy-looking Toyota Land Cruiser. "Call your family," he said as he backed down the drive. "If they answer, tell them to be on the lookout."

"Okay."

He had his own phone out and was already dialing. No answer. He ended the call and pressed another number, scarcely glancing at the keypad as he sped down the street. "Report," he barked at whoever answered. "Good. Stay alert. We have a possible Code E at primary."

On my phone, Jace didn't answer. Neither did my mother or father. My breath came faster. My heartbeats thundered in my ears. For some reason I kept thinking of the dark-haired woman and all that blood.

"Ava," Ritter was saying into his phone. "Possible Code E at primary. Communication down. Backup to primary and secondary. Stat." He paused. "She's with me."

I was dialing Chris now. "Hello?"

"It's Blondie," I said, hoping he'd remember the nickname, too. At seven years older, he'd left home long before I was in high school. "Look, don't say anything. I need you to take Lorrie and the kids to a safe place. Get your gun and be careful."

"What's going on?"

"Please, Chris. Just do it. We're coming to help."

"Okay."

I hung up. "Chris is all right," I told Ritter.

"My men there haven't seen anything unusual, but there's no answer from those at your parents' house."

"It's the Emporium, isn't it?" My throat was closed with fear, and the words came with difficulty.

Ritter's face was tight as he stared at the road. "Probably. Tell me what the Unbounded at the restaurant looked like."

"The man had dark hair, going gray. He wore a gray suit, shirt open at the neck. His face was long, hard. Brown eyes, I think. No beard. Mid-fifties. He wore a big gold ring."

"Mid-fifties would put him at fifteen hundred years. Experienced. And the woman?"

"Pale face. Lots of auburn hair. Darker than Laurence's. More brown. I didn't get a good look. She's about my build, though."

"The hair could be a disguise. Maybe she was hiding from Cort." He brought the Land Cruiser to a stop before the house in my neighborhood that sat directly behind my parents' property. The streets were empty of children, and I knew it was dinnertime. Still, it was broad daylight. Who attacked in the daylight?

People who believed they were above the law.

"You stay here." Ritter opened my purse and took out the handgun he'd given me earlier, fitting a silencer to the top. "Shoot anything that tries to get in."

"I can't stay here. I'm too exposed. There's a bunch of bushes in the back of my neighbor's yard. That would be a better place to hide."

He nodded. Reaching inside his duffel, he pulled out a couple green shirts. "Put on one of these." I chose the cleanest, pulling it on over my dress. The shirt was far too large, obscuring half the ruffled skirt of my red dress, but I knew that was the point.

Ritter passed me an extra magazine for my gun, which I tucked into my bra.

We kept to the line of bushes marking the side property line, running until we reached thicker shrubbery in the back. Together, we peered over the fence at the deceptively quiet house.

He turned to me. "I'm going in. Don't move from here. Got it?"

"Got it."

"Good." Still, he hesitated.

We were standing close, almost touching. I started to step back, mistrusting the uncontrolled emotions that were bubbling up inside me, but he leaned into me, his powerful arms pulling me close enough that his machine gun jabbed into my chest. His lips came down on mine. Not a tentative kiss, but one that burst into full passion from the beginning touch. I could feel my response echoing through every nerve as my mouth opened to his. A rush of warmth, my skin tingling. His hands on my back trailed fire. We were both breathing hard when we pulled away.

"What defense was that?" I challenged, my voice surprisingly steady despite the erratic pulsing of my veins.

He shook his head. "No defense in the world for that. That's the problem. But you never know when it might be your last chance."

He vaulted over the fence before I could reply. I sagged against the wood, trying to catch my breath. Trying to understand. Ritter both repulsed and attracted me, but for those few seconds, I'd lost myself in him. I hadn't done that since college, not even with Tom. It scared me.

I waited for the sound of bullets. I knew the Unbounded and those who worked for them had silencers, but if Jace had his army-issued handgun, or had managed to get to our father's hunting rifle, the noise would echo throughout the entire neighborhood.

Scooting behind the bushes, I found an old knot in the wood fence that I could see through. Ritter was scaling the back of my parents' house, heading to the second floor on the opposite side from where my parents had their adjoined sitting room and bedroom. I wondered why he chose there.

My heart tightened as gunfire burst like thunder through the silence of the neighborhood, spattering in rapid succession. *Jace!* I thought. More shots continued, slower now, but still coming one after the other.

My mother's scream pierced the air. Then everything fell silent.

CHAPTER 12

Tears slid down my cheeks. My pulse raced. I had to do something! I was practically immortal, yet here I hid while someone terrorized my family. What if Ritter couldn't save them? What if he was killed or captured? I might not be as powerful as he was, but I had a gun and I knew how to shoot.

I was standing before I realized it, kicking off my useless heels and climbing the neighbor's tree. From there I stepped out onto the fence and jumped down into the safety of the bushes on our side of the fence.

The yard was empty. Not even Max was out where he should be. I swallowed hard, but that did nothing for the lump of fear in my throat. I forced myself to run across the lawn to the flowerbed near the house. I was glad now that I'd neglected to trim the overgrown snowball bush. Ducking behind it, I took a deep breath, willing my nerves to be calm.

Movement. I brought up my gun, hoping the silencer worked well enough not to alert anyone if I had to shoot. Carefully, I worked my way farther into the bushes. My foot hit something. I was about to step over it, when I saw what it was—a body.

No, two bodies. Both lying at unnatural angles. One obviously had a broken neck; the other was missing half his face.

I gasped, biting my lip to stop further reaction. I'd never seen the men before, but since they were dead and I hadn't seen Ritter fire any shots outside, I bet they belonged to his mortal security team. Probably assigned to watch my family.

"Come out," said a voice I didn't recognize.

I didn't move.

"Shall I just shoot through the bushes?"

Maybe that's what *I* should do. But what if I shot one of Ritter's men who could help my family? Slowly, I worked my way out, switching my gun to my left hand so I could keep it hidden until the last moment.

I peeked around the bush to see an Unbounded man waiting. Not just any Unbounded, but the gray-haired man from the restaurant. He chuckled when he saw me. "Well, look who's here. You've saved us the trouble of finding you. Come out slowly, and I won't hurt you."

I didn't believe him for a minute. My finger tightened on the trigger. A soft thud came as he jerked back.

I kept firing. Bullet after bullet went into his body. I knew I couldn't kill him with this gun, but I might be able to damage him enough that he wouldn't be able to follow me. One of my bullets hit the middle of his chest. He staggered, squeezing his own trigger belatedly. To my relief, his shot went wild. Then he was down.

Swiftly, I retrieved my spare key from the frog in the flowerbed and went downstairs to my apartment, but the door was unlocked. Inside, the curtains were drawn shut, the room only dimly illuminated by the light that managed to bend around the edges of the material. Sensing movement at the end of the room near the stairs, I dove behind my couch.

There was a soft whimper, and I looked to see Max lying next to me, blood glistening on his golden coat. He put his nose into my hand and licked me weakly. I could feel his hurt and puzzlement at being shot, and the rage that boiled under the surface of his happy-go-lucky self. Or maybe the rage came from my heart. I wasn't a dog person, but I didn't like anyone making any animal suffer, much less one that so foolishly loved me.

"Von? That you? I tell you, there's no one outside. Would you stop being so paranoid? No one knows we're here. We got them cornered in the bedroom. Julio is sweet-talking them out now."

I sat up and fired. My shot missed, but I caught a glimpse of a Nordic-looking man, sliding toward me with that familiar Unbounded confidence. He jumped for cover as I let off another shot. He didn't make a sound, but I knew I'd hit him.

He was still coming, though, so I had to act. I crawled to the end of the couch and lifted my head to gauge where he was.

A body slammed into me, knocking me to the soft carpet. I pulled the trigger again, and my attacker grunted as the bullet sank into his chest. He brought his own weapon to my heart but stopped abruptly. "You," he muttered. "You weren't supposed to be here."

He knew me? But I'd never seen him before. "Tough luck for you." I fired again. Nothing. I was out of bullets.

Chuckling, the man switched his gun to his other hand, balling his fist. I knew what was coming. Now I'd be the one out of commission while he took care of my family, after Julio or whoever got them out of the bedroom. Where was Ritter?

Gathering my strength, I twisted at the last moment, and he hit me off-center. Even so, I reeled with the pain that spread through my jaw. This man wasn't nearly as fast as Ritter, but he was experienced and strong. I had only seconds to decide what to do. He was on top of me, easily half again my weight. I wouldn't be able to beat him in hand-to-hand combat, even if I were properly trained. But like the man outside, his orders didn't seem to be to kill or to even seriously wound me. If I could get to my knives, they might give me an upper hand.

I started reaching, but his leg was in the way. His fist came up again.

A low growl was the only warning before a golden shape sailed into the blond man. A scream burst from him as Max's heavy body knocked him to the side, freeing me. I grabbed a knife as Max snapped at his throat. The Unbounded hit Max's jaws away with his gun, bringing the weapon into position to fire at the dog's head.

"No!" I swung the knife, missing Max by inches but successfully embedding it into the man's gun shoulder. He winced and dropped the gun. By then I was slapping the new magazine into my gun. I fired once, twice.

That was enough. He lay still. I didn't know how long it would take him to revive, but I didn't worry about tying him up. Instead, I pulled off Ritter's shirt, used my teeth to rip it, and tied the cloth around the bloody wound in Max's body. "You stay here, buddy. I'll be back for you."

Yelling from upstairs spurred me to action. I had to be in time to help my family. Fighting the urge to vomit, I pulled my knife from the man's shoulder and gingerly wiped the blade on his shirt before replacing it in my sheath. I hurried up to the kitchen and around to the front entryway stairs. I took them two at a time.

Ritter was in my parents' sitting room behind the sofa, shooting into the short hallway that led to my parents' bedroom. Return fire came, the rapid shots so muffled as to seem surreal. I couldn't see the Emporium men from the top of the stairs, and they couldn't see me, but Ritter could.

He scowled and motioned me away. At that moment, a bullet slammed into his exposed shoulder and he fell. At once three men pounced on him.

Shaking, I lifted my gun to do something, anything to help, but Ritter threw off the men and was up and moving like the wind, unheeding of the blood streaming down his arm. He knocked down one opponent, then another. The first man got up again as Ritter faced the third, who didn't move with the Unbounded confidence his companions possessed. Ritter sent an uppercut to the man's chin, felling him heavily, before whipping around to land a powerful kick in the midsection of the first, slamming the man into the wall with a sickening thump. I could only watch in horrified amazement. Then the second man was coming at Ritter again.

Something was behind me. I whirled, barely catching a glimpse of the gray-haired man as a hot, slicing pain bit into my thigh. He was halfway up the staircase, blood spattered over his chest. His gun pointed at my chest. I fired and he fell, tumbling backwards down the stairs. Once at the bottom, he didn't move. I turned back to the other fight.

All Ritter's opponents were down. Ritter stood over one of them, aiming his gun at his heart. He fired. He moved to the next and did the same thing. When he reached the third, I called out, "He's not Unbounded."

Ritter's hand wavered, though his face was like granite. He didn't ask me how I knew, and I couldn't tell him. "Fine." He hit the man in the head with the gun instead before striding to my side. "You okay?"

The gentleness in his voice was more unnerving than my gunshot wound, but I was determined not to turn all weepy now. Never mind the blood dripping down my leg. "Yeah. Mostly. You?"

He flashed me a grin before glancing at his shoulder. "Perfect." A moment later the mirth left his face as he stared down at the man I'd shot, noting the many bullets holes in his chest. "He'll have already called others so we don't have much time to get your family out of here. At this point it's a guess who will come first, the police or more Emporium Unbounded. Depends on how many strings the Emporium can pull to delay law enforcement. So go talk to your family. We need them to open the door."

My hurt leg screamed in agony as I forced myself into the sitting room where the attackers lay sprawled, but the pain had already subsided from the initial impact, as though my body had rushed natural painkillers to the spot in order to allow me to keep functioning. I'd have to ask about that. I didn't remember it from before, so maybe my body was getting the hang of this Unbounded thing.

On my way to the short, bullet-riddled hallway to my parents' bedroom, I passed the mortal Ritter had almost killed. His face was deathly pale, and I saw that at some point he had been shot in the calf, but the bleeding didn't look serious. He had straight, chin-length brown hair and a nice face. Young and handsome. About my age. What was he doing with Unbounded?

"Jace?" I called. "Mom, Dad? It's me, Erin." The bedroom door was splattered with bullet holes and several jagged fist-sized openings. The barrel of a rifle poked from one of these.

"Erin?" It was my mother.

"Mom, you can open the door now."

"Are they threatening to hurt you if I don't?"

"No, we've taken care of the guys who attacked you, but they could be sending more. Or the police will come. Either way, we have to get out of here. It's safe to unlock the door—I promise."

My mother's eye appeared briefly in one of the larger holes. The door flung open, and she ran into my arms, sobbing loudly. "They shot your father! In the chest. We could barely get him up here, and Jace, he's been shot, too. So much blood! I didn't know what I was going to do if they started shooting again."

I wanted to rush to my dad and Jace, but my mother clung to me as though she were drowning. I held her tightly for a moment, my tears flowing into hers. "It's okay, Mom. Help is coming."

She stiffened, and I looked behind me to see Ritter. The bleeding of his wound had slowed, but the bloodstains down his arm made him look gruesome. "He's with me," I said. "Come, let's get to Dad and Jace. See what we can do." I kept my arm around her. All my life, she'd been the rock of the family, the source of all organization and determination, and I'd mostly resented her strength because of how weak and directionless it made me feel. But in an instant our roles had been reversed. Everything was different now. I couldn't give in to my urge to scream and weep. I had to be strong for her as she'd always been for me.

As I passed through the door to the bedroom, I heard Ava calling to Ritter from the main floor. "Up here," he directed.

My father and Jace were sprawled several feet from the door. My father lay with his arms askew, his chest covered in blood. Jace was also unconscious, his hands clutched over his stomach, blood welling between his fingers. More blood pooled beneath his head. Beyond them the pristine expanse of tan carpet and the untouched bed made a startling contrast to the blood and gore. A sound escaped me that was a mixture of horror and despair. Releasing my mother, I fell to my knees between the still forms of Jace and my father. In one hand I still carried my gun, which seemed to gleam at me accusingly.

Ava hurried into the room, followed by Stella and Dimitri and two mortal men I didn't recognize. One was stocky, with olive skin and dark hair; the other was a very dark black man with a wiry body and corded muscles. Both Unbounded and mortals alike were armed with silenced handguns and rifles that weren't much smaller than Ritter's machine gun. Dimitri went at once to check the wounded.

"What can we do to help?" I asked through my tears.

"Get towels," Dimitri ordered. "Press them over the wounds."

I hurried to my parents' bathroom. When I returned, my mother was kneeling near my father and brother, alternately stroking their cheeks while her own ran with tears and blood. Horror washed over me anew, followed by a tremendous load of guilt.

This is my fault, I thought. *If I hadn't been so impatient to see them, they would all still be safe.*

I gave Dimitri the towels. "Are they going to be okay?" I asked in a trembling voice I didn't recognize as my own.

"Your brother should make it if we can stop the bleeding, but your father's chest wound is bad. If I don't operate within the hour, he'll die. Even with the operation . . ." Dimitri shook his head. As he spoke, he had me press a towel over Jace's head wound. My brother looked so pale. My father was worse, though, his face now a grayish color. Without machines or a thorough examination, I didn't know how Dimitri could be so certain about their diagnoses, but I believed him completely. He'd had a thousand years to develop his skill in medicine.

"Oh, Grant, please don't leave me," my mother moaned, grabbing my father's hand.

"Go then," Ava told Dimitri. "Take Grant to the clinic. You'll have to come up with an explanation, but you've saved enough lives there this past year that they ought to cut you some slack. I'll work on Jace and bring him as soon as he's stable. I know enough. Go."

I hadn't realized Dimitri was working regularly as a doctor, but it made sense. Like Ava, he'd want to be useful during their down time. And he'd somehow been able to get me out of the burn center.

Dimitri gave a short nod and motioned to the men I didn't know. "Marco, Gaven, help me get him to the van. And I'll need you, too, Stella," he added. "You'll have to call ahead, let them know we're coming and make up some excuse for the emergency surgery, something that doesn't include bullets. Meanwhile, I'll try to slow the bleeding with what I've got in the car. Ritter, come down to the van with me. I have supplies Ava will need for Jace." His voice became gentle. "Annie," he said to my mother, using her name though to my knowledge they had never officially met, "you can come with us."

Everyone jumped into motion. After Ava took over with Jace, my mother hugged me and gave a last pat to my brother's still face. "He protected us," she murmured. "Without him, we would all be dead."

I nodded, guilt now the only feeling coming through the hazy numbness that had settled in my heart. My family was being ripped apart—and it was all my fault. "Go with Dad. We'll take care of Jace."

She nodded blindly. As she left, I wondered if she would ever forgive me for what I'd done.

Ritter returned with the medical supplies, and Ava deftly wrapped the wounds on Jace's stomach and head, and the smaller flesh wound on his upper arm. Afterward, she gave him a shot of antibiotic and morphine. "This'll hold him until Dimitri or Laurence can look at him."

"What about Chris?" I looked up from where Ritter was tying my still-bleeding leg, his fingers so gentle I felt almost no pain. Or maybe that was because of the painkiller he'd injected into my flesh.

"We sent Cort and Laurence and the others there," Ava said. "They'll check in soon."

Relief came through the numbness. "And my grandmother?"

Ava shook her head. "Our people got her out. At any rate, no one came for her. Probably because there's no chance of her having more children. I'm sure they came here primarily for Jace."

"We need to get these guys out of here before their backup arrives," Ritter said. "But there are four of them—"

"Five," I interrupted. "There's another one in the basement. Four Unbounded, one mortal, altogether." Apparently, they didn't plan to leave any of the Emporium operatives behind, unlike the Hunters who'd attacked us. That alone told me how much more dangerous they viewed the Emporium.

"Five, then, plus Jace, but Dimitri took his van." Ritter shoved a wad of gauze under his shirt to mop up his own wound. Apparently, real men didn't have time for bandages.

"We'll have to use my mom's car," I said. "It's got a big trunk and a backseat we can put down. Might be big enough. We can recline the front seat for Jace."

"Get the keys." Ava had prepared two more needles, handing one to Ritter. "Enough for two. Give half to each Unbounded."

"What is it?" I asked.

"Something to keep them out for a few days until we can transfer them."

"Transfer them?"

Ava's voice was ice-cold. "To Mexico. We have our own courts there and enact our own justice. If they can't be made to understand their wrongs, they will be executed for their crimes."

I understood the reasoning, and even welcomed such a sentence after what they'd done to my family, but after seeing her compassion for the Hunters, I hadn't expected this detached brutality.

"Good. I want them to pay." I stumbled out to the blood-stained sitting room to help move the men, noticing immediately that something was wrong. The two Unbounded were still unconscious, but the mortal I'd stopped Ritter from killing was missing.

Ritter swore under his breath. "I'll find him."

He checked the house, while Ava and I hurried to move the unconscious men to the car. They were heavy, but Ava was strong, and I surprised myself by being able to support the load. Muscles always at the peak of performance, despite my wound. Being Unbounded definitely had its perks.

The trunk and backseat of the car were smaller than I remembered, and several of the blood-drenched men ended up on their sides, but we managed to fit them in. I felt sick by the time we'd finished and heaved several times in the main floor bathroom. Nothing came up but bile.

We carried Jace last, and much more carefully. "I'll drive him to the clinic first," Ava said. "You and Ritter can meet me there, and then we'll deal with the others."

I put blankets around Jace to make the ride more comfortable. "I'm so sorry," I whispered to him. He didn't seem to hear me.

Ritter joined us in the garage carrying Max, who tried to greet me with his tongue. "The mortal is long gone, but look what I found downstairs behind the couch. He's going to need attention."

I'd completely forgotten Max, though Ava and I had gone to the apartment below for the last body. Worry about Jace and my father had crowded everything else out. "He saved me," I said. "I hope he'll be all right."

"Dogs are tough." A shadow of pain touched Ritter's face. Or was that a trick of the light? I wished I knew. Our eyes locked. Emotions roiled inside me, so many I couldn't differentiate them.

"Go," Ava told Ritter. "I'll meet you two at the clinic."

"I want to stay with Jace." My leg was throbbing again painfully, and I suspected my body was quickly ridding itself of the painkiller as it would any drug.

Ava shook her head. "As long as we have these men with us we are exposed to both the Emporium and local authorities. I don't want to risk you. Go on out the back. I'll meet you at the clinic. Move!"

My second magazine was half empty, but I picked up my gun from the floor of the car near Jace's feet where I'd stashed it. I stared at it for several seconds. I'd shot two men with this weapon today, and though they weren't dead, it had been the most horrible thing I'd ever had to do. How many more would I have to shoot?

Ritter carried Max as we went outside, this time using the gate between our yard and the neighbor's. Wordlessly we slipped into the bushes, which we planned to use for cover until we got as close as we could to the Land Cruiser. We hadn't gone far when I realized my neighbors were out in their front drive, talking to others and pointing in the general direction of my house. "We'll never make it to the car without being seen," Ritter said. "We'll have to make a run for it."

I put a hand on his arm. It felt warm and alive and I had the silly urge to rub my face against it. "Listen, there's a siren. If we wait a minute they might leave to go take a look, but if you go out there with that machine gun and all that blood on you, everyone will see us and tell the police exactly where we are."

"Okay. We wait. But not too long. Sooner or later they're going to realize my car doesn't belong here."

We crouched in the bushes at the side of the house, with Max emitting a tiny whine every so often. I stroked his blood-matted fur to calm him. The numbness I felt was growing inside. "It's all my fault," I whispered. "All of this. How do I live with that?"

He was silent a moment and then, "It isn't your fault. It's them. It's always them."

"If that's true, why do you blame yourself for what happened to your family?"

He frowned. "That's different."

"You didn't know any more than I did."

"So maybe we both aren't responsible."

"We're still the cause, so it doesn't change anything, does it?"

"Right." His voice grated against my ears.

I thought of the headless girl. I wanted to ask him if he knew who she was, or if I was going crazy. Instead, I said, "All I feel is nothing." A very painful nothing. A void as deep and wide as the ocean.

He put a hand on my arm. "That will pass. Then you'll just be angry. I'll teach you how to fight, to get back at them. Sometimes it's enough."

Would I become like him? An angry, hunting, killing machine? It didn't sound too bad at the moment. My past, my job, my life with Tom all seemed like a dream. "Okay."

The growing crowd gravitated to my neighbor's backyard, and everyone stood peering over the fence. Someone called out that the police were going inside my parents' house. Ritter tossed me the keys. "You drive. I'll carry Max."

It was ridiculously simple, waiting until the last of them passed us and then walking briskly to the Land Cruiser. As we drove from the area, we could see more neighbors out in the streets and on porches. Already the news of my parents' disappearance would be spreading over the once-quiet neighborhood. I wondered how long it would take before any of them felt safe again. I doubted I ever would.

Fifteen minutes later we pulled up at the clinic where Ava was coming out the front door. I sprang from the Land Cruiser. "How are they?"

"Dimitri's working on your dad, and Jace is being prepped for surgery. No use going inside now. You'll only raise more questions looking like that."

I glanced down to see splotches of darker red marring the dress. Not my blood but the Unbounded we'd carried. And Jace's. My own dried blood also covered my left leg. I resembled something from a slasher film.

Ava handed her keys to Ritter. "I parked the car in the back. Tossed a blanket over them so the orderly could help me take in Jace. Better transfer them to your vehicle. There were neighbors outside Erin's house when I left. The police will be looking for the car."

"I need to check in with Cort first," Ritter said. "I haven't heard anything."

"Stella has. He's on his way here. Look, there he is now, and Charles is with him."

Cort and another man emerged from the Lexus. Charles, obviously part of our mortal security detail, was a strong-looking man with pale skin, brown hair, and a serious expression. "What happened?" Ava asked Cort.

"We got there just after the Emporium went in," he said.

I sucked in a breath as Ava asked, "Chris?"

"He's okay. The kids were at a cast party or something, so they weren't even there. Nice bit of incompetence for us. First stroke of luck we've had all day. Laurence has gone to pick up the kids, and the others are bringing in an Unbounded we captured. We killed two mortals, but two Unbounded got away."

"Where's Chris?" I asked anxiously.

"With Laurence. We'll have to hide him and the kids, give them new identities. The Emporium will be after them again if we don't. Laurence is going to take care of it."

There was something he wasn't saying. I could feel it as though he were screaming the words. "What about Lorrie?"

Cort frowned and his eyes were sorrowful. "I'm sorry, but your sister-in-law was shot. She's dead. As soon as we're safely away, we'll have to report it. She has family."

Lorrie dead?

I couldn't take it in. Not Lorrie. Not the mother of my niece and nephew, the woman who was my brother's entire world. Tears blurred my vision. My father might die, my brother was seriously wounded, and Lorrie was already dead.

"It's not your fault," Ava said.

But it was. Cort put an arm around me, and I leaned into him gratefully. For once my hormones didn't send any signals. I was too numb. Maybe they'd never send signals again.

Ritter stood watching me and I knew that of them all, only he really understood. Well, possibly Ava, but it was different with her. She'd come to terms with her losses.

"We could use your help with the men we caught," Ava said to Cort.

Cort shook his head. "Stella's going to need her laptop so she can figure out how to hide our involvement here. If we can plant electronic evidence of drug trafficking, the authorities might think some drug dealer took the family to force Chris to fly them someplace."

I closed my eyes tightly, wishing I could block out all sound. How could he talk so calmly when Lorrie was dead? When my father and Jace were fighting for their lives?

"You take Erin to Stella's then," Ava said. "Let her clean up. Ritter and Charles will deal with the men."

I pushed away from Cort. "I'd rather stay with Jace if we can find a medical jacket or something I could wear over my dress. Even if the Emporium tracks me here, they don't want to kill me."

"What do you mean?" Ritter's eyes gleamed darkly.

"The two Unbounded I shot. They could have easily shot me first, but they didn't."

Ritter and Ava exchanged a glance with Cort, and I knew they were hiding something.

Anger cut through the numbness in my heart. "What?" I said. "Just tell me! Why is that important?"

"Go with Cort," Ritter said. "As soon as Ava and I are finished, we'll all sit down and talk."

"Fine." I turned back to the Land Cruiser. "But I have to get Max." I'd forgotten the dog once. I wouldn't do it again.

Ritter's hand stopped me. "I'll take care of him."

I hesitated, tears pricking my eyes despite my determination not to show weakness. "Thanks," I whispered.

He nodded and let me go.

"How's your leg?" Cort asked as he helped me into his car. "I've got some curequick if you need it."

"I'm okay." My leg was aching horribly, but I didn't want his drug.

"You sure?"

Lifting my dress, I examined the bandages and the wound. The bleeding was almost stopped now, though it burned with every tiny movement. "The bullet's still in there." I smoothed down my skirt, where a blood-soaked hole marred the red material. I put my finger through the hole, fighting tears. I wasn't crying for the dress, but for all the losses it represented.

"It'll be okay, Erin. You'll see."

It wouldn't ever be okay. Not for Lorrie.

I sat back as he drove through town. I tried closing my eyes, but every time I did, I saw blood and the determined faces of the Unbounded who'd attacked my family.

Because of me.

At least I was no longer seeing the headless girl.

"We should go to my place before Stella's," Cort said. "With so much of our warehouse equipment packed, Stella's going to need some of the stuff I left for the movers. If you don't mind a detour, it'll save me time."

"I don't mind." Anything we could do to help Stella figure out how we'd been compromised was a step in the right direction.

We drove for a long time, and I figured Cort was doubling back often in case anyone followed us. I dozed in my seat, thinking bleakly about everything that had happened. Feeling so helpless made me angry, resentful, and filled with despair. Ritter's kiss was the only bright spot in the afternoon, but it was only a kiss after all. A kiss before going into battle. It didn't really count.

Thinking of the kiss reminded me of Tom. We'd shared a lot of kisses in the past months, and once he'd been everything I wanted. He'd said on the phone that he still loved me, but so much had changed between us.

At last Cort stopped the car and triggered a garage door remote. I sat up and looked around. The garage was detached from the main house, so I couldn't see what his home looked like, but from the little I'd noticed on our drive, the nearest neighbor was some distance away. I suspected we'd left Kansas City and were in an outlying town.

The garage was vaulted and could easily fit ten cars. There were five there now, or six counting Cort's Lexus. "All yours?" I asked.

He grinned. "Yes. Want to take a peek?"

What was it with men and their cars? You'd think after five hundred years his enthusiasm for vehicles would get old. "Not now. Let's just hurry. I need to know how my dad and Jace are doing."

"Give me a hand. It'll only take a minute. And I'll get you something to drink."

At least my grief was contained by numbness. At the moment, I wasn't feeling anything besides mental exhaustion and pain in my thigh.

We moved slowly from the garage and down a short cement path to the house. The moment I hobbled into the kitchen, I knew something wasn't right. I lifted my gun, which for some absurd reason I still carried in my hand.

"Someone's here," I whispered. I wished I didn't sound so panicked.

They stepped out of doorways and came inside from the door behind us. Two Unbounded and four mortals. Each was armed, but if Cort acted fast, we might have a slim chance.

Cort set his rifle on the table.

"Cort!" I hissed. "What are you doing?"

"It's no use, Erin. Put down your weapon."

Ritter wouldn't have given up so easily.

"Do as he says," said another man, coming in from the hallway. "I really would hate to have to shoot you." His eyes went to the hole in my dress as he added dryly. "Again."

I knew him. The chin-length brown hair, the good-looking

face—which now had its color back—the darkening bruise on his temple made by Ritter's gun. The right leg of his jeans were cut off at the knee, exposing a bandage.

Bright green eyes met mine. "Hello, Erin. I'm Keene McIntyre. Glad to officially make your acquaintance."

"I saved your life!" I spat.

"How did you know I wasn't Unbounded?"

"None of your business."

He came slowly toward me, his eyes traveling the length of my body. "Oh, it is very much my business. Emporium business."

I should have let Ritter kill him.

Well, I'd just do it myself. I brought my gun up and squeezed the trigger, but shock made me slow and Keene grabbed the gun before it went off, causing the bullet to slam into the cupboard behind him.

"Are you finished?" Keene asked, giving me a flat, amused stare.

"Erin needs medical attention," Cort cut in. "The bullet's still in her leg."

"I'll get my bag." A tall Unbounded with ebony skin started for the door. I memorized his large nose and close-cropped black hair in case I found out he was the one who'd killed Lorrie.

Two of the mortals left with him. That left one Unbounded and two mortals. We could take them. I hoped Cort was ready. Surely after five hundred years he knew enough about combat to get a weapon away from one of them.

I made a dive for Cort's rifle on the table. Keene was faster, slamming his body into mine, which sent shudders of agony through my wounded leg. I didn't see what Cort had done during my attempt, but I had the impression he'd remained motionless.

Pain caused blackness to gnaw at the edges of my vision.

I let it take me.

CHAPTER 13

I WAS TRAPPED IN THE BURNING CAR, WITH JUSTINE'S FACE MELTING in front of me. "Help me, Erin," she cried. I knew I had only to reach out my hand to free her, but my hand wouldn't move. My breath came faster. A scream caught in my throat.

The car vanished and I became aware that I was lying on a bed. No one was around me, but I could hear angry voices. I focused on them in the same way I focused on pulling nutrients from the air. Absorbing them. Anything was better than the nightmare about Justine.

"I don't care what argument or excuses you use. This wasn't the plan." It was Cort's voice, fury oozing from the words.

"*This,* as you call it, might just make up for the disaster earlier this evening." Keene's voice was equally angry. "We lost five Unbounded to the Renegades."

"You should never have moved on her family. You think she's going to want to join the Emporium now?"

"If you hadn't dragged your feet about turning over information, we wouldn't have had to take that step. Besides, you think Tihalt or Stefan care about them? They've spent centuries searching for Ava's line. The whole family's death certificates were signed the minute we discovered Erin had Changed."

I opened one eye the merest sliver. They were face to face outside the half-closed door, talking fast and loud. I felt stunned. Cort knew this man. Knew him well enough to yell at him without fear of retribution.

"I had everything under control," Cort said tightly. "You didn't need to waste our men."

"That wasn't my choice. Our father is tired of waiting, brother dear."

I sucked in air, struggling to understand. What was it Keene had said? *Our father. Brother?* Did that mean they were actually related by blood or only by association? One thing was clear: Cort was Emporium and in league with the man who'd attacked my family.

I'm going to kill you, Cort, I thought. He was a traitor of the worst kind. The Renegades had befriended him. *I* had befriended him. And he had betrayed us all.

"Look, I'll be running this organization when you're rotting in the grave," Cort retorted. "The only reason you're even allowed to be a part of this is that your mother happened to have a pretty face."

"Tihalt loved her."

"Oh?" Cort sneered. "That must be why he let her die when we so easily could have cured her cancer."

Keene was quiet a moment. "He couldn't stand seeing her grow old."

"As he won't be able to stand seeing his favorite son grow old." The words hung between them.

"I did what I had to do." Keene spoke bitterly. "For what it's worth, I wasn't trying to kill anyone. The plan was to hold the family and use them for leverage. Unfortunately, the Unbounded under my command had another agenda. In fact, we were hashing out that little difference in opinion when the Renegades showed up." He motioned to his leg. "See what Wilhelm did? I should thank the Renegades for ridding me of men who don't follow orders."

Cort's body relaxed. "They were following someone's orders."

"I think we both know whose."

"I need to get back to the Renegades, feed them a story about Erin giving me the slip. There are still Stella's relatives to pin down. I know they're in Portland somewhere, but she's careful about their location, even around us. More importantly, there's that exchange with John Halden coming up tomorrow. You know how vital that is."

"Good old Halden. Now that's a man the Emporium wants dead." Keene's voice sounded almost boyish. "So are you actually going to report the information once you find out?"

"That's my job."

"Oh, so you remember the job. It's just that you've been an awful long time gaining their trust, big brother. A little too long, if you get my drift. One might think you've actually defected to the other side."

"Don't joke around," Cort growled. "They've kept information about the exchange on a need to know basis only, but I'll find out everything in plenty of time." His voice sounded odd, and I had the impression he was hiding something. If only I was closer maybe I could pick up a hint as to what.

"Just make sure you get our dear old dad and his cronies what they want."

The more they talked, the more I was sure they were actually related. If that was true, Cort's entire background was a lie.

"What if she won't have anything to do with the Emporium?" Cort asked after a brief lull in the conversation.

"Stefan will convince her. He has a way with women." A pause, and then, "Over here, Edgel."

The door swung wide and before I shut my eyes, I caught a glimpse of the large-nosed Unbounded who'd volunteered to get his medical supplies before Keene tackled me in the kitchen.

"She's still out cold," Cort said. "But you'd better give her something for the pain, or she's going to wake up in a hurry after you start cutting into her leg."

I was fully awake now and debating whether I should pretend to be out, or if I should take one of my knives and slash Cort's throat. No, that wouldn't kill him. I'd have to do something worse. I felt sick thinking about it. A week ago I would have never considered slitting anyone's throat, much less cutting them into three pieces. I hated him even more for that.

I opened my eyes a slit as they lifted up my dress high enough to see the wound on my thigh. Unfortunately, that also lifted the other side so they could see the sheath of knives on my other leg.

"Hello." Keene unbuckled the leather as the other two men watched with more than a little interest. You'd think they'd never seen a woman's bare leg before. Or maybe it was the knives they were admiring.

I pretended to come to as Edgel injected my leg with a numbing solution. "What are you doing?" I asked groggily.

Cort knelt beside me, taking my hand. "They're getting the bullet out. The man's not a doctor, but he seems to know what he's doing." He leaned closer and whispered in my ear. "Don't worry. I'll get us out of this. May take some time, so go along with them. Trust me." It was all I could do not to jerk my hand away. Better to play along for now.

The surgery on my leg was over within fifteen minutes. My leg was thoroughly numb, and I wished it could be my heart. Ritter was right. As the numbness I'd felt after the attack on my parents wore off, it was being replaced by hatred and anger. And worry.

Cort looked at Keene. "I have something that will help her heal in the fridge."

"I don't want it!" I wished I could add that I didn't want anything from him, but I'd save that little speech until later. Preferably when I had Ritter around to hold him for me while I took out my anger on his nerdy face.

Keene laughed. "Smart. If it's anything like our version, the stuff's poison. But like it or not, Edgel did inject some around your wound already." He turned to the Unbounded who'd performed the operation. "I'll take it from here, Edgel. Get to work. We move in an hour."

"What about him?" Edgel motioned to Cort, obviously unsure of his status.

"I'll take care of him." Keene casually leveled his gun at his brother.

Cort's blue eyes narrowed, and the brothers stared at each other for a long moment in silent challenge. They didn't look much alike, except perhaps in their build and the coloring of their hair. Keene appeared stronger, more capable, better looking, and his green eyes were every bit as compelling as Cort's blue ones. By rights he should have the Unbounded gene.

"Don't even think about it," Keene said to Cort for my benefit.

Cort shook his head. "I'm not stupid."

This whole little act was stupid.

Keene pulled two sets of handcuffs from a pocket in his tan cargo pants, and using only one hand, he set one pair around Cort's hands, locking him to the headboard, and the second around his ankles.

I couldn't have planned it better myself.

I had reserves of energy that had been gathering in my body since I left my parents' house. Maybe I could take Keene down and get away before Cort could alert the others. I opened myself, absorbing nutrients that came through the air. I took in as much as I had time for.

Now.

While Keene was still bent over, I kicked out at his gun with my good leg, using one of the moves Ritter had taught me. I executed it perfectly and the weapon went flying. I followed the move by coming to my feet and slicing down on Keene with a chop that should have sent him crashing to the floor, writhing in pain.

He moved too fast. With near Ritter-like speed, he avoided my attack and came back with one of his own, aimed at my mid-section. I jumped to the side, clumsy because of my leg, but managing to block with one hand while slamming my foot into his wounded calf. He grunted but blocked my next attempt by shoving my body up against the wall and grabbing my fist. Too late I remembered Ritter's warning about letting myself be pinned against a wall. For a moment we were locked together, bodies touching, breath coming fast. With his hair falling back, I could clearly see an ugly scar that ran the length of his right cheek near the hairline. Worse than being pinned against the wall was the fact that my overactive imagination was suddenly giving me another vision of why we might be so close. My head ached with sudden pressure.

"You can't beat me," Keene scoffed, his voice unnervingly calm, though there was something akin to admiration under the surface. "At least not yet, even if you have a combat ability. I've worked too long and too hard. I may not have my father's Unbounded gene, but that also means I don't have his aptitude for science." His voice became derisive. "I've been in training since I was five. Unlike you, I can't rely on family talent." He spoke as if it were a dirty thing.

I relaxed my body and gradually we let our arms fall to our sides, stepping apart. I was relieved that the strange attraction I'd felt for him seeped away. "Who are you?" I whispered.

It was Cort who answered. "He's the son of one of the most powerful men running the Emporium. At least that's what it says in our files. The rumor is that he's better at fighting than even Ritter."

That I seriously doubted.

"What do you want with me?"

Keene shook his head. "I don't want anything with you. I'm following orders. But there is someone who does want you."

"Who?"

"Your father."

"My father?" I clenched my fists, ready to make another attack. "Thanks to you my father is struggling for his life."

In a quick motion, he bent down and swept up his gun from the floor, leveling it at me. "No, Erin. Your father, like mine, is one of the three Triad members who run the Emporium." He saw my surprise and emitted a bitter laugh. "You didn't know? See? Just when I think I'm disgusted enough with the Emporium that I might join your Renegades, I find another reason to stay. Your friends lied to you, Erin. You are as much engineered as I was. Only my engineering failed."

Engineered? What on earth was he talking about? I had no way to reference anything he was saying. It meant nothing.

"Tell her, Cort," ordered Keene. Then he added, "You might as well. That's the reason we were able to find her in the first place."

Cort sighed. "He's right, Erin. At least to a point. You aren't who you think you are."

"Liar!" I spat.

For an instant, Cort flinched, but then he went on as though I hadn't spoken. "Ava wanted an Unbounded descendant, but you were seventh generation, and there wasn't much chance of that."

I remembered Stella saying something about the sixth generation being the last possibility for Unbounded, but I hadn't bothered with the math. Ava was my fourth great-grandmother. Four plus my grandmother and my mother did mean I was seventh generation.

"So when your mother had fertility treatments, it was too good an opportunity to pass up," Cort continued. "Ava decided to give you a better chance of being Unbounded."

"My mother has a tipped uterus," I said. "That was the only reason she went to the doctor."

"Well, what your doctor didn't know, or couldn't tell, is that your father's sperm would never have resulted in another child. He was lucky to have fathered Chris. So when the time came for the insemination, Ava replaced the sperm."

Replaced the sperm? Horror bled into my thoughts. "What does this have to do with the Emporium?" I managed to say.

"Oh, they didn't replace it with just any sperm." Keene's tone was still bitter. "Ava had her Renegades raid our facility. She knew we'd been able to engineer Unbounded sperm to result in the highest percentage of Unbounded offspring, and also that it would join only with a likely ovum, rejecting those with markers for genetic defects. Of course, that still left a lot open because none of us have managed to actually alter the eggs themselves to show which will result in an Unbounded child, but it was nearing a forty percent possibility with a mother like Erin's who at least carries the latent gene. Of course, with an Unbounded mother, the results are far higher."

Cort nodded. "Ava knew the Emporium sperm would bounce the odds up, and it was either that or start over with a new baby of her own, which I still think she should do, by the way."

I sagged against the wall. My father wasn't my father after all. The man who'd raised me, the man who'd come to all my soccer games, the man who'd taken a hundred pictures the night of my first prom. The man whose footsteps I'd once wanted to follow into the courtroom. And he didn't even know. Neither did my mother. Ava had never given them a choice. And what about Jace who'd been born after me?

There wasn't any overt difference in my physical features compared with my brothers, nothing to lend suspicion. Chris had darker blond hair, but we both had our mother's gray eyes.

Despite Jace's lighter hair and the blue eyes we'd always joked must be a throwback to some past relative, his face was similar to ours. As I pictured his face now, I realized that while Jace and I looked like Chris, we didn't resemble our father at all.

I wanted to be furious. I wanted to hate Ava. But if what they were saying was true, Ava had given me a chance at life. An Unbounded life. I wasn't yet sure if that weighed for or against her. Then again, if I hadn't been Unbounded, I would be decidedly dead. I owed her my life. Twice.

"I stole the sperm," Cort confessed. "Ritter and me. I'm sorry, but I still think it was the right thing to do."

Swallowing hard, I looked from one to the other. I could feel their expectation like a weight on my shoulders. Okay, I'd oblige them. "How did the Emporium find me?"

Keene smiled. "We had tracking devices on the sperm container. We followed it to the clinic, and it was easy enough after that to discover which of the clients had the procedure that day and which were likely candidates. After a little research, we knew it was your family, though we didn't realize you were Ava's descendant until more recently. Then we watched and waited."

"We didn't find the tracking device until later," Cort added. "That was my fault. We did as much damage control as we could, and we thought your family was in the clear, but apparently it wasn't enough."

It sounded like the truth, not a cover up for his own betrayal, but I knew better than to believe him. The Emporium had me now because of Cort. End of story.

"Are you sure I'm really my mother's child?" I asked. The idea was haunting. If switching sperm was seen as acceptable, then why not the ovum? If they'd used an egg cell from an Unbounded mother, they would have had a likelier chance of creating an Unbounded child.

"Of course," Cort said. "We would never force a woman to give birth to another woman's child."

"Only because it's impossible," Keene sneered. "An Unbounded ovum only survives in the body it was created in."

Relief flooded me. At least my entire life was not a lie—that is, if Keene was telling the truth. There was no way to be sure.

I stepped toward the door and Keene followed me with his gun. "What matters is that we want Unbounded offspring, Erin. You are a prize." Regret tinged his voice, and I knew he desperately wished to be in my place, to be the Unbounded his father desired.

"I don't want to join the Emporium."

Keene snorted. "You want to be with people who lied to you?"

"Lied to me? You tried to kill my family!" I yelled this despite the gun in his hand. "You work for monsters, and I will *never* be part of that." That went for Cort, too, but I didn't spare him a glance.

Keene and I glared at each other for long seconds before he

shrugged. "You'll come around as I had to. But since you're feeling so chipper, I think I'll move you down the hall."

So Cort could get away without me, of course. To further betray Ava and her friends. I wanted to dive for his gun in an effort to fight the separation, but for the moment I couldn't emotionally face another bullet.

Thinking of Ava reminded me of something important. Back at Stella's, Ritter had said I wasn't talented at fighting, and yet everyone else, even Keene, indicated that I was. I turned back to where Cort sat shackled on the bed, his face ghostly in the light of the lamp on the nightstand. "Ava isn't talented at combat, is she?"

He slowly shook his head. "No, but your father is. His genes should be the stronger because they're less removed, though it doesn't always happen that way. A lot depends on your other Unbounded ancestors."

"What's Ava's talent?"

Cort's jaw worked but nothing emerged.

"Tell her!" Keene hissed, white-lipped with fury. "Enough with the lies."

"Fine." Cort's eyes flashed anger of his own. "Ava is sensitive to thoughts and feelings. We call it sensing."

Sensing? Did he mean some sort of ESP? She'd mentioned the talent, but never related it to herself or our family line. "You're saying she knows what people are thinking?"

"More like she senses their emotions. There's a wide range of ability within the talent. And of course there's a way to block." Cort spoke confidently, and I knew he was right. After all, Ava hadn't known he was working for the Emporium.

Which was, of course, why Cort had wanted me to tell him when my ability kicked in. He hadn't wanted to record it for the sake of research, he was simply trying to cover himself in case I took after Ava instead of my biological father. "Why didn't anyone tell me?"

Cort shrugged. "Ava believes that knowing before the sensing ability manifests sometimes delays or skews the ability. She wanted to wait and see in the off chance that you developed that talent instead of combat."

Emotions were sliding off Cort now, a mixture of frustration and anger. I couldn't tell which was directed toward me and which were for Keene, or possibly Ava. But at that moment everything fell into place. Maybe the Change or curequick hadn't made my hormones go wild. Maybe the feelings—the out of control ones for Ritter, and the lesser ones for Cort and Keene—weren't mine but belonged to virile men who just happened to be somewhat attracted to a woman. Me.

If sensing was my ability, that might also explain why I could tell at a glance if someone was Unbounded. The more I thought about it, the more certain I was that I'd taken after Ava, not my illustrious sperm donor. The explanation fit all the emotions I'd experienced these past days—the strange thoughts and visions, and headaches.

Better yet, since everyone was still unaware of my ability, perhaps I could somehow use their ignorance to my advantage.

"So, I take after my biological father," I said. "That's why all the focus on combat training."

"You certainly have the guts for it," Keene replied.

Cort nodded. "You would have been trained anyway to some extent, but after seeing you attacking Keene, I'm pretty sure."

I didn't see the point in telling either of them that my actions had come solely from desperation and not from talent. Ritter would have known the difference. No wonder he'd believed me when I talked about the Unbounded at the restaurant. After training me, he'd suspected my true nature.

Keene reached out and pushed me gently but insistently toward the door. I had the sense of anger from him now, nothing more. No attraction. Well, that made two of us.

Without a glance at Cort, I moved out the door and down the hall. My leg was still numb from the medication, but that was better than pain from the freshly stitched wound. At least without the bullet, I'd heal faster.

Meanwhile, I'd watch for the opportunity to escape.

Keene stopped and patted me down in front of the door at the end of the hallway. His hands went methodically over every inch of the blood-streaked dress.

"Making sure I don't have more hidden knives?" I arched a brow. "I still might, you know. Better check again. I tend to stick things in my bra."

A rush of feeling from him about knocked me over, but this time I recognized the attraction wasn't my own; my hatred for him burned far too bright to mistake that.

Ah.

Not that it was really me he desired. I'd dated enough men in my thirty-one years to know that attraction for any halfway pretty girl was something men felt on a regular basis—even ones they didn't necessarily like.

The emotion vanished almost as soon as it appeared. "Shut up and go inside." He leaned past me and opened the door. It was a bedroom similar to the one we'd just left. Queen-sized bed, dresser, window. Nothing elaborate or beautiful. Cort obviously hadn't planned to stay here long term.

"My, the lengths you'll go through to get a girl alone."

"Aren't you forgetting who has the gun?" Keene lifted the weapon slightly for emphasis.

I leaned closer to him. "Aren't *you* forgetting that my so-called father is running this little kidnapping scheme? Besides, it's not like you can actually kill me with that thing."

I'd struck a nerve because he was glaring at me again, anger peeling off him in sheets. He really should learn to control his temper. "Both our fathers are running this show—and the Emporium. Now, as pleasant as this conversation is, there might still be a chance to rescue some of my men before I take you to your father. Plus, the faster I get rid of you, the faster I can get to Oregon and hunt more Renegades." He shoved me through the door, and it was all I could do to stay on my feet.

"You sure know how to show a girl a good time." I didn't know what had come over my mouth, but it was better than giving into hysteria.

Keene laughed tightly. "I do. Make no mistake about that." He paused before he shut the door. "Oh, and Erin, don't be too sure you know what's going on here. You've only just begun to uncover the lies."

I wasn't about to beg him to explain, but I wished I knew better how sensing worked. This far away from him, I wasn't receiving anything except anger—and that made my head hurt.

The door banged shut, and I stood there, tempted to wrench it open and scream obscenities at him until I was hoarse. *The Unbounded side of me,* I thought. No doubt that would give whoever he assigned to stand guard over me a good laugh. I turned resolutely from the door.

I heard water running, the sound coming from a connecting door that was slightly ajar. Carefully, I pushed it open to reveal a full bathroom. The water noise became louder.

"Who's there?" A man called, his voice freezing me in place.

The water turned off and his hand emerged from behind the shower curtain to grab a towel. Seconds later the curtain opened.

Tom.

Things just got better and better.

CHAPTER 14

ONE OF TOM'S EYES WAS BLACK, AND BRUISES LINED THE RIGHT SIDE of his jaw, but otherwise he appeared healthy. He smiled, and my heart did an unexpected jump, which didn't please me at all.

"Good, you're here. I've been worried." He stepped out of the shower and reached for me, his chest muscles rippling under his bare flesh. I moved away; Tom in a towel was not what I needed right now.

"Get dressed. I'll wait out there."

A few minutes later he came from the bathroom, wearing jeans and pulling on a T-shirt. His hair was still wet and he was smiling.

"What's going on?" I asked "Why are you here?"

"Because of you."

"How did they find you?"

"They didn't. I found them."

"I don't understand. Are you working with these people? Do you know they kidnapped me?"

"Come sit down. You're shaking. Is any of that blood yours?" He felt odd to me, more so than the night I'd come to his house to tell him I was alive, but I couldn't pinpoint the difference.

Of course Justine's death and funeral couldn't have been easy on him.

I sat down on the bed because my knees were feeling unsteady. I drew up my bloodstained dress to examine the bandage. My scuffle with Keene hadn't helped the wound, and the previously white bandage was soaked with crimson. "Nothing serious."

"Looks serious to me."

"Not for an Unbounded." I didn't mean to do it, but that put a wedge between us as surely as if I'd confessed I'd kissed Ritter—and that a part of me hoped to do it again. I was glad for the wedge. Once I would have loved being in a room alone with Tom, but that was before. Our old relationship was over, and I didn't know if we could salvage anything from the wreckage—or if I even wanted to try.

"You said on the phone that the Renegades weren't what I thought they were," I continued. "What did you mean? What did you find out? And why are you here?"

Tom sighed and gazed at me unhappily. "Look, I wasn't honest with you the other day at your parents' house."

I felt a chill. "You made it clear you didn't want anything to do with my new life."

Tom's jaw worked a moment before he said, "Seeing Justine dead was hard, as hard as seeing you lying in that hospital. She's all the family I've ever known." His eyes dropped from mine.

"You're lucky to have had her. Not all sisters would feel responsible for an eighteen-year-old brother about to age out of foster care."

"She was like a mother to me." Tom sat next to me on the bed and for the space of several heartbeats there was restfulness between us. "Without her I might never have finished college. And she certainly kept life interesting. You know, every time I started dating someone steadily, she'd say it was time to move to another state. That didn't bother me because I wasn't ready to settle down, but if it weren't for the million boyfriends she always had panting at our door, I would have thought she was jealous."

"She liked me, though."

"Yeah, she did. The first day we met she said you were the woman I should marry. In fact, she was the one who gave me the courage to ask such a stunning woman out." Tom hesitated, as if wondering how to go on.

I extended my hand and laid it over his. Images of Justine filled my head. Justine standing in the nightclub, Justine biking with us. The images shocked me with their clarity, and I had to fight to breathe. I pulled my hand away and came to my feet, unable to bear thinking about Justine for another minute.

"I don't care how you got here," I said, forcing myself to hobble to the window, "or what lies they've fed you, but we have to get out of here. Look, no bars. The window seems to be stuck, but I bet we can get it open if we both pull."

"Wait." He stepped close, his chest against my back, arms wrapping around my body. I felt a flare of emotion, but it wasn't mine: love, desire, uncertainty. All Tom's. Nothing from my own heart. I wanted to cry aloud at the loss.

"Erin." His mouth was by my ear, his voice low and husky. "Please forgive me for the other night. I didn't mean any of it. It doesn't matter that I'm not Unbounded. You and I can still make this work."

I shook my head, trying to block the rising wave of his emotions. "No."

"But a few days ago you—" He broke off, his arms falling away.

I'd lived a lifetime in those few days.

The emotions that weren't mine ceased when he released me. I turned slowly around to face him, wanting to offer him—and perhaps myself—some excuse for my emotional withdrawal.

"The Emporium attacked my family tonight. Jace and my father were shot—my father might not make it through surgery. Lorrie's dead. Murdered. And I don't know about Chris and the kids." For all I knew, Cort had killed both Chris and Laurence, and the children as well.

Tom's face showed shock. "Lorrie's dead?"

Cort could have lied, but I didn't see why he would, so I nodded. "If I don't get out of here, they might do the same thing to other families of potential Unbounded. The Renegades are moving tonight to Oregon. We have to warn them."

"But this doesn't make sense. They're the people you can't trust."

"Well, I certainly can't trust the men who brought me here." If he wouldn't help me, I'd do it without him.

First, I needed more energy. Turning to the window, I closed my eyes, absorbing everything I could. Somewhere I could feel curequick, and though I didn't want to risk an addiction, I let myself take the bits of it floating from the air. I also breathed in plants and the faint sensation of unripe apples without the sourness. There was an advantage in not using taste buds.

"What are you doing?" Tom asked.

He didn't need to know. "Are you going to help or not?"

"No."

I glared at him. "Why?"

"You've got it all wrong. The Emporium is the one who upholds order and protects the world. The Renegades are the troublemakers."

"I saw what the Emporium did to my family."

"It was a setup, then. Something contrived by the Renegades to make you believe in them."

I clenched my fist, the fingernails digging into my skin. "It wasn't a setup! That man out there—Keene—he was at my parents' house. He attacked my family." I stepped closer to the window, exasperated with his stubbornness. "Fine. Don't help me. I'll do it myself." I gave a mighty tug and the window came open. I pushed out the screen, wondering briefly what kind of security Cort had set up, but decided it really didn't matter. I needed to get out of here now, especially with a deluded Tom staring down my back.

A stab of icy pain spread through my arm. I turned and saw the needle in Tom's hand. "Sorry, love. Can't let you leave." Sorrowful brown eyes met mine, eyes that had once pulled me into their depths so far that I'd never wanted to leave.

My limbs were quickly losing all strength. I tried to speak, but my mouth wouldn't form the words. He caught me before I fell.

As he carried me to the bed, I thought of a dozen self-defense moves that would get me away from him. Unfortunately, Ritter hadn't taught me a defense against drugs.

My breathing was shallow and I wondered if I was going to suffocate. The horrible pressure in my chest felt like I was. If I died, would I awake when my body healed itself?

"Tom," I whispered. My vision was going dark. I seemed to have to claw for each breath.

"What, darling?" He kissed my cheek, my neck, and smoothed my hair with his hand.

"I'm . . . going to . . . kill you."

He laughed, though I could sense nervousness in it. "Don't be ridiculous. You don't kill people. Besides, when you know everything, you'll thank me. I did it to protect you." He kissed my lips lightly, and I was powerless to stop him.

Too bad he wasn't Unbounded. I'd kill him twice.

He walked to the door and spoke to someone outside. Within minutes I heard pounding at the window as it was nailed shut from the outside.

The pressure in my chest was leaving now, and I could see again. Either whatever Tom had given me wasn't lasting, or my Unbounded genes knew how to dispose of it. I struggled to a sitting position.

"Slowly, there." Tom sat next to me, but far enough away so that we didn't touch. Lucky for him.

"Have you been a part of this all along?" I demanded.

"I swear this is all as new to me as it is to you, but I'm convinced the Renegades will do anything to get what they want—including hurting you and your family."

"Who told you that?" I kept my voice low and steady, though I felt like screaming. Or strangling him.

"I did." There was a movement in the doorway and a slim figure came into view. The woman wore a scarf over her head, tied gypsy-style, which emphasized her enormous hazel eyes and gave her a wide-eyed, childlike appeal.

I'd know her anywhere.

Justine.

She grinned with fun-loving innocence. "Surprise!"

My arms curled protectively around my stomach as I tried to take it all in. I'd seen Justine burn, but she wasn't dead and that could only mean one thing: she was Unbounded. I didn't know whether to rejoice or feel betrayed.

"But . . ." I came to my feet, feeling slow and stupid. Justine being Unbounded explained a lot—her notable confidence, my admiration of her, her tirelessness when it came to physical activity, and even her lack of appetite. No other woman I knew had less interest in chocolate. She'd fooled us both for a very long time. Compared to what must be her several lifetimes of experience, Tom and I were children.

"Sorry for the shock. Don't blame Tom. I told him to stall and let me explain everything." She dropped the shopping bags she held in both hands and came forward to hug me, her signature spicy scent filling my nose. In typical Justine fashion, she wore black pants and a bright green fluttering duster blouse that emphasized her figure. Her ankles were clad in strappy, ridiculously high heels.

Gladness quickly eclipsed the shock. My friend was alive!

I hugged her back. She'd always been several inches shorter than me, and thin, but she felt smaller in my arms now, and I wondered how badly she'd been burned.

She held me back and eyed me critically. "Baby, your hair's marvelous! Or will be once we even it out a bit. Didn't I say you'd look great with a short cut? Nice dress. Too bad it was ruined. But that color is fabulous on you. Did you pick it out?"

"Why didn't you tell me?" I asked.

"I couldn't. Not until I knew about you for sure. Tom didn't even know."

He was grinning. "All those questions I asked at your parents' house? It wasn't because of you. I started thinking about Justine and how she never changed in all these years. How sometimes she'd go days without eating and still beat me in a bicycle marathon. All the long business trips she'd take without telling me where she'd been. The final proof was when I remembered the death certificate listing her age as thirty-five. But Justine was thirty-five when she came to get me at the foster home all those years ago."

"You were furious." I shivered at the memory of the moment when I'd realized I didn't know him as well as I thought.

"Because she'd lied to me." He cast a dark look at his sister that she met with a bland smile. "So I went looking for her. I tried to break into the funeral home and was arrested by police. At the precinct I called a number she'd given me for emergencies. In the morning two guys showed up and got me out. I had a little argument with them"—he touched his bruised jaw—"but they finally took me to her."

"Bet you wished you would have taken those self-defense classes I've always wanted you to take." There was a hint of spitefulness in Justine's tone. Those classes were the only continuing source of irritation between them, and the only time Tom had ever ignored one of her requests.

"The Emporium got you out of the hospital, didn't they?" I asked Justine, remembering the tampering Stella had found.

Justine grimaced. "The morgue, you mean. They would have gotten you out, too, if we'd realized you were Unbounded."

"You didn't know?"

"Not until the restaurant." She pulled off her scarf to expose a beautiful length of auburn hair. "It was all I could do not to throw my arms around you, but I didn't want to spook you."

Now I knew why the woman at the restaurant had taken such pains not to let me see her face, and why she'd seemed familiar, but I hadn't been looking for my blond friend who was supposedly dead and buried.

"I was almost certain you would be Unbounded," Justine continued, "but it's really hard to tell in the beginning, even for people who know what to look for. They wanted proof. Because my face isn't well known to our enemies, I was sent here to look after you until you Changed. Or until you didn't. Like I said, it was hard to tell because you had nothing wrong with you." She grinned. "Well, nothing a little fun couldn't remedy. I kept waiting for you to ask me about changes you might be experiencing."

So her choosing me from a crowd at the club wasn't coincidence. Ava's people had watched over me, and now it seemed Justine had been recruiting, too—for the other side.

I should have known, I thought. According to Ava, I might have been Unbounded for a month or more, but my sensing ability either hadn't kicked in, or Justine had carefully held her feelings in check because I'd believed she was exactly what she'd presented herself to be. Even if I'd felt something odd from her, like the incredible confidence of the Unbounded, I wouldn't have known what it meant.

What else had she lied about? The numbness in my leg had spread to fill my entire body.

"I take it that getting hit by that van wasn't part of the plan," I said.

The first hint of a frown tugged at her lips. "I noticed a few Hunters following us earlier, but something like that crash isn't usually their style. They must have done something to my car to cause it to explode when they hit us because the impact wasn't that great. Plus, the police never found the van. That alone tells me it wasn't really an accident."

Great. More Hunters.

"What are Hunters?" Tom asked.

Justine's gaze rested on her brother's face. "Just a few nasty pests that pop up from time to time. They hunt Unbounded. Fortunately, they're mortal and die rather easily."

Tom blanched, and I thought the better of him for it. "We should be leaving," he said. "We almost lost Erin to those Renegades, and this is going to be one of the first places they'll look once they realize she's gone."

Justine nodded agreement. "I have a private plane scheduled for the morning, but it's a bit of a drive to reach it, so as soon as Erin has a chance to clean up, we'll be on our way."

A private plane? I didn't know her at all.

"Renegades won't hurt me," I said. "Their leader is one of my ancestors."

"Forget that. Your place is with the Emporium." Beneath Justine's sweetness, there was a steel edge. "Darling, you know me. I'm your best friend. I wouldn't lead you astray."

After what I'd been through this past week, I knew I'd be a fool to believe anything she said. "You didn't tell them about my family, did you?"

Her brows creased. "They weren't supposed to be hurt. I know it looked bad, but everyone's going to be okay. Your father's stable now. I checked myself."

"What about Lorrie?"

"What about her? She's fine."

For a brief instance, I felt an inconsistency in her words, but the feeling vanished so quickly, I wasn't sure I could trust it.

Justine put a hand on each of us. "The important thing is that you and Tom are together again. Your father and the rest of the Triad will try to convince you to choose an Unbounded mate, but they'll see reason enough if you insist. Our mother was Unbounded, so Tom carries the latent gene. With a little help from our genetics lab, your children will have a very good chance of being Unbounded. They will be the future leaders of the Emporium."

"I want nothing to do with the Emporium after what they did to my family." I backed away from her and Tom.

Justine arched a brow. "I told you, they're fine. Everything is fine." A sense of calm radiated from her, but I didn't want to be calm. I knew what I'd seen.

"That's enough, Justine. Leave her alone." Tom stepped near me and put a hand on my back, a show of solidarity, a glimpse of the man I'd admired. Too late.

I shrugged off his hand. "Don't touch me ever again."

I was rewarded by a brief explosion of hurt before his face hardened.

"Don't be ridiculous, Erin," Justine said. "You and Tom were meant to be together."

"No, we weren't."

"Tell her, Tom."

He glared at her. "I love Erin, but she'll make her own choice once she understands everything."

Justine's lips curled as she lifted her eyes to his. "Everything I do, I do for you. You had every bit as much a chance to be Unbounded as I had, but you didn't Change, and now you need to do this right. For me."

I realized Justine wasn't simply disappointed that Tom was thirty-five and hadn't Changed. She was furious. No wonder she'd leapt at the chance to throw me and Tom together. From our chance meeting to his subsequent pursuit of me, just how much of our relationship had she engineered?

Maybe the real question was why had she gone to such effort? Why would it matter to her if Tom and I had Unbounded children? I knew the Emporium wanted new Unbounded, but why was she so particularly interested in Tom succeeding with *me?* I tried to sense the answer, but nothing came past the dull aching in my head.

"Let me go," I said. "Please, Justine."

"Before you've met your father?" She gave me her wide-eyed, innocent stare. "Of course not." She bent down to get the bags. "I've brought some clothes I picked up for you yesterday."

Anger squashed the hurt. "I don't care about meeting the monster you think is my father. I want to leave."

"It really doesn't matter what you want," Justine said in the calm voice that grated on my nerves. "Like it or not, you are a member of the Emporium now. You're better off accepting that because if you don't you won't stay alive very long."

CHAPTER 15

WITH POORLY HIDDEN IRRITATION, I WENT THROUGH JUSTINE'S shopping bags, finding a sleeveless, one-piece body suit made of black stretch material that promised comfort if not the familiarity of my usual jeans. No place for weapons, but I knew they weren't about to give me any, so that hardly mattered. Justine tried to insist that I wear a red half blouse over the top, but I refused. Mostly because it made her angry.

I was no longer beholden to this woman who'd pretended to be my friend. I wasn't aware of the politics involved in the Emporium hierarchy, but I wasn't about to be anyone's pawn. Not anymore. I would meet the man claiming to be my father, and I would pretend to go along with anything they threw my way. I'd watch and wait and learn, and when the moment was right, I'd leave, bringing down as many of them as I could before I vanished. What better way to fight the Emporium than from the inside?

Unwrapping my leg, I saw that the edges of the wound were healing rapidly, the bleeding long stopped. Inside would take more time, but as long as I didn't reopen the wound, I wouldn't need the bandage.

They let me shower, though Justine stayed in the bathroom with me, and another Unbounded was stationed outside the tiny window. As I rinsed the day's grime from my body, I wondered what Justine's ability was. Not combat, I didn't think. She didn't move with the same fluidity Ritter, or even the mortal Keene, had displayed. So what was her talent? Maybe she was like Laurence, fighting the family gene until she was ready to deal with it.

I told myself I needed to know her strength in order to arm myself, and that I didn't really care about her as a person. I knew I was lying.

"So what's your ability?" I asked as I wrapped myself in a towel and emerged from the shower.

Justine met my eyes in the mirror, wrinkling her small nose. "Ah, they told you about that."

"I'm supposed to fight."

"That's natural—given who your father is."

"Well?"

"I influence people. I'm an inspiration. A muse, you might say."

"I don't understand. How?"

She gave me a feline smile that didn't reach her eyes. "You will soon enough. For now, let's get you fixed up."

I recognized by the set of her jaw that the subject was closed. In a way it made sense that she could influence people—she certainly had Tom eating out of her hand, and I had once been every bit as blind. Even now I felt the silliest urge to please her.

She helped me get ready, combing my short hair and trimming the uneven parts, babbling all the time as though we were simply going on a shopping trip together.

I hated and loved her.

I was glad she wasn't dead.

Furious knocking at the door stopped Justine's prattle. "What is it?" she called. "I'm busy here."

"The other prisoner has escaped. Keene wants us ready to go in five."

She opened the door to reveal the Unbounded Edgel, his large nose jutting sharply from his ebony face. "My brother?" she demanded.

"Of course not. I meant the Unbounded prisoner."

Her lips tightened. "I see."

"How long has he been gone?" I asked.

When he didn't respond to my question, Justine said, "Edgel, darling, she's one of us. Give her an answer."

His sternness melted before her, something I wouldn't have thought possible of the big man. If he'd been a dog, he'd be rolling over on his back and asking for a rub. "We're not sure. Could have been as long as half an hour."

Justine tossed her head. "Keene's incompetence is unacceptable. The Triad will hear about this."

Was she trying to cover Cort's involvement, or did she even know about him? I reached out to touch her, to see if I could sense something, but she spun out of the bathroom, leaving Edgel and me staring after her. Edgel with longing, and me with growing anger. She and Keene were taking me somewhere against my will, and that meant she was the enemy now.

Meanwhile, Cort would be wreaking havoc with Stella's relatives or digging into the exchange with John Halden. Knowing this added to my determination to help the Renegades—despite the lies they'd told me. Or the truths they hadn't. Same thing.

I started after Justine, but Edgel clamped down on me before I'd gone a step, his face once again expressionless, as though carved from black granite.

Combat, I thought, but I doubted he was as fast as Ritter.

I was loaded into a fifteen-passenger van with Tom, Justine, Keene, three mortal guards, and the two Unbounded guards I'd seen earlier, including Edgel, who was driving. Tom sat next to me but didn't try to talk, for which I was glad. He also didn't appear to notice that Justine treated him as if he were nothing more than a cute pet she'd picked up for amusement. She treated the other mortals in the same way, except for Keene. She seemed to be strangely fascinated by the man, and demonstrated this by alternately insulting and flirting with him.

"Where are we going?" I asked no one in particular.

"Tulsa." Justine's eyes were bright, even from the front seat where she sat. "Ever been? There's a really great hotel I stay at. Great night life, though you'd never guess it."

Keene scowled from the far backseat where I knew he was keeping a good eye on me. "Only temporary. From there we'll be going . . . elsewhere." His flat tone dared me to beg for more, but I wouldn't give him the satisfaction. Not yet.

I dozed as much as I could on the three and a half-hour trip to Tulsa, Oklahoma, careful not to touch Tom. This time the headless woman in the blue dress didn't disturb my sleep. In fact, I hadn't seen her since I'd been separated from Ritter.

Separated from Ritter.

Sleep fled my grasp. If I'd only seen the woman when I was with Ritter, did that mean I'd picked up the vision from him? My guess was that she was his fiancée. Or had been. I shuddered. The gruesome reality of her fate and that of his family was far worse than simply hearing about it. The blood, the staring eyes, the help-less fury I felt—no, that Ritter felt. He still lived with the horror every day.

As I would live with the images of my father and brother lying in their own blood.

Ritter's feelings for the dead woman moved me more than I expected. Almost, I felt I understood him. I swallowed hard, not knowing what to make of Ritter or my thoughts.

"Can't sleep?" Tom whispered.

I didn't answer.

"For what it's worth, I'm sorry about all this."

Not sorry enough.

"You should have helped me." So many losses made my voice hard, though I tried to keep my voice down so Justine and the others wouldn't hear. They all appeared to be sleeping, but I knew Keene was alert. I could feel his nerves humming even from two seats back. "You believed Justine after she lied to you all these years. Doesn't that bother you—so many lies?"

"Of course it does, but she's my sister. I know she loves me."

I knew that, too. I might have completely imagined her affection for me, but not for Tom. No one was that good. Regardless of who she really was, Justine loved Tom.

"I care about you," he added.

He was telling the truth, but it wasn't enough. "Justine manipulated us." It was hard to make yourself stop loving someone, but I would do it—was doing it.

"Maybe at first. Not now." He tried to reach out to me, but I pulled my hand away.

"You've changed, maybe more than I have." With every minute that passed, he seemed more and more like someone I didn't know. "Because of Justine we never really had a chance."

"Without Justine, we never would have met. Would you give that up?"

"Yes." I turned my face to the window and shut my eyes.

He didn't try to talk again.

When we arrived at the hotel, Keene sent the mortals off with the van, but that still left the two Unbounded, Justine, Tom, and Keene. Ritter, I knew, would have somehow escaped, but I didn't stand a chance. I vowed that, talent or no, I'd never feel this helpless again. If I survived this mess, I would learn everything Ritter was willing to teach me. I would become at least as good as Keene.

Tom and I spent what little was left of Friday night in a hotel room, with two Unbounded keeping watch. Justine and Keene disappeared for hours, but at dawn Keene returned alone. I was sitting up in my queen bed staring at the curtained window, wondering if I could overcome my fear of heights long enough to force myself to jump. The three-story fall wouldn't kill me, of course, but I didn't know if I'd be able to get up and run before they got to me.

It would also hurt.

"Good morning," Keene said. Today the spot on his temple

where Ritter hit him was mottled an ugly green and black. "You want to spar a little?"

There was a kindness in the gesture I hadn't expected. Perhaps he knew that someone like Ritter would go insane without the release.

I bit back my first response—"I'd rather see you dead"—and forced myself to say, "No. I'm okay."

He gave me a flat grin. "My orders are to test you, see where you're at in training."

So much for being nice.

I debated refusing, but doing so wouldn't go far toward deceiving them that I was willing to accept my birth father's legacy. I also had a better chance at fooling Keene about my fighting abilities than an Unbounded who had the combat ability. Better to go along now and let Keene report—favorably, I hoped. That might delay any testing by an Unbounded, who, like Ritter, would recognize at once my lack of talent.

Besides, going to the hotel gym might offer a chance of escape, which would be better than playing along or attempting a three-story jump for freedom.

What would the Emporium do when they discovered I took after Ava instead of my father? She'd said the gift was rare and valuable, but because I didn't know the scope of the ability, I had no idea how the Emporium would use it to their advantage.

"Fine," I barked at Keene, who waited with a smirk on his handsome face. "But remember I'm new at this."

I changed into some exercise clothes Justine had so kindly provided. The top was too tight over my chest, and I had to unzip it a bit to allow my arms more freedom of movement. I still favored my leg ever so slightly but was determined not to show it. After all, Keene had also been shot, and he wouldn't be anywhere near as healed as I was.

To my disappointment, Edgel accompanied us into the hall, his dark face impassive, and we went not to the hotel gym but up two more flights to a large, empty meeting room, the chairs stacked neatly against one wall. So much for a chance of escape. Once again proof of the Emporium's power. Not every guest, I knew, would be allowed this privilege.

From his bag, Keene threw me an escrima stick. He attacked without warning, and I was barely able to prevent him from jabbing my stomach. I blocked him one, twice, and many more until I lost count, completely unable to go on the offensive. I knew he was holding back, and that if this was a real fight, I would have been on the floor within the first minute. Would he see my glaring lack of talent? If he did, any advantage I might have with my sensing would vanish.

Keene fought with single-minded intensity. The only feeling I received from him besides a fiery pain licking at his wound, was his determination to improve. I wasn't much help with that, and when he tossed me another stick instead of kicking me out of the room, I was actually surprised.

"You learn fast," he said, his breath coming fast. His hair hung in moist sections around his face. "Better than most mortals."

Any other Unbounded might have seen his compliment as backhanded, but it made me feel good. Apparently Keene wasn't familiar enough with new Unbounded to know the talent should have kicked in by now. Or what form it took when it did. Emporium Unbounded likely trained with other Unbounded, not with a lowly mortal like Keene, however exalted his father was in the Triad.

Finally, Keene slumped to the carpet in exhaustion, and I followed suit. He grunted as he straightened his wounded leg. I dragged a hand over my forehead, wiping the slickness on my shorts. Across the room, Edgel stood watching us, his hand on his weapon.

"What would you do," I asked Keene casually, "if I jumped out that window over there?"

He blinked.

"It wouldn't kill me, and I might get away."

All his muscles were tense, and I knew I'd never have a chance to make it to the window now, though it was mere feet away. Unless he was more tired than I was.

I began absorbing. You'd be surprised how many nutrients were floating around a hotel near breakfast. In minutes I'd feel ready for another match.

"I guess I'd have to shoot you," he said.

I shrugged. "That would only make a temporary dent, like the one the Hunters put into me a few days ago." I pulled the sleeve of my top aside, the wet material more flexible now, to show my healed shoulder. "See, all gone."

His eyes followed the motion, lingered on my smooth, very white skin, especially where the swell of my breast disappeared beneath the material. I yanked the top back up. "Was that little surprise with the Hunters your doing?" I asked.

Now he radiated emotion—rage—but his expression didn't change. "You might not be too far off," he said, slowly and carefully. "I used to work undercover for the Hunters, mainly to keep them away from us. I quit two years ago, but I'm sure the Emporium has new spies in place. They might have passed information as to your whereabouts. Not to harm you, of course, but the Renegades."

I had to admire the brilliance of the plan, using Hunters to attack their enemies and having someone in place to warn of potential attacks on your own people. If I ever made it back to Ava and the others, I'd recommend that we get our own spies in place among the Hunters, if they hadn't already thought of it.

"Working with Hunters is a difficult assignment," Keene said. "You're likely to get killed, especially if you're Unbounded. They have no sympathy for any Unbounded or those they employ. Their fear is too great."

"If half of what I've heard of the Emporium is true, the Hunters have every reason to be afraid."

His anger was gone, replaced by confusion, but again the emotion didn't register on his face. Though they looked nothing alike, he reminded me of Ritter in that respect.

"Everything you've heard about the Emporium is true," he said. "And more."

"Then why are you working for them?" I glanced across the room at Edgel to make sure he wasn't within hearing range.

"Because when the dust settles, I want to be on the winning side. Unlike you, I don't have unlimited lives." His green eyes were unreadable, but I felt he told the truth. At least part of it. He was holding something back.

"Why do you really stay?"

He shook his head. "None of your business."

At least he didn't lie. "You could let me go."

"Are you telling me you're not curious? You don't want to meet your father?"

"My *father* is in a hospital, struggling for his life." I didn't mean the tears to come to my eyes.

Keene's jaw tightened. "I'm sorry about that."

I didn't challenge his statement because I knew he was sorry. I sensed it. What a messed up world I'd stumbled into, where friends were betrayers and the enemy was the one who was sorry. Where friends lied and the enemy told the truth.

Another emotion stemmed from him now: attraction. Unwilling, but attraction nonetheless. And this time for who I was, rather than for any curves or beauty I might claim. His eyes were on my mouth when I asked, "What now?"

He dragged his gaze back to mine. In another time and place and different circumstances, I might have been sorry to distract him, but now he was the enemy, and I needed as much information as possible. If his attraction made his lips loose, then so much the better.

"We're flying out," he said. "We would have gone already if we could have used a commercial flight."

"You're afraid I'd escape."

He smiled and it made him look younger, less intense. Handsome. Not a trace of nerdiness like his brother. "You already tried at the house and threatened to again just now."

"So where are we going? Paris, I hope."

"Nope. California."

"Why didn't we fly there from Kansas City?"

"Because we have a pilot in place here. Besides, it gave me time to make a stab at convincing our fathers to meet you elsewhere. I think you're too dangerous to take to any of our headquarters."

I arched a brow, genuinely amused. *"I'm* too dangerous?"

"You'll be followed."

"How?"

"Your friend got away."

I studied him, my anger building. "You mean your *brother?"* I twisted the last word with disgust. So much for keeping my knowledge secret. Maybe I was the one who needed to control my anger.

"You *were* awake." He laughed. "I thought so. Cort's fault. He wouldn't let me drug you."

"Why'd you keep talking?"

"Because it doesn't matter if you know about his involvement. You would have figured it out anyway. And it's not as if you can warn anyone."

"I'm still going to kill Cort—if Ritter doesn't beat me to it."

"From what I've seen of Ritter's file, he's likely to do just that. Provided he finds out, of course."

"Are you and Cort really brothers?"

"Yes. But make no mistake, our Emporium connection is far stronger than blood." Keene's smile faded. "The truth is, Cort hasn't been very helpful. First, he didn't want to identify which family used the stolen sperm, so we did our own research. Then over the years, despite all his inside information, we've remained one step behind the Renegades. After your Change, he didn't want to bring you in. He wanted to wait until he found out more about the business with Halden and the whereabouts of the potential Unbounded in Oregon. But the Triad doesn't trust anyone implicitly, and when Cort dragged his feet a little too much, they called in the backup plan. They never fail to have a backup."

"You mean you and Justine."

"This time—yes."

"So you were telling the truth about the tracking device on the stolen container?"

"I always tell the truth."

"Maybe. But not the whole truth."

He shrugged. "We found out where you were and allowed you to stay in place until you were grown. Less trouble for us. No foster home to arrange."

"What if I hadn't been Unbounded?"

"You're still Stefan's child."

"But they'd found Ava's family. You said yourself their deaths were inevitable. That would mean me, too."

He shrugged. "I can't say what might have happened. They might have waited, observed your children. Or brought you in to see if they could get Unbounded offspring from you."

"My brothers and my niece and nephew, they would have died."

"Or something."

I inclined my head, acknowledging his honesty.

"When the car accident occurred," he continued, "Justine's locator went off, and we rescued her. Before that, the Triad had assigned her to watch you—though marrying you off to her mortal brother wasn't part of the deal. I wonder what your father would say if he knew."

"No reason to tell him." Why I felt compelled to protect Justine, I might never know.

Keene snorted. "That's the influence of her pheromones talking. She manipulates people, you know. Makes them want to please and protect her. It's primarily sexual and it works on everyone, no matter your orientation. It's a weak ability, though. Once you know, you can ignore it, if you're determined. For what it's worth, you really can't blame your boyfriend for following her so blindly."

Sexual attraction? Well, that explained Edgel's reaction to her, but I didn't want to think about Tom's. Or mine. Or how she might have influenced my relationship with Tom.

"How'd you find me after the accident?"

"Cort is tagged with one of our locators. It doesn't broadcast anywhere near Renegade strongholds—the Renegades are set up to protect against that like we are—but we can track him everywhere else. Once Justine followed him to the restaurant and saw that you'd Changed, the order went out to bring you and your family in."

"So Cort's tag is why you knew we were heading to his place."

"Yep. And a good thing. Makes it look like he brought you in."

"Maybe he wanted to wait so he could bring us all in." I couldn't keep the bitterness from my words.

"He might still be able to do that." Keene took my arm and began massaging it. His touch was warm and gentle and surprisingly pleasant. I wondered if this was prelude to an advance, but his next words surprised me. "The Renegades use a similar tagging method for tracking their operatives. They probably put one in you—another reason we needed to get out of Kansas so quickly." When I stared in surprise, he added, "Guess that's one more thing they didn't tell you." His fingers found something under the skin in my upper arm. "There. We'll deactivate it first thing when we get to LA, though we have our own signal disrupters in place so it won't work there anyway. I'd have deactivated it already if I had the equipment, but instead, we've been using a portable jammer here at the hotel. Not quite as effective, especially when we're on the move. We'll have to leave here before your friends show up."

The transmitter felt like a tiny square underneath my skin. Ava must have tagged me before I'd regained consciousness at the warehouse. It made sense, but I felt outraged that she hadn't asked my consent. "I'd have thought my body would reject it, push it out or something."

"We've learned to send electrical impulses that encourage the brain to ignore minor insertions. Lasts as long as your movement keeps recharging the micro battery." Keene laughed. "Actually, from what Cort told me, you Renegades have advanced further than that. He said Stella changes her appearance using nanotechnology—

the one thing that can keep ahead of our natural regeneration. They need constant, multi-level program updates, though, so on a long-term basis using nanites for appearances or things like, say, birth control is impractical for Unbounded unless they happen to be technopaths. And there aren't many of those around these days."

"Stella hasn't always looked like that?"

"Not according to Cort, but who can blame her? If you're going to live for two thousand years, there's no point spending that time looking less than perfect."

I laughed. "You can't know how relieved I feel hearing that. I really like Stella, but she's intimidating."

"Brains and beauty," he agreed.

We were sitting close together, but these few minutes had actually made me like him, and that was dangerous, so I climbed to my feet. "Well, let's get on with it then."

"We won't be ready to go for another hour."

"I didn't mean that." I picked up my sticks and lunged.

Somersaulting away from my attack, he swooped up his own sticks, blocking me easily. But he was tired and his wound hampered his movements, whereas I felt perfectly fine. That meant I moved slightly closer to giving him a real workout.

After another half hour, I excused myself to use the bathroom down a narrow hallway, though with the amount of sweat dripping from my body, he might suspect there couldn't be an ounce of liquid inside me. Of course, he'd be wrong because I'd been absorbing moisture from the air. I'd never thirst again.

Inside the small, windowless room, I dug with my fingernail into the skin of my arm, extracting the tiny Renegade transmitter. "Ouch!" I mouthed. Though it was barely under the skin and the pain was nothing compared to a gunshot wound, self-inflicted pain was the worst.

Setting the device on the counter, I rinsed the wound and held the edges together tightly. I waited as long as I dared before going to a stall and flushing a toilet with one bare foot, knowing Keene and Edgel were keeping guard outside. I used my chin to turn on the water for another few minutes. Let Keene think I had a hand-washing fetish. On second thought, still holding the tiny wound, I stuck my head under the water. The cool liquid felt good running down my hot body but was too cold on my scalp and neck. I slapped the hand dryer on and rubbed my scalp under the flow until I wasn't quite so dripping.

Time had run out. I looked at my arm. A thin line of blood curved along the small wound, but it wasn't immediately notice-able. Picking up the transmitter on the tip of my finger, and pinching it against my thumb, I opened the door. "Sorry," I said. "I was hot. And now I'm hungry. You?" Well, hungry wasn't exactly the right word, but it was what he'd understand.

"Famished."

Keene led the way back down the short hall to the meeting room where I picked up the sticks he'd lent me and casually dropped them into his bag, flicking the transmitter inside as well. There. With any luck, he'd store the bag away from the Emporium headquarters and Stella and Ritter could track me through him.

It was a long shot, so I didn't let myself hope too much. If I was going to get out of this, it would be up to me. The best thing I had going for me was that they wanted me alive and cooperating. I could do that. Pretend.

Justine and Tom were waiting when we arrived back at the room, a breakfast feast spread on the table near where they sat. "Join us?" Justine purred at Keene, crossing the room to greet us.

He shook his head. "I need to get things ready to leave."

"Plenty of time for a shower first." Her finger ran down his bare arm, still glistening with his sweat. "There's even a larger one in my room down the hall. I could show you." Her tone and expression left no doubt as to the meaning of her invitation.

"I'd better see if the plane's ready." Either he was immune to her pheromones or he really didn't like her, which raised him further in my estimation.

She rolled her eyes. "Whatever. They'll be ready or they'll be very sorry." She made a shooing motion. "Go ahead. Do what you have to. Just be sure to stay downwind." She smirked.

Without another word, Keene turned and vanished from the room.

Justine's mouth tightened. "Fool," she said under her breath.

"You okay?" Tom asked me as he left the table and joined us near the door.

"No one's cut me into three yet, if that's what you mean." A mean thing to say, but couldn't he see I was fine? Physically anyway. I didn't know if I'd ever be emotionally okay again. Thanks to him and Justine—and that wasn't ever for him to know.

Justine laughed. "Don't mind him, Erin. He can't possibly know what it means to be Unbounded."

She had a point. It was a completely new mind-set, one I'd have never caught onto so fast if I hadn't died in the fire.

Almost died. I shivered, trying not to let my emotion show, but Justine regarded me with interest. "Something wrong?" she asked.

"I'm drenched." I shook droplets off my hair to demonstrate.

"Better change," Tom said. "You don't want to catch a cold." His hair had been cut this morning, though it wasn't yet seven. Justine was taking care of her little brother as she always had.

Her brother or her pet? My thoughts were too caustic this morning, even for me.

Neither Justine nor I responded to Tom's comment, though near the door Edgel let out a soft laugh.

Tom's face hardened. "I guess Unbounded don't get sick, do they?"

"Of course not." Justine's hand fluttered to his shoulder. He looked irritated and I was glad.

"Ten minutes before we leave," Keene said, appearing at the door.

I picked up my black pantsuit from the night before and went to take a quick shower.

JUSTINE INSISTED ON SITTING NEXT TO ME IN THE SMALL PRIVATE PLANE. "I need to tell you about your father before you meet him."

I glanced at Keene, who sat in front of us next to Tom. They were talking easily, and I envied them. Though they both had brown hair and a similar build, the resemblance ended there. Tom's face was tanner and more square. Keene's green eyes were more alert, his body more graceful, and his scar lent a dangerous look to his face. By comparison Tom seemed gentle and innocent. Yeah, right. I'd seen how good he was with a needle.

"Are you listening, Erin?" Justine asked.

I refocused. "Go ahead. Something about my father?"

"Stefan Carrington is one of the world's most powerful men, for more reasons than one. Not only is he smart, but he's got sex appeal that won't quit."

Ugh, not something I wanted to know about my supposed birth father, but that was Justine for you. "God's gift to women, huh?"

"Exactly."

I'd meant it as a joke, but Justine didn't seem to notice. She rambled on. "You're lucky to be his daughter. I mean, Stefan has a lot of children, but children mean power, so you're important to him. Being Unbounded, you can hopefully give him Unbounded grandchildren. I don't think he'll force you into an alliance, so if you fight for Tom, he'll probably give in. With genetic manipulation, Tom's chances to father Unbounded will be at least as good as if you conceived with an Unbounded who didn't have gene therapy. And it's not as if your relationship will have to be for long."

Her words made my blood feel cold. Tom would grow old and die before I aged another year. Even after all that had happened between us, the knowledge was hard to take in.

"I am not going to have children with Tom," I said.

"I know you're mad at him now, but you'll see he only has your best interest at heart. Always has."

"Why are you trying to control his life? You could have your own children every bit as much as I could. You didn't need to interfere with us."

She didn't respond for long seconds, her face frozen into the pleasant expression she'd adopted at Cort's when she told me it didn't matter what I wanted. I had the sense she was struggling not to lash out at me physically.

I drew back from her, practically plastering myself against the side of the plane. I managed to swallow with difficulty, waiting for what would happen next.

"I care about Tom," she said finally, her body relaxing. Not a natural process but a conscious effort on her part. At the same time, my senses were flooded with warmth, a desire to please. An urge to make her happy. *Pheromones.* I gritted my teeth and ignored the sensation.

An image flashed into my mind. Justine holding a baby I instinctively knew was Tom. The emotions in her face, the way she cradled him, the mixture of triumph and sadness that filled her heart. My breath came faster as I understood. She wasn't Tom's sister, she was his mother.

"I know you love Tom," I said, letting a conciliatory note creep into my voice. Inside I was numb. I was not the only one who'd been lied to about my parentage.

If I ever decided to bring children into this mad world, which I was beginning to seriously doubt, I would never lie to them. And Unbounded or mortal, I would be the one to raise them.

If I lived long enough.

Still, why me? Justine could have chosen any potential Unbounded to throw at Tom. Why all the effort to force us together without the Triad's knowledge?

Maybe because I was Stefan Carrington's daughter. He was a leader in the Emporium, and as Justine had pointed out, his children and grandchildren would have power. Or maybe it was for some reason I wasn't seeing now. Regardless, I knew that despite the love Justine felt for Tom, he and I were nothing more than tools to get her where she wanted to be in the organization.

Could I really have been so blind? Could Tom? I pitied him now; he had no idea about her ability. For all I knew he imagined himself half in love with her and her pheromones.

Justine began talking again as if nothing out of the ordinary had occurred. The warmth and desire seeped away, leaving me cold and depressed. I stared out the window, biting my tongue so hard it bled, and let her words flow over me without connecting to them. There didn't seem to be enough room inside me to contain my hurts, but somehow I didn't explode.

Find me, Ritter. I knew he'd come. Somehow he and Ava and the others would come. They wouldn't give up easily.

I hoped.

Several cars awaited us at the airport. To my relief, Keene ushered me into one of them with only him and Edgel, whom I didn't like, but who at least didn't cause my emotions to fluctuate so rampantly.

As we drove through LA, I tried to notice landmarks, but I'd never been there before and the task proved fruitless. I was fascinated with the palm trees emerging from the ground like some alien plant, so different from what I was accustomed to. Definitely, I wasn't in Kansas anymore.

We reached a tall building, and I looked around again to mark its place, but the building was simply one in the midst of several other tall buildings. Nothing to differentiate it except a tiny variation of gray. An Unbounded man in a suit opened one of the glass doors, locking it behind us. Inside, we went to the reception area where two women—a brunette mortal and a blonde Unbounded—manned the desk.

"Hello, Keene," the dark-haired mortal said, her smile wide and real. "We've been waiting for you."

"We need a tag check first." Keene leaned on the desk, and I could feel his exhaustion.

The blonde removed a set of keys from a drawer. She was smiling but not nearly with the warmth of the brunette. I couldn't help wondering if she thought Keene was beneath her. "This way."

She led us to a tiny back room where a machine took up most of the space. "Lie down, please," she said to me.

Great, now for the moment of truth, when Keene would know what I had done in the bathroom at the hotel. I lay on the padded surface, which slowly fed into the machine, like the CAT scan my mother had a few years ago to investigate a numbness in her arm.

"She's clean," the blonde announced as I came out of the tunnel.

Keene helped me up, his hand going to the place where I'd once had the transmitter. I thought he was going to say something, but he nodded. "Thanks, Langly."

"You can go on up," the brunette told us as we returned from the lobby. "You're expected." She was beautiful, and I bet she was another failed attempt at creating Unbounded.

Tom and Justine were nowhere to be seen, and Edgel remained below while Keene took me up in the elevator. He was staring hard at me, and I shrugged. "No use keeping it if it's going to be deactivated."

"I see."

I knew he wondered what I'd done with it, but did it really matter? If what he'd told me was true, it wouldn't work here anyway. Besides, I was about to become Daddy's precious little girl.

We stared at each other for several long seconds. As the elevator was about to reach the top, I couldn't resist saying, "You should leave here, Keene. You should get out and go as far away as possible. You don't belong here."

His eyes narrowed. "What makes you think they'd ever let me leave?" There was that. "I suppose you think I could join the Renegades—as if they're any better."

"They don't kill whole families."

"How do you know?"

"Because you didn't die at my house yesterday." Besides, I simply couldn't see Ava or any of the Renegades killing children or other innocents. That meant I had to help them fight the Emporium.

The door opened and without another word, Keene passed the

two guards there—one mortal, one Unbounded—and hurried down the hallway so fast, I had to run to catch up. Despite his rapid steps, exhaustion radiated from every line of his body, and for the first time my pity was accompanied by a sense of superiority, which I quelled as fast as I recognized it. Being Unbounded didn't mean I was better; it meant I had the responsibility to help and protect those who weren't as strong.

Still, I might be able to take him now, especially since we'd turned a corner and the guards could no longer see us. I could use him as a shield to get past the guards, down the elevator, and out the door before anyone could stop me.

Instead, I followed Keene obediently to the double doors at the end of the hallway. "Good choice," Keene said softly. "You wouldn't have made it."

"I don't know what you're talking about."

"You were thinking about making a run for it. I know that much about you by now. Besides, your muscles don't lie. You were as tense as when you went for the gun at Cort's."

"Don't let it go to your head."

With the barest of smiles in my direction, he knocked on the door.

"Come in!"

Keene opened one of the doors. We were barely three steps inside when a knife hurtled toward us—or more exactly toward Keene. He ducked to the side casually, allowing the knife to plunge into the second door, at the same time whipping out his gun and pointing it at his attacker.

The blond man who'd thrown the knife laughed. "Haven't lost it, I see, Keene. Good to know you're on your toes."

Keene didn't look amused, but whatever his feelings, they were not revealed on his face or exuded in any emotion I could detect. He'd gone completely dark.

"Erin," Keene said. "This is Stefan Carrington, your father."

CHAPTER 16

STEFAN CARRINGTON WAS EVERYTHING JUSTINE HAD INTIMATED she would be. He was tall and well built, and the magnetism in his sky-blue eyes was palpable. His short hair was so blond I couldn't tell if there was any gray. His broad, tanned face showed fine lines, but instead of aging him they lent his face character and experience.

He was the type of man even a teenage girl would have been proud to claim as a father, and whose friends would have sighed over with girlish longing every time they were in his presence. He looked familiar to me, not as father being instinctively recognized by a child, but as someone I'd seen somewhere before. I hadn't expected that.

"Erin," he said, holding out his arms in welcome. "I'm so glad to finally meet you." He hugged me warmly before holding me out at arms' length, studying my features. "Your pictures don't do you justice. You're a beautiful, beautiful young woman. Not much of me in your face, but the hair, that's mine."

"My mother's too," I said stiffly, the anger building inside me as I remembered the last time I'd seen her.

"And your Unbounded ancestor's." He laughed. "I wish I could see Ava's face now."

I smiled, though I felt absolutely no joy in the comment. I couldn't tell if what he said was sincere or not. I could sense nothing from him. His mind was as dark to me as Keene had gone.

"Ah, but let me introduce you to Tihalt McIntyre." With a hand on my shoulder he angled me to several large windows where a man waited, a mug of something in his hands. "Tihalt is one of my two partners who help run this great organization."

I caught an impression of brown hair washed with gray, a narrow face, slim build—definitely Unbounded—and then he was offering his hand. "Welcome, Erin. Very nice to meet you." To my surprise, he took my hand and kissed it, all the while holding my gaze with green eyes that reminded me of Keene's. "My son has told me good things about you," Tihalt added. His gaze went to where Keene stood stiffly by the door. They hadn't greeted each other in any way that I had seen, but I'd been a little occupied.

Like Stefan, Tihalt exuded no emotion I could sense. Tihalt resembled Keene more than Cort, though his expression was decidedly more on the intellectual side like his Unbounded son. He let my hand go. To Stefan, he said, "I'll take my son for debriefing and let you two get acquainted. I'm sure I'll have many opportunities to get to know your beautiful daughter."

Stefan inclined his head. "Maybe we'll have another alliance soon."

Tihalt smiled. "Perhaps."

Tihalt walked to the door and without a word, Keene followed. He glanced at me once, and I thought he might be silently wishing me good luck.

I didn't need it or anything else from him. My plan was securely in place.

"I'll bet you could use a drink after your flight," Stefan said.

I followed him to the bar in an alcove on the same wall as the entry door. As I waited for him to pour, I took the opportunity to scan his office. There were exquisite paintings and art objects, carved wooden panels, clever lighting, and a comfortable couch arrangement. The only thing that signaled it was a work place was the enormous cherry desk, complete with carved legs, and a black leather swivel chair that must have pivoted around when Stefan arose because all I could see of it was the tall back.

"You like it?"

"It's beautiful." I accepted the drink, took a sip, and nearly choked. "Isn't it a little early for whisky?" Strong stuff, by the taste. Too strong.

He laughed. "Never too early for a good scotch. Besides, it's not as if we'll get drunk." I heard the remorse in his voice. "It's strong enough to give you a little buzz, but getting drunk would take far more than I have here."

"Another Unbounded trait?"

He cocked a brow. "Actually, yes. Whatever keeps us alive so long, also removes poisons from our bodies, and whisky is definitely a poison."

"Tastes like it."

He laughed again. "I keep forgetting you're so newly an Unbounded. There's a great deal you will learn here, Erin. A great deal I can teach you."

I nodded, not sure what to say to that. I took the opportunity to study him closely. Why did he seem so familiar? Was it because I saw myself in him? If I did, I couldn't identify any particular feature I could claim. Perhaps the recognition was on a more primitive level, the same level as the Unbounded gene. I concentrated until my head pounded, but I couldn't catch any of his thoughts.

"So, are you impressed with our organization?" Stefan asked.

"I haven't seen much."

"Of course not. Come, have a seat." He sat on a brown leather couch, patting the space beside him. "Are you happy to be here? Are you as happy to meet me as I am to meet you?"

I felt nothing for him or about him. Perhaps the fact that I couldn't sense any of his emotions caused my apathy. So what if he appeared happy to see me? I couldn't sense that he really was.

It was as though I was blind to him, made so intentionally by his own control. But why couldn't I sense anything? I remembered Cort talking about protecting his thoughts, and I wondered if Stefan was doing that and if he suspected my real talent.

"I'm happy to meet you, Stefan," I forced myself to say, "and to take my place among the Unbounded here."

His grin spread. "That will happen very soon, and meanwhile we'll be spending a lot of time together. Keene tells me you have the family ability."

"I guess so."

His turn to sit back and take a drink, looking both smug and in control.

My apathy instantly vanished, replaced by a burning anger. *This man's responsible for what happened to my real father. To Lorrie and Jace.* If I'd had a gun in my hand that moment, I would have easily pulled the trigger.

"She's lying." Across the room, the black chair behind the desk swiveled to reveal a small woman with gray hair swept into an elaborate twist at the back of her neck.

I was stunned to see her, taken completely by surprise, and I realized I'd become overconfident of at least being able to sense all the people in a room, even if I couldn't see inside them. Yet somehow I hadn't caught even an inkling of this woman's presence.

Stefan set his drink on the coffee table and came to his feet. "Erin, meet Delia Vesey. She's the third partner in the Triad."

Delia's face was lined, giving me the impression of great age, but she had an air of royalty that not even Stefan could match. Confidence, power, knowledge. Definitely Unbounded, though far older than the others. While I knew both Stefan and Tihalt were powerful, I had no doubt this diminutive woman was the true force behind the Emporium Triad.

She stood with a graceful motion that reminded me of a dancer, her gray dress flowing like water around her. The regal face must once have been beautiful but was now simply striking. Her brown eyes dominated her face and my attention. I arose, feeling like a bug in a jar.

"She believes she would kill you," Delia said without a change in expression, "given the chance. Fortunately for you, I don't think she has the guts for such an act. There is more she's hiding, but without a proper examination it's useless to guess. She seems to have learned a little about blocking." She crossed the space that separated her from Stefan. "This is not a good idea, as I've said from the beginning. She has already been poisoned against us."

"I'm sure once Erin understands what we are doing here, she'll join us willingly," Stefan said mildly.

"Will you?" The woman's gaze turned to me, and I felt a probing in my head, as though someone was touching the inside with feather-like strokes.

I pushed back at the touches, felt them subside. No sooner did I feel triumph than thoughts tumbled into my head. *I'm still here. You may hide things, but you cannot push me out entirely. You are untrained, and I am the strongest sensing Unbounded alive today. Even Stefan has a hard time keeping me away.*

I glared at her, pushing against the intrusion until suddenly it was gone. I didn't know if I'd pushed her out, or if she'd withdrawn on her own. Or if she was simply there without making herself known. A chill tingled down my back.

"Erin?" Stefan asked. "Are you willing to give this a try?"

I looked at him, still sensing nothing from him. It dawned on me that his darkness hadn't been for my benefit at all but because he didn't want Delia in his head any more than I wanted her in mine. Yet in my thoughts she'd been, and she had exposed my plan to play along with Stefan. What I didn't know was if she'd learned of my true ability.

"I need more answers before I can make a decision." My voice was steady but held a touch of venom. "My sister-in-law is dead, my brother's wounded, and my father is dying in a hospital. I have no idea where my other brother and his children are. If I'm so important to you, why would you do these things to everyone I love?"

Delia gave him a smirk that said, "See?"

Stefan ignored her. "I promise I have no idea what you are talking about. I ordered your family brought in for safety because I was afraid the Renegades would use them against you. Erin, you have to believe that we want the best for you."

I don't have to believe anything. My jaw clenched back the words before they could escape. I searched for something else to say instead. Something logical that might give him a way out of the mess, even if it meant lying to me. Then, as long as I could keep Delia out of my thoughts, my plan might still work. "Someone ordered them killed. Someone from the Emporium."

Stefan crossed to the desk and lifted the phone, punching in a number. "Tihalt, I'm sorry for the interruption, but I need to ask Keene a question immediately. Would you please send him back to us? Thank you."

I stood awkwardly, staring alternately at Delia and Stefan. He smiled; she remained expressionless. I kept up the outward pushing sensation in my mind, but I didn't know if it was working. I wished Ava had been more forthcoming about our gift, or at least had taught me how to protect my mind.

Tihalt's office must have been close because less than a minute later a knock came on the door. "Come," Stefan ordered.

Keene stood in the doorway, looking from Stefan to Delia and me. "How can I help?"

"Who was responsible for the attack on Erin's family?"

Keene's jaw twitched, but he didn't speak. Was that because he didn't want to lie? His mind was dark, and I could read nothing of his thoughts or feelings. I moved toward him. "Please, Keene, tell me who it was." I was still three feet away from him when I heard a thought as plainly as if it were a word: *Justine.*

Just when I thought I knew the extent of Justine's duplicity, she surprised me again. Aware of Delia's presence, I fought not to gasp aloud.

Delia walked toward Keene, a slight smile on her aged face. "It was Justine. She and several others acted against Keene's orders."

Her eyes flicked toward Stefan and then toward me. "I've changed my mind, Stefan. It may be a very good thing to bring your daughter here. A very good thing."

She knows, I thought, my stomach queasy.

Yes. Her thought came to my mind, shutting off as I pushed outward again.

"She will need a strong hand to be of value to us," Delia added aloud. "I will help with that. Until I clear her, keep her confined. There is too much at stake to let her roam." Without another word, she swept out the door, her gray dress fluttering in her wake.

I watched her vanish with relief. More than any other Unbounded I'd met, she frightened me, especially now that she knew my secret.

Why hadn't she told Stefan?

"Thank you, Keene." Stefan said. "You may go."

Keene looked at me, his mouth parted as though he wanted to speak. Then, as though thinking better of it, he whirled and marched away.

I watched him go, shaken by everything that had happened, but most of all by the information that Justine had ordered the attack on my family.

A touch on my arm, and I turned to face Stefan. "I will take care of this matter, Erin. I promise."

"Don't hurt her. Please." As much as I hated what she'd done, I didn't want her dead—or worse.

His nostrils flared. "I will do as I see best. You are family, and I will protect you." He was still touching me, and this time I received images of his strong connection with family, his loyalty to them, and his hope for me. I blinked at the emotions, but when he lifted his hand from my arm, all the images vanished instantly and there was only blackness again.

"For now, let's trust each other, shall we?" He smiled. "I hope to have a training session with you soon. We'll get to know each other better."

Just what I was afraid of. "I'm really new at this."

"I'm aware of your former occupation. But don't worry. Even if you aren't talented at combat, there are other variations of the gift, as you will soon learn." He paused a moment before adding. "I suppose it really would be too much to hope that you had your other ancestor's ability. Now that would be extremely useful. Well, no matter, there may be a possibility of enhancing that gene in your children."

In my children? I felt a shiver of dread.

Crossing the room, Stefan picked up his phone again. "I'll have you escorted to your suite. I have something for you there. I think you'll be pleasantly surprised."

"Jonny, please come to my office. Erin is ready to see her room." He'd no sooner hung up the phone than a slightly built Unbounded opened the door. He had blond hair and a ready smile, but he looked a bit young to have Changed.

"Jonny's your half-brother," Stefan said. "He'll take good care of you." He leaned over and kissed my cheek, a quick gesture that was over before I realized what he intended. "We'll talk later. Jonny, answer any questions she has. She's one of us now."

As the door shut behind us, Jonny gave me a winning smile. "You're not going to try to run away are you? Because it really wouldn't do you any good." With that, he practically disappeared. A blur streaked down the hall and back again. "See? No one can outrun me. I'm even faster than those with the ability for combat. I'd rather have their intuition for fighting, but this variation comes in handy at times."

For a moment, my mouth hung open at his display, but then I laughed at his infectious nature. He seemed a child in an adult body. "I bet it does." I matched his step down the hallway—his much slowed step, that is. "So what other abilities are there?"

He shrugged. "Just about anything anyone in the world is good at, but it boils down to about six main talents—science, math, art, combat, healing, and extrasensory. Each has variations. Like math has technology and building and computer skills. Accounting. You know, anything related. One guy here can multiply numbers faster than you can say them. It's pretty amazing." We'd reached the elevator, and he jabbed at the button. "Science has a lot of cross-over with math and healing, just as combat does with physical arts such as dancing. Some argue they are part of the same skill. They claim there are really only three basic skills—physical, mental, and extrasensory—which contain many variations. Can you believe people actually argue about such things?"

"I guess they have a lot of time on their hands." People were really talented at dancing? Art? It seemed too much to take in. Yet from the sincerity I sensed in him, I could tell Jonny wasn't saying anything unusual. I hoped I'd get the chance to see some of the more artsy abilities in action one day.

Jonny grinned, his blue eyes crinkling at the sides as though he'd laughed a great deal in his life. "Yeah, time is something we have a lot of." Unlike his father—our father—his face was small and had a crunched sort of look, as though his features hadn't time to fully develop and expand. Yet the way he moved showed all the confidence of an Unbounded.

We stepped inside the elevator. "What about the extrasensory variations?"

"Well, there's sensing, of course, which has different levels of ability. Different variations, too, like influencing people with pheromones, though some say that's more a physical ability. Then there's pre-cognition, telekinesis, teleporting—"

"You've got to be kidding."

"Well, I've never personally met anyone who has visions of the future or can lift things with their minds or transport themselves to another location—and I don't know anyone who actually knows anyone with those abilities, though I've heard tales from the old days. Some say those gifts would be a variation of the science or math talents. You know, going through space and time and defying gravity and all that." He grinned. "But like you say, some people have way too much time on their hands."

"Can anyone tell someone's an Unbounded by looking at them?"

"That's related to sensing." He looked at me closely. "Why do you ask?"

"One of my ancestors has that ability."

"I see."

I felt an unexpected surge of jealousy and hatred from him that threatened to overwhelm me. I put my hand against the elevator shaft to steady myself. I wanted to ask him why he hated me so much, but I didn't want to give myself away. Besides, he was looking at me with concern now.

"Are you all right?" He seemed solicitous and sincere, so maybe his previous emotions hadn't been directed toward me but simply stemmed from frustration at his life.

"I'm fine." To my relief the bell rang and the elevator doors slid open.

"Your quarters are below ground, I'm sorry to say. Near the nurseries."

"Nurseries?"

"That's where the offspring of our female Unbounded stay while their mothers are at work or on assignment. Sort of a daycare."

"So they keep their children with them."

He shrugged. "Some do and some don't. It's up to them. Mostly. Some prefer to adopt them out and wait to see if they're Unbounded. It really depends. Right now we have more children here than usual because the Triad's pushing for babies, and with the progress we've had recently, more children are Unbounded than before. That makes it easier to keep them. Unfortunately, there are only so many children a woman wants to have, as I'm sure you understand."

Thinking of my own conception I said, "With all the genetic research I'm surprised they haven't started a bunch of test tube babies and put the embryos in the general population."

"Oh, they've tried, believe me." A strange glee emanated from him now. "But eggs from Unbounded women don't survive unless they are in the original mother. It's been quite a problem."

So Keene hadn't lied—I really was my mother's child, and

unsuspecting women the world over weren't being tricked into birthing the offspring of female Unbounded.

We emerged from the elevator, passing two more guards, both Unbounded this time. Jonny's pace quickened as we moved down the corridor. "These are only the babies," he said, pausing before a large window that reminded me of a hospital nursery. "Older children are in another room, but they're taken out during the day. Can't have them cooped up down here all the time."

Inside the room, women—not Unbounded—were rocking, playing with, or bottle-feeding tiny infants. About ten babies if my count was correct. "What's their chance of being Unbounded?"

"We're talking up to fifty percent," Jonny said. "If we could manipulate the egg, it'd be more like seventy or eighty, but those experiments keep failing."

Half of these babies wouldn't be Unbounded, but they'd know the Unbounded secret and be forced to serve the Emporium. They'd be second-class citizens in an organization that looked down upon ordinary mortals. I felt saddened at the thought. No wonder some Unbounded women might choose to have their child adopted at birth rather than subject them to that life.

If I had a child, I'd want her or him with me.

Even if he or she had to endure prejudice?

Even if I had to watch the child grow old and die before I'd aged another year?

In the corner I saw a dark-haired Unbounded woman I hadn't noticed before. She sat in a rocking chair, her back mostly toward us as she rocked an infant in her arms. Something in the way she stared down at her child made me pay attention. I sensed love, the deep love of a new mother. She lifted the baby, and I caught a glimpse of unruly dark hair before she resettled the infant on the other side.

She's nursing, I thought. I could see the side of the mother's face now as she watched her baby suckle. Logically, I knew she served the Emporium and their questionable agenda, but for that moment she could have been any loving mother anywhere in the world—an Unbounded mother who desperately hoped her daughter would also be Unbounded.

"Come on," Jonny said.

I followed him, my thinking changed by what I'd seen. So many victims on both sides of this conflict. "How old are you, anyway, Jonny?"

"A hundred and fifteen."

That meant if he'd changed at thirty-one, biologically he'd be thirty-three. "Really? You look younger."

"That's because I Changed at eighteen."

I stopped walking. "But I thought—"

"Gene manipulation. They wanted to see if they could force the Change to come earlier. Hard to determine because the gene can't even be isolated until well into adulthood. But by giving the therapy to a bunch of potential Unbounded, they succeeded in speeding up the process in a few of us. Unfortunately, there are side effects."

"Side effects?"

His smile was gone. "I'm aging at five times the rate of normal Unbounded. Biologically, I'm twenty-eight. I've aged ten years in the past century, when I should have aged only two."

I felt his anger at being cheated. I supposed living only four hundred years seemed short for someone who'd expected two thousand. "I'm sorry, Jonny."

He shrugged. "Anything for the Emporium." There was no sincerity in his words now.

I caught another glimpse of a thought from him, and I knew that at least one of the other potential Unbounded had died from the experience. A girl Jonny had loved. But try as I might, I could sense nothing more.

We started walking again down the wide hallways, which were extremely well lit and at least a full foot taller than normal ceilings. Large paintings of the outdoors lined the whole corridor. Not like your usual claustrophobic underground office building.

"Jonny, how many siblings do we have?"

"Dozens. A hundred. Maybe more." He shrugged. "I really don't know. Stefan keeps those of us who are Unbounded or in the organization a little busy for family reunions. Some of the mortals work for us, but most were adopted out as babies and are on the outside living regular lives. They have no idea we exist. We check up on their children, usually around thirty-two, but often not until thirty-five. A lot of our people have been changing close to the outer age limit these days. Unfortunately, there have been far fewer Unbounded from our genetically altered lines than we expected."

"Wait. Are you saying that if the genetic alteration results in a mortal, the children of that person are usually mortal, too?"

"That's right. Still, it's worth it to get more Unbounded up front. So far those who do turn out to be Unbounded seem to be able to pass on the active gene to their children at the same rate as any other Unbounded. Stefan's been pleased."

When I'd been with Stefan, I'd felt his strong connection to his family, but I realized now that he wasn't raising and loving a family so much as he was making creations, bricks to be used to build his empire. I doubted either he or any of his offspring could understand how much I loved my own family. How much I wanted to be with them. How readily I would give my life to save theirs.

We walked in silence a few more feet before I said, "I have two brothers, Chris and Jace. Chris is older than me. Jace is younger."

"I know."

Of course. They knew everything about me. Jonny's openness was likely one more part in Stefan's plan to win me over.

"I'm sorry about what happened to them," Jonny added quietly.

"Thank you."

Around the next corner, he stopped and put his hand on a pad to the side of a door. The door made a buzzing sound as the lock came open. He leaned closer to me. "Look, you'd do best to forget your old life. You could really *be* someone here."

"What if I can't agree with the Emporium's agenda?"

He blinked. "We want the survival of our species. That's all we're fighting for." I knew he believed what he was saying. Maybe he *had* to believe in order to justify what had been done to him. He pushed open the door. "I'll see you again, Sis." He smiled and gestured for me to go inside.

I went in, not surprised when he pulled the door shut behind me and the lock slid into place. I had no illusions but that this was one more gilded prison until I could convince Stefan—and probably Delia—that I was on their side.

Of course, if they kept me locked in here alone for a hundred years, I might begin seeing things their way in order to preserve what little might remain of my sanity. Yet thinking of my father's still figure and Jace's pale face, the idea made me ill.

I walked down a short entry hall, and into a large sitting room with pristine, off-white furniture and decorations. There were three doors leading elsewhere. One door revealed a kitchen, the second a hallway, and from the third, partially-open door came the blare of a TV.

I'd been wrong. I wasn't alone after all.

CHAPTER 17

I FOLLOWED THE SOUND OF THE TV, STOPPING CAUTIOUSLY AT THE door. I had no weapon, nothing to defend myself. Laying my hand flat on the door, I pushed it open a little at time. My stomach relaxed as I saw two blond-headed children lying on the carpet playing video games, their gazes fixed on a huge screen hanging on the left wall.

I opened the door wider and stepped inside, relief flooding my senses. They were safe. My niece and nephew were safe.

"Erin!" A man jumped up from the couch from my right. He'd been obscured by the door, but I knew him as well.

"Chris!" I flung myself toward my older brother, who looked as though he hadn't slept in days. He held me tightly as my head buried into his shoulder. The video game paused, and the children turned in our direction.

"Hi, Aunt Erin." Kathy waved a hand, as though nothing out of the ordinary were happening. The slight twelve-year-old was a miniature of her pretty mother.

And what of Lorrie? Was she really dead? Did they know? Her absence seemed to indicate that Cort had been telling the truth.

"This is a way cool game." Spencer was two years younger than his sister, but he looked even younger than ten, his face still plump with baby fat.

"Cool," I forced myself to say.

They took that as permission to keep playing, and I let them, though I really wanted to examine them inch by inch to make sure they hadn't been hurt. Or maybe to hug them as tightly as I was hugging my brother.

Chris pulled away. "I'll be right back, kids." He dragged me to the door and into the sitting room. Once out of the children's view, his face crumpled. "I didn't think I'd ever see you again. I can't believe this is happening. They shot Lorrie!" Sobs convulsed his body, his grief a palpable thing. "She's dead!" he whispered hoarsely. "Dead!"

Pain—his and my own—knifed through my heart so deeply I wondered if I would survive the onslaught. How could Lorrie be gone? The future was utterly bleak. Only the children made life worth continuing at all. Barely. The barrage of Chris's emotions made me feel weak and desperate. Like dying. Giving up. Instinctively, I pushed his emotions away like I had with Delia's thoughts, stopping when they lessened to a tolerable level. My head ached from the effort, but that was nothing in comparison to his terrible grief.

There was nothing I could do but hold him until the convulsing eased. He pressed his hand against his mouth in an attempt to smother his cries, and I knew that despite his pain, his first thought was for the children. Tears wet his cheeks and mine, mixing together. I'd never seen my brother so distressed, and my hatred for the Emporium rose to a new level.

"What happened?" I whispered, needing to know every bit as much as he needed to tell me.

"They broke in right after you called. They shot her." He gasped between each whispered sentence as he struggled for composure. "If not for your other friends, Laurence and the blond guy, they would have killed me, too." He darted a glance toward the door, where the sounds of the TV hopefully covered our tears. "The children were at a party—I haven't told them yet. I don't know what to say."

"I'm so sorry."

"What the hell is going on? Why have they brought us here?" His eyes begged for answers.

"I don't know. I didn't even know you were here. Last I heard, you'd left your house after the break-in and were on your way to pick up the kids."

He heaved a shuddering sigh. "Laurence went with me, but before I could get the kids out to the car, some people drove up and made us go with them. They had guns. It was broad daylight, and there were people watching, but no one did a thing." He scrubbed a hand over the day-old growth on his face.

"Did you recognize them? The people with the guns?" I wondered if Laurence had tried to stop them, or if they'd taken care of him first in Chris's car. A bullet to the heart would have put him out of commission long enough to do something more permanent.

"No. Two men and a woman with long red hair."

Justine. My thoughts raged, but I tried to keep my face impassive.

"The woman was definitely in charge, but it was the men who brought us here. We took a commercial flight without going home for anything, which I guess was a blessing because the children didn't have to see what happened there. They had IDs for us and everything, so it was well-planned. They kept me separated from the kids, and no way would I leave them, so I couldn't break away or risk asking for help. Never felt so helpless in my life." He was breathing hard from both grief and anger, the wave of new emotions briefly breaking through the block I'd placed in my mind. I was glad for the anger. It helped with the pain.

He struggled to get himself under control. "What about Mom and Dad? Jace? Are they okay? The men said something about things going wrong at the house."

"Dad and Jace were both shot. They think Jace will be fine, but Dad needed surgery. That's all I found out before they got to me. Mom's safe, though. And Grandma."

"Why are they doing this? Who are these people?"

"The Emporium, the group Ava told us about."

"They're like you—Unbounded."

I nodded, not trusting my voice. Whether intentionally, or not, my existence had put my entire family at risk.

"How did they find us?"

"The woman you saw is Tom's sister, Justine. Apparently she's been spying on me for a lot of years, but up close for at least the past six months."

His eyes widened with the implication. "You mean she didn't die in the accident?"

"Turns out she's Unbounded. She had a locating device that was activated when her vitals vanished, so her people got her out, like Ava did for me." This led to telling him the rest: Cort's and Tom's betrayals, Justine overstepping her orders, the stolen sperm and the identity of my birth father.

Chris was shaking his head before I was finished. "I can't believe Ava took advantage of our family like that. What about Jace? Who's his father? The same as yours, or someone else?"

"I don't know. Unless a miracle happened, he's also engineered."

"It still doesn't make sense why they'd attack us now. Not when they want you on their side."

"Maybe Justine thought she could blame your deaths on the Renegades and that it would bind me more tightly to the Emporium." Or to her and Tom.

Chris ran his hands through his hair, pacing a few feet away and then back again. Tears stained his cheeks, and his eyes were swollen. "I can understand why they'd want you, but what do they want with me and the kids?"

Unfortunately, I knew. "They do a lot of genetic experimentation here. I think they might try to use the kids to create more Unbounded with a certain talent that runs in our family."

"Talent?"

"Sort of like ESP. Ava has it, and—" I'd been about to say, "and so do I," but I wondered belatedly if someone might be listening to our conversation. So far we hadn't talked about anything that would jeopardize my plan to fit in, but I wanted my ability to remain a secret for now. "Where's the bathroom?" I asked.

"The bathroom?" He blinked.

"Take me there."

He led me through the far door, which opened to a hallway and three bedrooms, each with an attached bathroom. Inside one, I flipped on the overhead fan and turned on the water as far as it would go. Then I flushed the toilet for good measure. "In case they're listening," I half-mouthed, half-whispered. "What I was going to say is that they think I'm talented in combat like my biological father, but I'm not. I can sense like Ava."

"You're saying you can read my thoughts?"

"Sh, not so loud. More like I can sense what you're feeling. Sometimes I see flashes of scenes. Some people can block me, though. A lot of people." I grimaced. "Okay, pretty much everyone, if they try. But that might be because I'm so new at it."

Chris, ever the pragmatist, didn't believe me. "What am I feeling now?"

I released the pushing out sensation in my mind, the block that had started to become second nature. I touched Chris's arm and fleeting sensations slid before me, in no apparent order. Rapidly, as though my brother didn't know what to think about first. Then a flash of someone aiming a gun at Chris. His numbing fear of dying. To his side a movement as Lorrie threw herself in front of him. The weight of her body collapsing against him, blood seeping from her wound. It was the clearest image I'd seen from anyone.

I withdrew my hand. "Lorrie," I whispered, my voice barely audible above the running water. "You thought you were going to die, but she saved your life. You wish it had been you instead." The impact of reliving that moment was like being punched in the stomach. The agony, the guilt. I fought to find something coherent to say. "Chris, it wasn't your fault. It wasn't! If anyone is to blame, it's me."

He stared at me for long seconds before gathering me into his arms as he had when I was a child and had fallen off my bike and skinned my knees. My big brother who wanted to protect me. I'd forgotten that relationship. "No, Erin, not you. You're right. None of us is to blame for any of this, except the monsters who brought us here."

"We'll get out. I have a plan."

"A plan?"

I nodded, pulling away and wiping my tears. I flushed the toilet again. "My plan is to do everything they say, to become my so-called father's daughter, and when I get enough power and freedom and information, I'll get us out of here. Then you'll take the kids so far away that no Unbounded, Emporium or Renegade, will ever bother you again. But you can't tell anyone about the sensing. Not the kids or anyone. If the Emporium finds out, they'll be guarding their minds, and I won't learn as much."

Of course, Delia might decide to tell my father the truth. That she hadn't done so led me to believe she had a use for me, perhaps to strengthen her position in the Triad. Or maybe she was simply toying with me. I had the feeling she enjoyed making people squirm.

Chris gave me a sad smile. "It's a good plan to a point, but even if we get out of here, I think I'm going to have to pick sides in this battle."

"This isn't your fight."

"And it's yours? No, little sister, we all do a lot of things we don't want to do. This is something big, something important." His voice became deadly. "They killed Lorrie, messed with my family, and that makes it my business. Even we lowly mortals have the right to fight for our family and friends." Tears rolled down his cheeks again, but there was no convulsing this time, no out-of-control despair.

He was right, and at this point the Renegades, though they'd lied to me, were the lesser of the two evils. "The Renegades may try to rescue us," I said, reaching to scoop a bit of water to splash over my face. "They had a tracking device on me that might have led them at least to L.A. But if they do try to save us, it'll only be one big trap for all of them, since Cort is really working for his father and the Triad."

Chris closed his eyes for a moment, considering. "You'd better tell Laurence when he gets back. Maybe he'll have some ideas."

I jerked my hands from the water and looked at him. "Laurence is here?"

"I'm sorry. Didn't I say? He came with us on the plane. Fortunately. He sat with the kids and entertained them."

I was more than glad to learn Laurence was here instead of dead or in an Emporium laboratory somewhere. "Where is he now?"

Chris snorted. "That is one man who loves his food. The first thing he demanded when they brought us breakfast this morning was groceries to make what he called 'decent food.' Believe it or not, they took him shopping. Not sure if they actually took him out of the building or to their supply closet or whatever. He should be back soon. He promised to make us lunch."

I'd been absorbing, most of the nutrients going to heal my wounded leg, but at this news I suddenly craved the comfort of normal food, preferably something loaded with fat. "Let's hope he really does come back," I said quietly. I didn't like thinking of the alternative.

"I'd better go check on the children."

"Wash your face first."

Chris grimaced at the mirror. "Yeah, I'm not ready to tell them yet."

We had no sooner resumed watching the children play than Laurence arrived, accompanied by an armed Unbounded guard and two teenage boys carrying plastic bags filled with groceries.

"Hi, Erin," Laurence said brightly, as though my presence was nothing out of the ordinary. "Heard you were here."

"Good to see you, Laurence." I meant it. His round face,

framed by his curly bright red hair was a welcome sight. He might be a little odd in the view of Ava and the others, but to me he was real.

"These boys brought your children a nice game," Laurence told Chris. "It's one they've been trying out for a company." To me he added, "Come into the kitchen while I cook us something to eat." Laurence's request seemed odd, since he was chewing on a large piece of pizza in his free hand, but I followed him to the kitchen anyway.

"I'll be there in a minute." Chris eyed the Unbounded guard with suspicion, and I knew he had no intention of leaving his children alone with any members of the Emporium, regardless of how many new video games they brought.

We left Chris to play protector, though I had no idea what he could do if they decided to take the children. Or what any of us could do. Still, I left the kitchen door open so I could hear what was going on. I'd die before I'd let anything happen to my niece and nephew.

The teenage boys set the bags on the round table in the kitchen and vanished, the taller pulling a disk from the pocket of his jeans. Laurence began moving about, putting things away in the cupboards and the fridge, piling a few items on the counter that he was apparently planning to use. "How does lasagna sound for lunch?"

"Fine." I eyed the bags of food with dismay. "Do you really think we're going to be here long enough to use all this?"

Laurence laughed. "It's only enough for a few days. I eat when I worry." He paused and added, "Well, I eat when I'm not worried. Or when I'm happy or tired or anxious or any other time." He heaved a sigh. "You know, one of the saddest things about becoming Unbounded is that I never really feel hungry anymore."

"That's a bad thing?"

"What I mean is I can't crave a huge meal and eat and be satisfied. I used to love Thanksgiving dinner. I'd grow hungrier all day as I smelled the food cooking, and then I'd eat until my stomach was about to burst and they'd have to roll me to the couch to watch TV. Then they'd bring the pie." He looked at the ceiling with an expression of utter joy.

I felt it all as he spoke, the fond memory of food and feeling full. How easy it was to identify these emotions as his, not mine; I'd spent my lifetime trying *not* to think about food.

"Now my body doesn't hunger for food," he continued, "and I'm never really satisfied when I eat. So I eat more, but my body hurries and gets rid of the bloated feeling, so I have to eat even more."

"Ah, Laurence, that's the part I love about being Unbounded." I sat down at the table, the first moment of rest since I'd arrived. "Not having to worry about making food, my body repairing itself. It's a miracle."

He flopped down heavily in the chair opposite me, and for a moment I wondered if the chair would hold his weight. "I watched my first wife die in childbirth," he said. "We had six children before Dimitri showed up to let me know I was Unbounded and that anything we did to avoid conception pretty much wasn't going to work. She was only twenty-five when I married her and we had six kids in six years." His eyes left mine and focused on a point beyond me. "Then she got pregnant again."

I didn't even have to touch him to know what happened. The terrible images were bright in his thoughts. "I'm really sorry, Laurence." I pushed his emotions away, shutting my mind to his sadness, hoping the block would stay in place. For an instant as I readjusted to sensing nothing, I felt oddly as though my sight or my sense of smell had been taken away.

"The child lived, at least." He smiled sadly as his eyes found mine again. "I'm sorry. I didn't mean to make you sad. I meant to show you that being Unbounded is sometimes a curse."

"You didn't make me sad. I mean, I am, but not for me. It must have been very difficult."

"She was a good, good woman." He came to his feet, a yellow onion in his hand. "I missed her terribly. I didn't think I'd ever marry again. I've had women friends over the years, of course, but those weren't real relationships. I did fall in love with Teresa, though. We have one child. A little girl. She's beautiful."

"What about your other children?"

"Two died in their teens—a son during military service and a daughter from smallpox. Another son and daughter died from old age. Only one of my children was Unbounded, but she was killed by the Hunters three years ago. Left behind two little girls who are being raised by their mortal father. My youngest two daughters are in their eighties. I don't see them often."

"They know about you, then?"

"Always did, right from the first. But not their children. We pretended I was dead." Coming to his feet, he took a knife from the drawer and began chopping an onion. "It was for the best. One of their boys did turn out to be Unbounded, but he was killed last year in New York during a battle."

I was glad my mind was blocked because though he spoke casually, his hand holding the knife shook.

"Did you know about my biological father?"

He threw the chopped onion in a pan with a tablespoon of olive oil. "I knew. For the record, I was against it."

"They were worried the blood had thinned too much. I was seventh generation."

"Ah, yes. The bloodlines. We must protect them as long as the Emporium exists." The irony in his words was clear, but I didn't understand the subtle meaning. Was he implying that by using Emporium engineered sperm we were as bad as the Emporium? Or something else altogether?

He continued adding garlic, herbs, and tomatoes to the fresh sauce he was making for the lasagna. He took out another pan to fry Italian sausage.

"I don't know if I'm mad at Ava or grateful," I said. "I love the idea of being something, of making a difference. Doing something important. But I don't want to watch my family die, I don't want to worry about losing every mortal I love, and the idea of having a child who might become an outcast among his own people is horribly sad."

For a long moment Laurence didn't reply. At last he turned to me. "I told you at Stella's that I planned to do research, but what I didn't tell you is that once I get the facilities and assistants I need, my research will be dedicated solely to either making everyone in the world Unbounded or doing away with the gene altogether. No one else will have to endure what so many of us have endured."

I was stunned. "That's wonderful, Laurence!"

He smiled. "I knew you would understand, but there are many Unbounded who won't be willing to give up what they see as near godhood. They've become hardened because of so much loss."

"But if you could make everyone Unbounded—"

"Not my preference of solutions."

"Why not? It's perfect."

"Not once you've had decades to think about it. If the world were full of Unbounded, every social security system in the world would be bankrupt in a very short time. Without birth control options, we would soon overrun the earth and its resources, and then where would we go? And that's just the beginning of the problems."

"Then make it so only those being born now have the gene, and by the time the world is crowded, we will have found a way to colonize space or something."

He laughed. "Or something. But that's what the plan would entail—something involving new Unbounded. We couldn't change the old humans. Unfortunately, we're not close to space travel or being able to colonize other worlds, and I can't be sure such a thing is even possible. No," he shook his head, "I really think the reverse is the better solution."

"You mean to make sure none of our descendants are Unbounded."

"Exactly."

It was a solution, but I felt opposed to the idea of making sure my posterity died on time. "How close are you?"

He made a face. "I'm not sure. Most of my research has been on paper instead of in the lab, but with the right resources, I'm sure I'll be able to come up with a cure eventually."

"Being Unbounded isn't a disease," I protested.

"Isn't it?" His broad face took on a flush of color. "The Emporium has a finger in every major corporation and political organization in the world. It's only a matter of time before they take their power one step further. The human world is much closer to genuine slavery than any of us realizes."

Surely he couldn't believe such a thing. I dissolved my barrier and sent out my thoughts. But he was dark, now, of his own will. Interesting. But if he didn't know about my talent, then who was he trying to block? Maybe he was worried about Delia.

"Ava thinks we come from another race who visited earth," I said.

"Most Unbounded scientists and doctors believe we are the result of a simple gene mutation."

I gave him a wry smile. "Frankly, given the choice between being an alien or a mutant, neither sounds very appealing."

Laurence laughed. "That's why I like you so much, Erin. You and I are a lot alike." He turned to stir the sauce.

"Is there anything I can do? To help with lunch, I mean."

"Find a big pan and boil some water for the noodles."

The noodles were nearly cooked by the time Chris showed up in the kitchen. "Sorry. Those teenagers wanted to watch the kids play that new game they brought, and I had to wait for them to leave. I wasn't going to leave them alone with Kathy and Spencer, no matter how much fun they seem to be having."

"It's good they're having fun," I said absently. To myself I was wondering how long Laurence would remain intact if the Emporium and the Renegades knew his ultimate goal. Or maybe they would laugh at the impossibility.

"Laurence, do you think they're listening to us in here?" I looked at him significantly.

He shook his large head. "I spent hours checking for bugs this morning. The place doesn't even have a camera except out in the halls. Still, we can be careful if you like." He reached over and turned on the empty blender.

"So how are we going to get out of here?" Chris slumped down at the table. "I've got to get my children somewhere safe. They're really taking to those other kids. All these games. They're incredible, nothing like I've seen on the market."

"If you think these are good, you should see what the Renegades have been working on," Laurence said.

Chris didn't seem to hear him, but it was hard to hear anything over the shrill noise of the blender. "Those boys were telling the kids about a special game room here and all the activities they have for the youth. I had the strangest feeling that if I were to disappear, Kathy and Spencer would be absorbed into this life and they wouldn't even miss me."

"They'd eventually serve the Emporium," I said, thinking of Keene and also of Tom, who likely had no idea what he'd gotten himself into, though that would change quickly.

Chris sighed. "The longer we're here, the more danger we're all in."

Laurence poured the noodles into a metal strainer in the sink and began laying them in the lasagna pan. "We'll just wait it out. Ava will send someone after us—Ritter and probably one or two of the others. Not Stella. They can replace Ritter for the meeting, but Stella will have to be in New York tonight to keep the appointment with Halden."

The appointment I was supposed to attend. "Will they even know you're here?" I asked Laurence. "Do you have a transmitter they can check?"

"Huh?" he asked, frowning at the blender.

I raised my voice to be heard. "Do you have a transmitter?"

"I had one, but they disabled it when I got here. What about you?"

"I took mine out before I arrived. I hope Ava will be able to track it at least to L.A."

"Then they'll find us," Laurence said confidently.

"That might not be a good thing," Going to stand closer to Laurence so he could hear me better, I told him about Cort and Justine and Tom. Chris sat silently at the table, mentally only half there. I knew he was thinking of Lorrie.

"I can't believe it." Laurence seated himself heavily on a chair by the table, leaving the pan of unfinished lasagna on the counter. "All this time Cort's been part of the Emporium? I thought it was suspicious, him showing up after an old college roommate of mine wrote an article about running into me and how I hadn't appeared to age."

"How long ago was that exactly?" I asked, picking up his abandoned sauce spoon.

Laurence thought a moment. "Thirty-five. But he's been very helpful to our cause all these years. He's the last person I'd ever peg for a traitor—except maybe Ritter. Everyone knows that any day he kills an Emporium agent is a good day for him."

"Do you think Cort knows about this place?" Chris recovered enough to ask.

I chewed my bottom lip. "He'd have to, I'd think. He's the son of one of the Triad. From what I heard him tell his brother, he's planning on running the Emporium someday."

"Then he'll set a trap for the others," Laurence said.

I spooned the sauce over the last layer of noodles before going back to the table. "So maybe the question isn't how we escape, but how do we stop the others from falling into the trap?"

"Ava and the others aren't new at this," Laurence said. "They'll be careful."

"But they have no idea Cort's a traitor." I licked a bit of sauce from my finger. A bit spicy but good.

Laurence heaved a sigh. "That could be a big problem."

"If they had a helicopter or something," Chris said, "I could fly it out of here."

"I'm sure they have one. The problem will be getting to it." Laurence came to his feet and slid the lasagna into the heated oven.

Back where we began—locked in a room with no chance of escape.

"Well, there's nothing we can do now." Laurence reached for a bag of flour and a jar of yeast. He turned off the blender, much to everyone's relief. "Do you know how to knead bread by hand? I know an awesome bread stick recipe. If we hurry, they'll be ready to pop in the oven just after the lasagna's finished."

We spent the next hour and a half helping Laurence with dinner and watching the children. When we finally sat down to eat, I wasn't hungry, but the smell of the bread sticks made my mouth water all the same. I ate one of the sticks and a piece of lasagna in record time.

Moments later, I sensed Keene's presence before he appeared in the kitchen doorway. I put down my second bread stick and met his gaze slowly. "Hello, Keene."

Laurence and Chris looked up from their plates, and the children stopped drinking root beer to stare at him.

Keene ignored everyone but me. "Delia Vesey wants to see you."

"That didn't take long." I glanced at Chris and Laurence for their reactions.

"I'll go with you," Laurence said.

I shook my head. "I'd feel better if you'd stay here with Chris and the kids." Chris was strong, but Laurence had been trained to fight Unbounded. Even overweight as he was and with only his bare hands, he'd be better protection for them than I would be. Or better at talking his way out of trouble. Of course, if an attacker had a gun, Laurence would be immobilized almost instantly.

"I'd feel better if you didn't go at all." Chris's voice was haunted and made me recall the horrifying images I'd seen in his mind.

"I have to," I said, though thinking of Delia made me shudder. "Okay. I'm ready."

CHAPTER 18

"WHAT'S GOING TO HAPPEN TO JUSTINE?" I ASKED AS KEENE AND I walked down the corridor. "Stefan said he'd deal with her."

If I saw her myself, I might rip her apart, especially now that I'd felt my brother's anguish.

He glanced at me but kept walking. "I don't know."

I tried to sense his thoughts, and this time he wasn't dark, but he really didn't know. The strongest emotion I felt from him was readiness in case I tried anything, but I could have told that from his body language. His arm was bent so the hand was closer to his gun; his muscles were poised with alertness. It made me smile that I could make him so nervous.

"What?" he asked, noticing my stare.

"I'm not going to try to get away."

"Why not?"

"A lot of reasons. But for one, you're holding my brother and my niece and nephew."

"Not me."

I glared at him. "You're the reason I'm here."

"If it weren't me, it would have been someone else."

He had a point. The Emporium would have sent someone else, perhaps someone who might not have minded putting a bullet through my heart to make me easier to handle. Even so, I didn't intend to be nice to Keene for only being halfway decent. "You're still wrong. Kidnapping people is wrong."

He didn't speak, and I felt maybe I'd been too hard on him. After all, how could he compete with an Unbounded father and brother? Probably he had even more Unbounded siblings, and he was the lowest on the family totem pole.

"How's your leg?" I asked.

He shrugged. "I'll live." Again he was telling the truth. He would live, but the pain was all too apparent to me, as was his struggle not to limp. Our workout this morning had obviously not helped his condition, but I had the feeling he wouldn't have any rest soon. Weakness was not something appreciated or encouraged here.

"How many sub floors are there?" I asked. From the visit with Stefan, I remembered there were five above ground, but I hadn't noticed when Jonny had brought me down here how far the basement levels reached.

He smirked. "Trying to figure out how many floors between you and freedom?"

"I'm trying to find out about the organization I'm going to be a part of, maybe even run one of these days."

The smirk turned into a full laugh. "You gotta be kidding. One minute you want me to release you and the next you're planning to be my boss."

"I told you I had many reasons for *not* running. My father is glad to see me. I would be a fool to turn down his hospitality." The lie came so easily it almost scared me. One more change within. If I'd been able to lie like this in law school, I might have actually graduated.

He gave me a strange look, but said nothing more as we walked into the elevator that was guarded by two men.

"Two sub levels," I said, eying the numbers on the control

panel. "We're on the first." Now it was my turn to smirk—and to realize I was finding our barbed exchange amusing. Was this enjoyment related to the confidence the Unbounded carried with them?

Whatever. Being here still beat being burned to a crisp in Justine's little car.

"What floor is Tom on?" I asked as the elevator doors closed.

"He's with Justine on four." Keene's eyes pinned mine. "Don't tell me you still love him?"

"Does it matter?"

"I guess not." He looked away.

Several moments ticked by before I whispered, "Our whole relationship was based on a lie."

He nodded and I knew he understood exactly how I felt.

We exited on the top floor, where two more guards stood outside the elevator. Not the same guards as that morning, I noticed. We passed the doors to Stefan's office and rounded a bend. I noticed a door with a picture of stairs on them and a notice reading *roof access*. Not a place I'd want to visit, not with my acrophobia.

"What does Delia want with you?" Keene asked.

"Why don't you tell me? You're the one taking me to her."

He shrugged. "I don't know."

I sensed nothing from him now and took the cue to put up my own mental barriers, though I had no idea how strong they might be. Strong enough, I hoped.

Keene stopped in front of a set of double doors. "You might be able to block her," he said in a low voice. "It won't be easy."

"Thanks."

He placed his hand on the pad outside the door, which slid open. Delia stood in front of us. "Ah, Erin. I trust you've had time to eat and rest a bit?"

"Yes, thank you."

"Come in, then. We have things to discuss." To Keene, she added, "We won't be long. Please wait."

Turning, she urged me inside and shut the door in his face. Before he was obscured from view, I saw him watching me, the green of his eyes a stark contrast against the dark bruises on his face.

Delia's apartment was nothing like those below or even like Stefan's tasteful office. Rather it resembled a luxury suite at a plush hotel. The vaulted room she led me into was filled with floor-length windows, and the furniture and carpets radiated color: deep reds and browns, even some orange and green. All boldly and exquisitely decorated. A huge chandelier dominated the ceiling.

Vastly different from the Renegades' common warehouse. "My home away from home," Delia said, seating herself on a red-toned couch.

"Not bad." Fear made my words stilted.

"Sit here." She patted the couch beside her.

I'd been about to sit in a chair some distance away. Instead, I moved a patterned throw pillow and sat on the couch as far away from her as I felt I could in the situation, placing the pillow between us.

"So, Erin, you are special."

"I'm Unbounded, if that's what you mean." I wished my heart would stop racing and that my mind would quit telling me to run.

"That's not what I mean. Of course you're Unbounded. Like you, I can sense that by looking at you."

"What are you talking about?" I said. "I mean, sure the Unbounded have good genes, and they tend to stand out in a crowd."

"Oh? Look more carefully at me."

I did as she asked. My first impression of her had been that she was striking and had once been a great beauty, but now I saw that wasn't true. She was no more or less than millions of women in the world. And yet, her bearing, her confidence made her more than what she was. Taken as a whole, she was impressive.

Belatedly I thought of my half-brother Jonny. He definitely didn't have anything going for him in the looks department, but I bet ordinary women were crazy about him.

"The Unbounded do come from the strongest genetic building

blocks," Delia said. "But not always are the strongest genes the most beautiful. It is what's inside the shell—the attitude, the self-belief, the awareness of immortality that makes the difference."

"I see."

"Do you?" Her dark eyes glittered as they studied me. "Do you feel the changes in your body? Do you understand the power you have at your fingertips?"

"What do you want from me?" I felt her touch on my mind, and I shook my head. "If you want my cooperation, do not rape my mind."

She cocked her head as if considering. "Very well—for now. As for what I want, you are one of only a few who have an extra-sensory ability, a rare gift these days. The Emporium as a whole has been so focused on trying to create more Unbounded, that for a time we lost sight of what abilities we were producing. As our Unbounded have bred together, many of the mundane talents have taken over the special, rare gifts, with combat naturally being the most prevalent because fighting was necessary for our survival. In fact, most variations of the special talents have disappeared alto-gether, but I believe with careful planning we can recreate them. We'll be able to recapture lost abilities and perhaps discover a few that even older Unbounded have never dreamed of."

Her chin lifted slightly, her face glowing as though she preached a sermon of great religious value. "Of course it'll take time finding the right combination—a grandfather talented with science, a grandmother with sensing, a sensing mother, a mathematical father. I don't know exactly what, but I believe we can find the right combination. You will be of great help."

Me or my genes? I figured she meant the latter, but I wasn't about to ask for clarification. Either way I had no intention of being part of her breeding program.

"Can an Unbounded have both his parents' talents?" I asked. "I mean, if both his parents are Unbounded."

Delia laughed. "My, aren't we greedy? But no, it doesn't work that way. Or at least not that I've ever known. We are unfortunately limited to one. However, there are some who have several variations within the one." She shrugged. "I believe it's really a matter of determination for the most part. We will see with you. You are, after all, very determined."

To live, maybe.

And to protect my family.

"It's also possible that a child may develop a talent passed on by Unbounded grandparents if they are duplicated in both the father's and the mother's lines, even if the father and mother themselves took after their other grandparent. Genetics is not entirely predictable. But trial and failure eventually lead to success."

"And if I don't want to be your guinea pig?"

She gave me a flat smile. "It doesn't really matter what you want, but I hope you will do your part willingly."

"For the Emporium."

"For the Emporium and for Stefan."

Was that a threat? Surely she couldn't think I felt anything for the man I'd only met once. A sperm donor did not a father make.

When I didn't reply, she bent closer to me. I caught the faint aroma of something, an herb perhaps, that I didn't recognize. "I know you think we're strong, but what you see here is the largest of only five facilities like it throughout the world. Five, Erin. We have succeeded in increasing our numbers in the past century, it's true. We have several hundred Unbounded and many mortal children like Keene who serve us loyally. But our encounters with the Renegades, and even with the Hunters whom we once had under our control, have diminished our numbers."

"By several hundred you mean what, two? Three? Four?" This was surely something Ava would want to know. Immediately, I stifled the thought in case Delia was already in my mind without my knowledge. I wished I could tell for sure.

"That isn't your concern. Suffice to say that we have grown, though not without price. Many of our numbers are in government or political positions and do not work with us on a daily basis. Many are young and have not yet Changed."

"I don't know much about the Renegade situation, but I believe they don't have nearly that many Unbounded."

"We do have the advantage of numbers and resources, but we have come to a crisis." She leaned back and crossed her legs, causing her gray dress to flutter around her bare ankles. "We learned some time ago that the Renegades plan to develop a new technology in connection with a certain man named John Halden, but only this morning did we learn the importance of the technology."

So Cort had finally learned the details of the exchange and passed them on to the Emporium. "John Halden?" I asked. "You mean the man the Emporium tried to assassinate a few days ago?"

Her lips pursed. "That man has been a danger to us for many years. He has cut into our profits with his inventions, and with several advances he's made it harder and harder to get new identities. But this latest technology could be the undoing of the entire Emporium organization."

"What could be so dangerous?"

She arose, walked to the window behind us, and stood looking out. I twisted on the couch so I could see her better. The harsh midday light on her profile was not flattering. She looked to be in her mid-sixties, and if she'd become Unbounded at thirty-one, she would be about seventeen hundred years old. The sheer enormity of the number made my mouth go dry. This woman had many lifetimes of experience behind her. I had only thirty-one years.

"It's not a faster computer chip or a smart house or a new medicine," she said. "This is an identification plan that will essentially eliminate identity theft."

"Sounds like a good thing."

"Not for the Unbounded." She faced me, framed in the light, looking more ethereal than human. "The general mortal population has no idea we exist, but if the world is forced to use this technology, it will eliminate our ability to create false identities. Some in our organization believe this is the mark of the beast foretold in the Bible, though that is irrelevant to me. What is relevant is that whether it's a chip put in at birth or an eye scan, if such is required for all commerce, it would be only a matter of time before our longevity is noticed. We're not ready to go public yet. Can you imagine the panic, the witch hunts that would ensue?" She paused and added, "Having suffered death by fire yourself, you know what that's like. We will not be hunted as we have been in the past. Not again."

I went to join her at the window. "Why would the Renegades develop such technology? It would put them in as much danger of discovery as the Emporium."

"We believe they will create hidden side programs that would allow them not only to protect themselves, but to track the identities of our people."

Now I finally understood why the Emporium was concerned. They weren't really worried about the general population but the Renegade Unbounded. If this program became active, they would be picked off one by one until they were all gone or until they were forced to abandon their goals and join with the Renegades. Unless they discovered a way to live outside the bounds of regular human interaction.

"Anyway," I said. "It'd take years to enact something like that."

Delia waved her hand as if erasing my words. "Child, that is but a blink of the eye in our life spans. We would all live to see it, even if the implementation took a hundred years. This is one of the reasons we've fought to keep certain technologies from the mortals."

"So you plan to stop the Renegades?"

"The deal is to take place in New York this evening, and I understand you were to attend. What do you know of the meeting?"

I shrugged with a nonchalance I was far from feeling. "I was to have helped with security, that's all. I was never told any details. They didn't trust me any more than you do."

Her thin lips curled in a predatory smile. "So, you refuse to help us."

"No, I'm saying I don't know anything. Smart move on their part—I can't tell you what I don't know."

"I don't believe you. But no matter. We will soon have the information we need, with or without your help. Our informants have given us a Renegade safe house in New York where Renegade Unbounded will be gathering in preparation for this deal. We will surprise them."

"You're planning an attack?" I spoke casually, but I hoped she couldn't sense my real emotions because at that moment my hatred for her and the Emporium burned brighter than ever.

She nodded, her eyes triumphant. "When our work is done this night, we will not have to worry about Renegades for at least a century, if ever again. We'll obtain the technology they seek to use against us, and you can be sure we will implement it in their stead. Only then can we protect ourselves forever."

I hated Cort even more now. With this new information he'd given to the Emporium, they'd not only slaughter the Unbounded gathered in New York, but they would soon be able to murder every Unbounded anywhere who opposed them. Laurence was right when he'd said that the world was well on its way to being enslaved.

I unsuccessfully fought my anger. I knew Delia could see it in my face, and that I was probably mentally broadcasting my feelings by now. They were too strong to contain.

"You must not resist," she said softly, stepping closer to me. Her large eyes dominated the tiny face. "I can help, you know. I have the power to smooth out the losses, make it so they do not hurt so much."

"Is that what you do for your people?" I retorted. "Is that why they continue to serve an organization that uses them as breeders or slaves?"

"Their contributions are of their own will." Delia motioned around her. "In return, we give them what they need to live as gods. But you and I are special, Erin, even among Unbounded. Nothing is out of our reach."

"As long as you get rid of the Renegades."

Her thin smile vanished. "We've been at war with them for

thousands of years. I do not think that will end in one night's work. It will only be the beginning of the end."

"I won't help you. They're my friends." I realized that was true. However briefly I'd known them, I'd grown to care for Ava, Dimitri, Ritter, Stella, and Laurence. And even Cort, who'd betrayed us all.

"Yes," Delia said. "You most certainly will help us."

She was in my mind then, a leap I hadn't expected. *Not a problem,* I found myself thinking. After all, the Emporium wanted only the best for all Unbounded. I should be grateful to help them. They didn't want to replace mortals but only to demand the rights all people deserved without persecution, without having to hide in the darkness or constantly changing identities. It was natural the Unbounded, with their greater wisdom, should assure that humanity stayed on track. It was only responsible to take control.

I found myself nodding before I realized I was being manipulated. I rejected her message, pushed against it. *I'm stronger than that,* I thought, but I knew it wasn't true. I was weak and inexperienced. Delia could teach me to be strong. We would oust Stefan and Tihalt and run the Emporium together, amassing great fortunes; the world would be at our feet. I could have anything, even my family if that was my desire.

No! With a massive effort I backed away, putting space between us. I made a humming noise in my head, the same one I'd used as a child when my brothers were teasing me. *I can't hear you, I can't hear you.*

Her touch was gone, and I smiled in triumph. Her lips grew white with rage. "You will have to choose sides, Erin. Everyone must choose. The point is choosing wisely."

"I think I just did," I said with far more calm than I was feeling. "Though that will remain between you and me. Your word against mine."

"Your father will not believe you. I will tell him the truth."

"That's okay. Because I'm going to tell him the truth, too— that you wanted to use me against him and Tihalt." I turned and started toward the door.

Her frustration slammed into me like pummeling fists, stealing my breath away. Each step I took felt like a thousand, as though I struggled through waist-deep mud. One, two, three, four. My progress was achingly slow. Pain hammered at my head. I forced one foot in front of the other, pushing outward with my mind, though I had no idea if this did any good. Silently, I cursed Ava for not better preparing me.

Somehow I reached the door. Delia laughed, and with a soft buzz, the door unlocked, though no one had used the hand panel by the door. Apparently, Delia's talent was stronger than I'd guessed. Either that or she had a remote. The power that had held me vanished, and I nearly fell.

"Run, little mouse," Delia called after me. "For now. There's no place you can go inside this building that's out of my reach. The minute you relax your guard, I will be there. You will not be able to resist me long. No one can."

I was shaking as I opened the door. Keene pushed himself off the wall where he was lounging in the hall, one brow arching in surprise. Inclining his head at Delia who was glaring at me from across the room, he pulled the door shut.

"A little early, aren't we?"

"I didn't like what she had to say."

"You don't seem to like anyone around here." He started down the hall, and my weary muscles rebelled as I followed.

"Except for you." Relief crept over me at the increasing distance from Delia, but I didn't dare let down my mental barriers yet.

"Me? You hate me most of all."

"At least you tell the truth."

He met my gaze. "Well, then here's another. You look like hell."

"That's better than I feel. She's a tough old bird."

"Vulture," he agreed.

Keene nodded at the two Unbounded guards as we entered the elevator, jabbing at a button, while I staggered near the wall. My head throbbed, and I didn't feel I could take another step.

"Look, I haven't been totally honest about Justine," Keene said into the silence. "Stefan demanded a name, and I thought of one. I couldn't do anything else with Delia there. She would have taken the true information, and used it to her advantage. I gave up the obvious person."

"What are you saying?"

He crossed the two steps that separated us. "Justine was responsible for your sister-in-law's death, but what you have to understand is that she would not have acted without approval from the Triad, especially from Stefan."

"Why especially?"

"Justine craves power more than anything else. At present, Stefan is the only Triad member strong enough to stand against Delia, and it's no secret that Justine wants into his bed. Creating a child with Stefan would give her power in the Emporium, especially if she's lucky enough to have a child with a sensing ability—which could happen, given that she has a weak variation of the ability herself. Getting such a child from you and Tom would be every bit as good, and a lot more likely given your genetic relationship with Ava."

I must have reached my surprise limit, because I didn't even feel shock. His explanation fit with Justine's near worship of Stefan on the plane and her plans for Tom and me.

"If Delia had tried harder to get the truth from me," Keene continued, "she would have been able to pin the attack on Stefan and put a wedge between you. I didn't want to be responsible for that. Or for causing more instability in the Triad. So I focused on Justine. I'm telling you now because I decided you have a right to know."

"Why would Stefan order my family killed?" My voice sounded strangled.

Keene's gaze was gentle. "My guess is that he wanted to be sure you had nothing pulling you away from him."

"What he's done is given me no reason to stay. There can never be a relationship between us now." Had a part of me hoped for such? I didn't know.

"I reported to my father after the attack," Keene continued. "Told him that his orders to bring them in alive had been over-ridden by Justine. Because he knows Stefan so well, he knew exactly what that meant. He was furious at the effect the attack would have on you and your willingness to join us. Besides a few useless variations, all of our sensing Unbounded are well over a thousand years old—when the ability to bear Unbounded children starts to diminish. Paired with men who have the right genes, you could have very powerful children and grandchildren for the Emporium."

I felt sickened at the idea of being used as a breeder, possibly for centuries, and at the thought of having as many children as possible to help those who gave so little value to human life. My father didn't care about me as a person. He never had. "At least Justine didn't hurt Chris and the kids once she caught up to them."

"My father convinced Stefan to spare their lives. He agreed, but only if they were brought here. He thinks they might also be useful."

So I'd been right about the Emporium's plan for the children, and Chris as well. As long as my brother or his children were prisoners, I could be made to do anything the Emporium wanted.

Keene reached past me and hit the stop button on the elevator. "What are you doing?"

"Giving you a little time to recover."

"Thanks." I sagged against the metal wall of the elevator. His arm was still there in front of me, stretched out toward the controls, but it felt good to touch another person. For a long moment we stood motionless, looking into each other's eyes.

In an instant, the mood changed and the air became charged. I saw him swallow, once, twice. His face came close, his intention to kiss me quite clear. After being so honest about my feeling regarding the Emporium, I couldn't have been more surprised if he'd stripped naked and stood on his head.

For a second, I considered resisting his advances, yet shouldn't I use any opportunity offered me? If he thought I was attracted to him, he might be willing to overlook my loyalties and help me at some point.

His lips met mine. Without thinking, I let my defenses fall and his emotions flooded over me, through me. Sensations rippled inside my body. I didn't have to pretend as much as I thought I would. In fact, it was pleasant—exhilarating even—to kiss a man who in this moment didn't want anything from me except what I was willing to give. Not like Tom, who wanted me blindly because of Justine, or even like Ritter, whose wanting made me lose myself.

So completely had I let down my defenses, becoming attuned with Keene's emotions, that I felt a stab of disappointment when he pulled away.

"Sorry, I didn't plan that," he said in a low voice. With one arm still around me, he traced my lip with his thumb. I could feel the slight roughness of his skin. "I know this place makes no sense to you. About as much sense as what I'm feeling now, but I'm glad you're here, Erin. You—I feel different around you. I know that doesn't mean anything for the future, and I don't expect anything to ever come from this moment. For the first time in a long time, I'm seeing what's really around me. What I'm involved in. For that, I thank you."

Now it was my turn to grip his arms. "If I don't do something to stop the Emporium, a lot of Unbounded are going to die tonight, including at least one of my friends—Stella. She's supposed to be in New York today. I have to warn her somehow."

His hands dropped to his sides. "I haven't heard anything about an attack."

"Remember Cort talking about a meeting with Halden? Well, he found out what they were negotiating—an identification program that will be able to track Unbounded. He didn't know where the meeting would be, but he's given them a location of a Renegade safe house. Delia's sure to get the location of the meeting with Halden from one of the Renegades there—and right after, she's going to slaughter everyone."

Was I trusting Keene too much? I didn't know. At this moment he was all I had. The idea of all those people dying made me desperate. Especially Stella, who'd been so kind to me.

"Cort usually keeps me in the loop." Keene shook his head in disbelief, as repulsed at the idea as I was. "This isn't like him."

"Well, it's happening. All those people will die and once the Emporium has the technology to track anyone anywhere, there'll be no going back. You see that, don't you? I need your help."

He considered me for a moment. "There's a back exit. I can take you there, get you out. Maybe you can find a way to warn them."

"I need to take my brother and his kids, and Laurence, too. I can't leave them for Delia or Stefan to use."

"There's no time."

I hissed sharply, "We'll make time." A sharp pain flared in my mind and was gone.

He recoiled as if I'd slapped him, uttering an expression of astonishment. "What was that? I *felt* that. In my mind."

What was he saying? Then I understood, and my anger melted away. I felt unsteady on my feet. "Oh. I'm sorry. I didn't mean—"

He was looking at me with something else in his eyes now, something that made me uneasy. "No wonder Delia is interested in you. This changes everything. Stefan will never let you go once he knows."

"Look, I don't want to get you in trouble. I just need a way out—with the others. Chris could fly us, if there's a helicopter."

"Stefan and Justine took it out an hour ago."

"An hour ago? Could they have taken it to New York?"

His eyes grew wide. "They did take a team and were heading for the airport. They didn't tell me why."

"Then it's begun."

Our gazes met and held. "Meet me by the front desk," he said. "On the main level where we came in. In exactly thirty minutes I'll make sure the way is clear."

"What about the door to the apartment?"

He took something unidentifiable from his pocket. "It's a glove. It has my prints."

"Thank you."

He nodded and kissed me again, long and slow. Warmth slithered through my body.

"What was that for?" I asked. The emotion coming from him now wasn't the same as before, and it confused me. It spoke more of friendship than of desire of a man for a woman.

"That was goodbye."

"You could come with us."

"No."

"Why?"

"Because I don't belong."

"Where do you belong?"

"I don't know." He started the elevator again.

Thoughts raced through me, but there was nothing I could say that would help him.

We were quiet until we reached the door to the apartment where Chris and Laurence waited. "Thirty minutes," Keene reminded me.

"What time do you have now?"

He showed me his watch and I nodded. "You should keep your mind guarded," he said. "Or she'll be able to find you once she realizes something's wrong. At least until we're away from the building."

I pulled my mental barriers back into place, berating myself for my laxity. A few pleasant kisses and I forgot everything. What kind of Unbounded was I?

I went into the apartment where my brother greeted me, relief etched on his face. "Thank God, you're back," he said, casting his gaze briefly heavenward. I wondered what he'd say if I told him Delia considered the Unbounded gods. "I've been so worried."

"I'm fine," I assured him. "But I need your watch."

He gave it to me without explanation. I checked the time to make sure it was the same as Keene's before strapping it around my own wrist, cinching the leather band as tightly as I could. It was still large on me but wouldn't fall off.

Laurence and the children had come from the other room. Kathy's eyes looked red and I wondered if Chris had told her about her mother, or if she'd finally begun to understand that we weren't on an impromptu vacation. There wasn't time to worry about it now.

"Well?" Laurence asked.

"We have thirty minutes," I said. "And then we're getting out of here."

CHAPTER 19

THIRTY MINUTES AFTER KEENE LEFT ME, I PUT ON THE GLOVE AND used it to open the door. "We'll take the stairs," I said. "It'll be quieter that way."

"Are you sure this is wise?" Laurence whispered, his meaty hand coming to rest on my arm. "They might let us go eventually."

I placed my hand over his and lowered my voice. "Laurence, the only way they'll let you and me out of here is in three pieces. Besides, I'm not going to stand by and watch these kids be used by the Emporium." He nodded and removed his hand.

"What about the cameras?" Chris asked. "They have plenty of them."

"We have to hope that Keene's distraction has taken care of whoever's watching, or maybe the equipment. I don't know what he has planned."

Only my nephew, Spencer, seemed to be enjoying himself as we hurried down the hall in search of the stairs. As Keene had promised, there were no guards near the elevators.

"Here," Chris hissed. He opened the door to the stairs, and we hurried inside.

Only one flight up and we were on the ground floor where the receptionists had greeted us earlier. "The ladies at the desk aren't there," Chris said, opening the door an inch. "But the guards still are."

"Give him a few more minutes." I peeked through the doorway and saw Keene talking to the guards, gesturing with his hands. After the space of several more heartbeats, they entered the elevator and disappeared. "Let's go," I said to the others.

Keene smiled when he saw us. "Right on time. Come this way." We were halfway down a corridor when we heard shouting behind us.

The guards were back, and they didn't look happy.

Keene swore and pulled out his gun. "They must have checked their orders with the radio on the way up. Hurry. Follow me!"

Everyone ran. Down the hallway, through a large room, and out again to another hallway. Keene rounded a corner, and I heard a whizzing from ahead that sounded like a shot from a silenced gun. I hurried faster to make sure he was okay—only to trip over a fallen man in my path. A pop sounded in my ankle, sending sharp pains up my leg.

"Aunt Erin!" shouted Kathy as I fell. Blood seeped from under the body, and she forgot me, staring in fascination. Spencer let out a sob.

"Keep running!" On my knees, I pushed her past the sprawled figure. She grabbed Spencer's hand and pulled him down the hallway toward Keene.

Chris had bent to help me rise, but I slapped his hands away. "Go on. Take care of the kids. They aren't safe here. I'll be all right in a moment." I gave him a confident smile I was far from feeling.

He stared at me, and then nodded once and ran after the children. I knew how much it cost him because I'd felt the same way leaving an unconscious Jace. But the children had to come first. There was no one else to save them.

Laurence yanked me to my feet, but my ankle gave out again as I stumbled after the others. "Run," I told Laurence. "Help Chris and the kids get out. They won't kill me." We shared a glance that said more than words, both understanding that there were far worse things than dying. Nodding, he lumbered on, surprisingly quick for his massive bulk.

Stupid, I thought. To come so close, only to fail. Already the pain in my swelling foot was lessening, but I could hear the guards approaching the turn in the hallway, and there was no way my ankle was going to hold up so soon. I could, however, buy Keene and the others more time. I leaned casually against the wall and waited, absorbing as rapidly as I could to help myself heal.

The guards did a double take as they rounded the corner, stumbling over the body as I had, though without such disastrous results. One guard was Unbounded, the other mortal, though he looked young so it was possible he hadn't yet Changed. The Unbounded pointed his gun at me, while the mortal bent down to feel the pulse of the fallen man. "Alive," he said under his breath.

I wasn't sure whether to be glad Keene wasn't a cold-blooded killer or depressed that the unconscious mortal would live to fight again.

"I couldn't catch them," I said with false brightness. "I tried. They had that big Renegade with them. They went in there." I pointed to a door down the hallway. I had no idea how well-informed the Emporium guards were about my position here, but the bluff was worth a try.

"You stay with her," the Unbounded barked at the mortal as he started down the hall. The misdirection wouldn't buy much time unless the door I'd indicated led to a hallway or a suite with possible hiding places, and that meant I had to get rid of the mortal. Unfortunately, he probably had more training than I did.

"I tripped over him," I said, indicating the sprawled man. "I hurt my ankle." I tested it, moaning softly, though I thought it might now hold my weight.

"You going to be okay?" the guard asked.

"In a while. Maybe you can help me back to my rooms, or at least to the front desk."

He holstered his gun and approached me cautiously. I tried another ginger step and this time let my leg collapse as though the pain was too much to bear. As I started to fall, he reached for me. I straightened suddenly and slammed my elbow down on his neck. He fell.

Even Ritter would have been proud.

I started down the hallway after Chris and the others. I hoped at some point they'd be able to wait for me.

Wishful thinking.

The Unbounded guard emerged from the room where I'd sent him, his gun ready. Confusion lit his face as I lunged toward him. The gun went off, the shot going wide. We struggled for the weapon, but he was stronger. Slowly, he brought the barrel to my stomach. I tensed for the pain I knew was coming.

A single silenced shot. But no pain.

The guard crumpled. Arms came around me—familiar arms.

I turned. Ritter stood there, looking angry and disheveled. My eyes fell greedily over his dark hair, his unshaven face, the black clothes that I knew hid more weapons than I'd ever begin to know what to do with. For a moment I leaned against him, not wanting to appear weak, but craving more than anything the comfort of his solid presence. His arms tightened around my body, holding me to the wide expanse of his chest. I felt safe for the first time in days.

More than safe. Other emotions came through every bit as strong. Not his feelings this time, but my own, because my mental barriers were tight and impenetrable—in case Delia was searching for me.

Not good. I couldn't fall for Ritter. Better the mortal Keene or Tom or anyone else. At least their hearts might be whole enough to be capable of real love. Ritter survived only to exact revenge.

I drew away and turned toward him. "I knew you couldn't pass up this party."

His eyes roamed my face, his expression fierce. "Can't let the new people have all the fun." An aura of danger emanated from him, in the hard lines of his chest and shoulders, the defined muscles of his legs. Or maybe it was in the fire in his eyes, that unending thirst for revenge. Even though I knew he was on my side, everything warned me to run.

He started down the hall and I followed as fast as I could, only limping slightly. "There's something you should know. Cort's a spy. He told them everything—about the technology from John Halden, the address of a safe house in New York, and probably more. He's been working for the Emporium all along."

"Impossible."

"Why do you think I'm here? His brother was waiting for us at his house."

"Cort's loyal to the Renegades. He's trying to knock out their systems now."

I gaped, my horror complete. "You brought Cort?"

"He's the one who tracked you here. Stella's in New York and Dimitri's still with your father."

My father? I'd become so accustomed to everyone here talking about Stefan as my father that it took me a moment to understand what he meant. "How is he?"

"Dimitri says if he leaves him, he'll die."

Blood rushed from my face, leaving me momentarily light-headed. "If my father's dying, why would it matter if Dimitri stays with him?"

Ritter stopped moving, his eyes meeting mine. "I can't explain it any more than I can explain what Ava does. It's part of his ability. Still, in the end it may not matter. He may be able to keep your father alive, but he can't make him another heart. Come on, we've got to get you out of here. Cort's waiting."

"He's not waiting!" I gritted. "He's the reason I'm in this mess. If he's here, he's plotting against us. Cort's father runs this place."

"I know that."

I blinked. "You know about Cort's father?"

"He told me, Ava, and Dimitri the truth before he joined us. I think Stella suspects his story, but she knows he's okay. His misfortune in fathers doesn't mean he's a traitor."

I backed away uneasily. "I heard Cort and his brother talking."

"Everything isn't always what it appears."

"I'm not putting my life in his hands."

He took a step toward me, closing the gap I'd put between us. "And how about in mine?"

I trusted him with more than my life. Crazy, maybe, but true. I wet my lower lip with my tongue. "I trust you, Ritter, but you have to trust me about this."

"You're wrong, and I'll prove it to you."

I opened my mind enough to sense his sincerity. Emotion slammed into me, the foremost was a deep and bitter hate. Not directed toward me, but partly because of me. I was one more person he'd almost lost. He noticed my stare and the emotions vanished as though I'd imagined them.

He smiled. "Trust me with your life, Erin. Nothing more."

Not my heart, he meant. Well, he didn't need to worry on that score. Slamming my barriers back into place, I turned and strode down the hall in the direction we'd been heading, ignoring the unpleasant pulsing of my ankle. I needed to find Chris and the kids, but I didn't know exactly what I was looking for. Would there be a flight of stairs to the second entrance? Or was it straight through one of these doors? I opened one but it only revealed a deserted office.

In two bounds, Ritter caught up with me. I risked a glance at him, but his face was unreadable. As I reached for another door, he paused at a new hallway leading off the first. "We can get to the control room through here. Cort should be finished there now, and he'll know the best way out."

I was about to tell Ritter I had no intention of leaving until I made sure my brother had escaped when we heard someone coming down the new hallway. Ritter motioned me behind him and took a fighting stance, his gun drawn.

Three long seconds passed before Cort came into view. He had his own weapon out, and for a tense moment, I thought they'd shoot each other, but when Cort saw us, he lowered his gun.

"Good, you found her. There was a fire on one of the lower floors, and no one was even in the control room when I got in to put up the fake camera feed, but I almost got caught getting out. We've got ten minutes to get to the roof before the feed runs out."

"You!" I came from behind Ritter and launched myself at Cort. "Traitor!"

Cort lifted his hands to ward off my blows. "What are you talking about? We came to save you!"

"I suppose you want me to believe you haven't been feeding your father information all this time? Tell the truth, Cort. Ritter doesn't believe me. You know, Keene may not be Unbounded, and he may have done a lot of bad things in his life, but at least he doesn't lie."

Cort's smile challenged me. "And you'd know the difference?"

Ritter pushed between us, his strong arm drawing me back. "Erin has Ava's talent, not her father's."

"You knew those people at the restaurant were Unbounded," I accused Cort. "You knew my family would be in danger once they saw me." I dug my nails into Ritter's arm in an attempt to get past him to Cort, but he didn't even flinch.

Cort shook his head. "I knew they were Unbounded, but I thought they were tracking me, not you. They often show up to let me know they're waiting for information. I didn't think they'd connect me with your brother."

"Liar!"

Ritter shoved me back and kept his arm out to keep me away. He brought up his gun, aiming it at Cort's temple. "I know this won't kill you, Cort, but it will hurt even more than the stakes those vampire hunters kept trying to put in our chests a hundred years ago."

"You know I'm not a traitor," Cort growled, his eyes growing angry. "You know what I've gone through for the Renegades."

To my horror, Ritter lowered his gun. "I do trust you. Now show Erin why she should. After what she's been through, she deserves that much."

"There's no time!" Cort's normal composure had deserted him, making him decidedly desperate. "I managed to fix their camera, but I couldn't do anything with the jamming system. I don't have Stella's skill. That means we can't communicate internally or radio Ava when we need her and the chopper. We'll have to signal her the old-fashioned way. Can't this wait?"

"Not if it saves us from another betrayal," I muttered.

Ritter shrugged. "You see how she is."

I tried not to take offense.

Cort looked at me. "Go ahead. Read me—if you can."

Read him? Oh, like Delia had done to me. I could try.

Ritter lowered his arm and motioned us into one of the empty rooms. I placed my hand on Cort's face. I expected him to fight, to hide his thoughts, anything to prevent Ritter from learning the truth through me. With centuries of experience, he'd know many tricks to keep me from his secrets.

To my surprise there were no barriers in his mind. "Be careful," he said. "You could damage me."

I hadn't known that. Gently, I pushed deeper, working by instinct and what I'd learned from Delia—a poor substitute for training, I decided as my head began to ache with the effort.

As his swirling emotions cleared, I saw images of Cort growing up, of him eventually leaving the Emporium and joining the Rene-gades. How he gave the Emporium enough to continue to trust him, but not enough to sever the ties that allowed him to work as a double agent. Even his own brother, for whom Cort felt an honest affection, had been kept in the dark, though Keene had apparently become suspicious of late—which explained why he'd been waiting for us at Cort's house.

There was more, much more. I saw glimpses of women he had loved and lost. A son who was now dead. A sister who became a Hunter. A mother he'd never known. A father he hated and rejected, but whom he still loved with a childlike doggedness. After the first few memories, I shied away from these more personal experiences.

I'd been wrong. Oh, so wrong! I wished the floor could open and swallow me whole.

I pulled away from Cort. "I'm sorry," I whispered.

He gave me a tight half smile in return, his mental shields springing into place and blacking out his real reply.

"Satisfied?" Ritter asked, his tone mocking.

I lifted my eyes slowly to his, struggling against the emotion of what I'd seen. "So when they told me they knew about the identification program and the location of the safe house in New York—that was false information you gave them, right? Or junk they were feeding me to see what I knew?"

Cort stared, his horrified gaze going to Ritter and then back to me. "What do you mean? The Emporium shouldn't know about the program, much less any safe house."

"Apparently they do." Ritter's body became taut. "Tell us everything."

Quickly I outlined what Delia had told me. My heart thundered in my chest and any moment I expected the door to bang open and a dozen guards to pounce on us. "She hoped I knew the location of the exchange, but I didn't."

"If they know about the technology and the safe house, our very existence is at risk," Cort said.

"So the Renegades *are* planning to develop the identification program?" I asked.

Cort shook his head. "Absolutely not. We're trying to stop Halden from developing it. When we got wind of what he was doing last year, Stella and some technopath friends of hers began creating the virtual reality program to exchange for the work he's done so far on the identification technology. The designers are coming together tonight to present it to him. On this one thing we agree with the Emporium. Nothing like this technology must ever be allowed to come into use. It's far too dangerous, not only for Unbounded, but for all humanity. We plan to destroy it."

I believed him, and that meant Delia had lied. I wasn't surprised at the lie, but the fact that it had been cloaked in half truths was disconcerting. I met Cort's gaze. "If you didn't tell the Emporium about the safe house or the technology, who did? Because someone had to."

"Only our group and a few key Renegade leaders know the full import of this exchange." Ritter's muscles flexed beneath his T-shirt as though he wanted to punch something. "Stella and I were supposed to brief you and the New York people there, along with the Unbounded delegations who are flying in from Italy and London. They should all be meeting at the safe house within the next hour or so."

Cort paced a few steps. "Ava and Dimitri would sooner die than betray us, and Stella's in New York. We're here. So that leaves only Laurence, and he wouldn't betray us. Besides, he called Ava this morning from Oregon. Maybe it's someone from the New York side."

I shook my head. "No, he's here." Or had been. Hopefully, he and the others had succeeded in making it out of the building.

Ritter frowned, his eyes glittering with suppressed violence. "Who's here?"

"Laurence. He was captured with Chris right after they picked up the kids. But hopefully they're outside by—"

"Wait a minute." Cort shifted his weight, glancing at the door. "Laurence told us he and Chris got the kids to one of our safe houses in Missouri. There's no way they could have been followed to the kids' party. I made sure of that after the attack."

His words were like a punch to my stomach. "Then Lawrence lied." Which could mean Chris and the children hadn't made it to safety after all.

"It's Laurence, then." Ritter's voice was deadly. "That explains a lot."

Had I trusted my brother's life to a traitor?

"We have to get up to the roof and signal Ava," Ritter said. "The sooner we warn New York the better. Too many will be at risk. Everyone was acting like it was an opportunity for a big reunion." There was self-deprecation in the words, as though he blamed himself for the oversight. He eased opened the door a crack and peered out. "Let's go."

"I can't," I said. "Laurence was with Chris and the kids. Keene was supposed to create a distraction and get them out a back exit."

"My brother did that?" Cort sounded doubtful.

I wanted to scream with impatience. "Do you know where that exit is? I have to make sure they got away. Laurence might have betrayed them."

"I know where it is, but the monitors showed a half-dozen armed guards heading that way before I put in the fake feed. They always reinforce the exits when something happens. That's why we chose the roof for our escape. If Keene's not out by now, they won't be getting out."

"Maybe they will with my help."

Ritter grabbed me before I went two steps. "You don't stand a chance."

"I'm not leaving them!"

He thrust a shiny disk into my hand. "Get to the roof. Signal Ava with this. Cort and I will see to your brother."

I shook my head.

"You'd trust your life to me." Ritter's grip on my arm tightened. "Why not your brother's?"

"I'll play the return of the prodigal son, if I have to," Cort added, "and I know my way around."

Ritter nodded. "Besides, if Laurence is still here, we can't allow him to tell them anything more."

I knew what Ritter wasn't saying: Laurence would have to be captured or die. "Fine," I said. "But don't leave Chris and the kids behind."

With a fierce glare, Ritter took weapons from his body, passing them to me—a gun, a knife, a grenade.

A grenade?

I handed him back the grenade. I had no idea how to use it or how far away I'd have to be to survive the blast.

Hesitating only a second, he tucked it back inside his pants.

My face flushed when I saw exactly where. He gave me a flat grin and started down the hall, his body moving like liquid, showing the same ease my new half-brother Jonny had displayed while running. It was all I could do not to stare.

Cort chuckled. "There's a service elevator by the control room, if you can get close enough. Might be easier to get to than the other one. That is, if it doesn't have a hand print lock. I've never used it myself."

"If it does, I have something to take care of it."

"Good. Don't get caught. Wouldn't want to have to save you again." He turned to go after Ritter.

"Cort?"

He stopped. "Yeah?"

"I'm sorry."

"You can make it up to me later." He lifted his brow suggestively.

I laughed. "In your dreams."

"I have pretty good dreams." Grinning, he sprinted after Ritter.

Was he really going to forgive me that easily? Somehow I doubted it.

I tucked the shiny disk Ritter had given me into my shirt, grateful to possess enough bust to secure the compact-sized object. The knife attached rather awkwardly to the fake belt on my stretch suit, but the gun I carried in my hands. What I'd have given for a big pocket.

I moved down the hallway toward the control room with none of Ritter's grace. At least my ankle was stronger. If I hadn't known I was Unbounded, I might have thought I'd imagined the sprain. I had no idea regarding the layout of the area, and my sense of direction had deserted me. How far was the service elevator?

Voices and running footsteps. I dived into a room, Ritter's gun ready in case it was occupied. It wasn't. I listened as the footsteps passed in the hallway. I slipped out and continued my search. I could hear voices now, and I wondered if the Emporium guards had reached the control room. If so, I should be close to the service elevator. I moved softly, glad for the comfortable flats

Justine had supplied with my suit. For once, both practical and attractive.

I found the elevator in a tiny alcove. It was much smaller than the main elevators, and was guarded only by a hand print reader.

I ran toward it, pulling on Keene's glove and pressing it to the panel. The numbers above lit up to show the elevator was on its way. I shut my eyes briefly in relief.

More footsteps. I brought up my gun and squeezed myself against the wall, hoping whoever it was would pass by without noticing me.

"Erin?"

Tom.

I lunged toward him, grabbing his shirt and pulling him farther into the alcove up against the wall, the gun pressed into his neck. Inside, I was shaking, but my gun hand was remarkably steady.

"What are you doing?" Tom didn't fight me, and for that I was glad. I didn't fool myself that I could actually pull the trigger.

A soft ding signaled the arrival of the elevator. I released him. "Get inside."

He obeyed. I punched the fifth floor and breathed a sigh of relief when the door shut without anyone else appearing. Now if I could only make it to the rooftop. But what would I do with Tom?

"I've been looking for you ever since I heard the commotion," Tom said. "Are you all right?"

"What do you care?"

"I care a lot. Look, you were right. These people aren't what they seem. I want to help you."

"You expect me to believe that? After what you gave me in that needle?"

He frowned. "I guess not. But for what it's worth, I thought I was protecting you from the Renegades."

"The Emporium wants to use Chris and the kids to breed more Unbounded. They want to use me. Justine was wrong about everything. They'd never let us be together, not in *your* lifetime." The words made him flinch.

"So we'll get out of here. Go somewhere. Just the two of us." He stepped toward me. "Put down the gun. I'm not the enemy here."

"Turn out your pockets." Holding the gun steady, I patted him down front and back to make sure he wasn't hiding any nasty surprises. He was clean. I relaxed slightly. "I'm going to the roof."

"There'll be guards by the door."

"I'll shoot my way through."

"I want to go with you."

Did I dare trust him?

No. Not without confirmation. I cracked opened my shield, let my thoughts reach out to him. The link wasn't strong enough to tell me much of anything, but the closer we got to the fifth floor, the more afraid I was of Delia finding me. I shoved my hand against his chest, my fingers splayed over his shirt. There, now I could feel his emotions.

He wanted to go with me.

I dropped my hand. "Fine. But if you betray me, I'll shoot you. I swear it."

He blinked and I felt sorrow emanating from him before I shut my mind. I told myself I didn't care about his sorrow. He was too weak and pliable, and I didn't want him back. Still, it hurt.

The elevator arrived, and I indicated for him to go first. No way would I turn my back on him.

He looked out. "No one's here. But it's a little alcove like downstairs so they might be out in the main hall."

We exited the elevator, and I cringed at the sound it made as it shut.

"I'm not sure how far the roof stairs are from here," Tom said.

"They were around the bend from the main elevator."

He pointed right. "That way, then."

Because his assumption matched my own, I nodded. No one was in the main hallway either, but we couldn't see around the next bend. I felt a tremor of fear. Was Delia nearby? Why was I so afraid of her? Or did I simply dread going to the roof?

Why did it have to be the roof?

"Go slowly," I warned Tom. My fingers holding the gun began to feel cramped and I loosened my grip slightly.

"They must have all gone to the genetics lab. A fire broke out there a little while ago. It spread to one of the nurseries above the lab."

Keene had been more efficient than I'd imagined. "Maybe that means we'll get lucky."

"Why the roof anyway? Shouldn't we try to get out downstairs?"

"Wait and see." My trust didn't extend far enough to confide in him. The only reason I didn't crack him over the head and leave him in the elevator was the fear that I'd be discovered more quickly. It wasn't because of our shared past.

Maybe.

We had arrived at a bend in the hallway. Tom peered around it, pulling back quickly. "I can see the door to the roof stairs, but two guards are in front of it. There's another turn in the hallway after that. I can't see what's there."

So much for luck.

Keeping space between us in case he acted against me, I peeked around the corner at the guards. Both were Unbounded. "If I don't get them, you hit them with this when they come around the corner," I told Tom, tossing him Ritter's knife, still in the scabbard. "Don't worry—they won't really die." I wondered if he heard the tremor in my voice. I desperately wished Ritter, or even Cort were with us. At least the gun Ritter had given me had a silencer, so we wouldn't alert any other guards who might be around that other bend.

Tom nodded curtly.

When he didn't try to attack me, I relaxed slightly and stepped into view. My first bullet slammed into the torso of a guard. He roared with pain but lunged toward us, his partner close behind. I fired a second shot, hitting the first Unbounded again—this time in the head. He went down. Horror washed over me, though I knew he'd survive.

My breath came fast. My pulse thundered in my ears. I fired once more, hitting the second guard in the chest. Before I could get off another shot, Tom dived for him. What if I shot Tom instead? It wasn't as if he'd have another chance to live.

The Unbounded heaved Tom against the wall with a loud crash. I pulled the trigger and the man fell.

Tom staggered toward me. "Are you sure he isn't dead?"

"Yes. Come on. We have to hurry." We ran. I felt sure we were going to make it.

When we were two feet from the door to the roof stairs, Delia rounded the far bend in the hallway— flanked by five Unbounded, all armed with machine guns.

She gave me a cold, triumphant smile. "Put down your weapons."

CHAPTER 20

WHEN I HESITATED IN GIVING UP RITTER'S GUN, DELIA GESTURED to Tom. "Do you really want to sacrifice his life? He means nothing to me, and his fool of a sister isn't here to protect him."

I laid down the pistol, but I didn't hand over the shiny compact. If they wanted that, they'd have to find it themselves. Thankfully, my snug outfit left little room for hiding weapons, and they didn't deem a pat-down necessary. Tom set down his knife, slightly streaked with blood, hopefully the guard's.

"Good choice," Delia said, her voice disdainful all the same. "But know that you will pay for what you've done. I don't know how you managed to start the fire or tamper with our equipment, but I *will* discover how. I will also find your brother and his children. They can't have gone far."

I struggled not to show the hope that flooded through me. Delia didn't know about Cort and Ritter, and for the moment, Chris still had a chance. I sent a silent thank-you to Keene, wherever he was.

Delia's eyes flicked to the Unbounded nearest her, a solid blonde with close-set eyes. "Put them in the conference room."

Surprise lit the woman's eyes. "Are you sure?"

Delia's mouth curved in a smile. "I'm sure Erin will enjoy the company."

I wasn't as sure as she was, but I was relieved she wasn't going to try to sense from me where Chris was. A good thing for her because I wouldn't have let her in easily. I'd shoot myself before I'd let her know Ritter and Cort were here.

The conference room was only a few steps down the hall through a set of double doors. Inside, a large oval table made of beautiful carved cherry was outlined by floor-to-ceiling windows like those in Delia's suite.

None of this held my attention. The only occupant of the room stood up from the table as we were thrust inside. He had a bleeding cut on his face, and a large patch of blood spilled over the left side of his chest, staining his white polo. I glared at him, but he met my gaze without flinching.

Laurence.

"Traitor!" I barked as the door closed.

Laurence sagged into one of the high-backed chairs. "How did you know?"

"Does it matter? All this time, I thought it was Cort, but it was you! *You're* the reason my brother and his children were captured. *You're* the reason our people are going to die today. The reason Stella's going to die! How could you do that to her? To any of us?"

"For the greater good." His voice was dull and lifeless. "It was the hardest decision I've ever made."

"You expect me to believe that? How many others have you murdered?"

"None. I swear! This is the first time I've ever given the Emporium information." He looked up at me where I stood over him, his eyes sincere and pleading.

I was trying not to cry, but I felt his betrayal deeply. I'd trusted Laurence. We'd had a connection from that first moment we'd met. It had been us against the rest in a playful but meaningful way.

"What about Chris?"

"He's fine. The kids, too. Probably out by now."

Could I believe him?

"Erin," Tom tried to touch my shoulder, but I shrugged him off. He walked around the table and sat watching us.

"Coming here—it was the only thing I could do," Laurence said. "Please believe me—I did it for you, and for all Unbounded."

"How can you think murdering Renegades will help Unbounded?"

He was slow in answering. "The Emporium has resources. With their background into genetics, I'm sure my virus will be ready soon."

"What virus?" Tom asked.

Laurence didn't even look at him but kept his pleading gaze on me. "I'm further along in my research than I led you to believe. There's this virus, you see. It—it only affects Unbounded."

Goose bumps broke out over my skin. "It makes them age normally?"

"Not exactly. It kills the active Unbounded gene once it matures. It's not quite finished, but I'm close. I just need to figure out a way to speed up the process so it'll get all the genes before the body regenerates them."

I didn't know much about genetics, but killing genes didn't sound healthy. "Wouldn't that hurt the Unbounded?"

He hesitated. "Yes."

"You mean we'd all be dead."

Laurence nodded. "The madness would be over."

"You're crazy!" I backed a step away from him, not hiding my horror. No wonder he hadn't cared about giving the addresses of the safe house. No wonder Stella's life hadn't been important. He planned on killing all Unbounded anyway. "That stuff you talked about downstairs—eliminating the Unbounded gene in future generations. That was all talk, wasn't it? A smokescreen for this virus. For murder!"

He stood up from the table, a flush of color coming to his face. "It's protecting humans! It's making sure no one ever again has to endure what we've endured. You've seen how much Stella suffers with Bronson. I know how she feels losing a mortal loved one—and we've lost too many Unbounded in these senseless battles for power." His voice was gruff and without even trying I sensed the pain in his mind. So much heartache and loss. But I'd been right about the madness, too. He was unbalanced.

Could I make him see reason? "Even if you can get it to work. The Unbounded gene may not show up for generations."

"That is a problem. The gene doesn't mutate into anything we can recognize until adulthood, but I believe I can make regular humans carriers. It won't affect anyone until the gene actually mutates."

"So someone would simply get sick and die? For no reason at all?" I could envision parents mourning children, and children their parents. Kindergarten teachers not finishing out the school year. A best friend at graveside services. All without explanation.

"We have unexpected deaths occurring all the time, so a few more in the beginning won't be too unusual." Laurence's anger had died and now his expression begged me to understand. "After six or seven generations, the gene should be gone from the human population, except for the occasional throwback. I won't take the virus myself until I'm sure it's working the way it should."

I put my hand on his arm. "Laurence, listen to what you're saying. I can't believe you're actually considering this. We may be a tiny minority, but it's still genocide."

Though he towered over me, his bulky figure looked small and withdrawn. "Don't look at it that way. Look at it as righting whatever wrong nature created. And you can help me, Erin. You probably have a talent for medicine, since Stefan isn't really your father. This will be our gift to mankind."

I stared at him. "What? Stefan's not my father?"

His expression was half a wince, half apology. "They were too late getting back from the Emporium genetics lab. Ritter and Cort hurried to the clinic but by the time they arrived, the procedure had already taken place."

I'd thought things couldn't get worse. I was wrong. Very wrong. "Are you saying *you're* my father?"

Laurence shook his head. "Dimitri is. You're my fourth great-aunt, practically my sister in Unbounded terms."

Dimitri? My father?

"Don't be upset," Laurence went on. "Only Ava, Dimitri, and I know what happened that day, and we never told anyone else. I was posing as a nurse at the clinic to help everything along. I tried to get your mother to wait, but she was impatient. Dimitri did what he had to do."

"You're lying!" Fury whipped through me. I took a step forward, reaching to place my hand on his arm. For a moment he was puzzled, but then understanding filled his eyes. Backing away from me, he hit a chair, which in turn pushed up against the table with a thump. My fingers touched his flesh. He put up a mental barrier, but it was a weak, hastily made thing, and I tossed it aside as though it were nothing more than tissue paper.

Perhaps I'd learned more from Delia than I realized.

In seconds I had my answer. Laurence was telling the truth. Dimitri was my father. I felt too stunned to react, though a part of me was relieved that Stefan and I weren't related after all.

Laurence laid his hand over mine where it rested on his arm. "I'll make sure you're okay, Erin. I'll take care of you. You won't die. You can watch and wait with me."

I jerked my hand from his and took two steps back. "You're no relative of mine, and no credit to Dimitri. He would never sacrifice his people because he's too weak to endure a little pain."

Laurence's bloated face darkened, and his voice rose in defense. "I watched my children die!"

"What about your little girl? Are you ready to kill her, too? Or her children?"

"It's better than seeing them cut into pieces. Or watching them mourn *their* children. It isn't natural." He squared his shoulders. "Someone has to put a stop to it."

He was a monster. "You have no right to play God!" I shouted.

"Why not? That's practically what we are." He gave a short, mirthless laugh. "Think of it. I'm killing gods to protect mankind. What irony."

I snorted. "Do you really think the Emporium is going to sit back and let you kill them? As soon as they realize what you're really doing, if they haven't already, they'll take your virus and use it against any Unbounded who doesn't serve them. Make no mistake, Laurence, the Renegades are the only ones who'll die from your virus. Except for you." My voice was calmer now, though inside my thoughts still churned erratically. "The Emporium will kill you the minute they have what they need, and then the world will see what true suffering is. The Emporium is using you like they do everyone. If I can break through to your mind, you can bet Delia Vesey already has."

His flaccid cheeks paled as understanding fell over him. He slumped back into his chair. "Oh, God," he whispered. "What have I done?"

God didn't answer.

I stalked to the window to prevent myself from venting more anger. He was a beaten, broken, sad man, and nothing I could fling at him would change the situation. I had to focus on how I could warn the Renegades.

Later I would deal with my parentage—if I survived long enough.

"I'm sorry," Tom said softly, coming up behind me. "You must feel like a yo-yo, bouncing around from one father to the next. Unfortunately, I know exactly how you feel, finding out your entire life is a lie."

I managed a bitter half smile. "You can't begin to know how relieved I am that I don't share any blood with Stefan." I was tempted to tell him that Justine was his mother, but I couldn't do it. Not yet. "We have to do something," I said instead.

"It'll be okay. Let's just wait."

"How can you say that?" He either had no clue of what was really going on, or he wanted the Emporium to succeed. Was that why he seemed so different to me? Was he hiding something? Maybe he was giving me only partial truths like Delia. Could I even trust my senses?

Tom opened his mouth to reply, but the sounds of a scuffle outside in the hall drew our attention. The door opened and Ritter was flung into the room, landing in a beaten, bloody mess on the carpet.

I ran to his side, but he was already pushing to his feet. "Chris?" I asked.

"Thanks, I'm okay."

"I can see that much." I wondered how many Emporium Unbounded he'd dispatched before they'd overwhelmed him with sheer numbers. "What about my brother?"

"He and the kids got out."

"And Cort?"

"I left him talking to his brother."

So Keene hadn't escaped with Chris. I wondered what kind of repercussions he might suffer because of us.

"Cort was planning to look for Laurence." Ritter's gaze went over my shoulder to where Laurence sat slumped at the table, apparently unseeing. "Looks like I beat him to it." Rage filled his voice. "I'm going to enjoy this."

"Forget Laurence," I said. "We have to find a way out of here." Our imprisonment was my fault. If I'd been able to trust Keene instead of sending Ritter after him, we might be on the roof right now with Cort. "Do you have any weapons left?" My eyes ran over his body, pausing on his pants. Given the heroic proportions, I was pretty sure something there didn't belong.

"They were thorough." He rubbed his hand over his chest and waist and hips, feeling for weapons.

"What's that?" I pointed.

His hands stopped, his eyes locking onto mine. A flare of emotion that battered against even my reinforced walls. "Well, gee, Erin," he drawled, "You want me to show you? Right here? Now? I'm not at all sure this is the right time, but if you insist."

I rolled my eyes. "I mean the grenade. You still have it, don't you?"

He brought it out and set it in my hand. "Fools them every time." The weapon was warm from his body and oddly reassuring.

"Isn't that too dangerous to use in here?" Tom had come up behind us, and I wondered how much he'd heard. The men stared at each other. Tom's eyes were hard and accusing, Ritter's like icy granite. Tom's boy-next-door good looks paled considerably next to Ritter's smoldering danger.

"Lover boy's right," Ritter said finally. "This would probably sever all three focus points."

"What does that mean?" Tom said. "I thought you were immortal."

"It would kill even us," I translated. "All of us. But maybe if we tipped over the table and dragged it to the other side, away from the glass, and put the curtains over us. Might give us enough protection."

Ritter shook his head. "The blast might still kill us. It's too close." He jerked his head at Tom. "He would die for sure." His eyes went to Laurence, glittering with intent. "Now if you'll excuse me, I want a word with my good friend over there."

The idea of him dismembering Laurence with his bare hands horrified me, and I hurried after him. "What are you going to do?"

No answer. I'd have better luck talking to an enraged bear.

Laurence had dragged himself from wherever his mind had gone and stood awaiting us. "I'll do it," he said. "Give me the grenade. I'll get them to let me out and explode it down the hall."

"No way," Ritter and I said together.

Laurence grabbed my hand. Ritter tensed, his arm flexing for a punch, but I held up my other hand. "Wait."

With a scowl, Ritter lowered his arm, the muscles in his body still taut, ready to move.

"I want to end the Unbounded gene," Laurence said, "but I don't want the Emporium to take over the world. You can trust me on this. Just like you did when I promised to help Chris and the kids get away. I took this for them." He pulled down the neck of his polo to reveal a congealed bullet wound.

He was still holding my hand, and I could sense the truth. Gratitude rushed through me, though I fought the feeling. Laurence met my gaze. "I swear to you that I want your brother and his kids to live a life where they won't be hunted. They are not the issue here."

"Then you shouldn't have allowed the Emporium to bring them here. Everything you stand for is wrong. Everything."

"Maybe. But I'm the only chance you guys have of getting out of here. Look into my mind, if you don't believe me."

I extended my thoughts, searching for hidden deceit. There seemed to be none, but what if the madness kicked in again? What if he'd had time to hide certain thoughts behind a barrier I couldn't detect?

I glanced at Ritter, whose eyes rested not on Laurence but on me. He seemed to be considering Laurence's offer. Of course he was. What other choice did we have? Short of ripping a leg from the table and using it to punch a hole through the wall—an act that would surely draw attention—we were stuck. Maybe if we had climbing skills, we could miraculously break what was probably bulletproof glass and climb five stories down to the street, dodging bullets from upset Emporium Unbounded along the way. For all I knew, Ritter was capable of doing just that. But I certainly wasn't. Neither could I sentence Tom to certain and final death by exploding the grenade in this room.

"Give me the grenade," Laurence said, "while you still have the chance of completing whatever escape Ritter has planned."

I shook my head.

Ritter's hands closed around mine. He took the grenade and gave it to Laurence. "If this is just a ploy to get away from me," he growled. "Know that regardless of what happens today, I won't rest until I hunt you down. You will never get near a lab again."

Laurence stared at Ritter for a long moment. Then he nodded slowly. "I wouldn't expect any less."

"This isn't a good idea," Tom said. "Let's wait. Maybe we can work it out with my sister."

Ritter turned on him. "There's no working it out with the Emporium. It is either kill or be killed. Now go pull down those curtains."

Tom glared at Ritter. "I know what you really want. You'll never have her."

A flash of the woman in the blue dress took me by surprise, but by the time I realized what it was, the vision was gone and Ritter's mind had returned to blankness.

"You don't know anything about what I want," Ritter spat. The bitterness in his voice was nothing compared to the hate I'd glimpsed in his mind. He turned his fiery gaze to me. "Let's get the table in place."

Laurence hadn't moved. He held my gaze, waiting. I turned away.

"Erin," he said.

I looked at him, arching a brow.

"If I don't make it out of here, if there's not enough of me left to regenerate . . . My wife. Will you tell her?"

I nodded. "Of course." I wouldn't give him absolution, but this I could do.

Tucking the grenade into his pocket, Laurence strode to the door.

"Walk a little ahead of them," I called after him. "Maybe you can sprint to the elevator and throw it behind you at the last moment."

His mouth curved in a smile. "I haven't sprinted in sixty years."

"I don't know. You ran pretty well downstairs."

Ritter gave no advice, and I knew Laurence had destroyed any measure of trust that had been between them. He was probably already having second thoughts about giving Laurence the grenade, but he was risking it for me, just as I was for Tom.

Laurence pounded on the door. Seconds later, the face of an Unbounded guard appeared in the doorway. "I have to talk to

Delia," Laurence said. "I've learned something from these people. It's vital that I see her now."

"Can't it wait? She's kind of busy."

"If you don't let me out, they're going to tear me to pieces with their bare hands, and I'll never be able to give her the information or work in your lab. Delia should know better than to put this killer in here with me. He knows I betrayed them."

The Unbounded relayed the information into his radio and then nodded. "Come on, then. I'll take you to her. She's down on main."

One of the guards went with him, leaving only one outside our door. Probably there were more near the elevator and stairs to the roof. Laurence would have to time this just right. Close enough to the elevator to involve the guards, but not too far away from this room so the explosion would set us free.

I reached out to him, but the few emotions I sensed faded quickly as the space between us grew. I hit the wall in frustration. Some talent this was.

"Get behind the table." Ritter pushed me in the right direction.

"We shouldn't have trusted him," I said. "He's just going to turn it over to her."

"Give it a moment." He and Tom pulled the curtain over our heads and shoulders.

No sooner had we squatted behind the table than an explosion rocked the entire building.

CHAPTER 21

THE FAR WALL BURST OPEN, BECOMING A MASS OF SMOKE AND DEBRIS. To our left, the glass in the windows shattered, pelting us with razor-sharp pieces that sliced through the curtains.

I felt a numb sort of surprise. *He really did it.*

"Hurry." Ritter shoved off the curtains, sending a shower of tinkling glass to the floor.

We stood and ran, crunching through the glass and rubble, the countless tiny cuts on my bare arms causing far more pain than I expected. Tiny wells of blood oozed and smeared from the wounds. We climbed through the new opening in the wall, and for a moment stood looking around, stunned at the devastation. Debris lay everywhere. Dust filled the air. I saw several unrecognizable body parts, mounds of tissue, blood dripping into the rubble. Overhead we could see the sky.

Where was Laurence? Could I find his remains? Were two of his focus parts still intact? Viewing the blood and carnage, it didn't seem possible, but even if I had stomach for the job, there was no time to search for him. The explosion would signal every Unbounded in the building, not to mention the local authorities.

I gagged on the sharp coppery smell of blood, knowing that if I stayed another minute I was going to be incapacitated for a long time while my stomach rebelled. *Goodbye, Laurence,* I thought. My brother, both martyr and would-be murderer.

"Which way?" Ritter asked.

Clenching my jaw, I held my breath and pointed. We dragged through the wreckage, moving or climbing over chunks of drywall and cement. Tom stumbled behind us. The door to the roof was missing and part of the wall, but the stairs were passable.

No one was on the roof, and the calm blue sky denied the horrors we'd witnessed. The only visible sign of the explosion was a gaping hole where the roof was simply gone. A large cloud from the debris floated up on the light breeze, vanishing almost instantly, though farther above us, a larger, thicker cloud from the initial explosion remained partially intact.

The openness of the roof, the gaping hole, the buildings stretching in every direction—it all bore down on me. I felt exposed and fragile and dizzy. *Crap, not now,* I thought. Of all the escape plans, we had to choose someplace up high. But maybe the vertigo and nausea wouldn't get any worse if I didn't make any sudden movements.

"Where's the signal?" Ritter asked.

I fumbled in my bra for the shiny disk.

"Need help?" Ritter asked with a smirk.

I gave him my best sneer and tossed it to him. "I have no idea how to use this."

"There are instructions printed right on it, but basically, you slap it hard against your hand." He demonstrated.

The next second, the disk emitted a powerful burst of light that nearly left me blind. Nausea flooded me. *Great.* I fought the urge to cringe and close my eyes. The disk throbbed again, and Ritter set it on the roof and backed away.

"Bright," Tom said, squinting. "But I don't see how anyone will see it in daylight."

"They'll see—" Ritter's voice was cut off as a blur slammed into him, knocking him to the ground. The blur became Jonny. Both men jumped to their feet, Jonny bringing up a gun.

"Jonny, no!" I said. "Please leave us alone. Just walk away."

Jonny shook his head, the wisps of blond hair moving in the breeze. "Stefan wouldn't be happy." He motioned to the door leading to the stairs. "Let's go inside, or I'll shoot both of you." When we didn't move, he shifted the gun to Tom. "Or should I shoot the mortal instead?"

I felt a fleeting disgust that Tom was so weak. A liability. No, it wasn't his fault. That was Emporium thinking.

Ritter kicked at Jonny's hand so fast, I barely saw him move. A bullet ricocheted off the rooftop. Smiling with grim satisfaction, Ritter sent a blow toward Jonny's head. Jonny blocked the move, jabbing his own foot into Ritter's middle. Ritter danced to the side, deflecting most of the strike. His muscular frame made Jonny seem fragile. His next blow sent Jonny halfway across the roof. Ritter dived toward him. They tangled together, rolled, and then Jonny was on his feet, streaking toward the stairs.

Ritter was right behind him. "Get on the chopper," he shouted. "I'm going to make sure he doesn't alert anyone." He reached Jonny, and in a flurry of limbs, they disappeared down the stairs together.

I could already hear helicopter blades beating in the distance. *Hurry,* I thought to both Ava and Ritter, though I knew they couldn't hear me. My nausea and vertigo had increased to the point that it was all I could do not to curl up in a ball and whimper.

Tom crossed the roof and picked up something. Jonny's gun.

"Good idea," I said. "We might need it." I could see the helicopter now, though looking at it made me dizzy. I hoped there was enough room for it to land. "Can you help me over there?"

Tom shifted the gun toward me. "I'm sorry. You're not going anywhere."

I gazed at him blankly, my fear of heights impeding my understanding. At last the meaning sank through. "You never planned to come with me at all."

"I may not live for thousands of years, but I can make something of myself here. These people have power, and I can be something. I can help them create another world. This is where I belong, where we both belong."

"You sound like Justine." I shook my head. "And that means I never really meant anything to you, except as something to use."

"That's not true. I love you. I wanted to make sure you were okay. That's why I agreed to come looking for you when Delia asked."

So that's how he'd found me. There'd been no accidental meeting. Delia must have sensed my general whereabouts when I'd let down my shield to examine Cort, and then sent Tom to find me. She'd likely been tracking him the entire time. And me through him.

"So you were keeping an eye on me until she found us." How strong the woman was if she'd made me believe Tom wanted to come with me.

"Haven't I always tried to take care of you?" His smile was gentle, his voice sincere.

To think that I'd once admired how careful he'd been of me. "People are going to die if I don't warn them." They'd cut them up into pieces like the woman in the blue dress.

"Not *our* people."

He was just like them. All of them. Tears came and I blinked them away.

"Go ahead. Shoot me, if you want. I'm leaving." I took a step toward where I thought the helicopter might land, a few small pebbles skidding away from my feet.

Tom laughed. "You can barely move, much less get to that chopper. Don't worry—this gun isn't for you. It's only in case your friend returns."

"Go to hell."

"Are you sleeping with him?" Tom moved closer. "Tell me, is it better with an Unbounded?"

I didn't answer. Would it be possible for me to distract him long enough to get his gun, maybe push him off the roof? My stomach revolted at the idea. Still I had to try something, even if we both went over the side together.

"He may be more experienced than I am with women, given how old he is," Tom continued, "but don't get your hopes up. He's a monster, incapable of love. Justine told me all about him. She was there that day when his family died. She almost got him."

Ritter didn't know that or Justine wouldn't still be alive.

"She's the real monster." I glared at him, my thoughts traversing the space between us. I might not be able to attack him physically, but what about distracting him with my sensing ability? I wasn't touching Tom, but all I needed was enough of a surprise to allow me to grab the gun.

I pushed at him mentally and came up with . . . nothing. What?

I tried again, pushing until my head threatened to burst apart. Still nothing.

He wouldn't have had time to learn to use a mental shield, or at least not one that strong, but there *was* something covering his real thoughts—something that had Delia written all over it. She'd tricked me. They both had. I wanted to crush him, hurt him as he had me, but I was powerless against whatever Delia had set in his mind. There was no chance of pushing in a suggestion, no glimpse of wavering to exploit, no chance of reaching the part of him that might really care for me.

"Walk toward the stairs," Tom said, his voice soft and reasonable, as though asking me if I wanted sugar with my tea.

Only seconds to decide what to do, and then I'd most likely end up with another bullet in some hurtful place in my body. I glanced toward the helicopter, now hovering above us. Where was Ritter?

Another wave of vertigo that sent a dozen frogs banging around inside my stomach. I was going to fall and keep falling forever. I sagged to my knees, gagging. Some Unbounded I was.

"Up. We don't have time for this!" Frustration laced Tom's voice.

I slumped into a miserable heap. If he wanted me, he'd have to carry me.

He hesitated a few seconds before placing the gun in his waistband. As he bent to pick me up, I tucked my head and rammed my shoulder into him. We tumbled and this time when we came up, I held the gun.

"Get out of here," I gritted.

Tom laughed. "Darling, you aren't going to shoot me. You love me. Remember all the time we've spent together? I know what you like. We're so good, you and I." His voice had become husky, promising. I focused on his face, knowing that if I saw the sky and buildings around us, I was going to puke.

"Stop." My hand holding the gun wavered.

He took another step.

"Please." I couldn't let him take me. I couldn't let Delia control my mind or permit the Emporium to use my body. It was him or me—and since I couldn't remove myself from their hands by means of a simple gunshot, I had to remove or incapacitate him.

His hands reached out. Another spell of dizziness took me.

The gun kicked in my hand. I'd been aiming for his shoulder, but vertigo had the last say. A hole appeared on the right side of his forehead, bits of tissue and blood spurting out onto the roof behind him. He crumbled backward.

"No!" I cried.

It seemed to take forever to crawl to his side, as though the entire world had slowed down. My body shook so badly that my arms gave out twice, and I scraped my cheek against the rooftop. I pulled myself forward. Blood gushed from Tom's wound, slashing across his forehead and streaming into his brown hair. More blood puddled on the cement under his head.

"Tom?" I touched him, hoping to sense him, but there was nothing. His mind was gone. Bile rose in my throat. What had I done? Tears wet my cheeks. I shut my eyes and wrapped my arms around myself, face pressed to my knees.

After several long moments, I became aware of the whirring

blades of the helicopter. I didn't know how I could possibly move toward it, but somehow I had to. Stella and the Renegades depended on me.

Biting my lip, I forced myself to a crouch. *Just stare at the rooftop,* I told myself. One step at a time. *Don't think about Tom.* A wave of nausea crashed down, and it was all I could do to keep my feet beneath me.

Ritter appeared at my side. He took in Tom's lifeless body and the gun in my hand with one glance. Peeling my fingers from the weapon, he put his arm around me and pushed me forward, carrying more of my weight than I was. "That kid was too fast for me to catch. He'll have the others here soon."

"What about Cort?" I asked in a strangled voice I didn't recognize. "We can't leave without him."

"The place is crawling with Unbounded. Cort will have to make it without us."

"But Delia. She'll see into his mind."

"No. He's strong enough to keep her out. Don't worry about him now."

A rope ladder with metal rungs fell from the helicopter overhead, the bottom rung clanging onto the rooftop. Panic swept through me. Wasn't it going to land? No way could I climb that ladder. Ritter might as well throw me off the roof and hope I survived.

Ritter glanced over his shoulder. "We're out of time," he yelled in my ear. "Climb!"

A shot whizzed by so close, I felt the air against my cheek. That was enough to unfreeze my limbs. Grasping the rungs tightly, I began to climb.

CHAPTER 22

I WANTED TO WRAP MY ARMS BETWEEN THE RUNGS, CLOSE MY EYES, and scream until I was rescued or unconscious, but Ritter kept pushing me from below. Only the idea of leaving him exposed to Emporium bullets kept me climbing. My breath was coming in rapid bursts, like the irrational fear inside my brain. Each second was an eternity. I made the mistake of looking down and saw Emporium Unbounded disgorging from the roof door, like ants from a hole in the ground.

Swallowing bile, I forced myself to take the next step. As I finally pulled myself inside, the helicopter rose abruptly, sprawling me onto the hard floor of what appeared to be a cargo area. Ava sat in one of the two seats at the front, her face a mask of concentration. The other seat was empty.

I looked outside for Ritter and saw people shooting at us from the rooftop. My eyes swept past them all, riveting on Tom's lifeless body. Fresh tears wet my cheeks before vertigo wiped the scene from my mind. I gagged and shut my eyes, gripping the metal bars under the empty front seat. Loud pings sounded as bullets battered the underside of the helicopter.

Help him! Ava's urgent voice said inside my head.

Digging my teeth into my bottom lip, I crawled back to the opening. Ritter had almost made it, but even as I watched, his body jerked once, twice. One hand came off the rungs.

"No!" Holding onto the edge of the opening with one hand, I leaned down and reached out to him. "Climb!" I screamed, both aloud and in my head. His eyes met mine as I tried to hold the dizziness at bay. *"Climb!"*

Ritter managed to grab the next rung. Slowly, he continued the climb. Finally, he was within reach, and I dragged him inside with strength founded in desperation. We crumpled in a tangled heap. The bright, coppery smell of blood filled my nose.

The helicopter veered violently, followed by a huge explosion off to our right. *Missed,* I thought, fighting the urge to vomit.

I could feel Ritter's heartbeat, his relief, echoes of the fear he'd experienced—mainly for me.

For me.

If I hadn't been so utterly exhausted, I might have smiled or said something sarcastic. If I hadn't been mourning Cort, Laurence, and even Tom.

"Thanks," Ritter whispered.

I couldn't hear him over the noise of the chopper, but I could see his mouth form the word, sense the feeling in his mind. For that brief instant nothing more was necessary.

I wanted to lie on the floor next to him forever, but he was already moving away, pulling himself into the passenger seat next to Ava. Four holes in his pants poured blood, darkening the black material. He put on headphones and began talking to Ava.

Images came to me: landing, a safe house, a cell phone. All of us knew that time was ticking away. Justine and Stefan had two hours on us, maybe more, and though they couldn't have arrived in New York yet, they had likely called in reinforcements who might already be in the city. Once they received word that we were onto them, they would step up proceedings and our allies would begin dying. The faster we landed, the faster we could warn someone. Even then we probably couldn't save all the Unbounded gathering at the safe house. I could only hope one of those we saved was Stella.

Cort. The images of him in Ava and Ritter's minds burned most brightly of all. They were worried about him. I was too. But we could do nothing for him at the moment except pray that his cover held. That he was strong enough to hold Delia from his thoughts.

I looked out of the chopper. The Emporium building was far in the distance, but I could still imagine Tom's body lying there.

He deserved it, I thought. *He made a choice.*

Maybe if I said it enough, I'd believe it.

What would Justine do when she returned and learned of his death? Tom had been her only weakness, the tiny bit of good left in her that I could see. I'd killed him, and she would never forgive me.

Which was fine; I didn't think I'd ever forgive myself. Worse, I knew if I had it all to do over, I would make the same choice.

Ava began calling the instant we landed, even while the chopper blades were still slowing. Marco from our security detail helped Ritter to a waiting rental car. I followed, my sickness completely gone now that we were on solid ground.

"What's going on?" Ava demanded into the phone. Her face paled as she listened for a long while. "What about Stella? Okay, let me know when you hear something. Look, Tenika, don't use any of your usual places. We'll be there as soon as we can. We've had some problems ourselves. Can you contact John Halden and delay the exchange? We'll need to convince him to move the location as well. I know your hypnosuggestion doesn't work as well over the phone, but do what you can. No, I can't call—he suspects me. But if the Emporium had access to the safe house and our people, I'm one hundred percent sure they'll be staking out his warehouse, and we don't want another blood bath. No, don't even hint why we want a change. That man's more paranoid than we are or he wouldn't still be alive. Make up something. If you have any problems, call me. I'll let you know what our plans are as soon as they're in place."

She hung up and gazed into space, her face tight.

"What happened?" Ritter asked from the backseat of the car where he and Marco were busy bandaging his injuries. I caught myself staring at his legs and the black boxer briefs that were so tight they defined every curve.

"Ava?" Ritter said a little louder. "What's going on?"

"Oh, sorry." Ava gave her head a shake. "The safe house was attacked fifteen minutes ago by a large force of Emporium Unbounded. At least twenty of our people were killed, including Shaddock." She glanced at me. "He was their leader. The fighting was over in a matter of minutes, but Tenika and some others escaped. She thinks they kept a few prisoners alive, but they killed everyone else."

"You mean really killed?" I grimaced as Marco, kneeling by the open car door, extracted a bullet from Ritter's leg with oversized tweezers. Ritter's face was white and his teeth clenched, but he didn't utter a sound. I'd seen Marco give him a shot of anesthesia and could only hope there'd been enough time for it to take at least partial effect.

Ava nodded. "They shot the mortals, but all the Unbounded they found in the safe house were cut."

I felt sick. "Then that means . . ." I couldn't finish. If only the Unbounded had been slaughtered, that meant someone like me had been there, someone who could tell Unbounded from mortals at a glance.

Ava nodded. "Our people are trained not to divulge information, but depending upon the strength of the sensing Unbounded the Emporium obviously brought with them, those they captured might break during examination or torture. We have to assume they know where the exchange was to have taken place, and we'll have to abandon all our safe houses for the time being."

"What about Stella?" I had no idea if she'd kept our original flight to New York, or if that had been delayed when I'd gone missing.

Ritter and Marco both paused in their ministration of Ritter's wounds, awaiting the answer. Ritter caught me staring and gave me a nod that made my heart jump a little.

I am so in trouble, I thought.

"No word yet." Ava's face showed no emotion, but her voice betrayed her concern. "But she's not among the victims. I'm betting your escape forced the Emporium to attack early, so some of the Renegades hadn't arrived yet, Stella and Gaven included. However, their flight touched down an hour ago and she still hasn't checked in. Our friends don't know if they arrived during the fight and were captured, or if they got away and are hiding out somewhere until we regroup."

At least Stella might still be alive, and Gaven as well. I remembered him from the mortal security force, the thin black man with rope-like muscles that stood out under the skin. I was glad Stella wasn't alone even if he wasn't Unbounded.

"She's resourceful," Ritter said as Marco took a needle from the suitcase of medical supplies and began injecting the area around one of his wounds with a yellow substance. Curequick, I assumed. Marco had a heavy hand, but Ritter didn't even flinch, so either the anesthesia was working well, or he was as tough as I thought.

"Unfortunately, they don't have enough manpower to search for her," Ava said. "But Tenika will try to change the meeting time with Halden. Anyway we look at this, it isn't going to be easy. The Emporium wants that technology as desperately as we do."

Ritter shifted so Marco could tend to a wound on the side of his leg. "If they don't have anything to offer, Halden won't deal with them."

"They could always kill him," Ava said.

Ritter nodded. "That would be a real tragedy. All this time protecting him and then we cause his death."

"Not us," I said. "Laurence."

Ava nodded solemnly. "The good news is that the attack in New York was put together hastily, and we had a lot of survivors.

The group from Italy hasn't even arrived, so they missed the attack altogether."

"We need to get there soon." Ritter finished taping a wound and passed the tape to Marco so he could wrap the last one.

"We have a plane," Ava said, staring at her cell phone. "We just need a pilot. I'll check into that now."

"You flew the helicopter." I looked over to where the rented chopper had been pulled next to a huge hanger. Someone was examining the bullet holes and dents on the bottom, and I wondered if they would ask about them.

"You learn a few things after three hundred years," Ava said. "Flying a helicopter is one thing—a plane is quite another. Cort flew us here. Dimitri could do it, too, but even Ritter here hasn't gotten around to learning how to fly my plane."

"How hard can it be?" Ritter asked.

"No way." I was relieved to have a problem to focus on, especially one that coincided with my secret worries about my brother. "I've flown many times, and even had a few lessons, but you're talking about crossing the entire continent. For that we need a real pilot. We need Chris. You said he got out, but where'd he go? Did Keene say?"

Ritter shrugged. "He said you'd know how to find them."

The surge of hope building inside me crashed. "I have no idea what he's talking about."

"Think," Ava said.

They looked at me expectantly, while I racked my brains. During my conversations with Keene, had he mentioned a place here in LA? Or had I? Nothing came to mind.

"Erin."

I looked up to see Ava holding out her hand. I knew what she wanted, and I felt some gratitude that she was at least asking permission. Placing my hand in hers, I thought back through all my meetings with Keene, feeling uncomfortable when we got to the part in the elevator when he'd kissed me. At least it had been an honest kiss.

She dropped my hand and shook her head. "Nothing."

"Wait." I held up a finger as I searched my memory again. For some reason I kept going back to how Keene hadn't exposed me when he'd discovered I'd removed the tracking device. "Do you have something with you that can track that chip you put in me?"

"Yes, it's right here." Ava opened the pack she carried from the chopper and withdrew a piece of equipment the size of a laptop. "But your chip stopped transmitting this morning, probably when you got to the building. Even if they didn't disable it, they have jamming signals in place around their buildings. Without Cort, we wouldn't have been able to pinpoint your location."

"Check it now," I said.

She didn't ask stupid questions. After several long seconds, her lips curved in a smile. "It's here. Strong, too. Not more than fifteen miles away."

"I planted my transmitter on Keene, but he must have found it and given it to Chris." I felt a new respect for Keene. If he'd told Ritter a location and Ritter had been captured, Chris and the children would have been at risk. Or Keene himself might have been taken and forced to reveal his whereabouts. But this way, only someone who knew what to look for and had the right frequency could find Chris wherever he chose to go.

Ava's gaze fell on Ritter's bare legs. "Are you finished yet? Let's hope we have something left in your size in the supplies."

Marco laughed. "I made sure we did. They're in the trunk."

Minutes later, Ritter sat next to me on the backseat as Ava steered us through traffic. The stocky Marco had taken shotgun. His gun was drawn and his dark eyes scanned every car we passed. His hair was thinning in the back, and I wondered if he at all resented the fact that if he'd been Unbounded he wouldn't have lost the hair, or at least not until the end of two thousand years. His brown eyes met mine briefly, his square chin dipping in a nod, the hint of a smile on his lips, and then the eyes rolled away again, ever searching for a potential threat.

"Looks like we're coming up on a beach," Ava announced.

I grinned. "Chris was always talking about taking the kids to see the ocean."

"Good place to hide." Ritter stared out the window, searching the faces walking along the sidewalks. "The busier, the safer."

Ava pulled the car to a stop. "I can't park here, but it looks like he's down by the water. Marco, go with Erin. Just head southwest of our position. About a hundred yards. Erin, you go find him, and we'll circle around and pick you all up right here."

"I'll go with her." Ritter opened his door.

"You'll limp," Ava said. "It'll be noticeable."

He scowled. "This is California. Anything goes."

Marco laughed, and I couldn't help smiling.

Ritter was right. People dressed in colorful clothes, or almost no clothing at all. I saw a green and orange Mohawk, piercings in every imaginable part of the body, and even a man in what I was reasonably certain was a Darth Vader outfit.

"We could walk behind him," I said to Ritter. "Everyone will be too busy staring at him to notice you."

"Until he collapses from heat exhaustion."

Ritter wasn't exaggerating. The heat was intense, focused even more because of the black clothing we both wore. My short hair was already sticking to my head and my underarms were wet with perspiration. My arms at least were bare to the sun, but I could feel the discomfort of dried blood on my skin from the shattered glass, though I'd rubbed off as much as I could from the nearly healed wounds. Each step on the sidewalk was an effort. Chris's watch said it was nearing five o'clock, but I felt as if I'd been awake all night.

Slowing to a standstill, I closed my eyes for a moment, absorbing the sustenance from the air around me, giving my body the nutrients it needed to repair whatever was making me so tired. I felt the distinct taste of salt on my tongue. Interesting. Within seconds I began to feel better.

Ritter had gone several paces without me. To his credit, he wasn't limping much, though the fluidity of his movements was severely hampered. He resembled any other person on the beach, except for his confident bearing, which screamed out his real identity as Unbounded. At least to me. I wondered how that translated to a regular mortal. Could they see a difference? No one seemed to be giving Ritter a second glance, except a group of high school girls who stared at him with longing eyes and whispered as they passed.

"You coming?" he asked, turning to see why I'd stopped. His hand went to where I knew he had a gun stashed in a holster sewn inside his pants.

I hurried to catch up. "About Keene. How was he when you saw him?"

Ritter's glittering eyes met mine. "Limping, but I left him alive, if that's what you're asking."

"He's not like the others. He proved that by helping Chris."

"He kidnapped you, so in my book that makes him someone we can't trust. Next time I see him, I *will* kill him. Especially if something happens to Cort because of him."

I thought about that and nodded. If Keene somehow managed to cover up his part in Chris's escape and continued his loyalty to his father and the Emporium, Ritter would have no choice.

"What is he to you?" Ritter asked.

It was an unexpected question. I shrugged.

Ritter stopped and put a hand on my arm. "Don't make the mistake of trusting him. You'll be better off."

"Better off if I keep everyone at arms' length like you do? Is that what you're saying?" I searched the hard planes of his face for any softening. We were inches apart and the closeness was doing odd things to my heart. That and the emotions of jealousy and desire I sensed even from behind the wall he'd erected to keep me out. I wondered if I was the only one who caused him so much turmoil and frustration that he couldn't always mask the feelings. Presumably he'd had enough years to perfect his mental barriers.

I took a step away, lengthening the space between us. "Maybe you're right. Every single man I've ever cared about outside my family has turned out to be nothing more than a spineless, self-centered lump of flesh."

The muscles in his jaw tightened. "Seems like you've learned a good lesson."

"Maybe." I wanted to bash in his self-satisfied face. "But keep in mind that not being able to deal with loss is what pushed Laurence over the edge, what made him willing to betray us. Living like that is no way to spend fifty years, much less two thousand. Then again, maybe after my first century, I'll be like you and bury my emotions so deep nothing will matter except revenge." I shook my head. "No. I don't want that. For now, I think I'll keep on dreaming of finding a man so crazy about me that I'm all he thinks about—even if it ends badly like with Bronson and Stella. I'll keep hoping for the chance to love someone so much that I feel like dying if he doesn't love me back. Whatever I do, it doesn't concern you. If you don't like it, well, you can just . . ."

I didn't know what he could do, and anything I said wouldn't be bad enough. "Forget it." I stalked away, reaching the sand and kicking off my shoes.

The insane thing was that at that moment I wanted Ritter more than I'd wanted anyone, and I knew he wanted me. But there was nothing I could do about his damaged heart, and for all my brave words, I *was* scared of losing again as I'd lost with Tom.

The sand burned my feet, so in the end I had to put my shoes on again. Ritter caught up to me and we ignored each other as we continued over the beach, but I could sense his emotions roiling under the surface of his mental shield, threatening to burst through.

It really wasn't fair that I should have to experience Ritter's emotions as well as my own, even in small glimpses. My attraction to him was strong enough on its own. At least he made no pretense of where he stood. He didn't want a family. He didn't want personal attachments. He didn't want to lose himself in anyone. Given the Unbounded virility, his lack of attachments probably made him a very frustrated man.

For some reason the thought cheered me immensely, and I began to smile.

"What?" Ritter growled. The hint of his emotions vanished as though he'd finally gained control.

"Not a thing. Hey, there's Chris." Ahead, I saw my brother at the water's edge. Kathy and Spencer had rolled up their pants and were playing in the gentle waves. Kathy held her face up to the sun and laughed. Spencer bent over and picked up a shell he'd found on the beach.

Hope shot through me. We would go on. Somehow we would make everything right for the children. For all of us.

Chris saw me and his face showed relief as he jogged across the sand and swept me into his arms. "You made it!"

"I had a little help." I jerked my head at Ritter.

Chris squeezed me tighter. "What do we do now?"

"We have to go to New York. We have a plane, but no pilot yet. Can you fly us?"

"What about the kids?"

"We'll have to take them with us."

"I don't want them in danger."

"Of course not. Once we're in New York, we'll stash you and the kids at a hotel somewhere."

"And you?"

My eyes flickered to Ritter standing beside me. "I'm going to do whatever I can to help. I have to, Chris," I added when he seemed about to protest. "It comes with being who I am now. I have no choice."

After a slight hesitation, he nodded. "I'll fly the plane, but I want to know everything that's going on. Like it or not, I'm in this as well. We have nowhere else to go."

"After this is over, you can go with us to Oregon and Ava can set you up with new identities. You can disappear wherever you want."

Chris's face hardened. "I'm not disappearing anywhere. We're family and we're sticking together. All of us. Especially now that

Lorrie's gone. I want to fight the people who did this to my wife, to my children."

I nodded solemnly, knowing exactly how he felt. "We have to be careful. Revenge can make us careless."

"It's not revenge," Ritter interrupted.

I'd been acutely aware of him during the entire exchange with my brother, but the comment surprised me. I smirked at him. "Then what is it?"

"It's making sure the deaths have a meaning, that the same thing doesn't happen to someone else."

I returned my gaze to Chris, but my words were also for Ritter. "The greatest revenge we will have is to go about our lives, raising our children, and finding happiness wherever we can."

Tears filled Chris's eyes, rain against gray clouds. "That may take some doing. I feel all numb inside. Without Lorrie I . . ."

I hugged him again. "I know. I know." I did know. At least to some extent. Though we'd been somewhat at odds this past week, Tom's loss left a hole inside my heart. I still couldn't believe he was dead, and that I'd been the one who killed him.

"We'd better hurry," Ritter said.

Chris drew away. "I'll call the kids." He sprinted to the water where the children had found a few friends and were playing with a ball.

I glanced at Ritter's face, but he was already turning to go. He cut a striking figure as he crossed the beach, a man full of raw, coiled power. He wasn't the kind of man to betray anyone, and I felt an unreasonable jealousy of the woman in the blue dress. She'd never had to doubt her lover's loyalty. I wondered if she would recognize the man he had become.

Back in the car, I held Spencer on my lap in the middle seat while Chris held Kathy on my right. Ritter sat on my left, his gun drawn in readiness. The children's gazes, and mine, kept sliding toward the weapon. The hard line of his leg touching mine was a constant distraction.

"What about Laurence?" Kathy asked in a small voice.

"He saved us, but then he disappeared. We thought he went back to help you. Did he?"

"Yes, he did help me." It was better this way, thinking of him as someone who protected those I loved instead of trying to murder them.

"Where is he?" Spencer asked.

I put my arms around him. "He didn't make it."

"Neither did Mommy," he said quietly. Kathy gave a little sob and buried her face in her father's chest.

I tightened my hold on Spencer, thinking of Lorrie. Thinking of my father and Jace. Of Laurence. Tom. So many losses.

Only the beginning. If we didn't succeed in our meeting with John Halden, all the Renegades and their families would die. There would be no one left to stand against the Emporium.

CHAPTER 23

"ERIN, WAKE UP." AVA'S VOICE CAME TO ME FROM FAR AWAY.

I sat up from the two airplane seats I was using as a bed, ashamed that I'd let myself sleep so soundly. What if Kathy or Spencer had needed me? I glanced toward the section of seats where I'd left my niece and nephew sleeping earlier, but they were still curled up like lost puppies, snoring softly.

"They're okay," Ava said, seated across from me. Between us was a table, and on it she set a steaming mug. "I've been keeping an eye on them."

"I guess you're every bit as related to them as I am."

"Well, a few times removed, and they don't know me as well as they do you."

"Looks like that will change."

Ava nodded. "Chris has asked if he could stay on. He wants to work for us."

"Us? Oh, you mean you and Dimitri."

"No, I mean the Renegades in general and our group specifically. We don't have many trained pilots, especially among our mortal security crew. I know I told you I didn't want to risk him and his family, but given what they've been through, I'm inclined to reconsider. He'd be a good addition."

"Then you said yes."

"I said I'd discuss it with the others, you included."

"And if I disagree?"

"Then I won't employ him." Ava gave me a wistful smile. "You are Unbounded and we need you more, though I feel it would be a mistake to turn Chris away. He's a good man, and we owe them our protection."

"They could get new identities."

Her brow creased. "They will have to anyway. I don't understand. Why is this a problem? I thought you wanted your family near."

I looked away from the gray eyes that were so much like mine—and like Chris's. "He shouldn't have to fight this battle. I don't want him hurt."

"None of our men are expendable. We fight for all of them, Unbounded or mortal. You can deny your brother this, but I don't think it'll stop him from searching for the Emporium, and you know what will happen once he finds them. If he's with us, we can train him, protect him, and keep him busy, give him a life of meaning. We have great hopes that at least one of Stella's relatives will be Unbounded and will add to our group, but a man like Chris, even though he's not Unbounded, could also make a real difference."

I sighed and looked out the small window into the darkness. "I know you're right, but I'm still worried."

"Then that's a yes?"

I nodded reluctantly. There was no other choice, not really. "Have you heard anything about my father and Jace?"

"Jace is recovering well. Your father, however, is still very ill. His condition has bumped him up on the heart transplant list, but you must prepare yourself for the worst."

My throat felt dry. "How's my mother?"

"I don't know. Dimitri says she rarely leaves your father's side."

"Does she know Chris and I escaped?"

Ava smiled. "We never let her know you'd been taken."

"Good." Still, a part of me was angry at one more deception. "You said you have great hopes that Stella's relatives will be Unbounded. Is that because you manipulated their conception like you did mine?"

Ava's mouth formed a thin, straight line. "Yes. Although we didn't steal from the Emporium as we did with you."

I waited for her to tell me Dimitri was really my father, but she didn't elaborate. "It's wrong," I said. "You have no right."

"Actually, with her great-nephew all we did was to arrange for his parents to meet. They were only second and third generation, meaning one had an Unbounded parent and the other an Unbounded grandparent—both of whom we lost far too soon in conflicts with the Emporium. We had to finagle things quite a bit to throw them together, and it took several years, but they eventually fell in love and married. We're hoping the gene is strong enough to cause at least one of their four adult children to be Unbounded. The odds are about the same as it is with the offspring of an Unbounded and a mortal union—twenty percent. The two oldest didn't Change, but the next one is coming up on the right age."

"I see." Nothing I could really object to there.

"As for the great-niece we're watching, Stella became close friends with her mother about the age when she would have Changed had she been Unbounded. In fact, Stella stuck around far too long for my comfort. She even gave her a house, though the woman had some means of her own. She was single, not very attractive or outgoing, and didn't have any marriage prospects, but she wanted a child, so Stella suggested she have one on her own. After a time, the woman decided to try artificial insemination, and we were able to manipulate the genetic material of an Unbounded in New York who matched the physical and mental aptitude she wanted, with far superior skills."

"And the possibility of immortality."

Ava shook her head. "Not immortality, Erin. We are not gods. We are not the Emporium. Regardless, we must take their example and actively try to increase our numbers. We need more Unbounded."

"Renegades, you mean. Would it be so bad if we just died out?"

She smiled. "You sound like Laurence."

That shocked me, but I still wanted an answer. "Well?"

"The Emporium wouldn't die out, would they? Only we would. Or we'd get to the point that only a handful would be born every couple hundred years, but the Emporium would continue on, increasing their numbers, and there would be no one to fight against them."

She was right. I hated it, but she was right.

To my surprise, she moved to the seat next to me, reaching out to draw me into her arms. Physically, she was only six years my senior, but at that moment I felt she was far closer to the real years she'd lived. My grandmother. My fourth great-grandmother. A tear trickled down my cheek and she brushed it away, running her hands along my cheek and over my ear and through my hair like my mother had done when I was small.

I've waited a long time for this. Her mental touch was gentle, not forceful or demanding. Simply comforting. *I'm sorry it's been so hard.*

I didn't respond in words but let my feelings of comfort touch her mind. She continued lightly stroking my cheek and smoothing my hair. *There's so much to teach you about our ability,* she added. *But you are already strong. I can tell. Usually it's harder for me to communicate by thought with other sensing Unbounded, even this close. Mostly we use scenes or emotions.*

We sat that way for a long time until my curiosity forced me to lift my head from her shoulder. "The virus I told you Laurence was working on. Do you think something like that could actually work?"

"It's always possible. But more stable minds than his have studied the Unbounded gene, and so far nothing has been able to kill it fast enough to make a difference." She shook her head sadly. "Poor, confused man. That's really all he was. He didn't have the experience to begin researching something like that. He spent too much time on other pursuits. We should have seen it, taken him in hand."

I sighed. "Then if he's really dead, he died for nothing."

"He died helping you get free."

I nodded, but my feelings for him were ambivalent. One moment I was furious at him, and the next I understood and almost agreed with his reasoning.

Chris's voice came over the intercom. "Okay, everyone, we've been cleared to land. Please return your chairs into an upright position and put on your safety belts."

"We'd better wake the kids." I stood, waiting for Ava to move into the aisle so I could pass. "Where are Ritter and Marco?"

"In the cockpit. Apparently Chris is giving them a flying lesson." Ava hesitated and I could tell there was more she wanted to say. I inclined my head expectantly.

"It's only fair to warn you," she said with the air of someone discharging an unpleasant duty. "Ritter doesn't stick around much. He trains us and comes when we need him for a job, but besides that he keeps to himself. Sometimes he'll disappear for months at a time. We keep training without him when he's gone because we know when he gets back he'll torture us with extra workouts if we don't keep in shape."

"Why don't you say what you mean?" Surely we'd moved past the need for cryptic statements. "Why should Ritter's habits mean anything to me?"

"I've sensed what you feel around him, Erin. I just want you to be careful. You're vulnerable, especially after what happened to Tom."

A burst of agony shot through me at the mention of Tom's name. Ava blinked, and I knew she'd felt it. I clamped down on my emotions.

She placed a hand on my shoulder. "We are not like regular

mortals. You are no longer the same. There are no casual relationships, no unplanned rolls in the hay, not when an act of intimacy
may create life that you must own and take responsibility for. That
changes everything."

"The end of the sexual revolution," I said dryly. "I knew there
had to be a drawback to near immortality." That and a bloodthirsty
bunch of control freaks out to use me as a breeder in their plan to
rule the world. "Thank you for the warning, Ava. Don't worry. I'm
not looking for anything from Ritter."

"Good."

She'd started into the aisle when my next words stopped her.
"But you did say it yourself—he always comes back."

Our eyes met, and she shook her head slowly. "Not worth it.
Don't go there."

There were all kinds of memories and pain in her eyes. I knew
she was right.

We woke the children and tightened their safety belts. I sat
between them, while Ava buckled into the row behind us.

Chris's voice came over the intercom. "Okay, we're going
to land in about one minute, but Ritter wanted me to tell you
some good news. He says he's picked up Stella's transmitter. And
Gaven's, too."

Ava closed her eyes, relief etched on her face.

"It could mean anything," I said, remembering my own transmitter fiasco.

"Yes," she agreed, "but this time let's believe something's going
our way for a change."

WE SAT IN THE RENTAL CAR IN A GROCERY STORE PARKING LOT NEAR
the airport, staring at the screen that showed Stella and Gaven's
tracking devices. They weren't moving or answering their cell
phones. The surviving Renegades in New York hadn't heard from
either of them, and we were all becoming worried.

"Our friends will be here soon, and we'll learn what they've planned for the meeting," Ava said. "Unfortunately, with Shaddock and most of the technopaths gone, we really need Stella. She's the only one left who can put together a full copy of the program we were to trade."

"What about the group from Italy?" I asked.

"Their technopath might be capable, if we can get Stella's hard drive, but Halden doesn't know her. He'll be suspicious with so many strangers."

"Let's split up." Ritter sat next to me in the back, the solid line of his arms touching mine as we leaned over the seat to study the dots that were Stella and Gaven. "You take Marco in case you need him." He gestured with his chin to the monitor. "I'll scout out this place and see what we're up against. Erin can come with me."

Ava didn't hide her surprise. "Are you sure?"

"No," he said, irritation seeping into his voice. "I still think she should have gone to the hotel with Chris, but since she's here, I might need her to sense something from whoever is still at the scene. She'll be safe enough because she'll be waiting in the car." His eyes narrowed as he made that last point.

Hopping between time zones had worn me down, and I was too tired to protest. That Ritter had glanced uncertainly in my direction as he spoke would have to be enough satisfaction for the moment.

"We'll need to be better armed," Ritter added.

"Tenika should have supplies. Look, there they are now."

A sleek black sedan rolled into the parking lot, which at 2:00 AM local time was deserted. I experienced a tremor of fear when two heavily armed Unbounded came toward us, but Ava and Ritter didn't seem concerned. The foremost was a tall, slender black woman with an array of tiny braids in her long hair. She wore faded jeans and a navy tank top. The woman looked somewhere in her late thirties, which would mean she was around four hundred years old, give or take a century. Her companion was a vaguely familiar Asian man with hair so short it must have been shaved recently. He was about my own age and only slightly taller. Dressed in black, he moved with the sinewy grace of an acrobat, strength masked in grace. Talented in combat, no doubt.

The man touched Ritter's outstretched fist with his own and bowed. From Ritter's expression I could tell he considered the man a respected ally, if not a friend. Ava and the woman shared a hug, and then Ava offered her fist to the man, who promptly kissed it. Ava smiled and leaned forward to touch her lips to his cheek. The woman ignored Ritter's outstretched hand and planted a firm kiss on his mouth. At his lack of a response, she tapped the semiautomatic rifle he wore slung over his neck and laughed.

"Still the same old Ritter, I see." She spoke with a slight accent I couldn't place.

"This is my granddaughter, Erin Radkey," Ava said, her hand on my shoulder. "And Marco Collins, who works for us. Erin, Marco, this is Tenika Vasco and Li Yuan-Xin. We call him Yuan-Xin." In my mind, she added, *Normally, some might call him by his surname Li, but that's too similar to his famous name. You might know him as Bruce. Yes, he is who you think he is. Both he and his son are Renegades. The shaved head and this lesser-known name help mask his identity.*

My eyes widened. She couldn't be talking about the martial arts icon who had died young before I'd been born. Maybe that explained the rumors that still surrounded his death. Yuan-Xin winked at me.

Tenika touched her closed fist to Marco's, inclining her head. Then she offered her fist to me, and I returned the gesture. "It is good to meet you, Erin," she said. "Ava has been waiting a long time for a descendant to Change. I'm sorry we meet under such terrible circumstances."

"So am I." I returned her nod and then touched fists with Yuan-Xin, feeling slightly relieved when he bowed but didn't kiss my hand.

"How was the call to Halden?" Ava asked.

Tenika's gaze shifted back to Ava. "He wanted time to think

about moving the exchange, but I'm expecting a call from him any minute. We should go. Will you drive with us or follow in your car?"

"We'll come with you. Erin and Ritter are tracking Stella in this car. They'll need weapons, though."

Tenika's eyes roamed over me and Ritter. I tried to sense what she was feeling but received nothing. "Yuan-Xin, take Ritter and let him choose what they need."

Yuan-Xin and Ritter crossed to the trunk of the sedan and returned within minutes, Ritter carrying several additional guns and full magazines. "We'll check in as soon as we know anything," he promised.

"We'll do the same." Ava glanced at me, as if she wanted to say something. Instead, she touched my arm, and a wave of well-wishes flooded my senses. I sent back the same to her and watched as she followed Tenika to the sedan.

"Let's go," Ritter said.

I watched Stella's dot on the monitor grow larger as we approached her location. The GPS on the device gave us clear directions where to turn, so there was no navigation involved for me. I had plenty of time to study Ritter's profile, lit periodically by passing cars. His hair had grown in the past week, now covering the mole on his right cheek. His face could have been carved in granite for all the expression he wore, and not a hint of emotion peeked through his mental shield.

Within twenty minutes we pulled in front of a ramshackle hotel. Ritter's frown increased. "Stella would never be here of her own accord, and this isn't the Emporium's style."

"You think Hunters took them?"

Ritter's jaw tightened. "Probably."

"You shouldn't go in. They'll recognize you from their files."

"I'll be careful." He was already checking the guns and shoving in magazines. He placed a handgun on my lap. "Try not to lose it like that last one I gave you."

I made a face at him. "I think I should go in and talk to the guy at the desk. He might have useful information."

Ritter's hand fell still, and I knew he was considering my suggestion. If he was any kind of a leader, he'd see the value of using my talent, however untried.

"Okay," he said finally. "But only the lobby. See what you can learn, and I'll meet you back here in a few minutes. Meanwhile, I'm going to check the layout."

"What if someone sees you?"

"No one will see me if I don't want them to."

I had to admire his confidence. On the other hand, I was already having second thoughts about my part. What if I did something to get us both killed? I shoved my uncertainties to the back of my mind because I owed it to Stella to try. If we didn't free her, she was as good as dead in the hands of the Hunters.

Unless they were working for an Emporium operative, and then her fate could be even worse. The more I thought about that, the more worried I became. Why would the Hunters show up now? And here? It was just too coincidental. Yet if the Emporium was behind Stella's capture, why wasn't she already in their hands?

Maybe she was and this was a trap.

I fought down my panic. "Is there anything I can carry this gun in?"

His eyes roamed over the snug pantsuit that I'd now been wearing for far too long. Unidentifiable stains marred the smooth fabric, which sported tiny rips from the shattered glass when we'd made our escape. I probably smelled like I hadn't taken a bath in a week.

"Take this." He emptied the remains of his duffel onto the rear seat and handed it to me. "It'll look natural going into a motel. Leave the zipper open enough for your hand, just in case."

"Okay." I took a deep breath and left the car.

My fear was so strong that I had to force myself to open the door to the motel lobby. My only comfort was that I really couldn't see Stefan or Justine at such a dump. After years of wealthy living, they'd become accustomed to opulence. That meant they were probably far from this place—and from me.

The night clerk lifted bleary eyes and watched me walk toward the desk. The man had beautiful dark skin and hair as black as Ritter's, though it was sleek and shiny and lay flat on his skull. He was a slight man, handsome, with striking, soulful eyes. If I had to guess, I'd say he was from India.

The lobby was tiny, so it didn't take much time to reach him. "Yes," he asked in heavily accented English. "You like a room?"

"I think so. But I'm looking for a friend of mine who might be here. She's slender, long dark hair. She may be with a thin black man, and maybe some others."

"Part Asian woman? Very beautiful?"

"That's her." I could see her face in his mind.

"She drove here in a van with maybe four men. Two of them left later in the vehicle. But she did not come inside, and I saw no black man. However, one man said you will come asking for the woman."

"Me?"

"Yes." His eyes traveled the length of my body. "He says you are thin and have very short blond hair. He wants me to call when you come. Shall I do this?"

I thought rapidly. If they were waiting for me, this was definitely a trap. I had to warn Ritter.

"I think I'll—"

"There he is now." The clerk's eyes went to the door behind me.

I slipped my hand inside the duffel, fingers tightening on the handle of my gun.

"The lady you talk about is here," the clerk called to the man.

"Oh good." The voice was very young, very American.

I turned slowly and saw a stolid, sandy-haired man with a thick neck and a red face. A mortal, but strong enough to break me in two pieces. Or three. He wore tight blue jeans with cowboy boots and a blue and white snap shirt that reminded me of a rodeo costume. His hair was longish, but fell flat around his face as though in need of a good washing. Obviously there was no woman in his life.

"Are you Erin?" he asked.

The pounding of my heart increased as my eyes riveted on the pocket of his shirt. The tiny embroidered insignia of a man with a rifle. He was a Hunter.

My hand tightened on the gun.

CHAPTER 24

I SWALLOWED AT THE SUDDEN DRYNESS IN MY MOUTH. BESIDES his beefy arms, I could see no weapon, though he might have one stashed somewhere. Not in the pocket of those ridiculously tight jeans, or I'd see the bulge. If I was properly trained, I'd laugh in his face, wrap him up in his own silly shirt, and give him as a present to Ava. As it was, I was shaking violently inside. Could I shoot another mortal? Tom's death already weighed heavily upon me.

I risked a glance at the Indian clerk, who was busying himself with paperwork but was probably listening to every word. Surely the Hunter wouldn't try anything in front of this witness.

Play along. "Yes, I'm Erin." Through the space between us I could feel relief pouring off the cowboy. I moved closer, trying to sense more detailed images. I caught a glimpse of Stella's face, but his fear blotted out almost everything else.

"Good." His voice lowered to a whisper. "I have that package for you. Ready for disposal."

Package? I had to know more, or I was going to blow my cover. How did he know who I was and why was he waiting for me? Only one way to find out for sure. Pulling my hand from the duffel, I took a few steps and offered my hand to the Hunter.

He hesitated only a second and then shook. Images burst into my mind. A warehouse, the cowboy crouching behind a Dumpster with three other men. Unbounded blowing each other to pieces. Satisfaction. Great gig for a relatively new Hunter. The woman from the picture approaching with a companion. He wasn't to let them go inside, according to his instructions. He needed to take them before they joined the fighting.

His hand dropped from mine. *Crap.* I wished I was better at this. I really didn't know what I'd seen, except that he and his partners had been waiting for Stella outside the warehouse. I hoped the motel clerk had been correct when he said some of the men had left.

"Come with me," the cowboy said, opening the door. "I'll show you where they are."

By "they" he must mean Stella and Gaven. If I wanted to learn more, I'd have to go with him. Ritter had better be watching.

As we traversed a dimly lit sidewalk, the cowboy looked me over. "Are you sure you can handle them alone? These Unbounded are very dangerous."

"What makes you think I'm alone? Anyway, of course I can handle them." I drew my gun from the duffel. "You have only one Unbounded anyway. The man is mortal. Easy to deal with."

His eyes widened. "How did you know that?"

"I keep informed."

"So you talked to Keene."

Keene. Now this whole situation was beginning to make sense. He'd told me he'd worked undercover with the Hunters, and somehow he must be behind this man's identification of me and his willingness to turn Stella and Gaven over. "We've been in touch," I said. "But why don't you tell me exactly what happened?"

The cowboy nodded. "Okay. Keene wasn't sure if we'd find anyone at the warehouse, but he thought his tip was good. When we got there, the place was loaded with Unbounded. You should have seen the creatures, still fighting when any normal man would have dropped dead." He shivered and crossed himself. "We almost left when the shooting started, but it got too dangerous so we hunkered down outside to wait it out. Just as things were winding down, these two come along. We recognized them from one of the pictures Keene sent us to keep watch for, so we jumped them. Black guy went down with one shot—got him in the stomach—but it took four of us to get the woman, even after we shot her. I sent Keene a picture from my phone, and he said to hold them until you got here."

I allowed myself a tight smile. So Keene had sent help through the Hunters, using the connections he'd formed when he'd been with them as an Emporium spy. That meant he had irreversibly chosen sides. Like his brother. Like me. Yet according to Ritter, Keene had still been inside Emporium headquarters after getting Chris out. What would the Triad do to him once they learned of his betrayal? Would he be able to get away?

I couldn't waste time thinking about that now, but I wished I had a way to contact him. Maybe he could help Cort before he fled.

I felt Ritter long before I saw him, murder in his heart. I reached out and shoved the Hunter against the wall. "Stay behind me," I ordered. To my surprise he obeyed, his eyes huge in his blocky face.

Ritter emerged from the shadows. "Ah, there you are," I said feigning calm. "I'd introduce everyone, but we all know it's better not to name names. At least not any more than we have already." To Ritter I said, "Cowboy here has the package Keene wants us to pick up. All ready for disposal." I hoped the Hunter was new enough that he didn't recognize Ritter. If not, we had a problem.

Ritter hesitated, his black look calculating. I willed him not to screw things up. "Good," he growled, sounding every bit the part of a man who was willing to dissect another man. Or a woman.

"I told you I wasn't alone," I added to the Hunter, who was eying Ritter, a worried crease in his brow. I sensed no recognition, only fear. "Show us where they are."

"This way." Cowboy hurried on ahead.

"Sensed you a mile away," I muttered at Ritter, who scowled. "Thought you'd want to know." I couldn't sense anything now. Good, he needed to be more careful. The Emporium had at least two sensing Unbounded that I knew of—and were out to breed more.

Cowboy led us up one flight of stairs to a door he opened with his key card. I started to follow him, but Ritter's arm flew out and stopped me. "I'll go first."

Inside the room lay two figures, one on each of the queen beds: Stella and Gaven. Both were trussed up like sacrificial lambs and were bleeding from at least one gunshot wound each. Someone had made only a half-hearted effort to wrap Stella's arm, but her color was good. Gaven looked worse. Blood seeped from a stomach wound despite the rags someone had tied around his middle.

"You should have been more careful," I told Cowboy. "We wanted to question them."

A man stepped out of the shadows behind us, a weapon in his hand. "They had to be convinced to come along."

Stella struggled to speak past the gag in her mouth. Her dark hair was messy, her clothes ripped and stained with blood, but she was as striking as ever. Cowboy couldn't drag his eyes away from her, and I was glad we'd come as soon as we did, or she might have had more to fear than a gunshot wound.

The second Hunter moved closer, his eyes fixing on Ritter. A sense of recognition flooded him—and me. Before I could call out a warning, he whipped his gun toward us. Ritter was faster, his hand blurred by rapid movement. A soft whoosh of a silenced gun. The Hunter fell dead, a stain spreading over his heart.

Cowboy swore and went for his own gun, tucked in the back of his waistband and hidden by his shirt.

"Don't," Ritter said, his voice flat and dangerous. "Leave it alone. Your friend got trigger happy."

"I don't know why he did that. We weren't supposed to—"

I reached out and touched him, an almost instinctive reaction.

Fear oozed from his body like a sickness. "It's okay," I said softly. "We're not going to hurt you. We only came for them. Your friend made a mistake. Everything is fine. Just be calm." To my amazement, his fear drained away, and the effort hadn't even made my head ache. I hadn't realized this was part of my sensing ability, though I should have suspected from what Delia tried to do to me. Maybe I was getting better at this.

"They're all yours," Cowboy said. "But what about him?" He gestured to his fallen companion.

"Leave him." Ritter dragged the body to the wall. "We'll call headquarters."

That seemed to satisfy Cowboy. "Then if you don't mind, I'd like to get out of here."

Ritter and I exchanged a glance. Letting him leave would be to our advantage, unless he suspected something and called for backup. I touched him again, straining to sense his intentions. An image of a bus came to me.

I nodded. "Good idea." *Hurry to your bus,* I added silently.

I had no idea if the suggestion reached him, but he grabbed a backpack by the dresser and started for the door. "Good luck and be careful. These people are dangerous."

That was when Ritter hit him over the head with his gun. Cowboy crumpled instantly.

"What did you do that for?" I demanded, checking to make sure he was still breathing.

"Too dangerous to let him go right now."

He was probably right. I set my gun on the table and hurried to loosen Stella's gag. "You took your sweet time getting here," she growled as I untied her hands.

Ritter laughed. "Same old Stella."

"Bronson know I was missing?"

"No," Ritter said. "No one told him."

"Good." Stella was untying her own feet, so I helped Ritter with Gaven. The man was conscious, but barely. He wouldn't be sitting up on his own anytime soon.

Ritter took a peek at his wound. "We have to get him to one of our doctors immediately. I wish we didn't have to move him, but it's not safe here."

"I'm fine," Gaven mumbled.

"Shut up." There was worry and affection in Stella's voice. "You're going to the doctor and that's that." She walked to the table, picked up my gun, and peeked out the blinds. "So why were they turning us over to you guys anyway?"

I explained to Stella as Ritter examined Gaven and retied his makeshift bandages. "I guess Keene felt bad enough about the Emporium attack that he sent someone to see if he could prevent you from falling into the trap. He gave them my description and told them I would be coming to pick you up. Probably told him I was another Hunter." I glanced at the unconscious cowboy. "Seems kind of risky. I mean, it could have been any of us following your tracking device."

Ritter snorted. "There were only two Hunters. Any of us would have been able to take them out. Keene only used your name to get our attention."

"He saved Stella's and Gaven's lives. That means he doesn't agree with the Emporium's slaughter any more than we do." Thinking of Keene staying at Emporium headquarters to call in favors on Stella's behalf made a hard knot form in my chest. I hoped he was all right, and that someday I could repay him.

Stella groaned. "Crappy way to save someone's life—have them shot."

"At least you're alive." Ritter handed me his gun and lifted Gaven carefully from the bed. "The New York group wasn't so lucky."

Stella sighed. "We heard. We were about to help when these bozos interrupted us."

"Good thing you didn't make it inside," Ritter said. "If you'd been captured by the Emporium, we might never get Halden's program."

She didn't reply to that. Instead, she scooped up a laptop case from the dresser and opened the door. "All clear."

"What about Cowboy?" I asked.

"He's seen you, and it's far too early for you to be in their database. You don't need to be looking over your shoulder for Hunters until you're fully trained." Ritter used a few extra rags to tie the unconscious man's hands. "There, that ought to hold him."

"Until when?" I didn't know why, but I felt sort of protective for this unsophisticated man, who looked like he'd be more at home on a farm than hunting Unbounded in the Big Apple.

Ritter sighed. "Don't worry. He won't be killed, if that's what you're asking. Though keep in mind, he intended just that for Stella and Gaven."

"We'll turn him over to our friends here in New York," Stella said. "There are ways to make him forget he ever wanted to be a Hunter."

"How?" I wasn't sure if I even wanted to know.

"Amnesia drugs usually work." Stella was checking outside again and the words came from over her shoulder. "Or if Ava has time, she can try to change the memory in his mind so he won't remember you."

"She can do that?" I remembered how she'd knelt by the Hunters outside the mansion. Is that what she had been doing there—changing their memories?

"Depends on the person. Some are easier than others. Unbounded are harder than mortals."

I don't know why I felt so amazed. It wouldn't surprise me at all to discover Delia might be able to do such things. With only a glimpse of my thoughts, the woman had been able to pinpoint my location in Emporium headquarters and send Tom in my direction.

The memory reopened the barely healing wound of Tom's death. Maybe on some unconscious level I'd wanted him to die for his betrayal. Maybe my so-called talent had aided that secret intent and made the bullet fly true.

No. I couldn't believe that. For all that I detested Tom for what he'd done, I didn't want him dead. I was not the monster Delia was.

Not yet. I pushed the thought away.

"Ritter, we'd better hurry," Stella said.

"Wait here while I get the car. I want to make sure no one's watching."

Less than five minutes passed before Ritter pulled the car closer to the motel room. When he flipped off the headlights, our predetermined signal, Stella and I helped Gaven down the steps. We made it without attracting unwanted attention, but Gaven passed out near the end, and Ritter had to help us get him inside the front passenger bucket seat, now lying back almost completely flat. Ritter and I made a second trip with the cowboy Hunter, dumping him rather unceremoniously in the trunk.

With Gaven so seriously wounded, Ritter didn't dare backtrack to make sure we weren't being followed. We stayed alert, carefully studying any car that came remotely near. Gaven moaned periodically, and his suffering was so great, I had to shut my mind so I wouldn't cry with his pain.

Stella talked to Ava on Ritter's cell phone, unwrapping the bandage on her arm with her free hand as she talked. "No, just a flesh wound. I'm fine now." In fact, she was no longer bleeding. She injected the site with curequick from the spilled contents of Ritter's bag. "Gaven needs a doctor, though. Right away. What? You're kidding!" She listened to Ava a long time before disconnecting.

"The New York group doesn't want us to take Gaven to their usual medical facility," Stella told us. "It could be compromised. Besides, both their doctors are dead. Ava says someone will meet us near the hospital and take him to the emergency room with a cover story. I'll go too, just in case there's trouble."

"You can't," Gaven said, his eyes fluttering open. "You have the meeting with Halden. Can't risk the cops getting in the way. Don't worry about me. I'll be fine."

"And if you're not?"

"What can you do, watch me die?" He smiled, his teeth white against the black of his skin. "I'm too tough for that. I may even outlive you."

"Next time get behind me and let me take the bullet," Stella retorted.

A weak smile filled Gaven's face. "Make me."

We all laughed, and I felt something soft and achy in my belly. Their relationship was familiar. It was family. Suddenly I wanted to know Gaven that well—I wanted to know all of them that well. And for them to know me.

We were quiet all the way to the meeting place, two streets over from the hospital, where I was surprised to see Tenika Vasco emerge from her sleek black sedan. This time she was alone. After greeting us with a nod, we moved Gaven to her car.

"Be careful," Stella said. "We can't afford to lose you now, not even temporarily."

Tenika Vasco grinned. "I'm a hypnopath, remember? They'll believe the suggestions I give them as long as they listen to me long enough."

"Good." Stella looked at me. "And to think by day she's a psychologist."

I laughed. Hypnosuggestion could be useful in that line of work.

"Wait here five minutes," Tenika said before driving away. "Someone's coming for the Hunter."

Sure enough, a few minutes later, a van pulled up and two Unbounded I didn't recognize loaded the cowboy inside. Ritter, who had gone to talk to them, touched his fist to each of theirs in farewell.

"Where to now?" he asked Stella when he slid again behind the wheel.

"The hotel. Ava will meet us there. They've managed to reschedule the meeting with Halden for tomorrow morning at nine, which means we have less than six hours to secure our position. However, Halden refuses to switch meeting places even though we've all but come out and told him the delay is due to an attempt to steal our program. He doesn't want to change his security plans."

"He's a fool," Ritter muttered.

"Maybe." Stella looked thoughtfully out of the window. "Why do I have the feeling there's something we're overlooking?"

"I'll make sure everyone's in place," Ritter said. "If the Emporium wants to break into our little party, they'll pay a stiff head charge." I had no doubt he would enjoy extracting every penny from their flesh.

At the hotel, we found Chris and the kids ensconced in a luxurious suite with two connecting bedrooms. The children were asleep in one, but Chris was dozing on the couch in the sitting room in front of the TV. He came to his feet as we entered and hugged me.

"Good, you're safe." His eyes slid past Ritter and focused on Stella, his jaw going lax for the space of a breath or two. I wasn't surprised at his reaction. I'd felt much the same when I'd met her, and I was heterosexual.

"Chris, this is Stella," I said. "She's one of our group." Our group. It felt good to say.

"Stella Davis." She offered her hand.

"Chris Radkey." He held her hand too long, but Stella didn't seem to mind. Or maybe she was accustomed to drooling men. Chris colored at his own reaction, and I was glad my barriers were up so that I didn't have to sense his thoughts.

"She knows who you are," I couldn't resist saying. "They were watching us for months."

Chris drew away then, and Stella gave me an unreadable look. Ritter's lips twitched with something that might have been amusement. He began pacing around the room, and it took a moment to realize he was looking at it not as a hotel room where he could rest, but as a place he might have to defend.

What a life.

Stella yawned prettily, covering her mouth with the back of one hand. "I need a shower."

"There are two bathrooms," Chris said. "One through that door and one connecting the bedrooms." His eyes caught on her unbandaged wound, which looked serious despite its shrinking size. "That's a pretty bad scrape."

Stella shrugged. "I gave it a jab of curequick. It'll be gone by morning."

Chris blinked at this blatant reminder of who she was. "Well, I'll go check on the kids. I'm staying in their room with them. I guess you guys can decide who'll take the other room. Two beds in there, and this couch folds down to a bed." His gaze went to Ritter as he said this, and then floated back to Stella, as if he couldn't bear to look away.

This might be a problem. I wanted to remind him that Lorrie had just died, and that at the moment Stella was very married.

I took my brother's arm, steering him toward the bedroom where he'd indicated the children were sleeping. "You're tired. Go to sleep."

"I can't," he said, his voice low. "I keep seeing Lorrie every time I shut my eyes."

"Yes, you can." I opened my mind to his. *Sleep. You're so tired.* As forcefully as I could manage, I thought of a nice, comfortable bed with downy pillows and a soft blanket. As close as we were, both physically and emotionally, I hoped some of my pushing would filter through.

He yawned. "Maybe now that you're back, I can sleep." Before disappearing into his room, he glanced once more at Stella, who had finished saying something to Ritter and was moving toward the bathroom for her shower. I understood then that it was the vision of life and beauty Chris craved, not necessarily Stella herself. And if seeing her gave him any measure of relief, I'd be happy for him to stare at her all day.

Once again, Ritter and I were alone. I couldn't help but notice how dim the lights were and how acute my senses felt. I dropped my barriers. No longer were there stray emotions zigzagging around for me to snag from the air like so many nutrients waiting for absorption. Just mine. I moved toward him, stopping several feet away. We stared at each other. He was dark to me, except for the impression of pulsing behind a black curtain. The exhaustion vanished. My nerves came to life, tingling from my fingertips to deep inside my body.

He took the steps between us and kissed me, his hand resting lightly on my shoulders. I strained toward him, my hands locking around his neck and pulling him closer. His arms came instantly around me. He felt so good, so solid, so real. Knowing that at any moment Ava could buzz the door or Stella could finish her shower added a delicious urgency to our kiss. I tasted his skin, his lips, his tongue. His mouth traveled down my neck, making me tremble. It made no difference that our clothes were dirty and we both needed a shower, or that we were exhausted from such a long and eventful day. This moment, this closeness, was the only thing that mattered.

Not a good idea. But if I was honest with myself, I had wanted this since our first training session.

There was a crack in the dark surrounding Ritter's mind. I pushed at it and his emotions began leaking, seeping over me. Quickly it grew to a flood, and I reeled at the onslaught. If I'd thought my emotions were powerful, Ritter's nearly caused me to burst into flames. He wanted to touch me, taste me, everywhere. He wanted to feel my hands on his body, to meld into me. I slid my hands under his shirt and pushed closer to him.

I'd regret this tomorrow. We both would.

He was regretting it already. In his mind I saw the woman in the blue dress, the sightless eyes staring at me. Ritter's desire for me was trying to suppress these thoughts, but his guilt was building to a deafening clamor in the background. So much loss and guilt. Pain similar to what I'd felt when I'd seen my father and Jace's prone figures. Like when I'd shot Tom.

Tom. My mind replayed the event. I saw his surprised stare as my bullet entered his head, the line of blood trickling between his eyes as he crumpled onto the rubble-strewn roof. I saw myself crawling to weep at his side.

With a muttered curse, Ritter stepped away, his hands dropping to his side. "What was that?"

"What?"

"I saw him. You sent it to me."

My face flushed. "I didn't mean to."

"I can't be Tom."

"I don't want Tom."

Ritter hadn't moved since breaking away from me, his entire body taut as though ready to do battle. "It's just a kiss, Erin. It doesn't mean anything."

I took a step and placed my hand on his hard chest. He didn't move away, but he didn't reach for me, either. "How many women have you kissed like that lately? Has it been years? Decades? Has it been since her? The woman in the blue dress? Did you even kiss *her* that way?"

His expression darkened as he growled, "I can't give you what you want."

"How do you know what I want?"

He didn't answer, so I reached out my mind. His mental shield was back in place, but when he saw my concentration, he gave a smirk and the barrier was gone.

I saw the dark-haired woman screaming in terror as a man slashed at her with a sword. Another man sliced off a young girl's head with a single blow, an older woman pulling helplessly at his sleeve. The barking of a dog and then sudden silence. More slicing. Swords through flesh. Blood pooling where the blade had gone through the first woman's neck. More blood slicking the floor where her torso is cut in half. The older woman sprawled beside her, and the young girl, both equally mangled. Gold rings glinted on their fingers—the same rings I felt now under Ritter's shirt. A sword raised, about to slash down toward Ritter where he lay recovering in bed. A man bursting into the room, sword raised. The others turning to meet him.

The memory vanished, Ritter's wall solidly in place once again, but I understood what he'd let me see. The only way he would seek a relationship was if there was a future, and the last thing he wanted was a future with someone who really mattered. Someone he could lose.

Ritter had nothing but revenge in his future. Tomorrow he would be back killing Emporium Unbounded, and he would not think about me or our kiss. He would see only the faces of his enemies and of his dead.

My breath was still coming fast, but from anger and frustration now instead of desire. I was silent for long seconds as I fought with myself. What should I say? What did I really want?

"Tell me," he said, almost casually, the amused glint back in his eyes, "are you ready to have my child? Because that's what this would mean. If not today, then tomorrow, or the next time we decide to have a little fun." He bent down and whispered next to my cheek. "There are no second chances. Death, life, or love— Unbounded always play for keeps."

The heat of his breath made me shiver. Things had been so simple when I was mortal. Now even the act of loving had a life-time of significance. Rules and consequences.

That didn't stop me from wanting him.

I clamped down on the longing arcing through my chest and gazed at Ritter through half-lidded eyes. "You're right," I said, my voice barely a whisper. "You can't give me what I want." I wasn't going to beg him to love me. If things ever happened between us, he would have to come to me of his own will. With his heart intact and ready for any possibility.

On the other hand, he was right that I wasn't ready for an Unbounded relationship. Maybe I'd never be ready for any rela-tionship. Maybe living for revenge was the right idea. That way I would never have to deal with another Tom. I would never have to see my children die of old age.

I turned from Ritter and stalked to the door leading to the unoccupied bedroom, leaving it open behind me. The slice of light from the sitting room illuminated the way to one of the two queen beds. Slowly, I stepped out of my clothes and slid under the covers, my bare skin tingling with the coolness of the sheets. I could feel Ritter's eyes still on me, emotions boiling behind his barriers.

More than anything, I wanted him to join me.

More than anything, I wanted him to leave me the hell alone.

He stood motionless in the outer room for the space of several heartbeats. Finally I heard him leave. It was a long time before I slept.

CHAPTER 25

WHEN I AWOKE THE NEXT MORNING, I FOUND I WAS ABSORBING without conscious thought. I let the sensation fall over me, feeling energy seep into my limbs. It was far too early for me to be awake, especially on a Sunday, but I felt rested after only a short few hours of sleep.

I could get used to this.

Stella lay in the next bed, wrapped in a white robe that had come loose over one shoulder. I saw her wound had become nothing more than a red spot on her skin.

At my movements, she opened her eyes, stretching. "Time already, huh?"

"It's only seven."

"Meeting's at nine. We'd better get ready." She sat up and swung her feet to the floor.

"Does that mean I'm still going?"

"Of course. With your ability, you'll be very valuable."

"What do I do?"

"Mostly try to get a sense of what Halden is feeling, and pass anything you learn to the rest of us, though that's kind of difficult since we can't sense. Ava can sometimes plant a word or two in our minds, but not all sensing Unbounded can do that." Stella arose and began going through a mound of clothing someone had placed on the chair. "No one's in the connecting bathroom if you need to shower," she said helpfully.

I gathered the blanket around me and stood, feeling a little self-conscious in my underwear. Stella apparently had no such inhibitions. She shucked off her robe and stood naked, her perfect body silhouetted by the morning light still filtering through the sheer curtains. Her abdomen was slightly rounded, and this surprised me because in her clothes her stomach had always seemed so flat and perfect. Maybe she'd been too busy for sit-ups this week. She reached for a pair of underwear.

Averting my gaze, I shut the sheer inner curtains to close out any prying eyes from the neighboring high rises, catching a glimpse of the city sprawled before me as I did, exciting and more than a little intimidating. The sun had risen and it was a glorious day, blue sky stretching as far as I could see until the buildings blocked it from view. So this was New York. I'd always wanted to visit. Too bad I wasn't here on vacation.

Then again, only one person had tried to murder me since my arrival, and he was lying on the floor of that motel room, never to see another blue sky. Maybe for Unbounded that was as close to a vacation as it came.

Stella was pulling on pants now, and I decided I'd better hurry.

My shower was delicious. I let the hot water run over my body for what was probably too long, sloughing off the dirt as well as the terrors I'd endured the past few days. As I used the hotel's body wash, my hands running over my skin, I thought of Ritter. I took a deep breath and turned the water a bit cooler.

Donning a soft, luxurious hotel bathrobe, I emerged, feeling energized. Stella was fully dressed in a black pinstriped power suit. Her dark hair was combed smooth and wound into a severe knot at the back. She'd used a light hand with her cosmetics and looked purposeful and competent—and as striking as ever.

"Aren't you going to be a little hot?" I asked.

She shrugged. "I like to meet powerful men on their own level. Otherwise they get too nervous."

"That's because you're gorgeous."

"I wasn't always like this."

I shrugged to show it meant no difference to me. "So do you have all the software you need to make the exchange with Halden?"

"Some of the others stopped by last night when you were asleep, and we were able to get everything ready. Even after all our technopaths' work and research, it'll still take Halden and his team another three to five years to be ready for release. But he agrees that it's going to revolutionize virtual reality and make all other platforms obsolete, especially those for video games."

"That's not going to make the game companies happy."

"Not our worry." She glanced at the alarm clock by the bed. "Ava's going to be knocking on that door any minute now."

"Anything look good for me?" I eyed the pile of clothing doubt-fully as I removed a new pair of white bikini underwear from a package.

"Another suit, a blue dress—nice cut on that, by the way—and this red blouse and black skirt combo."

I'd had enough red for a while, but the suit looked too confining and hot. That left the blue dress and the tallest blue heels I'd ever seen. I removed my robe and pulled the dress on.

"What happened between you and Ritter last night?" Stella asked.

I grimaced. "Nothing."

"Well, he's in a terrible mood."

I slipped my feet into the blue heels. "Good."

Stella regarded me silently for a minute before saying. "Maybe he'll mellow in a century or two."

I gave a dry laugh. "Maybe." The idea of waiting two hundred years wasn't appealing. Last night had been stupid anyway. I should have been throwing up barriers against Ritter, not trying to tear them down.

Stella was staring at the mirror again, smoothing the suit jacket over her hips and stomach, which once again looked flat under the material.

Understanding flooded me. "You're pregnant, aren't you?"

Stella held very still. "How do you know?"

I thought about mentioning the tiny swelling in her abdomen, but that was not what had triggered my suspicion. I'd sensed it. I walked up to her, my hand outstretched to touch her suit-clad stomach. She flinched slightly but didn't back away. I reached out my mind and there it was. So small and fluttering. Gentle. Difficult to explain except that it felt like something resembling trust. "I feel it," I said softly.

Tears formed in Stella's eyes. "I'm late this month, but I thought I could have miscalculated."

"You didn't." Of course not. Stella was too thorough, too good at what she did to miscalculate anything as simple as the date of her next period.

"Can you tell what sex it is?"

I shook my head. "I don't think that happens until later or if I'd be able to tell even then, but there's definitely something there. A presence." So faint it was almost undetectable.

She was crying now, and I pulled her into my arms much like Ava had done to me the previous day. A hug of comfort. With our contact, her feelings rushed over me: guilt, triumph, despair, joy, and fear. It was a lot to take in all at once.

"I wanted something of his," she whispered, "but I don't know if this is the right thing. I'm . . . I'm afraid."

Afraid of losing her child. Of watching her baby age and die.

"Death is part of life," I said. "You'll have many years to love your baby. Don't dwell on anything else today. You've made your decision."

She nodded fiercely. "It'll be such a shock for Bronson. All these years since his vasectomy. The past couple of years I was thinking of asking him to reverse it. I even talked to Dimitri about it, but I was worried the surgery would kill Bronson. He's so fragile now."

"I've heard of it reversing on its own."

Stella was quiet for a moment and then, "I think it was Dimitri. Maybe not even on purpose."

"What do you mean?" What other talents did my biological father hide?

"He can do more than see what's wrong with someone by looking at them, or how to create the medicine they need. He's been taking care of Bronson for years, and I've seen him give him the will to survive time and time again. He makes a body *want* to heal. His father was a doctor like him, but his mother could sense like you and Ava, and I think Dimitri ended up with a bit of something extra that enhances his predilection for medicine—possibly a type of biological manipulation."

Healing by the laying on of hands seemed more in the religious realm than I was willing to believe. Yet I believed in God, so who was I to doubt? After all, I could sense some people's private emotions, a thing I'd once believed impossible. Why shouldn't Dimitri have the talent to heal with his hands?

The added knowledge that my paternal grandmother could sense was another interesting thought altogether. I had the ability from both sides of the family. I wondered if that was significant.

There was a sharp rap on the door. "You ladies ready?" Ava's voice.

Stella picked up her cosmetics and headed for the bathroom. "Tell her I'll be out in a minute. I have to redo my makeup."

"Wait, Stella." She paused and I rushed on, "Have you and Ritter ever thought about—you know. I mean before Bronson."

She smiled. "I won't tell you I haven't been tempted to make a play for him. The idea of a man who won't grow old and die is tempting. Most days it's hard with Bronson because so often he can't give me what I need." She shook her head. "But Ritter's too angry, and I don't know how to live like that. I don't *want* to live like that."

I had no reply, so I nodded and watched her go into the bathroom. Part of me was relieved they'd never been together, but another part despaired. If the perfect Stella, with all her years of experience and logic, had deemed a relationship with Ritter impossible, I might as well give up now.

I opened the door to Ava, who looked cheery in a short-sleeve gold suit. Her eyes scanned me. "Nice fit. You look good. You need a little makeup, though." She pushed me over to the mirror inside the room and began working on me, using products from her bag.

"We're adhering as closely as possible to our original plan," she said as she worked. "You'll be posing as one of the New York programmers who died last night, which we'd planned to do anyway if you showed an ability for sensing. We need to make sure Halden turns over all the files regarding the identification program, keeping no copies. That's the deal. Ritter and Yuan-Xin were originally going in as guards and Tenika as the third programmer, but with so many of the Renegades hit last night, we need them on the outside. So Ritter will be both guard and programmer."

"It's just the three of us?"

She gave me a flat smile. "I can't send you all in there without another trained fighter, so despite the fact that Halden won't be pleased, I'm going, too. Halden's finally realized I don't age, but at least I'm familiar. He's dealt with Stella and the others before, but you and Ritter are new to him. New makes him more nervous than something he can't explain. Halden will be wary of me, and I probably won't get close enough to sense much from him, but between the two of us, we should be able to get the assurances we need."

I wasn't sure I'd be much help in a stressful situation. "Unless he decides not to deal at all."

"Oh, he'll deal. He wants Stella's program."

"What about the Emporium?"

"The rest of our people will be scattered over the area, watching for them. We'll need every experienced Renegade we have on the outside to keep the Emporium away. Don't worry. Stella or

I will do all the talking. Or Ritter." Her face contorted slightly. "That reminds me. Did something happen last night between you? Ritter's in a mood."

"Absolutely nothing." Unfortunately. Fortunately. I clenched my teeth together. I'd thrown up my barrier, so Ava probably couldn't sense any of my confusion. I hoped.

"Humph," she said, not fooled.

I examined her face. Unlined, clear, with high cheekbones and a nose that spread a tiny bit more than necessary. Familiar because it was my mother's face when she was younger, or as similar as you could expect with nearly three hundred years separating them. Yet my mother hadn't been Unbounded. I was. Though I had Ava's gray eyes and her blond hair, the rest of me looked more like Dimitri—a less-broad, feminine version. When would someone tell me the truth?

Ava stepped back to examine her efforts with the makeup. "That'll do. Your hair is growing, though. You'll have to decide if you're growing it out or keeping it short." She spoke absently, and I knew her mind had already moved on.

"Any news about my family?"

"I talked to Dimitri this morning. He says Jace was conscious last night and able to sit up with the support of the adjustable bed."

"My father?"

I'd meant the one who raised me, of course, but there was a slight hesitation in Ava's reply, as though she'd first thought I was asking if Dimitri was my father. "He's the same." She turned with obvious relief as Stella emerged from the bathroom. "Good, you're ready."

"Ritter's here?"

"He's with Tenika and Yuan-Xin going over last minute security details."

"It'll be okay," Stella said to no one in particular. "We're going to succeed."

I waited for Ava to sense the presence of Stella's child, but instead she said, "Something feels wrong, but I can't place my finger on it. I wish I'd been able to talk to Halden personally."

"Why?" Stella headed for the door that led to the sitting room. "Too much distance to get a read on his thoughts even if you'd called him yourself. Any food out there?"

Ava smiled. "Of course."

With all the absorbing I'd been doing, I wasn't hungry, but I ate anyway. The fruit was sweet, the hot chocolate rich, and the croissants the best I'd ever had, but Laurence was right when he said that eating wasn't the same. Lately I received more joy from absorbing than from ingesting real food. But to my view, it was a fair exchange. Almost a high. Why hadn't he been able to feel that?

We were finishing up when Chris stumbled from his room. "Up already?" His sleepy gaze skimmed past all of us and settled briefly on Stella, a wistful smile on his face. She was alive and vibrant, even more beautiful than ever in her pregnancy. A beacon of hope.

"We have to be somewhere at nine," I said.

Chris cocked his head to meet my gaze. "Will we be leaving New York after?"

I exchanged glances with Ava and Stella. None of us knew what this day would entail or if we'd emerge whole and alive. "Yes," Ava said finally. Chris didn't seem to notice her hesitation.

"I hear you're going to work for Ava." I pushed the last of my croissant in my mouth.

Ava met my eyes and frowned. I had agreed to his employment, but I was mentally broadcasting my uncertainty about Chris working for her—for us—in case she'd forgotten.

"Glad you're okay with it," Chris said. "I'll fly you guys wherever you want to go."

"What about the kids?"

"I'm hoping they can stay with Mom and Dad when I'm gone. Or maybe with you."

I had a sudden vision of Kathy and Spencer growing old before I physically aged another year. Not my thoughts, or at least not originating in my head. I narrowed my eyes at Ava before realizing that she hadn't meant to experience the emotions herself, much less send them to me. I forced a smile for my brother's benefit. "I'd be glad to help out."

We paused as Ritter threw open the door. He stood framed by the hallway, his face somber. His gaze slid over me, almost a physical touch.

I didn't look away.

Ava stood. "Guess it's time to go."

My heartbeat took that moment to increase its pace. I didn't know if it was because of Ritter or what we were walking into.

CHAPTER 26

ITTER AND I TOOK THE BACKSEAT AGAIN, WITH STELLA SHOTGUN and Ava driving. Ritter carried a handgun, though he knew it'd be taken from him before he was allowed to enter the meeting place.

"Do you have a knife in that bag?" I asked. "One with a leg strap, or whatever you call them."

"Sheath." One of his eyebrows rose questioningly. "I have two. Why?"

"I'd like to use one." I waited for a joke as to my competence with the weapon, and when none came, I felt strangely grateful.

He rummaged in his bag and handed me a dark blue arrangement. "This one might work. It only carries one knife, but the other isn't adjustable and won't fit you."

My eyes went to where his thigh touched mine on the seat, sending pulses of heat that I was trying to ignore. Obviously we were nowhere near the same size.

I unfastened the Velcro attachments. "I'm assuming we'll have to go through some kind of security before we see Halden. Won't they think it odd that we're armed?"

Ritter shook his head. "We told them there'd been trouble with pirates trying to steal the software. Besides, I'm playing the part of a game junkie and they love this stuff."

I lifted my dress to strap on the knife. I tried to hide my smile as Ritter averted his gaze, his nostrils flaring slightly. But then I couldn't get the sheath to adjust properly, and it was my turn to blush and look away as his roughened fingers made the adjustments. I wavered between slapping him away and begging him to keep his fingers right where they were.

When the sheath was finally in place, it felt strangely comforting against my skin.

We drove to the outskirts of town until we reached an area dotted with manufacturing plants. Small fields of grass and weeds had sprung up between some of the buildings. It was to one of the more isolated buildings we were heading, a squat, sprawling place with only one floor.

Each of us scanned the area as we strode up the cemented walk to the double front doors. At my side, Ritter was especially tense. He looked good in his dark suit, with his hair combed back from the hard lines of his face, but tiny beads of sweat dotted his forehead. Not a breeze in the air gave relief to the heat.

Ava gave Ritter a sidelong glance. "You think the Emporium's watching?"

"Our people have been in place for the past three hours. There's been no sign of them. I don't know whether to be relieved or more worried. They have to be here. With the information they have, it would be stupid for them not to be."

"Guess we'll find out." Ava opened one of the front doors.

Inside, we were met by two guards and the kind of metal detector I'd seen in airports. We began emptying our belongings into trays. "We'll have to hold this here for you," said a balding guard, hefting Ritter's gun. "Mr. Halden doesn't allow weapons." He divested Ritter also of a knife. "Interesting equipment for a programmer," he commented dryly.

"Game programmer," Ritter corrected. "I like weapons."

"Of course."

Meanwhile, the other guard, an attractive man with golden brown skin and short black dreadlocks, had passed Stella through the metal detector and motioned me over. The machine went off with a loud clang. I stiffened as he approached me. There was something different about him. Something difficult to place. Then I had it. He was Unbounded. Not old Unbounded like Ava and the others—he didn't quite have that confidence, but he was Unbounded all the same. Newer.

Fear shot through me. Was he from the Emporium?

I glanced at Ava who was awaiting her turn with the balding man, and she nodded at me. Her thoughts were shuttered, but I knew she wanted me to submit to his search. Easy to think, but quite another thing to stand still as the guard waved a wand over me, trying to determine the source of the metal. He found the knife, but to my surprise, he gave a quick flip of his arm and a metal anklet appeared in his palm. "You must have forgotten this," he said, pretending to unfasten it from my ankle.

"Oh, sorry." I shrugged delicately.

He was one of ours. My knees felt weak with relief.

The bald man laughed. "Not much of a weapon, but enough to set off the sensors. Better pick it up on your way out, miss."

"Thank you," I told the Unbounded guard, stumbling purposefully so I had to reach out and touch him.

He was dark. However new he was, he'd been trained that well at least.

Did that mean he might be a double agent? What if our trust in him was misplaced, as it had been with Laurence? We would have to kill him. If it came down to it, could I kill him to protect the others?

The guard winked and smiled. "You all right?"

I nodded, feeling guilty for my thoughts. I glanced at Ritter, understanding him better than I wanted to.

The bald guard motioned for Ava. "Okay, I'm done with Rambo, here. You can step through." Ava did so without a problem, and the man added, "Mr. Halden is waiting for you in the room at the end of the hall. I'll show you where."

Following the older guard, we walked purposefully down the hall. Ava was smiling, Stella, briefcase in hand, looked poised and beautiful, but Ritter's expression was grim. I found a smile and pasted it on my face.

"Smile," I hissed at Ritter. He looked startled for an instant before his lips moved upward at the corners. The effect wasn't very convincing, but when he took glasses out of the pocket of his shirt and put them on, I thought maybe he could pass. A computer nerd he wasn't, but there was an obvious intelligence in his eyes.

I didn't worry too much about his lack of a weapon. I'd seen him in action, and I knew his body was every bit as dangerous as a loaded gun. He glanced over at me, his eyes sliding down to where the knife was pressed against my thigh. That told me he'd been aware of what had happened with the guard. I wasn't surprised.

Despite my cool dress and the air-conditioned interior of the hallway, I was feeling rather hot under Ritter's stare. *Adrenaline,* I told myself.

Yeah, right.

Ritter's gaze left me as the guard knocked on the door. I took a deep breath. Without really meaning to, I sent my thoughts out to my companions. All were dark, even Ava, and I took that as my clue to be careful, but I wouldn't shut myself up entirely unless I felt threatened. If the Emporium was nearby, they would already know we were inside, and this far from their sensing agent we should be relatively safe. Sensing was the reason I was here, after all.

The door was opened by a stocky man with silver hair. He looked like security, probably loaded to the teeth. Another man stood to the side of the door, younger, but also with the air of security. A third man occupied the space near the window, his face turned away from us, and I knew immediately that this was John Halden. He was tall and thin, with coffee-colored skin and close-cropped black hair generously laced with gray. He wore jeans, Nikes, and a T-shirt with a logo I didn't recognize. When he turned, I saw a kind but unremarkable face with brown eyes that could have belonged to anyone.

Not at all the cutthroat businessman I'd expected.

He came toward us, hand outstretched. I felt more than saw the guards tense as he greeted us, as if they feared that was the moment we might try something.

Strange how sensing had evolved from disjointed flashes to a function as normal as breathing. Like absorbing. A limb I couldn't do without. For an absurd moment I wanted to laugh with joy for my newfound ability, like a blind man suddenly given sight. I squelched the emotion quickly, refocusing on Halden who had extended his hand to me.

"Nice to meet you," he said as Stella made our introduction. He had a generous mouth and with his smile, his face was utterly transformed. I was amazed at the difference between the ordinary man I'd first seen at the window and this man whose magnetism radiated sunlight.

I returned his smile. "My pleasure. I've heard a lot about you, and I'm pleased we can finally meet."

"Thank you for allowing us to reschedule, John," Ava added.

Halden's smile faltered, becoming a bit hard. "Well, we can't always predict life, can we?" I was sure there was a double meaning in the words, but his emotions didn't reveal what.

Halden motioned us to a large oval table that reminded me eerily of the one at the Emporium headquarters in California. "Please have a seat."

We did as we were told. He'd arranged it so the wide table was between him and us, and that gave me a sense of unease.

"I have been impressed with your project," Halden began, directing his gaze at Stella. His appeal went beyond power and magnetism; there was also a sensual energy in the lean lines of his body that he seemed unaware of. "You're right that it will completely revolutionize the entire gaming world. But there are also many other applications—medicine, education, law enforcement. And much more. I'm looking forward to developing it. When you showed me what your team was up to the last time we met, I was very impressed. Even more so with your latest reports. I've never seen anything like your work. We'll have to talk about whether or not you're paid enough at your current job." He smiled to show he was joking, though it was clear from his tone that he wasn't.

Something squeezed my thigh. Ritter's hand. I shook my head, as if shaking off the rain. I'd been so focused on Halden that I had no idea how long Ritter's hand had been on my thigh, which was strange because now that I was aware of it, my nerves were screaming at the contact.

Ritter's chin lifted toward Ava and Stella. The women's eyes were fixed on Halden, more caught up in him than they should be. Like I'd been. No wonder Halden had been so successful over the years. His magnetism was inescapable.

I glanced at Ritter and saw his eyes go to a second door to the room, located behind Halden. It was slightly ajar.

Something was wrong. Not just the door, but in Halden's demeanor, in his single-minded focus on his words. He was hiding something. I tried delving deeper into his mind, but besides a high level of anticipation, there was no clue to what he planned. Either he simply wasn't thinking about it, which I didn't believe for an instant, or someone had warned him not to think of anything he didn't want us to know.

But who?

I tried to probe further, but was rewarded only by a dull pain in my skull. I wondered if Ava was having better luck.

"I'm very happy where I am," Stella assured Halden. I was glad to see his eyes linger on the soft curves of her face. At least he wasn't immune to her charms. I wondered if there was a woman in his life.

"Too bad for me, I guess."

Checking first to make sure the guards weren't watching me, I pulled up the skirt of my dress enough to free the knife and pass it to Ritter. He could do far more damage with it than I could. To my surprise, he pushed it back, shaking his head almost imperceptibly.

"So the trade is acceptable to you?" Stella asked. "Of course, we'll want reassurances that you will not replicate the identification technology. We will do the same for our virtual reality program."

Halden hesitated. "I'm sorry, but there has been a complication. I can no longer trade, yet I would like to buy your technology from you. I promise to make it worth your while."

Ava blinked once as the information set in. "No."

"That was not the deal," Stella added. "I didn't put so much sweat into this project to give it away for money. We need the identification technology."

Halden arched a brow. "Need? That's a pretty strong word." He leaned forward. "And the thing is, it seems you're not the only ones who need it."

"You have another offer?" Ava's voice was curt.

"Actually, I do." He nodded to a guard, who walked to the partially open door behind Halden and motioned to someone we couldn't see.

Next to me Ritter's body was coiled, ready for action. Stella's face paled, and I wondered if it was fear or if the Unbounded experienced morning sickness. Everyone was standing now, except me. My eyes riveted on the door.

Stefan Carrington was the first to emerge, followed by Justine Carver, my once-best-friend. I should have known. Only Unbounded could have warned Halden about guarding his thoughts. With Stefan and Justine was the large-nosed Edgel who had operated on my leg at Cort's. They sauntered into the room, confident as though they owned the place. I had the urge to tug off Justine's auburn wig out of spite, but even if I did, it wouldn't expose the rot in her heart.

The last person emerged, and I bit my lip to keep from crying out. Cort!

He looked healthy, though rather frayed around the edges. His face sported a quickly fading bruise, his slacks were ill-fitting, and his white shirt rumpled. After the disaster at Emporium headquarters, he must have flown all night to get here. But he was alive.

Stefan was the first to speak. "Hello, Erin. I was sorry to hear you left California so abruptly."

"Guess I didn't like the idea of being anyone's puppet—yours or Delia's."

"So Cort was right. You do take after your maternal ancestor." Stefan's eyes flickered to Ava.

Now that Stefan was in the room, it was hard to decide who exuded more power, him or John Halden. I had the feeling none of this was going to end well.

"So," Ava said to Halden, "you've decided to sell out to this *animal*?"

"Animal?" Stefan's lips twitched with amusement.

"What matters here is that he's the man who tried to kill you this week," Stella said. "If it hadn't been for our organization and your own preparedness, you would have died."

Halden frowned. "Is this true, Stefan?"

Stefan shook his head. "I never heard of an attempt on your life. Did it really happen? If so, maybe you have the perpetrators right here."

Anger, frustration, and hopelessness flooded through me. "No," I whispered. "No."

Halden met my gaze. "You have something to say?"

All eyes turned toward me. "He's lying," I said. "You can't trust him."

Halden smiled and his magnetism was riveting. "You are in the company of a woman who hasn't appeared to age in the twenty years I've known her. How can I trust her? Or you? How do I know *you're* not the one lying? What information do you have that can sway me? Why are you even here? What personal stake do you have in all this?"

"You really want to know?" I asked because this wasn't about me, it was about the survival of the Renegades, and by extension John Halden and every other mortal in the world.

"I made my empire strong by listening. Try to convince me."

Many court trials had been won by focusing on the individual, and maybe it would help here. Halden was both judge and jury. At the very least, this distraction might provide an opportunity for the others to make a move. Smoothing my dress to be sure it hid my knife, I stood slowly, calculating my words.

"Last week," I began, "I had a boyfriend, a best friend I trusted, and I knew who my parents were. My brothers were happy and well. My niece and nephew had a mother. I'd never heard of you. I never cared about computer programs. I was like any other woman in America." I walked around the table until I stood in front of Justine. "Then I didn't die when I should have, and my best friend betrayed me by ordering the death of my family." I reached up and tugged off her wig. She gasped and lunged for it, but I tossed it over the table. We glared at each other for a moment. She wasn't bald. Like me, her hair had grown several inches; hers was a nice brown without her usual highlights or anything special. She must hate that, as she hated anything normal.

I pointed at Stefan and continued. "I was told this man was my biological father. Then he imprisoned me, and when I escaped in the attempt to save dozens of people from being slaughtered, the man I once thought I loved tried to stop me and . . ." I faltered, my throat tight with the memory. "And I shot him. He died right in front of me, and there was nothing I could do to save him."

"No!" Justine threw herself at me and started raking my face with her nails. Cort pulled her back.

"Didn't they tell you, Justine?" I mocked, though the pain in my chest made it difficult to breathe. "Delia used Tom. She did something to his mind so I wouldn't see until it was too late. I may have shot Tom, but in the end, you're to blame. You made Tom who he was. You chose to work for people who think they're above regular mortals."

"I loved Tom!" she cried.

So did I. "I know."

She crumpled against Cort, sobbing.

John Halden regarded me coldly. "Is there a point to all this?"

I could see from his thoughts that I'd taken his invitation to tell my personal stake too literally. I matched his aloofness, as years ago I'd practiced doing in mock courtrooms. "The point is if you give this technology to them, you are condemning many people to death—and all their descendants as well."

"It's murder," Ava added.

Stefan snorted. "Like you wouldn't use it against us."

"No. It's far too dangerous." Ava shook her head for emphasis. "We were going to destroy it."

Stefan looked from me to Ava and back again. I nodded. "It's true."

"And that," Halden said, the hint of a smile hovering on his lips, "is exactly why I will accept neither of your offers."

Ava and Stefan stiffened. "What do you mean?" Stefan demanded.

"There is another interested party." Halden nodded at the older guard, who walked to the door where we had entered. Minutes later he returned with four men, each armed with a semiautomatic rifle. I didn't know any of them, but I recognized the insignia on their uniforms.

Hunters.

CHAPTER 27

"A FTER I REALIZED AVA DIDN'T AGE, I DID A LITTLE RESEARCH," Halden said. "Actually, I put a whole team on it, and my trail eventually led to these gentlemen here. They were kind enough to explain the situation and show me the files they've collected over the years." His eyes scanned the room slowly. "With the exception of Erin, you are all in those files."

Stefan made a growl of disbelief in his throat. The other Unbounded appeared equally shocked. I hadn't seen any of this coming, either, though I'd maintained a link with Halden's mind. What he learned, he learned well.

When no one spoke, Halden continued. "These men have been telling me some very far-fetched stories. Interestingly enough, I'm inclined to believe them. After some discussion, they have agreed to completely fund my identification project. I might not earn as much money as I would have with either the virtual reality technology or the communication technology that your separate groups have offered, but it seems I'll be protecting humanity."

This attitude of morality was exactly what had caused the Renegades to back Halden, to feed his company technology over the years, but now his very goodness was to be our downfall. His emotions clearly confirmed his words; he believed what he was doing was right.

Silence reigned as everyone waited for what would happen next. I noticed Ritter had also come around the table and was within leaping distance of Halden. It was clear to me that not all of us would leave here alive. Perhaps none of us.

I faced Halden. "So you're a murderer."

"I'm not hurting anyone."

"Is that what they told you?"

The tallest of the Hunters started to speak, but Halden waved him to silence. "What do you mean?" he asked me.

I gestured to the Hunters. "They'll cut all of us in pieces as fast as they can identify us. All of us. That's what Hunters do. They don't care if some of us actually fight for humanity. They don't care if we hurt or love or have families. They kill us because we're different, like people once killed your race or the Jews." I was warming to my topic, presenting final arguments that meant my life and the lives of those I'd grown to care about. I'd been raised to argue, learning from the knees of the man who'd raised me. "They say they're protecting people, but killing an entire race because they're different is nothing short of genocide. And what happens when they're finished? Hatred like that doesn't just die. It's directed elsewhere. When they're through with us, they'll turn to whoever else might threaten their way of life. It won't stop with us. Racial targeting never does."

For the first time Halden seemed uncertain. "You told me the identification would make them go public," he said to the Hunters. "That it would allow them to live freely among us so they could be regulated like everyone else. You didn't say anything about murder."

When none of the Hunters replied, Ava said, "Oh, John, exposing us would mean the same thing. It will cause a division. Fear. Hatred. Genocide. But you can damn well bet we won't lie down and let ourselves be killed. My friends and I have been trying to protect humanity from abuses by our kind, but I am certain this move will force us to join hands with those who don't share that goal. What you are setting in motion today is a war that will encompass the entire world."

"She's right." Stefan flexed his arms, as though ready to pounce. "What's more, these monsters never planned to let us leave here today—at least not on our own feet."

"It's not as if a bullet would actually kill you," spat the tall Hunter.

"See?" Stefan flashed Halden a mirthless grin.

Halden ran a hand through his hair. Emotion radiated from him, so bright I didn't even have to try to discern his thought. An image came to me of the guard with the dreadlocks.

Halden's son.

Halden's Unbounded son who'd been trained by Renegade Unbounded. A son who'd gone against the advice of his tutors and had confessed his true nature to his father.

I reached out for the son now, stretching, pushing—driven to desperation by the situation. Stella had said Ava could sometimes plant a thought in a non-sensing mind. Was I strong enough? From Ava, I'd inherited the talent of sensing, but my paternal grandmother had it too. Perhaps I had enough strength to reach across the hall that separated us. Delia could reach across five floors. What about me? I strained and struggled. It felt like trying to bend a steel beam.

Nothing.

I tried to use John Halden's emotion as power to extend my reach, absorbing it like nutrition. It wasn't going to be enough. Tears of frustration filled my eyes. Soon the shooting would begin. I could tell by the tension radiating from every person in the room.

Then I found him, his shields still in place. I battered at them. Was that a tiny hole? *Danger. Your father needs you!* There was no answer, and I didn't expect one, because I'd have to be the one to take it from his mind, and at this distance I simply wasn't strong enough. I could only hope he received the impression.

If he did, I hoped I wasn't sending him to his death. When I pulled back, my head felt as though it had been cleaved in two.

Ritter had eased past Halden and was now a few steps closer to the Hunters, who were watching him carefully, prepared for any sudden movement. I knew he'd be able to take out two of them before any shots were fired, but that left the other two, plus Halden's guards. We had to somehow stop them from shooting us or the bullets might be our last memory before the cutting began.

Ava had taken several steps backward, preparing to attack Halden's guards from the side. Stella, however, seemed rooted to the spot, and I knew she was afraid. It was no longer only herself and us she had to defend. This time there was more to lose. A new life. A piece of her beloved Bronson.

Justine's eyes met mine, sending a message. My former best friend didn't agree with our cause, but she would fight these murdering bastards with us rather than go to her death willingly. Later she would personally take care of me. She wasn't sending out any pheromones that I could sense, and I wondered if she was afraid of distracting the Unbounded from the coming fight. I didn't think she needed to worry; we all knew what she was.

I looked from her to Ritter and the Hunters. Justine's head dipped slightly, showing her understanding. When Ritter attacked, she would, too. Cort shifted his weight, realigning himself in preparation. I knew he was with us and that he and Ritter had been together long enough to read each other completely.

The Hunters brought up their guns. "Easy now," said the one who seemed to be in charge. "We're taking you in for questioning, that's all."

"Right," Ritter sneered.

I'd left myself open to all the emotions in the room, but Ritter's came through stronger than anyone's. I focused more tightly on him and had a vision of my knife and Halden. Underneath barely concealed fury, he kept thinking the same thing over and over, which was crazy given that he should be focusing on what he planned to do himself.

Unless he'd expected me to see his thoughts. I delved further. My knife in my hand at Halden's throat. A threat only. An attempt to get the upper hand.

I could feel Ava's reticence at the images, which I echoed. I'd worked hard during my training sessions with both Ritter and Keene, but my experience was far too limited. Besides, though Halden was a trim man, he was a lot heavier than I was and had a good foot on me in height.

He was also sorry he'd made a mess of things. Maybe I could use that.

"Wait," I said, acting before I'd really decided that I would. "Nobody move. I have an idea." I crossed the few steps separating me from Halden. Faking a nonchalance I didn't feel, I reached out and touched his bare arm. *Sit,* I thought.

He looked at me, startled.

For your son. I pushed so hard with the thoughts that pain knifed through my head. I struggled not to cry out. Meeting Halden's gaze, I dropped my eyes once to his chair. He sat.

Instantly, I stepped behind him, pulling him back with one hand on his chest while the other whipped the knife out from under my dress and held it against his throat. Under his shirt I could feel a sort of hard rubbery material. Was that the body armor I'd heard Stella mention back in Kansas? Naturally he would be wearing it when he met with those he viewed as his enemies, but it couldn't save him from either the Hunters or the Unbounded. A slash on the neck or a shot to the head would snuff out his life instantly.

"Don't anyone move," I said in what I hoped was a deadly voice. "I swear I'll kill him and then all deals are off." All the while I was sending Halden peaceful, calming images. I couldn't tell if he felt any of them, but he didn't move. Needles of pain still pierced my skull.

The Hunters acted, but their delay was their undoing. As expected, Ritter took down two at once, his arms and legs little more than a blur. Justine and Cort removed the two remaining

Hunters. Ava disarmed one of Halden's guards, while Edgel put the other in a headlock.

Unfortunately, I hadn't kept track of my supposed dear old Dad. "Good thinking, Erin." Stefan's admiration was clear. Then in a blurred motion, he took the knife from my hand and pushed me out of the way, dragging Halden to his feet. I cursed under my breath, realizing I should have anticipated the move.

"Weapons down, everyone." Stefan pressed the knife against Halden's neck. "Except my people, of course."

Ritter snorted. "No way. What do we care if that fool dies?"

We stood at an impasse. Each side armed with guns, and Stefan with the knife. A thin line of blood appeared on Halden's dark throat. He was a victim here, as much as any of the Renegades.

"Let go of my father." The voice came from the second door to the room, the one behind Stefan and Halden where the Emporium Unbounded had been waiting earlier. Standing there now was the guard with the dreadlocks, and he was holding a gun less than a foot away from Stefan's head.

"Eric!" Halden said. "I thought I told you I didn't want you anywhere near here today."

Eric smiled grimly. "Sorry, Dad. When I knew what was at stake, I signed up for the whole weekend." To me, Eric added, "I let the knife through to help my dad, not to get him killed."

I made a face. "Sorry about that." Now what? Something had to break.

"Cort," Ritter said quietly.

Cort pulled the trigger.

CHAPTER 28

A STACCATO BURST SENT JUSTINE TO THE GROUND, FAR FROM DEAD, but in too much agony to retaliate. Ritter kicked Edgel's gun from his hand, at the same time bringing his weapon to point at Stefan. "Drop the knife. You know I don't care if I shoot you both."

Several heartbeats passed. Then Stefan released Halden, tossing the knife to the table. His eyes gleamed murderously at Cort. "I should have known. You may be Unbounded, but you're only half the man your brother is."

Cort gave him a chilly smile. "I have to agree. He's had a harder life all these years under your employ, though last I heard, he's finally had the courage to leave."

"Your father will hunt you down. Both of you!"

Cort shrugged. "That's entirely up to him. But I really doubt he'll come out of his lab long enough. You and I both know that he may be the brains behind the Emporium, but you and Delia control it."

"I'll hunt you down myself!" Stefan growled.

Ritter's laugh held no mirth. "Maybe I should kill you now and be done with it."

"My sensors stop transmitting my vitals and my men rush in," Stefan said. "You'd never make it out of here alive. They'll also kill the Renegades we captured last night. Is my death worth theirs? As it is, they may survive long enough to participate in our genetic research."

Ritter met his gaze. "One of these days, it'll be just you and me, Stefan. Then we'll see what happens."

"I'm looking forward to it." Stefan turned to me. "What about you, Erin? Are you coming with us?"

"I was never your daughter," I said, quite truthfully, though I knew he'd take it to mean that I'd made my choice. I didn't look at Ava.

"Get her," Stefan told Edgel. For a moment I thought he meant me, but Edgel bent to pick up Justine, who looked close to death.

We all knew better. Before two days were gone, she'd be plotting against us again, seeking revenge for Tom's death.

"Are we just letting them go?" This from Eric Halden, his words meant not for his father, but for Ava.

"Yes, but not until we're ready to leave ourselves." Ava crossed to the door Eric had come through and peered inside. "Lock them in here. Guard both doors."

"You should reconsider," Stefan said. "We could work well together."

Ava gave him a disparaging glance. "No, we couldn't." She was confident and beautiful and I was proud of her.

Halden's guards made a move to escort Stefan inside the room, but Ritter shook his head. "Stay out of our way. Cort, you're with me." The guards glanced at Halden who nodded.

When Ritter and Cort had disappeared with Stefan and the others, Ava faced Halden. "We're not going anywhere until we get what we came for. One way or another."

"It's yours." Halden slumped heavily in his chair, his dark skin drawn and his eyes hollow. "I'll need verification that you're really going to destroy it. I want my son protected."

Ava shook her head. "Our word will have to suffice. But know that any Renegade would protect Eric with their life, if necessary. To us, he is also family."

Of course he was. He would have ancestors, and even if they'd died last night, other Renegades would step up to take their place. Being a Renegade meant more than sharing the same blood.

Halden's gaze fell on his son who was searching the unconscious Hunters for additional weapons, piling them to one side. "I'm sorry, Eric. I thought I was helping you. I didn't know they would kill all of you." His eyes went to each of us in turn. "I thought I knew better."

"You've done great things in the past, John," Ava said. "We won't forget that."

"The technologies I've developed—those came from you?"

She shrugged. "Some of them."

"So Eric has been your connection, at least recently. He's been reporting to you."

"We wanted to make sure you remained safe."

Halden reached for the phone. When someone answered on the other end, he barked, "I want all of the identification files brought to the conference room and then delete them from our hard drives and backups. Yes, you heard me, all of them." To us he added. "I'll personally go down and make sure they do what I've asked."

"You'll have to excuse us if we send Eric instead," Ava said. "And wait here until he returns."

Halden inclined his head. "As you wish."

"Eric?" Ava said as the younger Halden moved toward the door. "Bring back the head programmer. Erin and I will need to talk to him to be sure."

Eric nodded and left the room, one of the guards trailing him at his father's request.

As Ava went to examine the Hunters, Stella handed Halden her briefcase. "The virtual reality files are in here."

"Thank you." He seemed surprised that she would still give them to him.

"A lot of good will come of this program," Stella said. "The medical applications, at least. You will save lives with it."

He nodded. "We'll get it out as soon as possible."

"These two are dead." Ava pointed to one of the Hunters Ritter had taken out and the one Justine had attacked. "The other two will probably make it."

Halden frowned. "What'll we do with them?"

"After we leave, you can call the police and tell them they tried to steal technology. That'll keep them occupied in court for a while and out of trouble. We do shoot to kill when we're attacked, but it's hard to kill them when they're helpless like this." She nudged one with her foot. "They have families who depend on them, who have no idea what they're up to, and for what it's worth, they're right about Stefan and his people. As much as we hate being hunted, these vigilantes help keep tabs on the bad guys."

Since I'd learned of the Emporium infiltration, I wasn't too sure about that, but I'd give that information to Ava later.

"So 'the enemy of my enemy is my friend,' " quoted Halden.

Ava smiled. "Something like that, though I won't be inviting them to dinner anytime soon, and if Ritter were in here right now, we might not be having this conversation."

"Do these Hunters ever tell the authorities about the Unbounded?" Halden asked.

"The last one who did ended up in psychiatric care."

"I see."

A new worry was working its way into my mind. "What if the Emporium makes a new identification program?"

Halden stared at me. "An excellent point. After reviewing their communication program, I'm sure they have the skills."

"No doubt," Ava said with a sigh. "But their focus hasn't been on computer skills, and it'll take them years to get anywhere with the idea. Don't sell yourself short, John. You run an amazing company. Even for a mortal." Her smile was unexpected, and Halden returned it.

"We'll keep tabs on them," Stella assured him. But we all knew a door had been opened, one we'd have to carefully monitor.

"Erin, come here." Ava was still kneeling by the Hunters. "Your first official lesson," she said as I knelt beside her. "We need to see if we can remove you from their memories. The process should be fairly simple since the time was so brief. Take my hand."

Once our minds were linked, she put her other hand on the unconscious Hunter's head. I saw nothing. He was completely out. How could she extract memories unless he was thinking of them?

Down, Ava thought. The next minute we were diving into a placid lake that appeared out of nowhere. I couldn't feel the water, but everything around us rippled and the images that sprang up appeared muted by water.

Don't touch anything, Ava said, as she sidestepped an image of a child in a swing.

Right. Wouldn't want him to forget his daughter. The memory of the child stunned me. One minute he threatened to kill us, and the next he was a doting father.

There. With quick hands Ava plucked several images from the man's mind. *So few. He won't even have the black spots that sometimes follow such extraction.*

Together we came up out of the lake, whose surface appeared undisturbed. We opened our eyes at the same time. "It's not always a lake," Ava said, "but that is usually the representation my mind creates."

We had finished with the second Hunter by the time the files arrived, and we wasted no time in exiting the building. Ritter walked several paces behind Stefan, watching him carefully. John Halden called a dozen more guards to the door, who stood at the ready. It was almost civil the way Stefan and Edgel, carrying Justine, got into their car as we climbed into ours. No shots were fired, no explosions, no screaming or threats. Once in the car, Ritter radioed our people to begin moving out with the utmost caution. As usual, Ava went through an evade routine, which included a car change.

"What about our people that Stefan captured?" I asked from the backseat between Ritter and Cort.

Ritter's jaw clenched. "They'll try to use them for information. It won't be pretty." Torture took on a whole new meaning for people who couldn't die in the usual way. "But we'll find them."

"They won't be killed right away," Cort said. "You heard Stefan. He wants to expand their Unbounded gene pool. Besides, they know we'll change all our safe houses and anything really important, so unless they get information from them quickly, it won't be of any use." He looked at me intently. "There's something else you should know." He hesitated for the space of several heartbeats. "Tom's alive."

I felt the blood drain from my face. "No. He was dead. I killed him." I looked at Ritter, who nodded his verification.

Cort shook his head. "We got up to the roof right after you two left. I'd already convinced them that I had come back because my cover was blown, and I saw Tom lying there, but the edges of his wound were closing. They got him into surgery right away and gave him a couple of injections of something similar to my curequick. Since he's barely coming into his Change, it'll take longer for him to recover, but he's going to survive."

Stunned was too weak a word for my surprise. I was finding it hard to breathe. "Justine didn't know. Not even that he'd been shot."

"That's right. I hadn't told her any of it yet. Or Stefan. Didn't want to give them the satisfaction."

Yes, it all made sense now. The difference I'd been feeling from Tom even in Kansas. The difference I'd either been too close to recognize or had blocked out of my rational mind. The beginning of the Change—both mental and physical. I wavered between joy that he was alive and horror that the Emporium had yet one more Unbounded. Justine had won that round, and Tom had lived to die another day.

Beside me Ritter shifted, and I glanced over at him. Even through my turmoil I was intensely aware of his presence.

The way his leg touched mine, the soft ache inside my chest. His look was shuttered, his emotions closed to me.

Ava took a phone call and her backward glance was full of pity. "What?" I asked.

"Your father isn't doing well. Dimitri wants you there as soon as possible. I'll arrange for Chris to fly us back."

"Thank you." I laid my head back against the seat and shut my eyes, fighting tears. Tom's betrayal, my father dying. I would kill Justine for all this—and Stefan, too. I would make Ritter and Ava teach me everything they knew about combat and sensing. The Emporium would attack again, and I would be ready when they did.

My mind felt battered, exhausted, and my emotions were careening all over the place. I barely noticed our arrival at the hotel. When I was slow to get out of the car, Ritter helped me stand. "Come on." His thoughts were still dark, but his voice was gentle.

I turned into his arms and let him guide me to the elevator. He took me not to the room where Chris waited but to another where we were all alone. Scooping me up at the door, he led me to the large bed that dominated the room, peeled back the covers, and set me inside.

"Rest. We'll have a few hours before our flight. I'll wake you when it's time."

My entire body had come to life at his closeness, the soft ache I'd felt in the car becoming a roar. I wanted to lose myself in his arms, to blot out last night's loneliness, my grief over my father, and the uncertainty of the future. "Don't leave," I whispered.

Ritter made a choked noise in his throat as he settled beside me, his arms drawing me to him until my back nestled in his chest. His lips rested briefly on my neck below my ear, sending fire through my veins. Fire that almost hurt with its intensity. All the images of death and fighting of the past days fled from my mind.

"You're exhausted," he said. "Ava told me what you did, calling to Eric like that. You weren't ready. She can't even project that far to an unsensing mind. Sleep now."

Sleep was the last thing my body wanted, but already my mind was starting to shut down without my approval. The sensations of fire faded, though Ritter's body still fit against mine as if it belonged. It was no promise for the future, I knew. Or a guarantee that what was between us this instant would exist tomorrow.

I didn't care. For once I was content not to think about tomorrow or any repercussions I might face for falling in love with a man who might never be able to love me back.

Besides, the steady thump of Ritter's heart against my back had given me an idea. A hope. There might be a way I could save my father after all.

I let sleep take me.

HOME TO KANSAS CITY WE WENT, THOUGH IT WASN'T REALLY HOME anymore. Or some of us went. Cort and Gaven flew to Oregon to supervise set up operations, while Ava, Ritter, and Stella accompanied Chris and me to the private clinic where my father had slipped into a coma and lay dying. My mother sat unwavering by his side.

Dimitri was there, too, and I felt shy seeing him again with the knowledge that he was my biological father. Did that explain how kind he'd been to me? No, I believed that was part of his personality, and he would have acted kindly toward me regardless. With Laurence gone, no one except Ava, Dimitri, and me knew what had happened at the fertility clinic the day I'd been conceived, but now wasn't the time to confront them.

I sat by the bed and touched my father's limp hand. "Isn't there anything you can do?" I whispered.

"He's dying," Dimitri said matter-of-factly. "I don't dare leave him for more than a few minutes. I don't know how much longer he'll last. He needs a new heart."

"Then let's give it to him."

Dimitri shook his head. "There isn't one."

"There's mine." I said it viciously, as though daring him or anyone to contradict me.

"What are you saying, Erin?" My mother's haggard face was frightened.

"I can grow a new one."

"No." Ritter spoke from the doorway. "You have no idea what you're saying." His hand went to his heart and I had the odd sensation that if Cort were present, he'd tease Ritter about vampire hunters.

"It has to be possible." I looked at Dimitri. "Isn't it? I'm the same blood type, just like my mother and the rest of my family. My father's not a big man. Why wouldn't it work? At least it could hold him over until you found something better." With all the dead Hunters in our wake, you'd think hearts shouldn't be that hard to find.

"It's not exactly that simple," Dimitri said. "Though I admit my research indicates an Unbounded organ might actually adjust itself to a recipient's body."

"Then it's worth a try. How long would it take me to grow a new one?"

"With a lot of curequick, about three days." Dimitri's jaw twitched in exactly the same way mine did when I was forced to confront something I wanted to reject. In fact, now that I studied him, the wide oval shape of his eyes was mine, too.

"I want to do this for him. What's three days compared to his life?" I waited for Dimitri to tell me the man on the bed wasn't my real father, for anyone to say it. To say that I had come from stolen sperm or to admit the truth about Dimitri. No one did.

I answered anyway. "Please. He's my dad. He was the first person to hold me after I was born. He took me for my first ice cream. He was at all of my soccer games when I was five, and even when I kept tripping over my own feet or sat down at the goal to wait for the ball, he acted like I was the best player on the team."

Tears slid down my face, made my vision blur. "He bought me my first book. He taught me about law. I can't stand here and watch him die if I have the means to save him."

Dimitri showed no emotion. "It might not work."

"But it could."

"He can have mine." This from Ritter.

We all turned toward him, surprised. I didn't like that idea at all, though if asked I wouldn't be able to say why.

"I'm bigger, and my heart's in excellent shape."

"Not a good idea," Dimitri said. "Or I'd have already figured out how to give him mine. We don't know enough about the procedure. It may adjust to him well enough, but for all we know once the Unbounded organ is no longer in an Unbounded body, it could very well degrade quickly to its natural age. That would kill him."

"You don't know that for sure," Ritter said. "The genes are in the heart, too. Maybe it would outlast all his other organs."

"The point is that there has been almost no research into Unbounded transplants in mortals, except for my own limited testing. We've been too busy patching up our people all these years so they can fight the Emporium to do much of anything else. If your heart failed, Grant wouldn't survive two surgeries close together. He has only one chance."

"My heart's the only option then," I said. "It wouldn't degenerate."

"No, Erin." My mother spoke with a fierceness born from years of protecting me. I never admired her more than at that moment for being willing to put me before my father, whom I knew she loved more than her own life.

I took her hand. "I really want to do this, Mom. It's his only chance."

"I don't want to lose you."

"You're not going to lose me."

"You'll just be in a hell of a lot of pain," Ritter muttered.

Ignoring him, I looked at Dimitri? "It will work, won't it?"

He nodded. "I believe it will."

"Will you do it?"

The hint of wistful smile touched his lips. "We'll give it a try."

My mother was crying in her chair by the bed, and I bent over and hugged her. "Everything's going to be okay. I promise." I hoped I was telling the truth.

"I can have things ready in an hour," Dimitri said.

Nodding, I walked out into the hall feeling both frightened and determined. Chris sat on a bench outside the door near his children, who were occupying themselves with activity books. Chris's eyes were focused down the hall to where Stella sat with Bronson.

I studied the pair as well. They were talking earnestly, Bronson looking every one of his seventy years and then some. In fact, he seemed to have shrunk in the few days we'd been gone. He held Stella's face in his gnarled hands and wiped tears from her cheeks before pulling her into a hug. No kiss. They had learned to be careful in public.

I wondered how Bronson felt at learning he was to become a father to a child he would never raise. Maybe never even meet. Not that I would try to find out. Under no circumstances was I even going to walk past them. Some emotions were better left private.

Chris apparently felt the same, because he'd looked away and was softly stroking Kathy's hair. She smiled up at him and said something. He laughed, though his face was still strained. It might take time, but I knew they would eventually be okay, even without Lorrie.

I waved at them and walked down the hall, heading toward Jace's room, where he was lying in a bed healing at the normal slow human rate. I wished my Unbounded blood could make a difference for either him or my father, but Dimitri had assured me it wouldn't.

Ritter came after me. "Erin," he said in a low voice.

I turned to him. "You can't talk me out of it."

"You're so new to being Unbounded. How do we know you'll heal?"

I blinked in amazement. "I burned to death and healed from two gunshot wounds practically overnight. I can absorb nutrients from the air. I can sometimes sense what people are feeling. I'm Unbounded every bit as much as you are, Ritter, and I'm not going to stand back and lose another person I love until I absolutely have to, which is going to happen soon enough. I'm going to lose them all eventually. Tell me, if you could go back, wouldn't you do anything you could to save your family?"

His angular face was ashen, his body tense, but he nodded.

"The real question is," I said, "will you be here when I wake up?"

His jaw worked silently, but before he could respond, a commotion down the hall caught our attention. "Please, sir," a nurse was saying to a patient, "you must go back to your room and lie down. You'll rip your stitches!"

The patient avoided her with a dexterous move that would have given credit to a skilled martial artist. "I'm fine. That's what I'm telling you!" Irritation dripped from his words. "And I've also been telling you for the past two hours that I need to see my doctor. Since no one will contact him, I'm going to find him myself. I know he's here somewhere with my father."

I knew that voice. "Jace!" I ran to him.

"It's okay," I told the nurse. "He's my brother. I'll take care of him." Her forehead knotted with concern, but she left him to me, shaking her head as she walked down the hall.

Jace looked drunk and happy. He pulled open the robe he wore over a pair of gray pajama pants. Bandages hung loosely from his chest and stomach. "I'm fine!" he said in a low, urgent voice. "Dimitri told me not to mess with the bandages, but they were itching, so I lifted them up, and my wounds are fifty percent better than yesterday. My insides still hurt, but look, I can walk! I think Dimitri suspected all along, the old fart. Maybe he didn't want to get my hopes up. This is the best day of my life! I'm like you, Erin. I'm like you!"

Ritter and I stared at each other and at Jace. I began to laugh and cry at the same time. The rest of my family might age and leave me, but I would always have Jace. I hugged him tightly. He wavered a little under the pressure, and I knew he was still far from well, but he'd definitely begun emitting a hint of the same odd feeling I'd sensed around Tom. A Changing.

Jace backed away from me and began tearing off his bandages.

"Shut that robe!" I ordered, noticing the stares of several nurses and visitors farther down the hall.

Jace laughed and hugged me again. "Oh, boy. I think I'm going to faint."

Ritter caught him as he fell and carried him to several nearby chairs where we could lay him down. "We'd better get some curequick from my bag. Actually, we'd better ask Dimitri about it first. He's probably been giving it to him already if he suspects Jace is Changing."

Changing!

"I'll ask him." I wanted to skip down the hall like a joyful child.

Before I could leave, Ritter's hand closed over mine. His skin felt warm. In that instant, his mind was open. I felt his happiness over Jace and worry at my pending operation. And more.

The more made me shiver with anticipation.

The next minute he was pushing me into a room behind us, kissing me, his hands pressing me against the hardness of his body. His mouth opened. He tasted of heat, of desire, or maybe that came from our minds. His hands made my skin tingle. I wanted to be a part of him, to feel him become a part of me. I didn't care that it was a terrible idea. I wanted to—

"Um, do you two mind?" came a quavering voice behind us.

We sprang apart to find a wrinkled old woman staring at us from her hospital bed. "Sorry," I muttered as Ritter groaned.

"Much better than what's on TV, mind you, but I have to be careful of my heart." She gave us a sly grin. "I have a pacemaker, you know."

I turned toward the door, but Ritter stopped me. "On the beach you said, you wanted . . ." He stopped and took a breath before rushing on, his voice nearly a growl. "You are in my every waking thought—and most of my sleeping ones, too. I don't know what that means exactly, but I'll be here when you wake up, Erin."

It was enough.

I leaned forward and whispered against his lips. "I know."

Together we opened the door and went to find Dimitri.

THE END

Be sure to follow more of Erin's story in *The Cure,* book two of the *Unbounded* series.

TEYLA BRANTON GREW UP AVIDLY READING SCIENCE FICTION AND fantasy and watching Star Trek reruns with her large family. They lived on a little farm where she loved to visit the solitary cow and collect (and juggle) the eggs, usually making it back to the house with most of them intact. On that same farm she once owned thirty-three gerbils and eighteen cats, not a good mix, as it turns out. Teyla always had her nose in a book and daydreamed about someday creating her own worlds.

Teyla is now married, mostly grown up, and has seven kids, so life at her house can be very interesting (and loud), but writing keeps her sane. She thrives on the energy and daily amusement offered by her children, the semi-ordered chaos giving her a constant source of writing material. Grabbing any snatch of free time from her hectic life, Teyla writes novels, often with a child on her lap. She warns her children that if they don't behave, they just might find themselves in her next book!

She's been known to wear pajamas all day when working on a deadline, and is often distracted enough to burn dinner. (Okay, pretty much 90% of the time.) A sign on her office door reads: DANGER. WRITER AT WORK. ENTER AT YOUR OWN RISK.

She loves writing fiction and traveling, and she hopes to write and travel a lot more. She also loves shooting guns, martial arts, and belly dancing. She has worked in the publishing business for over twenty years. Teyla also writes romance and suspense under the name Rachel Branton. For more information, please visit http://www.TeylaBranton.com.